FASTEN YOUR SEAT BELTS.
THIS RIDE IS…

v

"RIP-ROARING."
—Rocky Mountain News

v

"NAIL-BITING."
—Library Journal

v

"WICKED."
—The Denver Post

v

"UNFORGETTABLE."
—The Orlando Sentinel

Echo Burning

continued on next page . . .

Running Blind

"Swift and brutal."   —*The New York Times*

"A masterpiece."   —*Booklist*

"Spectacular . . . Muscular, energetic prose and pell-mell pacing."   —*The Seattle Times*

"Plan to stay up long past bedtime and do some serious hyper-ventilating toward the end."   —*Kirkus Reviews*

Tripwire

"*Tripwire* fills the bill. [It] makes the reader sit back and gasp with both wonder and understanding."   —*The Denver Post*

"The Reacher novels are like westerns spun into a thriller . . . Reacher is the quintessential loner, a kind of *High Noon* hero who comes into a town demanding justice."
—*Ft. Lauderdale Sun-Sentinel*

"A good villain . . . a great hero [and] a thriller good to the last drop."   —*Orlando Sentinel*

"Bang-on suspense . . . an insightful look into how humans work."   —*The Houston Chronicle*

"Fun . . . Reacher swashbuckles with the best of them."
—*Kirkus Reviews*

"A solid thriller that brings to mind the knight-errant adventures of John D. McDonald's Travis McGee."   —*Booklist*

"Page for page, there's probably more fisticuffs in a Lee Child thriller than anywhere else around."   —*Chicago Tribune*

"A sort of millennial reshaping of John D. McDonald's Travis McGee character and world view."
—*The Dallas Morning News*

Die Trying

"It takes a brave man to move into the macho territory of suspense writer Stephen Hunter, but Lee Child is making his move with this follow-up to *Killing Floor*."

—*Chicago Tribune*

"Tough, elegant, and thoughtful."

—Robert B. Parker, author of *Sudden Mischief*

"Speed and action . . . A thoroughly engrossing tale told by an author who doesn't miss a beat. Jack Reacher is one of the more fully realized and intelligently resourceful heroes to come along in years." —*Rocky Mountain News*

"A riveting thriller, brought to life with well-observed detail and paced with taut, evocative prose. It's a winner."

—Greg Iles, author of *Mortal Fear*

"[A] literate scenario-cum-thriller . . . the writing is way above average." —*The Philadelphia Inquirer*

"Child presents his tense, action-packed adventure in vivid prose, as lean and capable as his central character. Jack Reacher is not merely a terrific hero; he sets a new standard."

—Tom Savage, author of *The Inheritance*

"Lee Child's knowledge of the modern military and its combat tactics amazed me. A chilling and all-too-realistic story, and a damn good book." —Steve Thayer, author of *The Weatherman*

"Thoroughly convincing . . . The suspense here is nonstop. . . . A fast, solid, action-oriented thriller."

—*Mysterious Galaxy* newsletter

continued on next page . . .

Killing Floor
A *People* Magazine "Page-turner"

"Combines high suspense with almost nonstop action. Reacher is a wonderfully epic hero: tough, taciturn, yet vulnerable. From its jolting opening scene to its fiery final confrontation, *Killing Floor* is irresistible."
—*People*

"Great style and careful plotting. The talented first-time author . . . knows what he's doing. The violence is brutal . . . depicted with the kind of detail that builds dread and suspense."
—*The New York Times*

"A complex thriller, with layer upon layer of mystery and violence and intrigue . . . A long, unsettling trip that leaves your brain buzzing and your stomach knotted."
—*Philadelphia Inquirer*

"This is such a brilliantly written first novel that [Child] must be channeling Dashiell Hammett . . . Reacher handles the maze of clues and the criminal unfortunates with a flair that would make Sam Spade proud."
—*Playboy*

"A tough, compelling thriller with characters who jump off the page."
—*Houston Chronicle*

ECHO BURNING

LEE CHILD

JOVE BOOKS, NEW YORK

ECHO BURNING

A Jove Book / published by arrangement with
G. P. Putnam's Sons

PRINTING HISTORY
G. P. Putnam's Sons hardcover edition / June 2001
Jove edition / May 2002

Copyright © 2001 by Lee Child.
Excerpt from *Without Fail* copyright © 2002 by Lee Child.
Cover photograph by Jeremy Woodhouse/PhotoDisc.

Visit our website at
www.penguinputnam.com

ISBN: 0-515-13331-0

A JOVE BOOK®
Jove Books are published by The Berkley Publishing Group,
a division of Penguin Putnam Inc.,
375 Hudson Street, New York, New York 10014.
JOVE and the "J" design
are trademarks belonging to Penguin Putnam Inc.

PRINTED IN THE UNITED STATES OF AMERICA

10 9 8 7 6 5 4 3 2 1

People think that writing is a lonely, solitary trade. They're wrong. It's a team game, and I'm lucky enough to have charming and talented people on my side everywhere I'm published. Accordingly, if you ever worked on or sold one of my books, this one is dedicated to you. You're too numerous to mention individually, but too important not to mention at all.

There were three watchers, two men and a boy. They were
using telescopes, not field glasses. It was a question of distance. They were almost a mile from their target area, because of the terrain. There was no closer cover. It was low,
undulating country, burned khaki by the sun, grass and rock
and sandy soil alike. The nearest safe concealment was the
broad dip they were in, a bone-dry gulch scraped out a million years ago by a different climate, when there had been
rain and ferns and rushing rivers.

The men lay prone in the dust with the early heat on their
backs, their telescopes at their eyes. The boy scuttled around
on his knees, fetching water from the cooler, watching for
waking rattlesnakes, logging comments in a notebook. They
had arrived before first light in a dusty pick-up truck, the long
way around, across the empty land from the west. They had
thrown a dirty tarpaulin over the truck and held it down with
rocks. They had eased forward to the rim of the dip and settled in, raising their telescopes as the low morning sun
dawned to the east behind the red house almost a mile away.

This was Friday, their fifth consecutive morning, and they were low on conversation.

"Time?" one of the men asked. His voice was nasal, the effect of keeping one eye open and the other eye shut.

The boy checked his watch.

"Six-fifty," he answered.

"Any moment now," the man with the telescope said.

The boy opened his book and prepared to make the same notes he had made four times before.

"Kitchen light on," the man said.

The boy wrote it down. *6:50, kitchen light on*. The kitchen faced them, looking west away from the morning sun, so it stayed dark even after dawn.

"On her own?" the boy asked.

"Same as always," the second man said, squinting.

Maid prepares breakfast, the boy wrote. *Target still in bed.* The sun rose, inch by inch. It jacked itself higher into the sky and pulled the shadows shorter and shorter. The red house had a tall chimney coming out of the kitchen wing like the finger on a sundial. The shadow it made swung and shortened and the heat on the watchers' shoulders built higher. Seven o'clock in the morning, and it was already hot. By eight, it would be burning. By nine, it would be fearsome. And they were there all day, until dark, when they could slip away unseen.

"Bedroom drapes opening," the second man said. "She's up and about."

The boy wrote it down. *7:04, bedroom drapes open*.

"Now listen," the first man said.

They heard the well pump kick in, faintly from almost a mile away. A quiet mechanical click, and then a steady low drone.

"She's showering," the man said.

The boy wrote it down. *7:06, target starts to shower*.

The men rested their eyes. Nothing was going to happen while she was in the shower. How could it? They lowered their telescopes and blinked against the brassy sun in their eyes. The well pump clicked off after six minutes. The silence sounded louder than the faint noise had. The boy wrote:

7:12, target out of shower. The men raised their telescopes again.

"She's dressing, I guess," the first man said.

The boy giggled. "Can you see her naked?"

The second man was triangulated twenty feet to the south. He had the better view of the back of the house, where her bedroom window was.

"You're disgusting," he said. "You know that?"

The boy wrote: *7:15, probably dressing*. Then: *7:20, probably downstairs, probably eating breakfast*.

"She'll go back up, brush her teeth," he said.

The man on the left shifted on his elbows.

"For sure," he said. "Prissy little thing like that."

"She's closing her drapes again," the man on the right said.

It was standard practice in the west of Texas, in the summer, especially if your bedroom faced south, like this one did. Unless you wanted to sleep the next night in a room hotter than a pizza oven.

"Stand by," the man said. "A buck gets ten she goes out to the barn now."

It was a wager that nobody took, because so far four times out of four she had done exactly that, and watchers are paid to notice patterns.

"Kitchen door's open."

The boy wrote: *7:27, kitchen door opens*.

"Here she comes."

She came out, dressed in a blue gingham dress that reached to her knees and left her shoulders bare. Her hair was tied back behind her head. It was still damp from the shower.

"What do you call that sort of a dress?" the boy asked.

"Halter," the man on the left said.

7:28, comes out, blue halter dress, goes to barn, the boy wrote.

She walked across the yard, short hesitant steps against the uneven ruts in the baked earth, maybe seventy yards. She heaved the barn door open and disappeared in the gloom inside.

The boy wrote: *7:29, target in barn*.

"How hot is it?" the man on the left asked.

"Maybe a hundred degrees," the boy said.

"There'll be a storm soon. Heat like this, there has to be."

"Here comes her ride," the man on the right said.

Miles to the south, there was a dust cloud on the road. A vehicle, making slow and steady progress north.

"She's coming back," the man on the right said.

7:32, target comes out of barn, the boy wrote.

"Maid's at the door," the man said.

The target stopped at the kitchen door and took her lunch box from the maid. It was bright blue plastic with a cartoon picture on the side. She paused for a second. Her skin was pink and damp from the heat. She leaned down to adjust her socks and then trotted out to the gate, through the gate, to the shoulder of the road. The school bus slowed and stopped and the door opened with a sound the watchers heard clearly over the faint rattle of the idling engine. The chrome handrails flashed once in the sun. The diesel exhaust hung and drifted in the hot still air. The target heaved her lunch box onto the step and grasped the bright rails and clambered up after it. The door closed again and the watchers saw her corn-colored head bobbing along level with the base of the windows. Then the engine noise deepened and the gears caught and the bus moved away with a new cone of dust kicking up behind it.

7:36, target on bus to school, the boy wrote.

The road north was dead straight and he turned his head and watched the bus all the way until the heat on the horizon broke it up into a shimmering yellow mirage. Then he closed his notebook and secured it with a rubber band. Back at the red house, the maid stepped inside and closed the kitchen door. Nearly a mile away, the watchers lowered their telescopes and turned their collars up for protection from the sun.

Seven thirty-seven, Friday morning.

Seven thirty-eight.

Seven thirty-nine, more than three hundred miles to the north and east, Jack Reacher climbed out of his motel room window. One minute earlier, he had been in the bathroom, brushing his teeth. One minute before that, he had opened the door of his room to check the morning temperature. He had left it open, and the closet just inside the entrance passageway was faced with mirrored glass, and there was a shaving mirror in the bathroom on a cantilevered arm, and by a freak of optical chance he caught sight of four men getting out of a car and walking toward the motel office. Pure luck, but a guy as vigilant as Jack Reacher gets lucky more times than the average.

The car was a police cruiser. It had a shield on the door, and because of the bright sunlight and the double reflection he could read it clearly. At the top it said City Police, and then there was a fancy medallion in the middle with Lubbock, Texas, written underneath. All four men who got out were in uniform. They had bulky belts with guns and radios and nightsticks and handcuffs. Three of the men he had never seen before, but the fourth guy was familiar. The fourth guy was a tall heavyweight with a gelled blond brush-cut above a meaty red face. This morning the meaty red face was partially obscured by a glinting aluminum splint carefully taped over a shattered nose. His right hand was similarly bound up with a splint and bandages protecting a broken forefinger.

The guy had neither injury the night before. And Reacher had no idea the guy was a cop. He just looked like some idiot in a bar. Reacher had gone there because he heard the music was good, but it wasn't, so he had backed away from the band and ended up on a bar stool watching ESPN on a muted television fixed high on a wall. The place was crowded and noisy, and he was wedged in a space with a woman on his right and the heavyweight guy with the brush-cut on his left. He got bored with the sports and turned around to watch the room. As he turned, he saw how the guy was eating.

The guy was wearing a white tank-top shirt and he was eating chicken wings. The wings were greasy and the guy was a slob. He was dripping chicken fat off his chin and off his fingers onto his shirt. There was a dark teardrop shape right between his pecs. It was growing and spreading into an impressive stain. But the best barroom etiquette doesn't let you linger on such a sight, and the guy caught Reacher staring.

"Who you looking at?" he said.

It was said low and aggressively, but Reacher ignored it.

"Who you looking at?" the guy said again.

Reacher's experience was, they say it once, maybe nothing's going to happen. But they say it twice, then trouble's on the way. Fundamental problem is, they take a lack of response as evidence that you're worried. That they're winning. But then, they won't let you answer, anyway.

"You looking at me?" the guy said.

"No," Reacher answered.

"Don't you be looking at me, boy," the guy said.

The way he said *boy* made Reacher think he was maybe a foreman in a lumber mill or a cotton operation. Whatever muscle work was done around Lubbock. Some kind of a traditional trade passed down through the generations. Certainly the word *cop* never came to his mind. But then, he was relatively new to Texas.

"Don't you look at me," the guy said.

Reacher turned his head and looked at him. Not really to antagonize the guy. Just to size him up. Life is endlessly capable of surprises, so he knew one day he would come face to face with his physical equal. With somebody who might worry him. But he looked and saw this wasn't the day. So he just smiled and looked away again.

Then the guy jabbed him with his finger.

"I told you not to look at me," he said, and jabbed.

It was a meaty forefinger and it was covered in grease. It left a definite mark on Reacher's shirt.

"Don't do that," Reacher said.

The guy jabbed again.

"Or what?" he said. "You want to make something out of it?"

Reacher looked down. Now there were two marks. The guy jabbed again. Three jabs, three marks. Reacher clamped his teeth. What were three greasy marks on a shirt? He started a slow count to ten. Then the guy jabbed again, before he even reached eight.

"You deaf?" Reacher said. "I told you not to do that."

"You want to do something about it?"

"No," Reacher said. "I really don't. I just want you to stop doing it, is all."

The guy smiled. "Then you're a yellow-bellied piece of shit."

"Whatever," Reacher said. "Just keep your hands off me."

"Or what? What you going to do?"

Reacher restarted his count. *Eight, nine.*

"You want to take this outside?" the guy asked.

Ten.

"Touch me again and you'll find out," Reacher said. "I warned you four times."

The guy paused a second. Then, of course, he went for it again. Reacher caught the finger on the way in and snapped it at the first knuckle. Just folded it upward like he was turning a door handle. Then because he was irritated he leaned forward and headbutted the guy full in the face. It was a smooth move, well delivered, but it was backed off to maybe a half of what it might have been. No need to put a guy in a coma, over four grease marks on a shirt. He moved a pace to give the man room to fall, and backed into the woman on his right.

"Excuse me, ma'am," he said.

The woman nodded vaguely, disoriented by the noise, concentrating on her drink, unaware of what was happening. The big guy thumped silently on the floorboards and Reacher used the sole of his shoe to roll him half onto his front. Then he nudged him under the chin with his toe to pull his head back and straighten his airway. The recovery position, paramedics call it. Stops you choking while you're out.

Then he paid for his drinks and walked back to his motel, and didn't give the guy another thought until he was at the bathroom mirror and saw him out and about in a cop's uniform. Then he thought hard, and as fast as he could.

He spent the first second calculating reflected angles and figuring *if I can see him, does that mean he can see me?* The answer was *yes, of course he can.* If he was looking the right way, which he wasn't yet. He spent the next second mad at himself. He should have picked up the signs. They had been there. Who else would be poking at a guy built like him, except somebody with some kind of protected status? Some

kind of imagined invulnerability? He should have picked up
on it.

So what to do? The guy was a cop on his own turf. And
Reacher was an easily recognizable target. Apart from anything else he still had the four grease spots on his shirt, and a
brand-new bruise on his forehead. There were probably
forensics people who could match its shape to the bones in
the guy's nose.

So what to do? An angry cop bent on revenge could cause
trouble. A lot of trouble. A noisy public arrest, for sure,
maybe some wild gunshots, definitely some four-on-one fun
and games in an empty out-of-the-way cell down at the station house, where you can't fight back without multiplying
your original legal problem. Then all kinds of difficult questions, because Reacher habitually carried no ID and nothing
else at all except his toothbrush and a couple of thousand dollars cash in his pants pocket. So he would be regarded as a
suspicious character. Almost certainly he'd be charged with
attacking a law officer. That was probably a big deal in Texas.
All kinds of witnesses would materialize to swear it was ma-
licious and completely unprovoked. He could end up convicted and in the penitentiary, easy as anything. He could end
up with seven-to-ten in some tough establishment. Which
was definitely not number one on his wish list.

So discretion was going to be the better part of valor. He
put his toothbrush in his pocket and walked through the room
and opened the window. Unclipped the screen and dropped it
to the ground. Climbed out and closed the window and rested
the screen back in its frame and walked away across a vacant
lot to the nearest street. Turned right and kept on walking until he was hidden by a low building. He looked for buses.
There weren't any. He looked for taxis. Nothing doing. So he
stuck out his thumb. He figured he had ten minutes to find a
ride before they finished at the motel and started cruising the
streets. Ten minutes, maybe fifteen at the outside.

Which meant it wasn't going to work. It couldn't work.
Seven thirty-nine in the morning, the temperature was already over a hundred degrees. It was going to be impossible
to get a ride at all. In heat like that no driver on the planet

would open their door long enough for him to slide right in, never mind for any long prior discussions about destinations. So finding a getaway in time was going to be impossible. Absolutely impossible. He started planning alternatives, because he was so sure of it. But it turned out he was wrong. It turned out his whole day was a series of surprises.

There were three killers, two men and a woman. They were an out-of-state professional crew, based in Los Angeles, contactable through an intermediary in Dallas and a second cutout in Vegas. They had been in business ten years, and they were very good at what they did, which was take care of problems anywhere in the Southwest and survive to get paid and do it over again as many times as anybody asked them to. Ten years, and never once a hint of a problem. A good team. Meticulous, inventive, perfectionist. As good as it gets, in their strange little world. And perfectly suited to it. They were bland, forgettable, white, anonymous. To see them together, they looked like the branch office of a photocopier company on its way to a sales convention.

Not that they were ever seen together, except by their victims. They traveled separately. One always drove, and the other two flew, always by different routes. The driver was one of the men, because invisibility was their aim, and a woman driving a long distance alone was still slightly more memorable than a man. The car was always rented, always at LAX arrivals, which had the busiest rental counters in the world. It was always a generic family sedan, a mud-colored nothing car. The license and the credit card used to obtain it were always real, properly issued in a distant state to a person who had never existed. The driver would wait on the sidewalk and then line up when a busy flight was spilling out into baggage claim when he would be just one face among a hundred. He was small and dark and had a rolling duffel and a carry-on and a harassed expression, same as everybody else.

He did the paperwork at the counter and rode the bus to the rental compound and found his allotted car. He dumped his bags in the trunk, waited at the exit check, and drove out into the glare. He spent forty minutes on the freeways, driving a wide aimless circle around the whole of the metropolitan area, making sure he wasn't followed. Then he ducked off into West Hollywood and stopped at a lock-up garage in an alley behind a lingerie salon. He left the motor running and opened the garage door and opened the trunk and swapped his rolling duffel and his carry-on for two big valises made of thick black nylon. One of them was very heavy. The heavy valise was the reason he was driving, not flying. It contained things best kept away from airport scanners.

He closed up the garage and rolled east on Santa Monica Boulevard and turned south on 101 and hooked east again on 10. Squirmed in his seat and settled in for the two-day drive all the way out to Texas. He wasn't a smoker, but he lit numerous cigarettes and held them between his fingers and flicked ash on the carpets, on the dash, on the wheel. He let the cigarettes burn out and crushed the butts in the ashtray. That way, the rental company would have to vacuum the car very thoroughly, and spray it with air freshener, and wipe down the vinyl with detailing fluid. That would eliminate every trace of him later, including his fingerprints.

The second man was on the move, too. He was taller and heavier and fairer, but there was nothing memorable about him. He joined the end-of-the-workday crush at LAX and bought a ticket to Atlanta. When he got there, he swapped his wallet for one of the five spares in his carry-on and a completely different man bought another ticket for Dallas–Fort Worth.

The woman traveled a day later. That was her privilege, because she was the team leader. She was closing in on middle age, medium-sized, medium-blond. Nothing at all special about her, except she killed people for a living. She left her car in the LAX long-term parking, which wasn't dangerous because her car was registered to a Pasadena infant who had died of the measles thirty years previously. She rode the shuttle bus to the terminal and used a forged MasterCard to buy her ticket, and a genuine New York driver's license for photo

ID at the gate. She boarded her plane about the time the driver was starting his second day on the road.

After his second stop for gas on the first day, he had made a detour into the New Mexico hills and found a quiet dusty shoulder where he squatted in the cool thin air and changed the car's California plates for Arizona plates, which he took from the heavier valise. He wound his way back to the highway and drove another hour, then pulled off the road and found a motel. He paid cash, used a Tucson address, and let the desk clerk copy the Arizona plate number onto the registration form.

He slept six hours with the room air on low and was back on the road early. Made it to Dallas–Fort Worth at the end of the second day and parked in the airport long-term lot. Took his valises with him and used the shuttle bus to departures. Took the moving stairs straight down to arrivals and lined up at the Hertz counter. Hertz, because they rent Fords, and he needed a Crown Victoria.

He did the paperwork, with Illinois ID. Rode the bus to the Hertz lot and found his car. It was the plain-jane Crown Vic, in steel blue metallic, neither light nor dark. He was happy with it. He heaved his bags into the trunk and drove to a motel near the new ballpark on the road from Fort Worth to Dallas. Checked in with the same Illinois ID, ate, and slept a few hours. He woke early and met his two partners in the fierce morning heat outside the motel at exactly the same moment Jack Reacher first stuck out his thumb, more than four hundred miles away in Lubbock.

Second surprise after the cop showing up was he got a ride within three minutes. He wasn't even sweating yet. His shirt was still dry. Third surprise was the driver who stopped for him was a woman. Fourth and biggest surprise of all was the direction their subsequent conversation took.

He had been hitching rides for the best part of twenty-five years, in more countries than he could easily recall, and three minutes was about the shortest interval between sticking out his thumb and climbing into a car he could remember. As a mode of transportation, hitching rides was dying out. That was his conclusion, based on a lot of experience. Commercial drivers had insurance problems with it, and private citizens were getting worried about it. Because who knew what kind of a psycho you were? And in Reacher's case, it was worse than the average, especially right then. He wasn't some dapper little guy, neat and inoffensive. He was a giant, six-five, heavily built, close to two hundred and fifty pounds. Up close, he was usually scruffy, usually unshaven, and his hair was usually a mess. People worried about him. They stayed away from him. And now he had the fresh new bruise on his forehead. Which was why he was surprised about the three minutes.

And why he was surprised about the woman driver. There's usually a pecking order, based on some kind of subconscious assessment of risk. Top of the list, a young girl will get a ride from an older man easiest of all, because where's the threat in that? Although now, with some of the young girls turning into scam artists wanting a hundred bucks in exchange for dropping fake molestation claims, even that is getting harder. And whatever, right down there at the bottom of the list is a big scruffy guy getting a ride from a neat slender woman in an expensive coupe. But it happened. Within three minutes.

He was hurrying south and west of the motel strip, stunned by the heat, hard to see in the jagged morning shadows, his left thumb jammed out urgently, when she pulled over at his side with the wet hiss of wide tires on hot pavement. It was a big white car and the sun on the hood dazzled him. He turned blindly and she buzzed her far window down. Seven forty-two, Friday morning.

"Where to?" she called, like she was a cab driver, not a private citizen.

"Anywhere," he said.

He regretted it, instantly. It was a dumb thing to say, because to have no specific destination usually makes things worse. They think you're some kind of an aimless drifter, which makes them suspicious, and makes them worried they might never get rid of you. Makes them worried you'll want to ride all the way home with them. But this woman just nodded.

"O.K.," she said. "I'm headed down past Pecos."

He paused a beat, surprised. Her head was ducked down, her face tilted up, looking out at him through the window.

"Great," he said.

He stepped off the curb and opened the door and slid inside. The interior was freezing cold. She had the air roaring on maximum and the seat was leather and it felt like a block of ice. She buzzed the window up again with the button on her side as he swung the door shut behind him.

"Thanks," he said. "You don't know how much I appreciate this."

She said nothing. Just made some kind of all-purpose dismissive gesture away from him as she craned to look over her shoulder at the traffic stream behind her. People have their reasons for giving rides, all of them different. Maybe they hitched a lot when they were younger and now they're settled and comfortable they want to put back what they took out. Like a circular thing. Maybe they have charitable natures. Or maybe they're just lonely and want a little conversation.

But if this woman wanted conversation she was in no kind of a hurry to get it started. She just waited for a couple of trucks to labor past and pulled out behind them without a word. Reacher glanced around inside the car. It was a Cadillac, two doors, but as long as a boat, and very fancy. Maybe a couple of years old, but as clean as a whistle. The leather was the color of old bones and the glass was tinted like an empty bottle of French wine. There was a pocketbook and a small briefcase thrown on the backseat. The pocketbook was anonymous and black, maybe plastic. The briefcase was made from weathered cowhide, the sort of thing that already looks old when you buy it. It was zipped open and there was a lot of folded paper stuffed in it, the sort of thing you see in a lawyer's office.

"Move the seat back, if you want," the woman said. "Give yourself room."

"Thanks," he said again.

He found switches on the door shaped like seat cushions. He fiddled with them and quiet motors eased him rearward and reclined his backrest. Then he lowered the seat, to make himself inconspicuous from outside. The motors whirred. It was like being in a dentist's chair.

"That looks better," she said. "More comfortable for you."

Her own chair was tight up to the wheel, because she was small. He twisted in his seat so he could look her over without staring straight at her. She was short and slim, dark-skinned, fine-boned. Altogether a small person. Maybe a hundred pounds, maybe thirty years old. Long black wavy hair, dark eyes, small white teeth visible behind a tense half-smile. Mexican, he guessed, but not the type of Mexican who swims the Rio Grande looking for a better life. This woman's ancestors had enjoyed a better life for hundreds of years. That was pretty clear. It was in her genes. She looked like some kind of Aztec royalty. She was wearing a simple cotton dress, printed with a pale pattern. Not much to it, but it looked expensive. It was sleeveless and finished above her knees. Her arms and legs were dark and smooth, like they had been polished.

"So, where are you headed?" she asked.

Then she paused and smiled wider. "No, I already asked you that. You didn't seem very clear about where you want to go."

Her accent was pure American, maybe more western than southern. She was steering two-handed, and he could see rings on her fingers. There was a slim wedding band, and a platinum thing with a big diamond.

"Anywhere," Reacher said. "Anywhere I end up, that's where I want to go."

She paused and smiled again. "Are you running away from something? Have I picked up a dangerous fugitive?"

Her smile meant it wasn't a serious question, but he found himself thinking maybe it ought to have been. It wasn't too far-fetched, in the circumstances. She was taking a risk. The sort of risk that was killing the art of hitching rides, as a mode of transportation.

"I'm exploring," he said.

"Exploring Texas? They already discovered it."

"Like a tourist," he said.

"But you don't look like a tourist. The tourists we get wear polyester leisure suits and come in a bus."

She smiled again as she said it. She looked good when she smiled. She looked assured and self-possessed, and refined to the point of elegance. An elegant Mexican woman, wearing an expensive dress, clearly comfortable with talking. Driving a Cadillac. He was suddenly aware of his short answers, and his hair and his stubble and his stained shirt and his creased khaki pants. And the big bruise on his forehead.

"You live around here?" he asked, because she'd said *the tourists we get,* and he felt he needed something to say.

"I live south of Pecos," she said. "More than three hundred miles from here. I told you, that's where I'm headed."

"Never been there," he said.

She went quiet and waited at a light. Took off again through a wide junction and hugged the right lane. He watched her thigh move as she pressed on the gas pedal. Her bottom lip was caught between her teeth. Her eyes were narrowed. She was tense about something, but she had it under control.

"So, did you explore Lubbock?" she asked.

"I saw the Buddy Holly statue."

He saw her glance down at the radio, like she was thinking *this guy likes music, maybe I should put some on.*

"You like Buddy Holly?" she asked.

"Not really," Reacher said. "Too tame for me."

She nodded at the wheel. "I agree. I think Ritchie Valens was better. He was from Lubbock, too."

He nodded back. "I saw him in the Walk of Fame."

"How long were you in Lubbock?"

"A day."

"And now you're moving on."

"That's the plan."

"To wherever," she said.

"That's the plan," he said again.

They passed the city limit. There was a small metal sign on a pole on the sidewalk. He smiled to himself. City Police, the shield on the cop car had said. He turned his head and watched danger disappear behind him.

The two men sat in the front of the Crown Victoria, with the tall fair man driving to give the small dark man a break. The woman sat in the back. They rolled out of the motel lot and picked up speed on I-20, heading west, toward Fort Worth, away from Dallas. Nobody spoke. Thinking about the vast interior of Texas was oppressing them. The woman had read a guidebook in preparation for the mission that pointed out that the state makes up fully seven percent of America's land mass and is bigger than most European countries. That didn't impress her. Everybody knew all that standard-issue Texas-is-real-big bullshit. Everybody always has. But the guidebook also pointed out that side-to-side Texas is wider than the distance between New York and Chicago. That information had some impact. And it underlined why they were facing such a long drive, just to get from one nowhere interior location to another.

But the car was quiet and cool and comfortable, and it was as good a place to relax as any motel room would be. They had a little time to kill, after all.

The woman slowed and made a shallow right, toward New Mexico, then a mile later a left, straight south, toward old Mexico. Her dress was creased across the middle, like maybe she was wearing it a second day. Her perfume was subtle, mixed into the freezing air from the dashboard vents.

"So is Pecan worth seeing?" Reacher asked, in the silence.

"Pecos," she said.

"Right, Pecos."

She shrugged.

"I like it," she said. "It's mostly Mexican, so I'm comfortable there."

Her right hand tensed on the wheel. He saw tendons shifting under the skin.

"You like Mexican people?" she asked.

He shrugged back. "As much as I like any people, I guess."

"You don't like people?"

"It varies."

"You like cantaloupe?"

"As much as I like any fruit."

"Pecos grows the sweetest cantaloupe in the whole of Texas," she said. "And therefore, in their opinion, in the whole of the world. Also there's a rodeo there in July, but you've missed it for this year. And just north of Pecos is Loving County. You ever heard of Loving County?"

He shook his head. "Never been here before."

"It's the least-populated county in the whole of the United States," she said. "Well, if you leave out some of the places in Alaska, I guess. But also the richest, per capita. Population is a hundred and ten souls, but there are four hundred and twenty oil leases active."

He nodded. "So let me out in Pecos. It sounds like a fun place."

"It was the real Wild West," she said. "A long time ago, of course. The Texas and Pacific Railroad put a stop there. So there were saloons and all. Used to be a bad place. It was a word, too, as well as a town. A verb, and also a place. To pecos somebody meant to shoot them and throw them in the Pecos River."

"They still do that?"

She smiled again. A different smile. This smile traded some elegance for some mischief. It eased her tension. It made her appealing.

"No, they don't do that so much, now," she said.

"Your family from Pecos?"

"No, California," she said. "I came to Texas when I got married."

Keep talking, he thought. *She saved your ass.*

"Been married long?" he asked.

"Just under seven years."

"Your family been in California long?"

She paused and smiled again.

"Longer than any Californian, that's for sure," she said.

They were in flat empty country and she eased the silent

car faster down a dead-straight road. The hot sky was tinted bottle-green by the windshield. The instrumentation on her dashboard showed it was a hundred and ten degrees outside and sixty inside.

"You a lawyer?" he asked.

She was puzzled for a moment, and then she made the connection and craned to glance at her briefcase in the mirror.

"No," she said. "I'm a lawyer's client."

The conversation went dead again. She seemed nervous, and he felt awkward about it.

"And what else are you?" he asked.

She paused a beat.

"Somebody's wife and mother," she said. "And somebody's daughter and sister, I guess. And I keep a few horses. That's all. What are you?"

"Nothing in particular," Reacher said.

"You have to be something," she said.

"Well, I used to be things," he said. "I was somebody's son, and somebody's brother, and somebody's boyfriend."

"Was?"

"My parents died, my brother died, my girlfriend left me." *Not a great line,* he thought. She said nothing back.

"And I don't have any horses," he added.

"I'm very sorry," she said.

"That I don't have horses?"

"No, that you're all alone in the world."

"Water under the bridge," he said. "It's not as bad as it sounds."

"You're not lonely?"

He shrugged. "I like being alone."

She paused. "Why did your girlfriend leave you?"

"She went to work in Europe."

"And you couldn't go with her?"

"She didn't really want me to go with her."

"I see," she said. "Did *you* want to go with her?"

He was quiet for a beat.

"Not really, I guess," he said. "Too much like settling down."

"And you don't want to settle down?"

He shook his head. "Two nights in the same motel gives me the creeps."

"Hence one day in Lubbock," she said.

"And the next day in Pecos," he said.

"And after that?"

He smiled.

"After that, I have no idea," he said. "And that's the way I like it."

She drove on, silent as the car.

"So you *are* running away from something," she said. "Maybe you had a very settled life before and you want to escape from that particular feeling."

He shook his head again. "No, the exact opposite, really. I was in the army all my life, which is very *un*settled, and I grew to like the feeling."

"I see," she said. "You became habituated to chaos, maybe."

"I guess so."

She paused. "How is a person in the army all his life?"

"My father was in, too. So I grew up on military bases all over the world, and then I stayed in afterward."

"But now you're out."

He nodded. "All trained up and nowhere to go."

He saw her thinking about his answer. He saw her tension come back. She started stepping harder on the gas, maybe without realizing it, maybe like an involuntary reflex. He had the feeling her interest in him was quickening, like the car.

Ford builds Crown Victorias at its plant up in St. Thomas, Canada, tens of thousands a year, and almost all of them without exception are sold to police departments, taxicab companies, or rental fleets. Almost none of them are sold to private citizens. Full-size turnpike cruisers no longer earn much of a market share, and for those die-hards who still want one from the Ford Motor Company, the Mercury Grand Marquis is the same car in fancier clothes for about the same money, so it mops up the private sales. Which makes private Crown Vics rarer than red Rolls-Royces, so the subliminal re-

sponse when you see one that isn't taxicab yellow or black
and white with *Police* all over the doors is to think it's an unmarked detective's car. Or government issue of some other
kind, maybe U.S. Marshals, or FBI, or Secret Service, or a
courtesy vehicle given to a medical examiner or a big-city
fire chief.

That's the subliminal impression, and there are ways to en-
hance it a little.

In the empty country halfway to Abilene, the tall fair man
pulled off the highway and headed through vast fields and
past dense woodlands until he found a dusty turn-out probably ten miles from the nearest human being. He stopped there
and turned off the motor and popped the trunk. The small
dark man heaved the heavy valise out and laid it on the
ground. The woman zipped it open and handed a pair of Virginia plates to the tall fair man. He took a screwdriver from
the valise and removed the Texas plates, front and rear.
Bolted the Virginia issue in their place. The small dark man
pulled the plastic covers off all four wheels, leaving the
cheap black steel rims showing. He stacked the wheel covers
like plates and pitched them into the trunk. The woman took
radio antennas from the valise, four of them, CB whips and
cellular telephone items bought cheap at a Radio Shack in
L.A. The cellular antennas stuck to the rear window with
self-adhesive pads. She waited until the trunk was closed
again and placed the CB antennas on the lid. They had mag-
netic bases. They weren't wired up to anything. They were
just for show.

Then the small dark man took his rightful place behind the
wheel and U-turned through the dust and headed back to the
highway, cruising easily. A Crown Vic, plain steel wheels, a
forest of antennas, Virginia plates. Maybe an FBI pool car,
three agents inside, maybe on urgent business.

"What did you do in the army?" the woman asked, very casually.

"I was a cop," Reacher said.

"They have cops in the army?"

"Sure they do," he said. "Military police. Like cops, inside the service."

"I didn't know that," she said.

She went quiet again. She was thinking hard. She seemed excited.

"Would you mind if I asked you some questions?" she said.

He shrugged. "You're giving me a ride."

She nodded. "I wouldn't want to offend you."

"That would be hard to do, in the circumstances. Hundred and ten degrees out there, sixty in here."

"There'll be a storm soon. There has to be, with a temperature like this."

He glanced ahead at the sky. It was tinted bottle-green by the windshield glass, and it was blindingly clear.

"I don't see any sign of it," he said.

She smiled again, briefly. "May I ask where you live?"

"I don't live anywhere," he said. "I move around."

"You don't have a home somewhere?"

He shook his head. "What you see is what I've got."

"You travel light," she said.

"Light as I can."

She paused for a fast mile.

"Are you out of work?" she asked.

He nodded. "Usually."

"Were you a good cop? In the army?"

"Good enough, I guess. They made me a major, gave me some medals."

She paused. "So why did you leave?"

It felt like an interview. For a loan, or for a job.

"They downsized me out of there," he said. "End of the Cold War, they wanted a smaller army, not so many people in it, so they didn't need so many cops to look after them."

She nodded. "Like a town. If the population gets smaller, the police department gets smaller, too. Something to do with appropriations. Taxes, or something."

He said nothing.

"I live in a very small town," she said. "Echo, south of Pecos, like I told you. It's a lonely place. That's why they named it Echo. Not because it's echoey, like an empty room. It's from ancient Greek mythology. Echo was a young girl in love with Narcissus. But he loved himself, not her, so she pined away until just her voice was left. So that's why it's called Echo. Not many inhabitants. But it's a county, too. A county and a township. Not as empty as Loving County, but there's no police department at all. Just the county sheriff, on his own."

Something in her voice.

"Is that a problem?" he asked.

"It's a very *white* county," she said. "Not like Pecos at all."

"So?"

"So one feels there *might* be a problem, if push came to shove."

"And has push come to shove?"

She smiled, awkwardly.

"I can tell you were a cop," she said. "You ask so many questions. And it's me who wanted to ask all the questions."

She fell silent for a spell and just drove, slim dark hands light on the wheel, going fast but not hurrying. He used the cushion-shaped buttons again and laid his seat back another fraction. Watched her in the corner of his eye. She was pretty, but she was troubled. Ten years from now, she was going to have some excellent frown lines.

"What was life like in the army?" she asked.

"Different," he said. "Different from life outside the army."

"Different how?"

"Different rules, different situations. It was a world of its own. It was very regulated, but it was kind of lawless. Kind of rough and uncivilized."

"Like the Wild West," she said.

"I guess," he said back. "A million people trained first and foremost to do what needed doing. The rules came afterward."

"Like the Wild West," she said again. "I think you liked it."

He nodded. "Some of it."

She paused. "May I ask you a personal question?"

"Go ahead," he said.

"What's your name?"

"Reacher," he said.

"Is that your first name? Or your last?"

"People just call me Reacher," he said.

She paused again. "May I ask you another personal question?"

He nodded.

"Have you killed people, Reacher? In the army?"

He nodded again. "Some."

"That's what the army is all about, fundamentally, isn't it?" she said.

"I guess so," he said. "Fundamentally."

She went quiet again. Like she was struggling with a decision.

"There's a museum in Pecos," she said. "A real Wild West museum. It's partly in an old saloon, and partly in the old hotel next door. Out back is the site of Clay Allison's grave. You ever heard of Clay Allison?"

Reacher shook his head.

"They called him the Gentleman Gunfighter," she said. "He retired, actually, but then he fell under the wheels of a grain cart and he died from his injuries. They buried him there. There's a nice headstone, with 'Robert Clay Allison, 1840–1887' on it. I've seen it. And an inscription. The inscription says, 'He never killed a man that did not need killing.' What do you think of that?"

"I think it's a fine inscription," Reacher said.

"There's an old newspaper, too," she said. "In a glass case. From Kansas City, I think, with his obituary in it. It says, 'Certain it is that many of his stern deeds were for the right as he understood that right to be.'"

The Cadillac sped on south.

"A fine obituary," Reacher said.

"You think so?"

He nodded. "As good as you can get, probably."

"Would you like an obituary like that?"

"Well, not just yet," Reacher said.

She smiled again, apologetically.

"No," she said. "I guess not. But do you think you would like to *qualify* for an obituary like that? I mean, eventually?"

"I can think of worse things," he said.

She said nothing.

"You want to tell me where this is heading?" he asked.

"This road?" she said, nervously.

"No, this conversation."

She drove on for a spell, and then she lifted her foot off the gas pedal and coasted. The car slowed and she pulled off onto the dusty shoulder. The shoulder fell away into a dry irrigation ditch and it put the car at a crazy angle, tilted way down on his side. She put the transmission in park with a small delicate motion of her wrist, and she left the engine idling and the air roaring.

"My name is Carmen Greer," she said. "And I need your help."

2

"It wasn't an accident I picked you up, you know," Carmen Greer said.

Reacher's back was pressed against his door. The Cadillac was listing like a sinking ship, canted hard over on the shoulder. The slippery leather seat gave him no leverage to struggle upright. The woman had one hand on the wheel and the other on his seat back, propping herself above him. Her face was a foot away. It was unreadable. She was looking past him, out at the dust of the ditch.

"You going to be able to drive off this slope?" he asked.

She glanced back and up at the blacktop. Its rough surface was shimmering with heat, about level with the base of her window.

"I think so," she said. "I hope so."

"I hope so, too," he said.

She just stared at him.

"So why did you pick me up?" he asked.

"Why do you think?"

"I don't know," he said. "I thought I just got lucky. I guess I thought you were a kind person doing a stranger a favor."

She shook her head.

"No, I was looking for a guy like you," she said.

"Why?"

"I must have picked up a dozen guys," she said. "And I've seen hundreds. That's about all I've been doing, all month long. Cruising around West Texas, looking at who needs a ride."

"Why?"

She shrugged the question away. A dismissive little gesture.

"The miles I've put on this car," she said. "It's unbelievable. And the money I've spent on gas."

"Why?" he asked again.

She went quiet. Wouldn't answer. Just went into a long silence. The armrest on the door was digging into his kidney. He arched his back and pressed with his shoulders and adjusted his position. Found himself wishing somebody else had picked him up. Somebody content just to motor from A to B. He looked up at her.

"Can I call you Carmen?" he asked.

She nodded. "Sure. Please."

"O.K., Carmen," he said. "Tell me what's going on here, will you?"

Her mouth opened, and then it closed again. Opened, and closed.

"I don't know how to start," she said. "Now that it's come to it."

"Come to what?"

She wouldn't answer.

"You better tell me exactly what you want," he said. "Or I'm getting out of the car right here, right now."

"It's a hundred and ten degrees out there."

"I know it is."

"A person could die in this heat."

"I'll take my chances."

"You can't get your door open," she said. "The car is tilted too much."

"Then I'll punch out the windshield."

She paused a beat.

"I need your help," she said again.

"You never saw me before."

"Not personally," she said. "But you fit the bill."

"What bill?"

She went quiet again. Came up with a brief, ironic smile.

"It's so difficult," she said. "I've rehearsed this speech a million times, but now I don't know if it's going to come out right."

Reacher said nothing. Just waited.

"You ever had anything to do with lawyers?" she asked. "They don't do anything for you. They just want a lot of money and a lot of time, and then they tell you there's nothing much to be done."

"So get a new lawyer," he said.

"I've had four," she said. "Four, in a month. They're all the same. And they're all too expensive. I don't have enough money."

"You're driving a Cadillac."

"It's my mother-in-law's. I'm only borrowing it."

"You're wearing a big diamond ring."

She went quiet again. Her eyes clouded.

"My husband gave it to me," she said.

He looked at her. "So can't he help you?"

"No, he can't help me," she said. "Have you ever gone looking for a private detective?"

"Never needed one. I *was* a detective."

"They don't really exist," she said. "Not like you see in the movies. They just want to sit in their offices and work with the phone. Or on their computers, with their databases. They won't come out and actually *do* anything for you. I went all the way to Austin. A guy there said he could help, but he wanted to use six men and charge me nearly ten thousand dollars a week."

"For what?"

"So I got desperate. I was really panicking. Then I got this idea. I figured if I looked at people hitching rides, I might find somebody. One of them might turn out to be the right type of person, and willing to help me. I tried to choose pretty carefully. I only stopped for rough-looking men."

"Thanks, Carmen," Reacher said.

"I don't mean it badly," she said. "It's not uncomplimentary."

"But it could have been dangerous."

She nodded. "It nearly was, a couple of times. But I had to take the risk. I had to find *somebody*. I figured I might get rodeo guys, or men from the oil fields. You know, tough guys, roughnecks, maybe out of work, with a little time on their hands. Maybe a little anxious to earn some money, but I can't pay much. Is that going to be a problem?"

"So far, Carmen, everything is going to be a problem."

She went quiet again.

"I talked to them all," she said. "You know, chatted with them a little, discussed things, like we did. I was trying to make some kind of judgment about what they were like, inside, in terms of their characters. I was trying to assess their qualities. Maybe twelve of them. And none of them were really any good. But I think you are."

"You think I'm what?"

"I think you're my best chance so far," she said. "Really, I do. A former cop, been in the army, no ties anywhere, you couldn't be better."

"I'm not looking for a job, Carmen."

She nodded happily. "I know. I figured that out already. But that's better still, I think. It keeps it pure, don't you see that? Help for help's sake. No mercenary aspect to it. And your background is perfect. It obligates you."

He stared at her. "No, it doesn't."

"You were a soldier," she said. "And a *policeman*. It's perfect. You're *supposed* to help people. That's what cops *do*."

"We spent most of our time busting heads. Not a whole lot of helping went on."

"But it must have. That's what cops are *for*. It's like their fundamental duty. And an army cop is even better. You said it yourself, you do what's necessary."

"If you need a cop, go to the county sheriff. Pecos, or wherever it is."

"Echo," she said. "I live in Echo. South of Pecos."

"Wherever," he said. "Go to the sheriff."

She was shaking her head. "No, I can't do that."

Reacher said nothing more. Just lay half on his back, pressed up against the door by the car's steep angle. The engine was idling patiently, and the air was still roaring. The woman was still braced above him. She had gone silent. She was staring out past him and blinking, like she was about to cry. Like she was ready for a big flood of tears. Like she was tragically disappointed, maybe with him, maybe with herself.

"You must think I'm crazy," she said.

He turned his head and looked hard at her, top to toe. Strong slim legs, strong slim arms, the expensive dress. It was riding up on her thighs, and he could see her bra strap at her shoulder. It was snow white against the color of her skin. She had clean combed hair and trimmed painted nails. An elegant, intelligent face, tired eyes.

"I'm not crazy," she said.

Then she looked straight at him. Something in her face. Maybe an appeal. Or maybe hopelessness, or desperation.

"It's just that I've dreamed about this for a month," she said. "My last hope. It was a ridiculous plan, I guess, but it's all I had. And there was always the chance it would work, and with you I think maybe it could, and now I'm screwing it up by coming across like a crazy woman."

He paused a long time. Minutes. He thought back to a pancake house he'd seen in Lubbock, right across the strip from his motel. It had looked pretty good. He could have crossed the street, gone in there, had a big stack with bacon on the side. Lots of syrup. Maybe an egg. He would have come out a half hour after she blew town. He could be sitting next to some cheerful trucker now, listening to rock and roll on the radio. On the other hand, he could be bruised and bleeding in a police cell, with an arraignment date coming up.

"So start over," he said. "Just say what you've got to say. But first, drive us out of this damn ditch. I'm very uncomfortable. And I could use a cup of coffee. Is there anyplace up ahead where we could get coffee?"

"I think so," she said. "Yes, there is. About an hour, I think."

"So let's go there. Let's get a cup of coffee."

"You're going to dump me and run," she said.

It was an attractive possibility. She stared at him, maybe five long seconds, and then she nodded, like a decision was made. She put the transmission in D and hit the gas. The car had front-wheel drive, and all the weight was on the back, so the tires just clawed at nothing and spun. Gravel rattled against the underbody and a cloud of hot khaki dust rose up all around them. Then the tires caught and the car heaved itself out of the ditch and bounced up over the edge of the blacktop. She got it straight in the lane, and then she floored it and took off south.

"I don't know where to begin," she said.

"At the beginning," he said. "Always works best that way. Think about it, tell me over coffee. We've got the time."

She shook her head. Stared forward through the windshield, eyes locked on the empty shimmering road ahead. She was quiet for a mile, already doing seventy.

"No, we don't," she said. "It's real urgent."

Fifty miles southwest of Abilene, on a silent county road ten miles north of the main east-west highway, the Crown Victoria waited quietly on the shoulder, its engine idling, its hood unlatched and standing an inch open for better cooling. All around it was flatness so extreme the curvature of the earth was revealed, the dusty parched brush falling slowly away to the horizon in every direction. There was no traffic, and therefore no noise beyond the tick and whisper of the idling engine and the heavy buzz of the earth baking and cracking under the unbearable heat of the sun.

The driver had the electric door mirror racked all the way outward so he could see the whole of the road behind him. The Crown Vic's own dust had settled and the view was clear for about a mile, right back to the point where the blacktop and the sky mixed together and broke and boiled into a silvery shimmering mirage. The driver had his eyes focused on that distant glare, waiting for it to be pierced by the indistinct shape of a car.

He knew what car it would be. The team was well briefed. It would be a white Mercedes Benz, driven by a man on his own toward an appointment he couldn't miss. The man would be driving fast, because he would be running late, because he was habitually late for everything. They knew the time of his appointment, and they knew his destination was thirty miles farther on up the road, so simple arithmetic gave them a target time they could set their watches by. A target time that was fast approaching.

"So let's do it," the driver said.

He stepped out of the car into the heat and clicked the hood down into place. Slid back into the seat and took a ball cap from the woman. It was one of three bought from a souvenir vendor on Hollywood Boulevard, thirteen ninety-five each. It was dark blue, with *FBI* machine-embroidered in white cotton thread across the front. The driver squared it on his head and pulled the peak low over his eyes. Moved the transmission lever into drive and kept his foot hard on the brake. Leaned forward a fraction and kept his eyes on the mirror.

"Right on time," he said.

The silver mirage was boiling and wobbling and a white shape pulled free of it and speared out toward them like a fish leaping out of water. The shape settled and steadied on the road, moving fast, crouching low. A white Mercedes sedan, wide tires, dark windows.

The driver eased his foot off the brake and the Crown Vic crawled forward through the dust. He touched the gas when the Mercedes was still a hundred yards behind him. The Mercedes roared past and the Crown Vic pulled out into the hot blast of its slipstream. The driver straightened the wheel and accelerated. Smiled with his lips hard together. The killing crew was going to work again.

The Mercedes driver saw headlights flashing in his mirror and looked again and saw the sedan behind him. Two peaked caps silhouetted in the front seat. He dropped his eyes automatically to his speedometer, which was showing more than ninety. Felt the cold *oh-shit* stab in his chest. Eased off the

gas while he calculated how late he was already and how far
he still had to go and what his best approach to these guys
should be. Humility? Or maybe *I'm-too-important-to-be-
hassled*? Or what about a sort of *come-on-guys, I'm-work-
ing-too* camaraderie?

The sedan pulled alongside as he slowed and he saw three
people, one of them a woman. Radio antennas all over the
car. No lights, no siren. Not regular cops. The driver was
waving him to the shoulder. The woman was pressing an ID
wallet against her window. It had *FBI* in two-inch-high letters. Their caps said *FBI*. Serious-looking people, in some
kind of duty fatigues. Serious-looking squad car. He relaxed
a little. The FBI didn't stop you for speeding. Must be something else. Maybe some kind of security check, which made
sense considering what lay thirty miles up the road. He nodded to the woman and braked and eased right, onto the shoulder. He feathered the pedal and coasted to a stop in a big
cloud of dust. The Bureau car eased up and stopped behind
him, the brightness of its headlight beams dimmed by the
cloud.

The way to do it is to keep them quiet and alive as long as
possible. Postpone any kind of struggle. Struggling leads to
evidence, blood and fibers and body fluids spraying and leak-
ing all over the place. So they all three got out of the car at a
medium speed, like they were harassed professionals dealing
with something important, but not something right up there at
the top of their agenda.

"Mr. Eugene?" the woman called. "Al Eugene, right?"

The Mercedes driver opened his door and slid out of his
seat and stood up in the heat and the glare. He was around
thirty, not tall, dark and sallow, soft and rounded. He faced
the woman, and she saw some kind of innate southern courtesy toward women place him at an immediate disadvantage.

"What can I do for you, ma'am?" he asked.

"Your cellular phone not working, sir?" the woman asked.

Eugene patted at the pocket of his suit coat.

"Should be," he said.

"May I see it, sir?"

Eugene took it out of his pocket and handed it over. The woman dialed a number and looked surprised.

"Seems O.K.," she said. "Sir, can you spare us five minutes?"

"Maybe," Eugene said. "If you tell me what for."

"We have an FBI assistant director a mile up the road, needs to speak with you. Something urgent, I guess, or we wouldn't be here, and something pretty important, or we'd have been told what it's all about."

Eugene pulled back his cuff and looked at his watch.

"I have an appointment," he said.

The woman was nodding. "We know about that, sir. We took the liberty of calling ahead and rescheduling for you. Five minutes is all we need."

Eugene shrugged.

"Can I see some ID?" he asked.

The woman handed over her wallet. It was made of worn black leather and had a milky plastic window on the outside. There was an FBI photo-ID behind it, laminated and embossed and printed with the kind of slightly old-fashioned typeface the federal government might use. Like most people in the United States, Eugene had never seen an FBI ID. He assumed he was looking at his first.

"Up the road a-piece?" he said. "O.K., I'll follow you, I guess."

"We'll drive you," the woman said. "There's a checkpoint in place, and civilian cars make them real nervous. We'll bring you right back. Five minutes, is all."

Eugene shrugged again.

"O.K.," he said.

They all walked as a group back toward the Crown Vic. The driver held the front passenger door for Eugene.

"You ride up here, sir," he said. "They're listing you as a class-A individual, and if we put a class-A individual in the backseat, then we'll get our asses kicked but good, that's for damn sure."

They saw Eugene swell up a little from his assigned status. He nodded and ducked down and slid into the front seat. Either he hadn't noticed they still had his phone, or he didn't care. The driver closed the door on him and ducked around the hood to his own. The tall fair man and the woman climbed into the rear. The Crown Vic eased around the parked Benz and pulled left onto the blacktop. Accelerated up to about fifty-five.

"Ahead," the woman said.

The driver nodded.

"I see it," he said. "We'll make it."

There was a plume of dust on the road, three or four miles into the distance. It was rising up and dragging left in the faint breeze. The driver slowed, hunting the turn he had scouted thirty minutes before. He spotted it and pulled left and crossed the opposite shoulder and bumped down through a depression where the road was built up like a causeway. Then he slewed to the right, tight in behind a stand of brush tall enough to hide the car. The man and the woman in the rear seat came out with handguns and leaned forward and jammed them into Eugene's neck, right behind the ears where the structure of the human skull provides two nice muzzle-shaped sockets.

"Sit real still," the woman said.

Eugene sat real still. Two minutes later, a big dark vehicle blasted by above them. A truck, or a bus. Dust clouded the sky and the brush rustled in the moving air. The driver got out and approached Eugene's door with a gun in his hand. He opened the door and leaned in and jammed the muzzle into Eugene's throat, where the ends of the collarbones make another convenient socket.

"Get out," he said. "Real careful."

"What?" was all Eugene could say.

"We'll tell you what," the woman said. "Now get out."

Eugene got out, with three guns at his head.

"Step away from the car," the woman said. "Walk away from the road."

This was the tricky time. Eugene was glancing around as far and as fast as he dared move his head. His eyes were jumping. His body was twitching. He stepped away from the

car. One pace, two, three. Eyes everywhere. The woman
nodded.

"Al," she called loudly.

Her two partners jumped away, long sideways strides. Eugene's head snapped around to face the woman who had
called his name. She shot him through the right eye. The
sound of the gun clapped and rolled across the hot landscape
like thunder. The back of Eugene's head came off in a messy
cloud and he went straight down and sprawled in a loose tangle of arms and legs. The woman stepped around him and
crouched down and took a closer look. Then she stepped
away and stood up straight with her legs and arms spread,
like she was ready to be searched at the airport.

"Check," she said.

The two men stepped close and examined every inch of
her skin and clothing. They checked her hair and her hands.

"Clear," the small dark man said.

"Clear," the tall fair man said.

She nodded. A faint smile. No residue. No evidence. No
blood or bone or brains anywhere on her person.

"O.K.," she said.

The two men stepped back to Eugene and took an arm and
a leg each and dragged his body ten feet into the brush. They
had found a narrow limestone cleft there, a crack in the rock
maybe eight feet deep and a foot and a half across, wide
enough to take a man's corpse sideways, too narrow to admit
the six-foot wingspan of a vulture or a buzzard. They maneuvered the body until the trailing hand and the trailing foot fell
into the hole. Then they lowered away carefully until they
were sure the torso would fit. This guy was fatter than some.
But he slid in without snagging on the rock. As soon as they
were sure, they dropped him the rest of the way. He wedged
tight, about seven feet down.

The bloodstains were already drying and blackening. They
kicked desert dust over them and swept the area with a
mesquite branch to confuse the mass of footprints. Then they
walked over and climbed into the Crown Vic and the driver
backed up and swung through the brush. Bounced through

the dip and up the slope to the roadway. The big car nosed
back the way it had come and accelerated gently to fifty-five
miles an hour. Moments later it passed by Eugene's white
Mercedes, parked right where he'd left it, on the other side of
the road. It already looked abandoned and filmed with dust.

"**I have a** daughter," Carmen Greer said. "I told you that,
right?"

"You told me you were a mother," Reacher said.

She nodded at the wheel. "Of a daughter. She's six and a
half years old."

Then she went quiet for a minute.

"They called her Mary Ellen," she said.

"They?"

"My husband's family."

"They named your kid?"

"It just happened, I guess. I wasn't in a good position to
stop it."

Reacher was quiet for a beat.

"What would you have called her?" he asked.

She shrugged. "Gloria, maybe. I thought she was glorious."

She went quiet again.

"But she's Mary Ellen," he said.

She nodded. "They call her Ellie, for short. Miss Ellie,
sometimes."

"And she's six and a half?"

"But we've been married less than seven years. I told you
that, too, right? So you can do the math. Is that a problem?"

"Doing the math?"

"Thinking about the implication."

He shook his head at the windshield. "Not a problem to
me. Why would it be?"

"Not a problem to me, either," she said. "But it explains
why I wasn't in a good position."

He made no reply.

"We got off to all kinds of a bad start," she said. "Me and
his family."

She said it with a dying fall in her voice, the way a person might refer back to a tragedy in the past, a car wreck, a plane crash, a fatal diagnosis. The way a person might refer back to the day her life changed forever. She gripped the wheel and the car drove itself on, a cocoon of cold and quiet in the blazing landscape.

"Who are they?" he asked.

"The Greers," she said. "An old Echo County family. Been there since Texas was first stolen. Maybe they were there to steal some of it themselves."

"What are they like?"

"They're what you might expect," she said. "Old white Texans, big money from way back, a lot of it gone now but a lot of it still left, some history with oil and cattle ranching, river-baptized Protestants, not that they ever go to church or think about what the Lord might be saying to them. They hunt animals for pleasure. The father died some time ago, the mother is still alive, there are two sons, and there are cousins all over the county. My husband is the elder boy, Sloop Greer."

"Sloop?" Reacher said.

She smiled for the first time since driving out of the ditch.

"Sloop," she said again.

"What kind of a name is that?"

"An old family name," she said. "Some ancestor, I guess. Probably he was at the Alamo, fighting against mine."

"Sounds like a boat. What's the other boy called? Yacht? Tug? Ocean liner? Oil tanker?"

"Robert," she said. "People call him Bobby."

"Sloop," Reacher said again. "That's a new one to me."

"New to me, too," she said. "The whole thing was new to me. But I used to like his name. It marked him out, somehow."

"I guess it would."

"I met him in California," Carmen said. "We were in school together, UCLA."

"Off of his home turf," Reacher said.

She stopped smiling. "Correct. Only way it could have happened, looking back. If I'd have met him out here, you

know, with the whole package out in plain view, it would
never have happened. No way. I can promise you that. Always assuming I'd even *come* out here, in the first place,
which I hope I wouldn't have."

She stopped talking and squinted ahead into the glare of
the sun. There was a ribbon of black road and a bright shape
up ahead on the left, shiny aluminum broken into moving
fragments by the haze boiling up off the blacktop.

"There's the diner," she said. "They'll have coffee, I'm
sure."

"Strange kind of a diner if it didn't," he said.

"There are lots of strange things here," she said.

The diner sat alone on the side of the road, set on a slight
rise in the center of an acre of beaten dirt serving as its parking lot. There was a sign on a tall pole and no shade anywhere. There were two pick-up trucks, carelessly parked, far
from each other.

"O.K.," she said, hesitant, starting to slow the car. "Now
you're going to run. You figure one of those guys with the
pick-ups will give you a ride."

He said nothing.

"If you are, do it later, O.K.?" she said. "Please? I don't
want to be left alone in a place like this."

She slowed some more and bounced off the road onto the
dirt. Parked right next to the sign pole, as if it was a shade
tree offering protection from the sun. Its slender shadow fell
across the hood like a bar. She pushed the lever into Park and
switched off the engine. The air conditioner's compressor
hissed and gurgled in the sudden silence. Reacher opened his
door. The heat hit him like a steelyard furnace. It was so intense he could barely catch his breath. He stood dumb for a
second and waited for her and then they walked together
across the hot dirt. It was baked dry and hard, like concrete.
Beyond it was a tangle of mesquite brush and a blinding
white-hot sky as far as the eye could see. He let her walk half
a pace ahead of him, so he could watch her. She had her eyes
half-closed and her head bowed, like she didn't want to see or
be seen. The hem on her dress had fallen to a decorous knee-
length. She moved very gracefully, like a dancer, her upper

body erect and perfectly still and her bare legs scissoring elegantly below it.

The diner had a tiny foyer with a cigarette machine and a rack full of flyers about real estate and oil changes and small-town rodeos and gun shows. Inside the second door it was cold again. They stood together in the delicious chill for a moment. There was a register next to the door and a tired waitress sitting sideways on a counter stool. A cook visible in the kitchen. Two men in separate booths, eating. All four people looked up and paused, like there were things they could say but wouldn't.

Reacher looked at each of them for a second and then turned away and led Carmen to a booth at the far end of the room. He slid across sticky vinyl and tilted his head back into a jet of cold air coming down from a vent in the ceiling. Carmen sat opposite and raised her head and he looked at her face-on for the first time.

"My daughter looks nothing at all like me," she said. "Sometimes I think that's the cruelest irony in this whole situation. Those big old Greer genes just about steamrollered mine, that's for sure."

She had spectacular dark eyes with long lashes and a slight tilt to them, and a straight nose that made an open Y-shape against her brows. High cheekbones framed by thick black hair that shone navy in the light. A rosebud of a mouth with a subtle trace of red lipstick. Her skin was smooth and clear, the color of weak tea or dark honey, and it had a translucent glow behind it. It was actually a whole lot lighter in color than Reacher's own sunburned forearms, and he was white and she wasn't.

"So who does Ellie look like?" he asked.

"Them," she said.

The waitress brought ice water and a pad and a pencil and an upturned chin and no conversation. Carmen ordered iced coffee and Reacher ordered his hot and black.

"She doesn't look like she's mine at all," Carmen said. "Pink skin, yellow hair, a little chubby. But she's got my eyes."

"Lucky Ellie," Reacher said.

She smiled briefly. "Thank you. Plan is she should stay lucky."

She held the water glass flat against her face. Then she used a napkin to wipe the dew away. The waitress brought their drinks. The iced coffee was in a tall glass, and she spilled some of it as she put it down. Reacher's was in an insulated plastic carafe, and she shoved an empty china mug across the table next to it. She left the check facedown halfway between the two drinks, and walked away without saying anything at all.

"You need to understand I loved Sloop once," Carmen said.

Reacher made no reply, and she looked straight at him.

"Does it bother you to hear this kind of stuff?" she asked.

He shook his head, although the truth was it did bother him, a little. Loners aren't necessarily too comfortable with a stranger's intimacies.

"You told me to start at the beginning," she said.

"Yes," he said. "I did."

"So I will," she said. "I loved him once. You need to understand that. And you need to understand that wasn't hard to do. He was big, and he was handsome, and he smiled a lot, and he was casual, and he was relaxed. And we were in school and we were young, and L.A. is a very special place, where anything seems possible and nothing seems to matter very much."

She took a drinking straw from the canister on the table and unwrapped it.

"And you need to know where I was coming from," she said. "Truth is, I had it all completely backward. I wasn't some Mexican worrying about whether the white family would accept me. I was worrying about *my* family accepting this gringo boy. That's how it seemed to me. I come from a thousand acres in Napa, we've been there forever, we were always the richest people I knew. And the most cultured. We had the art, and the history, and the music. We gave to museums. We employed white people. So I spent my time worrying about what my folks would say about me marrying out."

He sipped his coffee. It was stewed and old, but it would do.

"And what did they say?" he asked.

"They went insane. I thought they were being foolish. Now I understand they weren't."

"So what happened?"

She sipped her drink through the straw. Took a napkin from a canister and dabbed her lips. It came away marked with her lipstick.

"Well, I was pregnant," she said. "And that made everything a million times worse, of course. My parents are very devout, and they're very traditional, and basically they cut me off, I guess. They disowned me. It was like the whole Victorian thing, expelled from the snowy doorstep with a bundle of rags, except it wasn't snowing, of course, and the bundle of rags was really a Louis Vuitton valise."

"So what did you do?"

"We got married. Nobody came, just a few friends from school. We lived a few months in L.A., we graduated, we stayed there until the baby was a month away. It was fun, actually. We were young and in love."

He poured himself a second cup of coffee.

"But?" he asked.

"But Sloop couldn't find a job. I began to realize he wasn't trying very hard. Getting a job wasn't in his plan. College was four years of fun for him, then it was back to the fold, go take over Daddy's business. His father was ready to retire by then. I didn't like that idea. I thought we were starting up fresh, on our own, you know, a new generation on both sides. I felt I'd given stuff up, and I thought he should, too. So we argued a lot. I couldn't work, because of being so pregnant, and I had no money of my own. So in the end we couldn't make the rent, so in the end he won the argument, and we trailed back here to Texas, and we moved in to the big old house with his folks and his brother and his cousins all around, and I'm still there."

The dying fall was back in her voice. The day her life changed forever.

"And?" he asked.

She looked straight at him. "And it was like the ground opens up and you fall straight through to hell. It was such a shock, I couldn't even react at all. They treated me strange, and the second day I suddenly realized what was going on. All my life I'd been like a princess, you know, and then I was just a hip kid among ten thousand others in L.A., but now I was suddenly just a piece of beaner trash. They never said it straight out, but it was *so* clear. They hated me, because I was the greaseball whore who'd hooked their darling boy. They were painfully polite, because I guess their strategy was to wait for Sloop to come to his senses and dump me. It happens, you know, in Texas. The good old boys, when they're young and foolish, they like a little dark meat. Sometimes it's like a rite of passage. Then they wise up and straighten out. I knew that's what they were thinking. And hoping. And it was a shock, believe me. I had never thought of myself like that. Never. I'd never had to. Never had to confront it. The whole world was turned upside down, in an instant. Like falling in freezing water. Couldn't breathe, couldn't think, couldn't even move."

"But he didn't dump you, evidently."

She looked down at the table.

"No," she said. "He didn't dump me. He started hitting me instead. First time, he punched me in the face. Then Ellie was born the next day."

The Crown Victoria turned back into a normal Hertz rental behind a stand of trees eight miles off the highway, halfway between Abilene and Big Spring. The Virginia plates came off, and the Texas plates went back on. The plastic wheel covers were kicked back into place. The cellular antennas were peeled off the rear glass and laid back in the valise. The CB whips pulled clear of the sheet metal and joined them. The souvenir ball caps were nested together and packed away with the handguns. Eugene's mobile phone was smashed against a rock and the pieces hurled deep into the thicket. A little grit from the shoulder of the road was sprinkled onto the front passenger seat, so that the rental people would have to vacuum up any of Eugene's stray hairs and fibers along with it.

Then the big sedan pulled back onto the blacktop and wound its way back to the highway. It cruised comfortably, heading west, a forgettable vehicle filled with three forgettable people. It made one more stop, at a comfort area named for the Colorado River, where sodas were consumed and a call was made from an untraceable payphone. The call was to Las Vegas, from where it was rerouted to Dallas, from where it was rerouted to an office in a small town in the west of Texas. The call reported complete success so far, and it was gratefully received.

"**He split my** lip and loosened my teeth," Carmen Greer said.

Reacher watched her face.

"That was the first time," she said. "He just lost it. But straight away he was full of remorse. He drove me to the emergency room himself. It's a long, long drive from the house, hours and hours, and the whole way he was begging me to forgive him. Then he was begging me not to tell the truth about what had happened. He seemed really ashamed, so I agreed. But I never had to say anything anyway, because as soon as we arrived I started into labor and they took me straight upstairs to the delivery unit. Ellie was born the next day."

"And then what?"

"And then it was O.K.," she said. "For a week, at least. Then he started hitting me again. I was doing everything wrong. I was paying too much attention to the baby, I didn't want sex because I was hurting from the stitches. He said I had gotten fat and ugly from the pregnancy."

Reacher said nothing.

"He got me believing it," she said. "For a long, long time. That happens, you know. You've got to be very self-confident to resist it. And I wasn't, in that situation. He took away all my self-esteem. Two or three years, I thought it *was* my fault, and I tried to do better."

"What did the family do?"

She pushed her glass away. Left the iced coffee half-finished.

"They didn't know about it," she said. "And then his father died, which made it worse. He was the only reasonable one. He was O.K. But now it's just his mother and his brother. He's awful, and she's a witch. And they still don't know. It happens in secret. It's a big house. It's like a compound, really. We're not all on top of each other. And it's all very complicated. He's way too stubborn and proud to ever agree with them he's made a mistake. So the more they're down on me, the more he pretends he loves me. He misleads them. He buys me things. He bought me this ring."

She held up her right hand, bent delicately at the wrist, showing off the platinum band with the big diamond. It looked like a hell of a thing. Reacher had never bought a diamond ring. He had no idea what they cost. A lot, he guessed.

"He bought me horses," she said. "They knew I wanted horses, and he bought them for me, so he could look good in front of them. But really to explain away the bruises. It was his stroke of genius. A permanent excuse. He makes me say I've fallen off. They know I'm still just learning to ride. And that explains a lot in rodeo country, bruises and broken bones. They take it for granted."

"He's broken your bones?"

She nodded, and started touching parts of her body, twisting and turning in the confines of the tight booth, silently recounting her injuries, hesitating slightly now and then like she couldn't recall them all.

"My ribs, first of all, I guess," she said. "He kicks me when I'm on the floor. He does that a lot, when he's mad. My left arm, by twisting it. My collarbone. My jaw. I've had three teeth reimplanted."

He stared at her.

She shrugged. "The emergency room people think I'm the worst rider in the history of the West."

"They believe it?"

"Maybe they just choose to."

"And his mother and brother?"

"Likewise," she said. "Obviously I'm not going to get the benefit of the doubt."

"Why the hell did you stick around? Why didn't you just get out, the very first time?"

She sighed, and she closed her eyes, and she turned her head away. Spread her hands on the table, palms down, and then turned them over, palms up.

"I can't explain it," she whispered. "Nobody can ever explain it. You have to know what it's like. I had no confidence in myself. I had a newborn baby and no money. Not a dime. I had no friends. I was watched all the time. I couldn't even make a call in private."

He said nothing. She opened her eyes and looked straight at him.

"And worst of all, I had nowhere to go," she said.

"Home?" he asked.

She shook her head.

"I never even thought about it," she said. "Taking the beatings was better than trying to crawl back to my family, with a white blond baby in my arms."

He said nothing.

"And the first time you pass up the chance, you've had it," she said. "That's how it is. It just gets worse. Whenever I thought about it, I still had no money, I still had a baby, then she was a one-year-old, then a two-year-old, then a three-year-old. The time is never right. If you stay that first time, you're trapped forever. And I stayed that first time. I wish I hadn't, but I did."

He said nothing. She looked at him, appealing for something.

"You have to take it on faith," she said. "You don't know how it is. You're a man, you're big and strong, somebody hits you, you hit him back. You're on your own, you don't like someplace, you move on. It's different for me. Even if you can't understand it, you have to believe it."

He said nothing.

"I could have gone if I'd left Ellie," she said. "Sloop told me if I left the baby with him, he'd pay my fare anyplace I wanted to go. First class. He said he'd call a limo all the way from Dallas, right there and then, to take me straight to the airport."

He said nothing.

"But I wouldn't do that," she said quietly. "I mean, how could I? So Sloop makes out this is my *choice*. Like I'm agreeing to it. Like I *want* it. So he keeps on hitting me. Punching me, kicking me, slapping me. Humiliating me, sexually. Every day, even if he isn't mad at me. And if he *is* mad at me, he just goes crazy."

There was silence. Just the rush of air from the cooling vents in the diner's ceiling. Vague noise from the kitchens. Carmen Greer's low breathing. The clink of fracturing ice in her abandoned glass. He looked across the table at her, tracing his gaze over her hands, her arms, her neck, her face. The neckline of her dress had shifted left, and he could see a thickened knot on her collarbone. A healed break, no doubt about it. But she was sitting absolutely straight, with her head up and her eyes defiant, and her posture was telling him something.

"He hits you *every* day?" he asked.

She closed her eyes. "Well, almost every day. Not literally, I guess. But three, four times in a week, usually. Sometimes more. It feels like every day."

He was quiet for a long moment, looking straight at her.

Then he shook his head.

"You're making it up," he said.

The watchers stayed resolutely on station, even though there was nothing much to watch. The red house baked under the sun and stayed quiet. The maid came out and got in a car and drove away in a cloud of dust, presumably to the market. There was some horse activity around the barn. A couple of listless ranch hands walked the animals out and around, brushed them down, put them back inside. There was a bunkhouse way back beyond the barn, same architecture, same blood-red siding. It looked mostly empty, because the barn was mostly empty. Maybe five horses in total, one of them the pony for the kid, mostly just resting in their stalls because of the terrible heat.

The maid came back and carried packages into the

kitchen. The boy made a note of it in his book. The dust from her wheels floated slowly back to earth and the men with the telescopes watched it, with their tractor caps reversed to keep the sun off their necks.

"You're lying to me," Reacher said.

Carmen turned away to the window. Red spots the size of quarters crept high into her cheeks. Anger, he thought. Or embarrassment, maybe.

"Why do you say that?" she asked, quietly.

"Physical evidence," he said. "You've got no bruising visible anywhere. Your skin is clear. Light makeup, too light to be hiding anything. It's certainly not hiding the fact you're blushing like crazy. You look like you've just stepped out of the beauty parlor. And you're moving easily. You skipped across that parking lot like a ballerina. So you're not hurting anyplace. You're not stiff and sore. If he's hitting you almost every day, he must be doing it with a feather."

She was quiet for a beat. Then she nodded.

"There's more to tell you," she said.

He looked away.

"The crucial part," she said. "The main point."

"Why should I listen?"

She took another drinking straw and unwrapped it. Flattened the paper tube that had covered it and began rolling it into a tight spiral, between her finger and thumb.

"I'm sorry," she said. "But I had to get your attention."

Reacher turned his head and looked out of the window, too. The sun was moving the bar of shadow across the Cadillac's hood like the finger on a clock. His attention? He recalled opening his motel room door that morning. A brand-new day, ready and waiting to be filled with whatever came his way. He recalled the reflection of the cop in the mirror and the sticky whisper of the Cadillac's tires on the hot pavement as they slowed alongside him.

"O.K., you got my attention," he said, looking out at the car.

"It happened for five whole years," she said. "Exactly like I told you, I promise. Almost every day. But then it stopped, a year and a half ago. But I had to tell it to you backward, because I needed you to listen to me."

He said nothing.

"This isn't easy," she said. "Telling this stuff to a stranger."

He turned back to face her. "It isn't easy listening to it."

She took a breath. "You going to run out on me?"

He shrugged. "I almost did, a minute ago."

She was quiet again.

"Please don't," she said. "At least not here. Please. Just listen a little more."

He looked straight at her.

"O.K., I'm listening," he said.

"But will you still help me?"

"With what?"

She said nothing.

"What did it feel like?" he asked. "Getting hit?"

"Feel like?" she repeated.

"Physically," he said.

She looked away. Thought about it.

"Depends where," she said.

He nodded. She knew it felt different in different places.

"The stomach," he said.

"I threw up a lot," she said. "I was worried, because there was blood."

He nodded again. She knew what it felt like to be hit in the stomach.

"I swear it's true," she said. "Five whole years. Why would I make it up?"

"So what happened?" he said. "Why did he stop?"

She paused, like she was aware people might be looking at her. Reacher glanced up, and saw heads turn away. The cook, the waitress, the two guys at the distant tables. The cook and the waitress were faster about it than the two guys chose to be. There was hostility in their faces.

"Can we go now?" she asked. "We need to get back. It's a long drive."

"I'm coming with you?"

"That's the whole point," she said.

He glanced away again, out of the window.

"Please, Reacher," she said. "At least hear the rest of the story, and then decide. I can let you out in Pecos, if you won't come all the way to Echo. You can see the museum. You can see Clay Allison's grave."

He watched the bar of shadow touch the Cadillac's windshield. The interior would be like a furnace by now.

"You should see it anyway," she said. "If you're exploring Texas."

"O.K.," he said.

"Thank you," she said.

He made no reply.

"Wait for me," she said. "I need to go to the bathroom. It's a long drive."

She slid out of the booth with uninjured grace and walked the length of the room, head down, looking neither left nor right. The two guys at the tables watched her until she was almost past them and then switched their blank gazes straight back to Reacher. He ignored them and turned the check over and dumped small change from his pocket on top of it, exact amount, no tip. He figured a waitress who didn't talk didn't want one. He slid out of the booth and walked to the door. The two guys watched him all the way. He stood in front of the glass and looked out beyond the parking lot. Watched the flat land bake under the sun for a minute or two until he heard her footsteps behind him. Her hair was combed and she had done something with her lipstick.

"I guess I'll use the bathroom too," he said.

She glanced right, halfway between the two guys.

"Wait until I'm in the car," she said. "I don't want to be left alone in here. I shouldn't have come in here in the first place."

She pushed out through the doors and he watched her to the car. She got in and he saw it shudder as she started the engine to run the air. He turned and walked back to the men's room. It was a fair-sized space, two porcelain urinals and one toilet cubicle. A chipped sink with a cold water faucet. A fat roll of paper towels sitting on top of the machine it should have been installed in. Not the cleanest facility he had ever seen.

He unzipped and used the left-hand urinal. Heard footsteps outside the door and glanced up at the chromium valve that fed the flush pipes. It was dirty, but it was rounded and it reflected what was behind him like a tiny security mirror. He saw the door open and a man step inside. He saw the door close again and the man settle back against it. He was one of the customers. Presumably one of the pick-up drivers. The chromium valve distorted the view, but the guy's head was nearly to the top of the door. Not a small person. And he was fiddling blindly behind his back. Reacher heard the click of the door lock. Then the guy shifted again and hung his hands loose by his sides. He was wearing a black T-shirt. There was writing on it, but Reacher couldn't read it backward. Some kind of an insignia. Maybe an oil company.

"You new around here?" the guy asked.

Reacher made no reply. Just watched the reflection.

"I asked you a question," the guy said.

Reacher ignored him.

"I'm talking to you," the guy said.

"Well, that's a big mistake," Reacher said. "All you know, I might be a polite type of person. I might feel obligated to turn around and listen, whereupon I'd be pissing all over your shoes."

The guy shuffled slightly, caught out. Clearly he had some kind of set speech prepared, which was what Reacher had been counting on. A little improvised interruption might slow him down some. Maybe enough to get zipped up and decent. The guy was still shuffling, deciding whether to react.

"So I guess it's down to me to tell you," he said. "Somebody's got to."

He wasn't reacting. No talent for repartee.

"Tell me what?" Reacher asked.

"How it is around here."

Reacher paused a beat. The only problem with coffee was its diuretic effect.

"And how is it around here?" he asked.

"Around here, you don't bring beaners into decent folks' places."

"What?" Reacher said.

"What part don't you understand?"

Reacher breathed out. Maybe ten seconds to go.

"I didn't understand any of it," he said.

"You don't bring beaners in a place like this."

"What's a beaner?" Reacher asked.

The guy took a step forward. His reflection grew disproportionately larger.

"Latinos," he said. "Eat beans all the time."

"Latina," Reacher said. "With an *a*. Gender counts with inflected languages. And she had iced coffee. Haven't seen her eat a bean all day."

"You some kind of a smart guy?"

Reacher finished and zipped up with a sigh. Didn't flush. A place like that, it didn't seem like standard practice. He just turned to the sink and operated the faucet.

"Well, I'm smarter than you," he said. "That's for damn sure. But then, that's not saying much. This roll of paper towels is smarter than you. A lot smarter. Each sheet on its own is practically a genius, compared to you. They could stroll into Harvard, one by one, full scholarships for each of them, while you're still struggling with your GED."

It was like taunting a dinosaur. Some kind of a brontosaurus, where the brain is a very long distance from anyplace else. The sound went in, and some time later it was received and understood. Four or five seconds, until it showed in the guy's face. Four or five seconds after that, he swung with his right. It was a ponderous slow swing with a big bunched fist on the end of a big heavy arm, aiming wide and high for Reacher's head. It could have caused some damage, if it had landed. But it didn't land. Reacher caught the guy's wrist in his left palm and stopped the swing dead. A loud wet *smack* echoed off the bathroom tile.

"The bacteria on this floor are smarter than you," he said.

He twisted his hips ninety degrees so his groin was protected and he squeezed the guy's wrist with his hand. There had been a time when he could break bones by squeezing with his hand. It was more about blind determination than sheer strength.

But right then, he didn't feel it.

"This is your lucky day," he said. "All I know, you could be a cop. So I'm going to let you go."

The guy was staring desperately at his wrist, watching it get crushed. The clammy flesh was swelling and going red.

"After you apologize," Reacher said.

The guy stared on, four or five seconds. Like a dinosaur.

"I'm sorry," he said. "I apologize."

"Not to me, asshole," Reacher said. "To the lady."

The guy said nothing. Reacher turned up the pressure. Felt his thumb go slick with sweat, sliding up over the tip of his index finger. Felt the bones in the guy's wrist click and move. The radius and the ulna, getting closer than nature intended.

"O.K.," the guy gasped. "Enough."

Reacher released the wrist. The guy snatched it back and cradled his hand, panting, looking up, looking down.

"Give me the keys to your truck," Reacher said.

The guy twisted awkwardly to get into his right pocket with his left hand. Held out a large bunch of keys.

"Now go wait for me in the parking lot," Reacher said.

The guy unlocked the door left-handed and shuffled out. Reacher dropped the keys in the unflushed urinal and washed his hands again. Dried them carefully with the paper towels and left the bathroom behind him. He found the guy out in the lot, halfway between the diner door and the Cadillac.

"Be real nice, now," Reacher called to him. "Maybe offer to wash her car or something. She'll say no, but it's the thought that counts, right? If you're creative enough, you get your keys back. Otherwise, you're walking home."

He could see through the tinted glass that she was watching them approach, not understanding. He motioned with his hand that she should let her window down. A circular motion, like winding a handle. She buzzed the glass down, maybe two inches, just wide enough to frame her eyes. They were wide and worried.

"This guy's got something to say to you," Reacher said.

He stepped back. The guy stepped up. Looked down at the ground, and then back at Reacher, like a whipped dog. Reacher nodded, encouragingly. The guy put his hand on his chest, like an operatic tenor or a fancy maître d'. Bent slightly from the waist, to address the two-inch gap in the glass.

"Ma'am," he said. "Just wanted to say we'd all be real pleased if y'all would come back real soon, and would you like me to wash your car, seeing as you're here right now?"

"What?" she said.

They both turned separately to Reacher, the guy pleading, Carmen astonished.

"Beat it," he said. "I left your keys in the bathroom."

Four, five seconds later, the guy was back on his way to the diner. Reacher stepped around the hood to his door. Pulled it open.

"I thought you were running out on me," Carmen said. "I thought you'd asked that guy for a ride."

"I'd rather ride with you," he said.

The Crown Victoria drove south to a lonely crossroads hamlet. There was an old diner on the right and a vacant lot on the left. A melted stop line on the road. Then a decrepit gas station, and opposite it a one-room schoolhouse. Dust and heat shimmer everywhere. The big car slowed and crawled through the junction at walking pace. It rolled past the school gate and then suddenly picked up speed and drove away.

Little Ellie Greer watched it go. She was in a wooden chair at the schoolroom window, halfway through raising the lid of her big blue lunch box. She heard the brief shriek of rubber as the car accelerated. She turned her head and stared after it. She was a serious, earnest child, much given to silent observation. She kept her big dark eyes on the road until the dust settled. Then she turned back to matters at hand and inspected her lunch, and wished her mom had been home to pack it, instead of the maid, who belonged to the Greers and was mean.

3

"**What happened a** year and a half ago?" Reacher asked.

She didn't answer. They were on a long straight deserted road, with the sun just about dead-center above them. Heading south and near noon, he figured. The road was made of patched blacktop, smooth enough, but the shoulders were ragged. There were lonely billboards at random intervals, advertising gas and accommodations and markets many miles ahead. Either side of the road the landscape was flat and parched and featureless, dotted here and there with still windmills in the middle distance. There were automobile engines mounted on concrete pads, closer to the road. Big V-8s, like you would see under the hood of an ancient Chevrolet or Chrysler, painted yellow and streaked with rust, with stubby black exhaust pipes standing vertically.

"Water pumps," Carmen said. "For irrigating the fields. There was agriculture here, in the old days. Back then, gasoline was cheaper than water, so those things ran all day and all night. Now there's no water left, and gas has gotten too expensive."

The land fell away on every side, covered with dry brush. On the far horizon southwest of the endless road, there might have been mountains a hundred miles away. Or it might have been a trick of the heat.

"Are you hungry?" she asked. "If we don't stop we could pick Ellie up from school, and I'd really like to do that. I haven't seen her since yesterday."

"Whatever you want," Reacher said.

She accelerated until the big Cadillac was doing eighty and wallowing heavily over the undulations in the road. He straightened in his seat and tightened his belt against the reel. She glanced across at him.

"Do you believe me yet?" she asked.

He glanced back at her. He had spent thirteen years as an investigator, and his natural instinct was to believe nothing at all.

"What happened a year and a half ago?" he asked. "Why did he stop?"

She adjusted her grip on the wheel. Opened her palms, stretched her fingers, closed them tight again on the rim.

"He went to prison," she said.

"For beating up on you?"

"In *Texas?*" she said. She laughed, just a yelp, like a short cry of pain. "Now I know you're new here."

He said nothing. Just watched Texas reel in through the windshield ahead of him, hot and brassy and yellow.

"It just doesn't happen," she said. "In Texas a gentleman would never raise his hand to a woman. Everybody knows that. Especially not a *white* gentleman whose family has been here over a hundred years. So if a greaseball whore wife dared to claim a thing like that, they'd lock *her* up, probably in a rubber room."

The day her life changed forever.

"So what did he do?"

"He evaded federal taxes," she said. "He made a lot of money trading oil leases and selling drilling equipment down in Mexico. He neglected to tell the IRS about it. In fact, he neglected to tell the IRS about anything. One day they caught him."

"They put you in jail for that?"

She made a face. "Actually, they try hard not to. A first-time thing like that, they were willing to let him pay, you know, make proposals and so forth. A clean breast and a pay-back plan is what they're looking for. But Sloop was way too stubborn for that. He made them dig everything out for themselves. He was hiding things right up to the trial. He refused to pay anything. He even disputed that he owed them anything, which was ridiculous. And all the money was hidden behind family trusts, so they couldn't just take it. It made them mad, I think."

"So they prosecuted?"

She nodded at the wheel.

"With a vengeance," she said. "A federal case. You know that expression? Making a federal case out of something? Now I see why people say that. Biggest fuss you ever saw. A real contest, the local good old boys against the Treasury Department. Sloop's lawyer is his best friend from high school, and his other best friend from high school is the DA in Pecos County, and he was advising them on strategy and stuff like that, but the IRS just rolled right over all of them. It was a massacre. He got three-to-five years. The judge set the minimum at thirty months in jail. And cut me a break."

Reacher said nothing. She accelerated past a truck, the first vehicle they had seen in more than twenty miles.

"I was so happy," she said. "I'll never forget it. A white-collar thing like that, after the verdict came in they just told him to present himself at the federal prison the next morning. They didn't drag him away in handcuffs or anything. He came home and packed a little suitcase. We had a big family meal, stayed up kind of late. Went upstairs, and that was the last time he hit me. Next morning, his friends drove him up to the jail, someplace near Abilene. A Club Fed is what they call it. Minimum security. It's supposed to be comfortable. I heard you can play tennis there."

"Do you visit him?"

She shook her head.

"I pretend he's dead," she said.

She went quiet, and the car sped on toward the haze on the

horizon. There *were* mountains visible to the southwest, unimaginably distant.

"The Trans-Pecos," she said. "Watch for the light to change color. It's very beautiful."

He looked ahead, but the light was so bright it had no color at all.

"Minimum thirty months is two and a half years," she said. "I thought it safest to bet on the minimum. He's probably behaving himself in there."

Reacher nodded. "Probably."

"So, two and a half years," she said. "I wasted the first one and a half."

"You've still got twelve months. That's plenty of time for anything."

She was quiet again.

"Talk me through it," she said. "We have to agree on what needs to be done. That's important. That way, you're seeing it exactly the same way I am."

He said nothing.

"Help me," she said. "Please. Just theoretically for now, if you want."

He shrugged. Then he thought about it, from her point of view. From his, it was too easy. Disappearing and living invisibly was second nature to him.

"You need to get away," he said. "An abusive marriage, that's all a person can do, I guess. So, a place to live, and an income. That's what you need."

"Doesn't sound much, when you say it."

"Any big city," he said. "They have shelters. All kinds of organizations."

"What about Ellie?"

"The shelters have baby-sitters," he said. "They'll look after her while you're working. There are lots of kids in those places. She'd have friends. And after a little while you could get a place of your own."

"What job could I get?"

"Anything," he said. "You can read and write. You went to college."

"How do I get there?"

"On a plane, on a train, in a bus. Two one-way tickets."

"I don't have any money."

"None at all?"

She shook her head. "What little I had ran out a week ago."

He looked away.

"What?" she said.

"You dress pretty sharp for a person with no money."

"Mail order," she said. "I have to get approval from Sloop's lawyer. He signs the checks. So I've got clothes. But what I haven't got is cash."

"You could sell the diamond."

"I tried to," she said. "It's a fake. He told me it was real, but it's stainless steel and cubic zirconium. The jeweler laughed at me. It's worth maybe thirty bucks."

He paused a beat.

"There must be money in the house," he said. "You could steal some."

She went quiet again, another fast mile south.

"Then I'm a double fugitive," she said. "You're forgetting about Ellie's legal status. And that's the whole problem. Always has been. Because she's Sloop's child, too. If I transport her across a state line without his consent, then I'm a kidnapper. They'll put her picture on milk cartons, and they'll find me, and they'll take her away from me, and I'll go to jail. They're very strict about it. Taking children out of a failed marriage is the number one reason for kidnapping today. The lawyers all warned me. They all say I need Sloop's agreement. And I'm not going to get it, am I? How can I even go up there and ask him if he'd consent to me disappearing forever with his baby? Someplace he'll never find either of us?"

"So don't cross the state line. Stay in Texas. Go to Dallas."

"I'm not staying in Texas," she said.

She said it with finality. Reacher said nothing back.

"It's not easy," she said. "His mother watches me, on his behalf. That's why I didn't go ahead and sell the ring, even though I could have used the thirty bucks. She'd notice, and it would put her on her guard. She'd know what I'm planning.

She's smart. So if one day money is missing and Ellie is missing, I might get a few hours start before she calls the sheriff and the sheriff calls the FBI. But a few hours isn't too much help, because Texas is real big, and buses are real slow. I wouldn't make it out."

"Got to be some way," he said.

She glanced back at her briefcase on the rear seat. The legal paperwork.

"There are lots of ways," she said. "Procedures, provisions, wards of the court, all kinds of things. But lawyers are slow, and very expensive, and I don't have any money. There are pro-bono people who do it for free, but they're always very busy. It's a mess. A big, complicated mess."

"I guess it is," he said.

"But it should be possible in a year," she said. "A year's a long time, right?"

"So?"

"So I need you to forgive me for wasting the first year and a half. I need you to understand why. It was all so daunting, I kept putting it off. I was safe. I said to myself, plenty of time to go. You just agreed, twelve months is plenty of time for anything. So even if I was starting cold, right now, I could be excused for that, right? Nobody could say I'd left it too late, could they?"

There was a polite beep from somewhere deep inside the dashboard. A little orange light started flashing in the stylized shape of a gas pump, right next to the speedometer.

"Low fuel," she said.

"There's Exxon up ahead," he said. "I saw a billboard. Maybe fifteen miles."

"I need Mobil," she said. "There's a card for Mobil in the glove box. I don't have any way of paying at Exxon."

"You don't even have money for gas?"

She shook her head. "I ran out. Now I'm charging it all to my mother-in-law's Mobil account. She won't get the bill for a month."

She steered one-handed and groped behind her for her pocketbook. Dragged it forward and dumped it on his lap.

"Check it out," she said.

He sat there, with the bag on his knees.

"I can't be poking through a lady's pocketbook," he said.

"I want you to," she said. "I need you to understand."

He paused a beat and snapped it open and a soft aroma came up at him. Perfume and makeup. There was a hairbrush, tangled with long black hairs. A nail clipper. And a thin wallet.

"Check it out," she said again.

There was a worn dollar bill in the money section. That was all. A solitary buck. No credit cards. A Texas driver's license, with a startled picture of her on it. There was a plastic window with a photograph of a little girl behind it. She was slightly chubby, with perfect pink skin. Shiny blond hair and bright lively eyes. A radiant smile filled with tiny square teeth.

"Ellie," she said.

"She's very cute."

"She is, isn't she?"

"Where did you sleep last night?"

"In the car," she said. "Motels are forty bucks."

"Mine was nearer twenty," he said.

She shrugged.

"Anything over a dollar, I haven't got it," she said. "So it's the car for me. It's comfortable enough. Then I wait for the breakfast rush and wash up in some diner's restroom, when they're too busy to notice."

"What about eating?"

"I don't eat."

She was slowing down, maybe trying to preserve the rest of her gas.

"I'll pay for it," Reacher said. "You're giving me a ride."

There was another billboard, on the right shoulder. Exxon, ten miles.

"O.K.," she said. "I'll let you pay. But only so I can get back to Ellie."

She accelerated again, confident the tank would last ten miles. Less than a gallon, Reacher figured, even with a big old engine like that. Even driving fast. He sat back and watched the horizon reel in. Then he suddenly realized what he should do.

"Stop the car," he said.

"Why?"

"Just do it, O.K.?"

She glanced at him, puzzled, but she pulled over on the ragged shoulder. Left it with two wheels on the blacktop, the engine running, the air blasting.

"Now wait," he said.

They waited in the cold until the truck she had passed came through.

"Now sit still," he said.

He unclipped his seat belt and squinted down and tore the pocket off his shirt. Cheap material, weak stitching, it came away with no trouble at all.

"What are you wearing?" he asked.

"What? What are you doing?"

"Tell me exactly what you're wearing."

She blushed. Fidgeted nervously.

"This dress," she said. "And underwear. And shoes."

"Show me your shoes."

She paused a second, and then leaned down and worked her shoes off. Passed them across to him, one at a time. He checked them carefully. Nothing in them. He passed them back. Then he leaned forward and unbuttoned his shirt. Took it off. Passed it to her.

"I'm getting out now," he said. "I'm going to turn my back. Take all your clothes off and put the shirt on. Leave your clothes on the seat and then get out, too."

"Why?"

"You want me to help you, just do it. All of them, O.K.?"

He got out of the car and walked away. Turned around and stared down the road, back the way they had come. It was very hot. He could feel the sun burning the skin on his shoulders. Then he heard the car door open. He turned back and saw her climbing out, barefoot, wearing his shirt. It was huge on her. She was hopping from foot to foot because the road was burning her feet.

"You can keep your shoes," he called.

She leaned in and picked them up and put them on.

"Now walk away and wait," he called.

She paused again, and then moved ten feet away. He stepped back to the car. Her clothes were neatly folded on her seat. He ignored them. Reached back and searched her pocketbook again, and then the briefcase. Nothing there. He turned back to the clothes and shook them out. They were warm from her body. The dress, a bra, underpants. Nothing hidden in them. He laid them on the roof of the car and searched the rest of it.

It took him twenty minutes. He covered it completely. Under the hood, the whole of the interior, under the carpets, in the seats, under the seats, in the trunk, under the fenders, everywhere. He found nothing at all, and he was absolutely prepared to bet his life no civilian could conceal anything from him in an automobile.

"O.K.," he called. "Get dressed now. Same routine."

He waited with his back turned until he heard her behind him. She was holding his shirt. He took it from her and put it back on.

"What was that about?" she asked.

"Now I'll help you," he said. "Because now I believe you."

"Why?"

"Because you really don't have any money," he said. "No credit cards, either. Not in your wallet, and not hidden anyplace else. And nobody travels three hundred miles from home, not overnight, with absolutely no money. Not unless they've got some real big problems. And a person with real big problems deserves some kind of help."

She said nothing. Just ducked her head slightly, like she was accepting a compliment. Or offering one. They climbed back in the car and shut the doors. Sat for a minute in the cool air, and then she maneuvered back onto the road again.

"So, you've got a year," he said. "That's plenty of time. A year from now, you could be a million miles away. New start, new life. Is that what you want me for? To help you get away?"

She said nothing for a couple of minutes. A couple of

miles. The road rolled down a slight hill, and then up again. There were buildings in the far distance, on the next crest. Probably the gas station. Maybe a tow-truck operation next to it.

"Right now just agree with me," she said. "A year is enough. So it's O.K. to have waited."

"Sure," he said. "A year is enough. It's O.K. to have waited."

She said nothing more. Just drove straight ahead for the gas station, like her life depended on it.

The first establishment was a junkyard. There was a long low shed made out of corrugated tin, with the front wall all covered with old hubcaps. Behind it was an acre of wrecked cars. They were piled five or six deep, with the older models at the bottom, like geological strata. Beyond the low shed was the turn for the gas station. It was old enough to have pumps with pointers instead of figures, and four public rest rooms instead of two. Old enough that a taciturn guy came out into the heat and filled your car for you.

The Cadillac took more than twenty gallons, which cost Reacher the price of a motel room. He passed the bills through his window and waved away a dollar in change. He figured the guy should have it. The outside temperature reading on the dash showed one hundred and eleven degrees. No wonder the guy didn't talk. Then he found himself wondering whether it was because the guy didn't like to see a beaner driving a white man around in a Cadillac.

"Gracias, señor," Carmen said. "Thank you."

"Pleasure," he said. *"De nada, señorita."*

"You speak Spanish?"

"Not really," he said. "I served all over, so I can say a few words in a lot of languages. But that's all. Except French. I speak French pretty well. My mother was French."

"From Louisiana or Canada?"

"From Paris, France."

"So you're half-foreign," she said.

"Sometimes I feel a lot more than half."

She smiled like she didn't believe him and eased back to the road. The gas needle jumped up to F, which seemed to reassure her. She got the car straight in her lane and accelerated back to a cruise.

"But you should call me *señora*," she said. "Not *señorita*. I'm a married woman."

"Yes," he said. "I guess you are."

She went quiet for a mile. Settled back in the seat and rested both hands lightly on the bottom curve of the wheel. Then she took a deep breath.

"O.K., here's the problem," she said. "I don't have a year."

"Why not?"

"Because a month ago his lawyer friend came out to the house. Told us there was some kind of deal on the table."

"What deal?"

"I don't know for sure. Nobody told me exactly. My guess is Sloop's going to rat out some business associates in exchange for early release. I think his other friend is brokering it through the DA's office."

"Shit," Reacher said.

Carmen nodded. "Yes, shit. They've all been working their asses off, getting it going. I've had to be all smiles, like oh great, Sloop's coming home early."

Reacher said nothing.

"But inside, I'm screaming," she said. "I left it too late, you see. A year and a half, I did nothing at all. I thought I was safe. I was wrong. I was stupid. I was sitting around in a trap without knowing it, and now it's sprung shut, and I'm still in it."

Reacher nodded slowly. *Hope for the best, plan for the worst.* That was his guiding principle.

"So what's the progress on the deal?" he asked.

The car sped on south.

"It's done," she said, in a small voice.

"So when does he get out?"

"Today's Friday," she said. "I don't think they can do it on the weekend. So it'll be Monday, I expect. A couple of days, is all."

"I see," Reacher said.

"So I'm scared," she said. "He's coming home."

"I see," Reacher said again.

"Do you?" she asked.

He said nothing.

"Monday night," she said. "He's going to start it all up again. It's going to be worse than ever."

"Maybe he's changed," Reacher said. "Prison can change people."

It was a useless thing to say. He could see it in her face. And in his experience, prison didn't change people for the better.

"No, it's going to be worse than ever," she said. "I know it. I know it for sure. I'm in big trouble, Reacher. I can promise you that."

Something in her voice.

"Why?"

She moved her hands on the wheel. Closed her eyes tight, even though she was doing seventy miles an hour.

"Because it was me who told the IRS about him," she said.

The Crown Victoria drove south, and then west, and then looped back north in a giant sweeping curve. It detoured over near the highway so it could fill up with gas at a self-service pump in a busy station. The driver used a stolen Amex card in the slot and then wiped his prints off it and dropped it in the trash next to the pump, with the empty oil bottles and the soda cans and the used paper towels covered with windshield dirt. The woman busied herself with a map and selected their next destination. Kept her finger on the spot until the driver got back in and squirmed around to take a look at it.

"Now?" he asked.

"Just to check it out," she replied. "For later."

"It seemed like such a good plan," Carmen said. "It seemed foolproof. I knew how stubborn he was, and how greedy he was, so I knew he wouldn't cooperate with them, so I knew he would go to jail, at least for a little while. Even if by some chance he didn't, I thought it might preoccupy him for a spell. And I thought it might shake some money loose for me, you know, when he was hiding it all. And it worked real well, apart from the money. But that seemed like such a small thing at the time."

"How did you do it?"

"I just called them. They're in the book. They have a whole section to take information from spouses. It's one of their big ways to get people. Normally it happens during divorces, when you're mad at each other. But I was already mad at him."

"Why haven't you gone ahead and *got* a divorce?" he asked. "Husband in jail is grounds, right? Some kind of desertion?"

She glanced in the mirror, at the briefcase on the rear seat.

"It doesn't solve the problem with Ellie," she said. "In fact, it makes it much worse. It alerts everybody to the possibility I'll leave the state. Legally, Sloop could require me to register her whereabouts, and I'm sure he would."

"You could stay in Texas," he said again.

She nodded.

"I know, I know," she said. "But I can't. I just can't. I know I'm being irrational, but I can't stay here, Reacher. It's a beautiful state, and there *are* nice people here, and it's very big, so I could get a long way away, but it's a *symbol*. Things have happened to me here that I have to get away from. Not just with Sloop."

He shrugged.

"Your call," he said.

She went quiet and concentrated on driving. The road reeled in. It was dropping down off of a wide flat mesa that looked the size of Rhode Island.

"The caprock," she said. "It's limestone, or something. All the water evaporated about a million years ago and left the rock behind. Geological deposits, or something."

She sounded vague. Her tour-guide explanation was less definitive than usual.

"So what do you want me to do?" he asked.

"I don't know," she said, although he was certain that she did.

"Help you run? I could do that, probably."

She said nothing.

"You picked me out," he said. "You must have had something in mind."

She said nothing. He fell to thinking about the potential target group she had outlined to him. Out-of-work rodeo riders and roughnecks. Men of various talents, but he wasn't sure if beating a federal manhunt would be among them. So she had chosen well. Or lucked out.

"You need to move fast," he said. "Two days, you need to get started right now. We should pick Ellie up and turn the car around and get going. Vegas, maybe, for the first stop."

"And do what there?"

"Pick up some ID," he said. "Place like Vegas, we could find something, even if it's only temporary. I've got some money. I can get more, if you need it."

"I can't take your money," she said. "That wouldn't be fair."

"Fair or not, you're going to need money. You can pay me back later. Then maybe you should go back to L.A. You could start building some new paperwork there."

She was quiet again, another mile.

"No, I can't run," she said. "I can't be a fugitive. I can't be an *illegal*. Whatever else I am, I've never been an illegal. I'm not going to start being one now. And neither is Ellie. She deserves better than that."

"You both deserve better than that," he said. "But you've got to do something."

"I'm a citizen," she said. "Think about what that means to a person like me. I'm not going to give it up. I'm not going to pretend to be somebody else."

"So what's your plan?"

"You're my plan," she said.

Bull riders, roughnecks, a six-foot-five two-hundred-fifty-pound ex-military cop.

"You want me to be your *bodyguard*?" he asked.

She made no reply.

"Carmen, I'm sorry about your situation," he said. "Believe me, I really am."

No response.

"But I can't be your bodyguard."

No reply.

"I can't be," he said again. "It's ridiculous. What do you think is going to happen? You think I'm going to be with you twenty-four hours a day? Seven days a week? Making sure he doesn't hit you?"

No reply. A huge highway interchange sprawled across the empty landscape, miles away in the haze.

"It's ridiculous," he said again. "I could warn him off, I guess. I could scare him. I could smack him around a little, to back up the message. But what happens when I'm gone? Because sooner or later, I'm going to be gone, Carmen. I'm not going to stay around. I don't like to stay anywhere. And it's not just me. Face it, *nobody* is going to stay around. Not long enough. Not ten years. Or twenty, or thirty or however long it is until he ups and dies of old age."

No reply. No effect, either. It wasn't like what he was saying was a big disappointment to her. She just listened and drove, fast and smooth, and silent, like she was biding her time. The highway cloverleaf grew larger and nearer and she swooped onto it and around it and headed due west, following a big green sign that said: Pecos 75 miles.

"I don't want a bodyguard," she said. "I agree, that would be ridiculous."

"So what am I supposed to be for?"

She settled onto the highway, center lane, driving faster than before. He watched her face. It was completely blank.

"What am I supposed to be for?" he asked again.

She hesitated. "I can't say it."

"Say what?"

She opened her mouth. Closed it again. Swallowed hard, and said nothing. He stared at her. *Bull riders, roughnecks, an ex-MP. Clay Allison's grave, the fancy inscription, the obituary in the Kansas City newspaper.*

"You *are* crazy," he said.

"Am I?" The spots of color came back to her face, the size of quarters, burning red high above her cheekbones.

"Totally crazy," he said. "And you can forget about it."

"I *can't* forget about it."

He said nothing.

"I want him dead, Reacher," she said. "I really do. It's my only way out, literally. And he deserves it."

"Tell me you're kidding."

"I'm not kidding," she said. "I want him killed."

He shook his head. Stared out of the window.

"Just forget all about it," he said. "It's absurd. This isn't the Wild West anymore."

"Isn't it? Isn't it still O.K. to kill a man who needs killing?"

Then she went quiet, just driving, like she was waiting him out. He stared at the speeding landscape in front of him. They were heading for the distant mountains. The blazing afternoon sun made them red and purple. It changed the color of the air. The Trans-Pecos, she had called them.

"Please, Reacher," she said. "Please. At least think about it."

He said nothing. *Please? Think about it?* He was beyond reaction. He dropped his eyes from the mountains and watched the highway. It was busy with traffic. A river of cars and trucks, crawling across the vastness. She was passing them all, one after another. Driving way too fast.

"I'm not crazy," she said. "Please. I tried to do this right. I really did. Soon as his lawyer told me about the deal, I saw a lawyer of my own, and then three more, and none of them could do anything for me as fast as a month. All they could do was tell me Ellie traps me exactly where I am. So then I looked for protection. I asked private detectives. They wouldn't do anything for me. I went to a security firm in Austin and they said yes, they could guard me around the clock, but it would be six men and nearly ten thousand dollars a week. Which is the same thing as saying no. So I tried, Reacher. I tried to do it right. But it's impossible."

He said nothing.

"So I bought a gun," she said.

"Wonderful," he said.

"And bullets," she said. "It took all the cash I had."

"You picked the wrong guy," he said.

"But why? You've killed people before. In the army. You told me that."

"This is different."

"How?"

"This would be murder. Cold-blooded murder. It would be an assassination."

"No, it would be just the same. Just like the army."

He shook his head. "Carmen, it wouldn't be the same."

"Don't you take an oath or something? To protect people?"

"It's not the same," he said again.

She passed an eighteen-wheeler bound for the coast, and the Cadillac rocked and shimmied through the superheated turbulent air.

"Slow down," he said.

She shook her head. "I can't slow down. I want to see Ellie."

He touched the dashboard in front of him, steadying himself. The freezing air from the vents blasted against his chest.

"Don't worry," she said. "I'm not going to crash. Ellie needs me. If it wasn't for Ellie, I'd have crashed a long time ago, believe me."

But she eased off a little, anyway. The big rig crept back alongside.

"I know this is a difficult conversation," she said.

"You think?"

"But you have to look at it from my point of view. Please, Reacher. I've been through it a million times. I've thought it through. I've been from A to B to C to D, all the way to Z. Then again, and again. And again. I've examined all the options. So this is all logical to me. And this is the only way. I *know* that. But it's hard to talk about, because it's new to you. You haven't thought about it before. It comes out of the blue. So I sound crazy and cold-blooded to you. I know that. I appreciate that. But I'm not crazy or cold-blooded. It's just that I've had the time to reach the conclusion, and you haven't. And this is the only conclusion, I promise you."

"Whatever, I'm not killing a guy I never saw before."

"He hits me, Reacher," she said. "He beats me, badly. Punches me, kicks me, hurts me. He enjoys it. He laughs while he does it. I live in fear, all the time."

"So go to the cops."

"The cop. There's only one. And he wouldn't believe me. And even if he did, he wouldn't do anything about it. They're all big buddies. You don't know how it is here."

Reacher said nothing.

"He's coming home," she said. "Can you *imagine* what he's going to do to me?"

He said nothing.

"I'm *trapped,* Reacher. I'm boxed in, because of Ellie. Do you see that?"

He said nothing.

"Why won't you help me? Is it the money? Is it because I can't pay you?"

He said nothing.

"I'm desperate," she said. "You're my only chance. I'm begging you. Why won't you do it? Is it because I'm Mexican?"

He said nothing.

"It's because I'm just a greaseball, right? A beaner? You'd do it for a white woman? Like your girlfriend? I bet she's a white woman. Probably a blonde, right?"

"Yes, she's a blonde," he said.

"Some guy was beating up on her, you'd kill him."

Yes, I would, he thought.

"And *she* ran off to Europe without you. Didn't want you to go with her. But you'd do it for her, and you won't do it for me."

"It's not the same," he said for the third time.

"I know," she said. "Because I'm just beaner trash. I'm not worth it."

He said nothing.

"What's her name?" she asked. "Your girlfriend?"

"Jodie," he said.

"O.K., imagine Jodie over there in Europe. She's trapped in some bad situation, getting beat up every day by some maniac sadist. She tells you all about it. Bares her soul. Every horrible humiliating detail. What are you going to do?"

Kill him, he thought.

She nodded like she could read his mind. "But you won't do that for me. You'd do it for the gringa, but not for me."

He paused a beat with his mouth halfway open. It was true. He would do it for Jodie Garber, but he wouldn't do it for Carmen Greer. *Why not?* Because it comes in a rush. You can't force it. It's a hot-blooded thing, like a drug in your veins, and you go with it. If it's not there, you can't go with it. Simple as that. He'd gone with it before in his life, many times. People mess with him, they get what they get. They mess with Jodie, that's the same thing as messing with him. Because Jodie *was* him. Or at least she used to be. In a way that Carmen wasn't. And never would be. So it just wasn't *there*.

"It's not about gringas or latinas," he said quietly.

She said nothing.

"Please, Carmen," he said. "You need to understand that."

"So what *is* it about?"

"It's about I know her and I don't know you."

"And that makes a difference?"

"Of course it does."

"Then get to know me," she said. "We've got two days. You're about to meet my daughter. Get to know us."

He said nothing. She drove on. Pecos 55 miles.

"You were a policeman," she said. "You should want to help people. Or are you scared? Is that it? Are you a coward?"

He said nothing.

"You could do it," she said. "You've done it before. So you know how. You could do it and get clean away. You could dump his body where nobody would find it. Out in the desert. Nobody would ever know. It wouldn't come back on you, if you were careful. You'd never get caught. You're smart enough."

He said nothing.

"Are you smart enough? Do you know how? Do you?"

"Of course I know how," he said. "But I won't do it."

"Why not?"

"I told you why not. Because I'm not an assassin."

"But I'm desperate," she said. "I need you to do this. I'm begging you. I'll do anything if you'll help me."

He said nothing.

"What do you want, Reacher? You want sex? We could do that."

"Stop the car," he said.

"Why?"

"Because I've had enough of this."

She jammed her foot down hard on the gas. The car leapt forward. He glanced back at the traffic and leaned over toward her and knocked the transmission into N. The engine unloaded and screamed and the car coasted and slowed. He used his left hand on the wheel and hauled it around against her desperate grip and steered the car to the shoulder. It bounced off the blacktop and the gravel bit against the tires and the speed washed away. He jammed the lever into P and opened his door, all in one movement. The car skidded to a stop with the transmission locked. He slid out and stood up unsteadily. Felt the heat on his body like a blow from a hammer and slammed the door and walked away from her.

4

He was sweating heavily twenty yards after getting out of the car. And already regretting his decision. He was in the middle of nowhere, on foot on a major highway, and the slowest vehicles were doing sixty. Nobody was going to want to stop for him. Even if they did want to, give them a little reaction time, give them a little time to check their mirrors, a little braking time, they'd be more than a mile away before they knew it, and then they'd shrug their shoulders and speed up again and keep on going. *Dumb place to hitch a ride,* they'd think.

It was worse than dumb. It was suicidal. The sun was fearsome and the temperature was easily a hundred and twelve degrees. The slipstream from the cars was like a hot gale, and the suction from the giant trucks wasn't far from pulling him off his feet. He had no water. He could barely breathe. There was a constant stream of people five yards away, but he was as alone as if he was stumbling blind through the desert. If a state trooper didn't come by and arrest him for jaywalking, he could die out there.

He turned and saw the Cadillac, still sitting inert on the

shoulder. But he kept on walking away from it. He made it about fifty yards and stopped. Turned to face east and stuck out his thumb. But it was hopeless, like he knew it would be. After five minutes, a hundred vehicles, the nearest thing he'd gotten to a response was some trucker blasting his air horn, a huge bass sound roaring past him with a whine of stressed tires and a hurricane of dust and grit. He was choking and burning up.

He turned again. Saw the Cadillac lurch backward and start up the shoulder toward him. Her steering was imprecise. The rear end was all over the place. It was close to slewing out into the traffic. He started walking back to it. It came on to meet him, fishtailing wildly. He started running. He stopped alongside the car as she braked hard. The suspension bounced. She buzzed the passenger window down.

"I'm sorry," she said.

He didn't hear it in the noise, but he caught the shape of the words.

"Get in," she said.

His shirt was sticking to his back. He had grit in his eyes. The howl of sound from the road was deafening him.

"Get in," she mouthed. "I'm sorry."

He got in. It felt exactly the same as the first time. The air roaring, the freezing leather seat. The small cowed woman at the wheel.

"I apologize," she said. "I'm sorry. I said stupid things."

He slammed the door. There was sudden silence. He put his hand in the chill stream from the vents.

"I didn't mean them," she said.

"Whatever," he said back.

"Really, I didn't mean them. I'm just so desperate I can't tell right from wrong anymore. And I'm very sorry for the thing about the sex. It was a crass thing to say."

Then her voice went small. "It's just that some of the guys I've picked up, I figured that was what it was going to have to be."

"You'd have sex with them so they'd kill your husband?"

She nodded. "I told you, I'm trapped and I'm scared and I'm desperate. And I don't have anything else to offer."

He said nothing.

"And I've seen movies where that happens," she said.

He nodded back.

"I've seen those movies, too," he said. "They never get away with it."

She paused a long moment.

"So you're not going to do it," she said, like a statement of fact.

"No, I'm not," he said.

She paused again, longer.

"O.K., I'll let you out in Pecos," she said. "You can't be out there walking. You could die in heat like this."

He paused too, much longer than she had. Then he shook his head. Because he had to be *somewhere*. When you live on the road, you learn pretty quick that any one place is about as good as any other place.

"No, I'll come with you," he said. "I'll hang out a couple of days. Because I'm sorry about your situation, Carmen. I really am. Just because I won't walk in and shoot the guy doesn't mean I don't want to help you some other way. If I can. And if you still want me to, that is."

She paused another beat.

"Yes, I still want you to," she said.

"And I want to meet Ellie. She looks like a great kid, from her picture."

"She is a great kid."

"But I'm not going to murder her father."

She said nothing.

"Is that completely clear?" he asked.

She nodded.

"I understand," she said. "I'm sorry I asked."

"It's not just me, Carmen," he said. "Nobody would do it. You were fooling yourself. It wasn't a good plan."

She looked small and lost.

"I thought nobody could refuse," she said. "If they knew."

She turned and watched the traffic coming up behind her. Waited for a gap. Six cars later, she pulled back onto the highway and gunned the motor. Within a minute she was doing eighty again, passing one car after another. The trucker who had used his air horn as he left Reacher in the dust lasted seven whole minutes, before she reeled him in.

The Crown Victoria made it to the destination the woman had selected within eighty minutes. It was an inch-wide empty brown stain on the map, and it was a forty-mile-wide empty brown stain in reality. One road ran through it, meandering roughly north and east in the lee of distant mountains. Hot, lonely, valueless country. But it had all the features she had predicted. It would serve her purposes. She smiled to herself. She had an instinct for terrain.

"O.K.," she said. "First thing tomorrow. Right here."

The big car turned and headed back south. The dust from its tires hung in the air for long minutes and then floated down to the powdery ground.

Carmen came off the highway just short of Pecos and speared south on a small county road that led down into total emptiness. Within five miles, they could have been on the surface of the moon.

"Tell me about Echo," he said.

She shrugged. "What's to tell? It's nothing. When they were first mapping Texas a hundred years ago, the Census Bureau called a place settled if it had more than six people to the square mile, and we *still* don't qualify. We're still the frontier."

"But it's very beautiful," he said.

And it was. The road was snaking and diving through endless contours, with red rock canyons either side of it, tall and noble to the east, fractured and pierced to the west, where ancient streams had sought the banks of the Rio Grande. Tall dry mountains reared beyond, with an immense technicolor sky above, and even in the speeding car he could sense the stunning silence of thousands of square miles of absolute emptiness.

"I hate it," she said.

"Where will I be?" he asked.

"On the property. In the bunkhouse, I guess. They'll hire you for the horses. We're always a man short. You show up with a pulse, they'll be interested. You can say you're a wrangler. It'll be a good disguise. It'll keep you close by."

"I don't know anything about horses."

She shrugged. "Maybe they won't notice. They don't notice much. Like me getting beaten half to death."

An hour later, they were tight for time. She was driving fast enough that the tire squeal from the curves was more or less continuous. They came up a long steep grade and then turned out between two rock pillars on a peak and suddenly there was flat land below them as far as the eye could see. The road fell away like a twisted tan ribbon and was crossed twenty miles ahead by another, just visible through the haze like a faint line on a map. The distant crossroads was studded with a handful of tiny buildings, and apart from them and the two roads there was no evidence humans had ever lived on the planet.

"Echo County," she said. "Everything you see, and a lot more besides. A thousand square miles, and a hundred and fifty people. Well, a hundred and forty-eight, because one of them is sitting right here with you, and one of them is still in jail."

Her mood had improved, because she said it with a wry smile. But she was looking at a tiny plume of dust on the road far below them. It was puffing out like a squirrel's tail, crawling slowly south, a quarter of the way to the crossroads.

"That must be the school bus," she said. "We have to beat it to town, or Ellie will get on and we'll miss her."

"Town?" Reacher said.

She smiled again, briefly.

"You're looking at it," she said. "Uptown Echo."

She accelerated down the grade and the Cadillac's own dust swirled and hung behind it. The landscape was so vast that speed seemed slowed to absurdity. Reacher figured the bus might be a half hour from the crossroads, and the Cadillac was traveling twice as fast, so they should catch it inside fifteen minutes, even though the elevation and the clear desert air made it look close enough to reach out and touch, like a child's toy on the floor of a room.

"It's good of you to be coming," she said. "Thank you. I mean it."

"No hay de que, señorita," he said.

"So you do know more than a few words."

He shrugged. "There were a lot of Spanish-speaking people in the army. Most of the new generation, in fact. Some of the best of them."

"Like baseball," she said.

"Yes," he said. "Like baseball."

"But you should call me *señora*. *Señorita* makes me too happy."

She accelerated again when the road leveled out and about a mile before they caught up with the bus she swung out into the wrong lane, ready to pass it. Safe enough, he figured. The chances of meeting oncoming traffic in that part of the world were worse than winning the lottery. She reeled in the bus and pulled through the cone of dust and blasted past and stayed on the left for another mile. Then she eased back right and five minutes later they were slowing as they approached the crossroads.

From ground level the hamlet looked ragged and defeated, the way small places do under the heat of the sun. There were lots partially overrun with dry thorny weeds, delineated with raw block walls, commercially zoned but never developed. There was a diner on the right on the northwest corner, nothing more than a long, low shack made of wood with all the color baked right out of it. Diagonally opposite was the school, a one-room building like something out of a history book. *The beginnings of rural education.* Opposite that on the southwest corner was a gas station with two pumps and a small yard filled with stalled cars behind it. Diagonally opposite the gas station and across the road from the school the northeast corner was an empty lot, with concrete blocks spilled randomly across it, like an optimistic new venture had been planned and then abandoned, maybe while LBJ was still in office. There were four other buildings, all one story, all plain concrete, all set back with thin rough driveways leading to them from the road. Houses, Reacher guessed. Their yards were littered with junk, children's bikes and tired automobiles on blocks and old living room furniture. The yards were baked dry and hard and had low chicken-wire fences around them, maybe to keep the big snakes out.

The crossroads itself had no stop signs, just thick lines on the blacktop, melted in the heat. Carmen drove straight through and past the school and U-turned across the full width of the road, bumping down into shallow drainage ditches on both shoulders. She came back and stopped with the school gate close to Reacher's window. The school yard was ringed by a wire hurricane fence like a dog pound, and the gate was an inexact hinged rectangle made of galvanized tubing and faced with the same wire.

She stared past him at the school door. The bus came laboring down from the north and stopped on its own side of the road, parallel to the Cadillac, facing the other direction. The schoolhouse door opened and a woman stepped out. She moved slow and looked tired. The teacher, Reacher guessed, ready to end her day. She saw the bus and waved to the children. They spilled out in a long stream. Seventeen of them, nine girls and eight boys, he counted. Ellie Greer was seventh in line. She was wearing a blue dress. She looked damp and hot. He recognized her from her photograph and by the way Carmen moved beside him. He heard her catch her breath and scrabble for the door handle.

She skipped around the hood and met her daughter outside the car on the beaten earth strip that passed for a sidewalk. She scooped her up in a wild hug. Spun her around and around. Her little feet windmilled outward and her blue lunch box swung and hit her mother on the back. Reacher could see the child laughing and tears in Carmen's eyes. They came back around the rear of the car clutched tight together. Carmen opened the door and Ellie scrambled straight into the driver's seat and stopped dead when she saw him. She went instantly silent and her eyes went wide.

"This is Mr. Reacher," Carmen said.

Ellie turned to look at her.

"He's my friend," Carmen said. "Say hello to him."

Ellie turned back.

"Hello," she said.

"Hey, Ellie," Reacher said. "School O.K.?"

Ellie paused. "It was O.K."

"Learn anything?"

"How to spell some words."

She paused again, and then tilted her chin upward a fraction.

"Not easy ones," she said. *"Ball* and *fall."*

Reacher nodded gravely.

"Four letters," he said. "That's pretty tough."

"I bet you can spell them."

"B-A-L-L," Reacher said. "F-A-L-L. Like that, right?"

"You're grown up," Ellie said, like he had passed a test. "But you know what? The teacher said four letters, but there's only three, because the L comes twice. Right there at the end."

"You're a smart kid," Reacher said. "Now hop in the back and let your mom in out of the heat."

She scrambled past his left shoulder and he caught the smell of elementary school. He had attended maybe fifteen different places, most of them in different countries and continents, and they all smelled the same. It was more than thirty years since he had last been in one, but he still remembered it clearly.

"Mom?" Ellie said.

Carmen slid in and shut the door. She looked flushed. Heat, sudden exertion, sudden brief happiness, Reacher didn't know.

"Mom, it's hot," Ellie said. "We should get ice cream sodas. From the diner."

Reacher saw Carmen about to smile and agree, and then he saw her glance back at her pocketbook and remember the lone dollar stashed inside it.

"From the diner, Mom," Ellie said. "Ice cream sodas. They're best when it's hot. Before we go home."

Carmen's face fell, and then it fell a little farther when she caught up to the end of Ellie's sentence. *Home.* Reacher stepped into the silence.

"Good idea," he said. "Let's get ice cream sodas. My treat."

Carmen glanced across, dependent on him and unhappy about it. But she put the car in drive anyway and pulled back through the crossroads and turned left into the diner's lot. She came around and parked in the shade tight against its north wall, right next to the only other car in the place, a steel blue Crown Victoria, new and shiny. Must be a state trooper's unmarked, or maybe a rental, Reacher thought.

The diner was cold inside, chilled by a big old-fashioned air conditioner that vented down through the roof. And it was empty, apart from a group Reacher took to be the Crown Victoria's occupants, a trio of ordinary indoor types at a window, two men and a woman. The woman was medium blond and pleasant looking. One guy was small and dark and the other was taller and fair. So the Crown Vic was a rental, not a cop car, and these guys were maybe some kind of a sales team heading between San Antonio and El Paso. Maybe they had heavy samples in the trunk that prevented them from flying. He glanced away and let Ellie lead him toward a booth at the opposite end of the room.

"This is the best table," she said. "All the others have torn seats, and they've sewed them up, and the thread is kind of thick and it can hurt the back of your leg."

"I guess you've been in here before," Reacher said.

"Of course I have." She giggled, like he was crazy. Two rows of tiny square teeth flashed at him. "I've been in here lots of times."

Then she jumped up and scooted sideways over the vinyl.

"Mommy, sit next to me," she said.

Carmen smiled. "I'm going to use the rest room first. I'll be right back. You stay here with Mr. Reacher, O.K.?"

The kid nodded gravely and Mr. Reacher sat himself down opposite her and they looked at each other quite openly. He wasn't sure what she was seeing, but he was seeing a living version of the photograph from her mother's wallet. Thick corn-colored hair tied back in a ponytail, incongruous dark eyes wide open and staring at him rather than at the camera's lens, a little snub of a nose, a serious mouth closed in a rather earnest way. Her skin was impossibly perfect, like pink damp velvet.

"Where did you go to school?" she asked. "Did you go here too?"

"No, I went to lots of different places," he said. "I moved around."

"You didn't go to the same school all the time?"

He shook his head. "Every few months, I went to a new one."

She concentrated hard. Didn't ask why. Just examined the proposition for its benefits and drawbacks.

"How could you remember where everything was? Like the bathrooms? You might forget who the teacher was. You might call her by the wrong name."

He shook his head again. "When you're young, you can remember stuff pretty well. It's when you get old that you start to forget things."

"I forget things," she said. "I forgot what my daddy looks like. He's in prison. But I think he's coming home soon."

"Yes, I think he is."

"Where did you go to school when you were six and a half like me?"

School, the center of her universe. He thought about it. When he was six and a half, the war in Vietnam was still well below its peak, but it was already big enough that his father was there or thereabouts at the time. So he figured that year would have been split between Guam and Manila. Manila, mostly, he thought, judging by his memories of the buildings and the vegetation, the places he hid out in and played around.

"The Philippines," he said.

"Is that in Texas too?" she asked.

"No, it's a bunch of islands between the Pacific and the South China Sea. Right out in the ocean, a long way from here."

"The ocean," she said, like she wasn't sure. "Is the ocean in America?"

"Is there a map on the wall in your school?"

"Yes, there is. A map of the whole world."

"O.K., the oceans are all the blue parts."

"There's a lot of blue parts."

He nodded. "That's for sure."

"My mom went to school in California."

"That'll be on the map, too. Find Texas and look to the left."

He saw her looking down at her hands, trying to remember which was left and which was right. Then he saw her look up beyond his shoulder, and he turned to see Carmen on her way back, trapped temporarily by the sales people getting up out of their booth. She waited until they had moved to the door and cleared the aisle and then she skipped back and sat down, all in one graceful movement. She pressed close to Ellie and hugged her one-armed and tickled her and got a squeal in exchange. The waitress finished with the sales people at the register and walked over, pad and pencil at the ready.

"Three Coke floats, please," Ellie said, loud and clear.

The waitress wrote it down.

"Coming right up, honey," she said, and walked away.

"Is that O.K. for you?" Carmen asked.

Reacher nodded. Like the smell of elementary school, he remembered the taste of a Coke float. He'd had his first ever in a PX canteen in Berlin, in a long low Quonset hut left over from the Four Powers occupation. It had been a warm summer's day in Europe, no air conditioning, and he remembered the heat on his skin and the bubbles in his nose.

"It's silly," Ellie said. "It's not the *Coke* that floats. It's the ice cream that floats *in* the Coke. They should call them ice cream floats."

Reacher smiled. He recalled thinking the same sorts of things, when he was her age. Outraged puzzlement at the illogicalities of the world he was being asked to join.

"Like elementary school," he said. "I found out that *elementary* means easy. So 'elementary school' means 'easy school.' I remember thinking, well, it seems pretty hard to me. 'Hard school' would be a better name."

Ellie looked at him, seriously.

"I don't think it's hard," she said. "But maybe it's harder in the ocean."

"Or maybe you're smarter than me."

She thought about it, earnestly.

"I'm smarter than some people," she said. "Like Peggy. She's still on the three-letter words. And she thinks you spell zoo with a Z."

Reacher had no answer to that. He waited for Carmen to pick it up, but before she could the waitress arrived back with a tin tray with three tall glasses on it. She put them on the table with great ceremony and whispered *"Enjoy"* to Ellie and backed away. But the glasses were almost a foot tall, and the drinking straws added another six inches, and Ellie's chin was about level with the table top, so her mouth was a long way from where it needed to be.

"You want me to hold it down?" Carmen asked her. "Or do you want to kneel up?"

Ellie thought about it. Reacher was starting to wonder if this kid ever made a quick, easy decision. He saw a little of himself in her. He had taken things too seriously. The kids in every new school had made fun of him for it. But usually only once.

"I'll kneel up," she said.

It was more than kneeling. She stood on the vinyl bench in a kind of crouch, with her hands planted palms-down on the table around the base of the glass, and her head ducked to the straw. As good a method as any, Reacher figured. She started sucking her drink and he turned to look at his own. The ice cream was a round greasy spoonful. He found the cola way too sweet, like it was mixed from syrup in the wrong proportions. The bubbles were huge and artificial. It tasted awful. A long way from a childhood summer's day in Germany.

"Don't you like it?" Ellie asked.

Her mouth was full, and she sprayed a little of the mixture onto his sleeve.

"I didn't say anything."

"You're making a funny face."

"Too sweet," he said. "It'll rot my teeth. Yours, too."

She came up with a huge grimace, like she was showing her teeth to a dentist.

"Doesn't matter," she said. "They're all going to fall out anyway. Peggy's got two out already."

Then she bent back to her straw and vacuumed up the rest

of the drink. She poked at the sludge in the bottom of the glass with her straw until it was liquid enough to suck.

"I'll finish yours, too, if you want," she said.

"No," her mother said back. "You'll throw up in the car."

"I won't. I promise."

"No," Carmen said again. "Now go to the bathroom, O.K.? It's a long way home."

"I went already," Ellie said. "We always go at school, last thing. We line up. We have to. The bus driver hates it if we pee on the seats."

Then she laughed delightedly.

"Ellie," her mother said.

"Sorry, Mommy. But it's only the boys who do that. I wouldn't do it."

"Go again anyway, O.K.?"

Ellie rolled her eyes theatrically and clambered over her mother's lap and ran to the back of the diner. Reacher put a five over the check.

"Great kid," he said.

"I think so," Carmen said. "Well, most of the time."

"Smart as anything."

She nodded. "Smarter than me, that's for sure."

He let that one go, too. Just sat in silence and watched her eyes cloud over.

"Thanks for the sodas," she said.

He shrugged. "My pleasure. And a new experience. I don't think I've ever bought a soda for a kid before."

"So you don't have any of your own, obviously."

"Never even got close."

"No nieces or nephews? No little cousins?"

He shook his head.

"I was a kid myself," he said. "Once upon a time, and a long time ago. Apart from what I remember about that, I don't know too much about it."

"Stick around a day or two and Ellie will teach you more than you ever wanted to know. As you've probably guessed."

Then she looked beyond his shoulder and he heard Ellie's footsteps behind him. The floor was old and there were obviously air pockets trapped under the buckled linoleum because her shoes made hollow slapping sounds.

"Mom, let's *go*," she said.

"Mr. Reacher is coming, too," Carmen said. "He's going to work with the horses."

He got up out of the booth and saw her watching him.

"O.K.," she said. "But let's *go*."

They pushed outside into the heat. Past the middle of the afternoon, and it was hotter than ever. The Crown Victoria was gone. They walked around to the Cadillac and Ellie climbed through to the backseat. Carmen sat for a long moment with her hand resting on the key. She closed her eyes. Then she opened them again and started the engine.

She drove back through the crossroads and past the school again and then more than sixty miles straight south. She went pretty slowly. Maybe half the speed she had used before. Ellie didn't complain. Reacher guessed she thought this was normal. He guessed Carmen never drove very fast on her way home.

They didn't pass much. There were power lines looping rhythmically between weathered poles on the left shoulder. There were windmills and oil pumps here and there in the distance, some of them working, most of them seized up and still. There were more V-8 irrigation rigs on the western side of the road, on the edges of old fields, but they were silent and rusted because the winds had scoured the earth shallow. Some places, it was cleaned right back to dry caliche ledges. Nothing much left to irrigate. The eastern side was better. There were whole square miles of mesquite, and sometimes broad patches of decent grassland running in irregular linear shapes, like there must be water underground.

Every ten or twelve miles there would be a ranch gate standing isolated by the side of the road. They were simple right-angle shapes, maybe fifteen feet wide, maybe fifteen feet high, with beaten earth tracks running through them into the distance. Some of them had names on them, made up from strips of wood nailed into the shapes of letters. Some of them had the names formed from iron, worked by hand into fancy script. Some of them had old bleached cattle skulls fixed centrally, with long horns curving outward like vulture's wings. Some of them were supplemented by old barbed wire strands running aimlessly into the middle distance, sketching the location of ancient boundaries. The wire was on wooden posts, and the posts were weathered and twisted into corkscrew shapes and looked as if they would turn to dust if you touched them.

Some of the ranch houses were visible, depending on the contours of the land. Where it was flat, Reacher could see clusters of buildings in the far distance. The houses were two-story, mostly painted white, crouching among huddles of low barns and sheds. They had windmills out back, and satellite dishes, and they looked quiet and stunned in the heat. The sun was getting low in the west, and the outside temperature was still showing a hundred and ten.

"It's the road, I think," Carmen said. "It soaks up the sun all day, and gives it back later."

Ellie had fallen asleep, sprawled across the rear seat. Her head was pillowed on the briefcase. Her cheek was touching the edges of the papers that outlined how her mother could best escape her father.

"Greer property starts here," Carmen said. "On the left. Next track is ours, about eight miles."

It was flat land, rising slightly on the right to a fragmented mesa about a mile away to the west. On the left, the Greers had better barbed wire than most. It looked like it might have been restrung less than fifty years ago. It ran reasonably straight into the east, enclosing patchy grassland that showed about equal parts green and brown. Miles away there was a forest of oil derricks visible against the skyline, all surrounded by tin huts and abandoned equipment.

"Greer Three," Carmen said. "Big field. It made Sloop's grandfather a lot of money, way back. Ran dry about forty years ago. But it's a famous family story, about that gusher coming in. Most exciting thing that ever happened to them."

She slowed a little more, clearly reluctant to make the final few miles. In the far distance the road rose into the boiling haze and Reacher could see the barbed wire change to an absurd picket fence. It was tight against the shoulder, like something you would see in New England, but it was painted dull red. It ran about half a mile to a ranch gate, which was also painted red, and then ran on again into the distance and out of sight. There were buildings behind the gate, much closer to the road than the ones he had seen before. There was a big old house with a two-story core and a tall chimney and sprawling one-story additions. There were low barns and sheds clustered loosely around it. There was ranch fencing enclosing arbitrary squares of territory. Everything was painted dull red, all the buildings and all the fences alike. The low orange sun blazed against them and made them glow and shimmer and split horizontally into bands of mirage.

She slowed still more where the red fence started. Coasted the last hundred yards with her foot off the gas and then turned in on a beaten dirt track running under the gate. There was a name on the gate, high above their heads, red-painted wood on red-painted wood. It said Red House. She glanced up at it as she passed through.

"Welcome to hell," she said.

The Red House itself was the main building in a compound of four impressive structures. It had a wide planked porch with wooden columns and a swinging seat hung from chains, and beyond it eighty yards farther on was a motor barn, but she couldn't drive down to it because a police cruiser was parked at an angle on the track, completely blocking her way. It was an old-model Chevy Caprice, painted black and white, with Echo County Sheriff on the door, where it had said something else before. Bought by the county secondhand, Reacher thought, maybe from Dallas or Houston, repainted and refurbished for easy duty out here in the sticks. It was empty and the driver's door was standing open. The light bar on the roof was flashing red and blue, whipping colors horizontally over the porch and the whole front of the house.

"What's this about?" Carmen said.

Then her hand went up to her mouth.

"God, he can't be home already," she said. "Please, no."

"Cops wouldn't bring him home," Reacher said. "They don't run a limo service."

Ellie was waking up behind them. No more hum from the engine, no more rocking from the springs. She struggled upright and gazed out, eyes wide.

"What's that?" she said.

"It's the sheriff," Carmen said.

"Why's *he* here?" Ellie asked.

"I don't know."

"Why are the lights flashing?"

"I don't know."

"Did somebody call 911? Maybe there's been a burglar. Maybe he wore a mask and stole something."

She crawled through and knelt on the padded armrest between the front seats. Reacher caught the school smell again and saw delighted curiosity in her face. Then he saw it change to extreme panic.

"Maybe he stole a horse," she said. "Maybe my pony, Mommy."

She scrambled across Carmen's lap and scrabbled at the door handle. Jumped out of the car and ran across the yard, as fast as her legs would carry her, her arms held stiff by her sides and her ponytail bouncing behind her.

"I don't think anybody stole a horse," Carmen said. "I think Sloop's come home."

"With the lights flashing?" Reacher said.

She unclipped her seat belt and swiveled sideways and placed her feet on the dirt of the yard. Stood up and stared toward the house, with her hands on the top of the door frame, like the door was shielding her from something. Reacher did the same, on his side. The fierce heat wrapped around him. He could hear bursts of radio chatter coming from the sheriff's car.

"Maybe they're looking for you," he said. "You've been away overnight. Maybe they reported you missing."

Across the Cadillac's roof, she shook her head. "Ellie was here, and as long as they know where she is, they don't care where I am."

She stood still for a moment longer, and then she took a sideways step and eased the door shut behind her. Reacher did the same. Twenty feet away, the house door opened and a uniformed man stepped out onto the porch. The sheriff, obviously. He was about sixty and overweight, with dark tanned skin and thin gray hair plastered to his head. He was walking half-backward, taking his leave of the gloom inside. He had black pants and a white uniform shirt with epaulettes and embroidered patches on the shoulders. A wide gun belt with a wooden-handled revolver secured into a holster with a leather strap. The door closed behind him and he turned toward his cruiser and stopped short when he saw Carmen. Touched his forefinger to his brow in a lazy imitation of a salute.

"Mrs. Greer," he said, like he was suggesting something was her fault.

"What happened?" she asked.

"Folks inside will tell you," the sheriff said. "Too damn hot for me to be repeating everything twice."

Then his gaze skipped the roof of the Cadillac and settled on Reacher.

"And who are you?" he asked.

Reacher said nothing.

"Who are you?" the guy said again.

"I'll tell the folks inside," Reacher replied. "Too damn hot for me to be repeating everything twice."

The guy gave him a long calm look, and finished with a slow nod of his head, like he'd seen it all before. He dumped himself inside his secondhand cruiser and fired it up and backed out to the road. Reacher let its dust settle on his shoes and watched Carmen drive the Cadillac down the track to the motor barn. It was a long low farm shed with no front wall, and it was painted red, like everything else. There were two pick-ups and a Jeep Cherokee in it. One of the pick-ups was recent and the other was sitting on flat tires and looked like it hadn't been moved in a decade. Beyond the building a narrow dirt track looped off into the infinite desert distance. Carmen eased the Cadillac in next to the Jeep and walked back out into the sun. She looked small and out of place in the yard, like an orchid in a trash pile.

"So where's the bunkhouse?" he asked.

"Stay with me," she said. "You need to meet them anyway. You need to get hired. You can't just show up in the bunkhouse."

"O.K.," he said.

She led him slowly to the bottom of the porch steps. She took them cautiously, one at a time. She arrived in front of the door and knocked.

"You have to knock?" Reacher asked.

She nodded.

"They never gave me a key," she said.

They waited, with Reacher a step behind her, appropriate for the hired help. He could hear footsteps inside. Then the door swung open. A guy was standing there, holding the inside handle. He looked to be in his middle twenties. He had a big square face, with the skin blotched red and white. He was bulky with frat-boy muscle turning to fat. He was wearing denim jeans and a dirty white T-shirt with the sleeves rolled tight over what was left of his biceps. He smelled of sweat and beer. He was wearing a red baseball cap backward on his head. A semicircle of forehead showed above the plastic strap. At the back, a shock of hair spilled out under the peak, exactly the same color and texture as Ellie's.

"It's you," he said, glancing at Carmen, glancing away.

"Bobby," she said.

Then his glance settled on Reacher.

"Who's your friend?"

"His name is Reacher. He's looking for work."

The guy paused.

"Well, come on in, I guess," he said. "Both of you. And close the door. It's hot."

He turned back into the gloom and Reacher saw the letter *T* on the ball cap. *Texas Rangers,* he thought. *Good ball club, but not good enough.* Carmen followed the guy three steps behind, entering her home of nearly seven years like an invited guest. Reacher stayed close to her shoulder.

"Sloop's brother," she whispered to him.

He nodded. The hallway was dark inside. He could see the red paint continued everywhere, over the wooden walls, the floors, the ceilings. Most places it was worn thin or worn away completely, just leaving traces of pigment behind like a stain. There was an ancient air conditioner running somewhere in the house, forcing the temperature down maybe a couple of degrees. It ran slowly, with a patient drone and rattle. It sounded peaceful, like the slow tick of a clock. The hallway was the size of a motel suite, filled with expensive stuff, but it was all old, like they'd run out of money decades ago. Or else they'd always had so much that the thrill of spending it had worn off a generation ago. There was a huge mirror on one wall, with the ornate frame painted red. Opposite to it was a rack filled with six bolt-action hunting rifles. The mirror reflected the rack and made the hallway seem full of guns.

"What did the sheriff want?" Carmen called.

"Come inside," Bobby called back.

We are inside, Reacher thought. But then he saw he meant "Come into the parlor." It was a big red room at the back of the house. It had been remodeled. It must have been a kitchen once. It opened out through the original wall of the house to a replacement kitchen easily fifty years old. The parlor had the same worn paint everywhere, including all over the furniture. There was a big farmhouse table and eight wheelback chairs, all made out of pine, all painted red, all worn back to shiny wood where human contact had been made.

One of the chairs was occupied by a woman. She looked to be somewhere in her middle fifties. She was the sort of person who still dresses the same way she always did despite her advancing age. She was wearing tight jeans with a belt and a blouse with a Western fringe. She had a young woman's hairstyle, colored a bright shade of orange and teased up off her scalp above a thin face. She looked like a twenty-year-old prematurely aged by some rare medical condition. Or by a shock. Maybe the sheriff had sat her down and given her some awkward news. She looked preoccupied and a little confused. But she showed a measure of vitality, too. A measure of authority. There was still vigor there. She looked like the part of Texas she owned, rangy and powerful, but temporarily laid low, with most of her good days behind her.

"What did the sheriff want?" Carmen asked again.

"Something happened," the woman said, and her tone meant it wasn't something good. Reacher saw a flicker of hope behind Carmen's eyes. Then the room went quiet and the woman turned to look in his direction.

"His name is Reacher," Carmen said. "He's looking for work."

"Where's he from?"

Her voice was like rawhide. *I'm the boss here,* it said.

"I found him on the road," Carmen answered.

"What can he do?"

"He's worked with horses before. He can do black-smithing."

Reacher looked out of the window while she lied about his skills. He had never been closer to a horse than walking past the ceremonial stables on the older army bases that still had them. He knew in principle that a blacksmith made horse-shoes, which were iron things horses had nailed to their feet. Or their hoofs. Hooves? He knew there was a charcoal bra-zier involved, and a bellows, and a great deal of rhythmic hammering. An anvil was required, and a trough of water. But he had never actually touched a horseshoe. He had seen them occasionally, nailed up over doors as a superstition. He knew some cultures nailed them upward, and some down-ward, all to achieve the same good luck. But that was all he knew about them.

"We'll talk about him later," the woman said. "Other things to talk about first."

Then she remembered her manners and sketched a wave across the table.

"I'm Rusty Greer," she said.

"Like the ballplayer?" Reacher asked.

"I was Rusty Greer before he was born," the woman said. Then she pointed at Bobby. "You already met my boy Robert Greer. Welcome to the Red House Ranch, Mr. Reacher. Maybe we can find you work. If you're willing and honest."

"What did the sheriff want?" Carmen asked for the third time.

Rusty Greer turned and looked straight at her.

"Sloop's lawyer's gone missing," she said.

"What?"

"He was on his way to the federal jail to see Sloop. He never got there. State police found his car abandoned on the road, south of Abilene. Just sitting there empty, miles from anywhere, keys still in it. Situation doesn't look good."

"Al Eugene?"

"How many lawyers you think Sloop had?"

Her tone added: *you idiot*. The room went totally silent and Carmen went pale and her hand jumped to her mouth, fingers rigid and extended, covering her lips.

"Maybe the car broke down," she said.

"Cops tried it," Rusty said. "It worked just fine."

"So where is he?"

"He's gone missing. I just told you that."

"Have they looked for him?"

"Of course they have. But they can't find him."

Carmen took a deep breath. Then another.

"Does it change anything?" she asked.

"You mean, is Sloop still coming home?"

Carmen nodded weakly, like she was terribly afraid of the answer.

"Don't you worry none," Rusty said. She was smiling. "Sloop will be back here Monday, just like he always was going to be. Al being missing doesn't change a thing. The sheriff made that clear. It was a done deal."

Carmen paused a long moment, with her eyes closed, and her hand on her lips. Then she forced the hand down and forced the lips into a trembling smile.

"Well, good," she said.

"Yes, good," her mother-in-law said.

Carmen nodded, vaguely. Reacher thought she was about to faint.

"What do you suppose happened to him?" she asked.

"How would I know? Some sort of trouble, I expect."

"But who would make trouble for Al?"

Rusty's smile thinned to a sneer.

"Well, take your best guess, dear," she said.

Carmen opened her eyes. "What does that mean?"

"It means, who would want to make trouble for their lawyer?"

"I don't know."

"Well, I do," Rusty said. "Somebody who buys them a big old Mercedes Benz and gets sent to jail anyhow, that's who."

"Well, who did that?"

"Anybody could have. Al Eugene takes anybody for a client. He has no *standards*. He's halfway to being plain crooked. Maybe all the way crooked, for all I know. Three-quarters of his clients are the wrong sort."

Carmen was still pale. "The wrong sort?"

"You know what I mean."

"You mean Mexican? Why don't you just come right out and say it?"

Rusty was still smiling.

"Well, tell me different," she said. "Some Mexican boy gets sent to jail, he doesn't just stand up and accept his punishment like we do. No, he blames his lawyer, and he gets all his brothers and his cousins all riled up about it, and of course he's got plenty of those come up here after him, all illegals, all *cholos,* all of them in gangs, and now you see exactly how that turns out. Just like it is down there in Mexico itself. You of all people should know what it's like."

"Why should I of all people? I've never even been to Mexico."

Nobody replied to that. Reacher watched her, standing up shaken and proud and alone like a prisoner in the enemy camp. The room was quiet. Just the thump and click of the old air conditioner running somewhere else.

"You got an opinion here, Mr. Reacher?" Rusty Greer asked.

It felt like a left-field question in a job interview. He wished he could think of something smart to say. Some diversion. But it wouldn't help any to start some big clumsy fight and get himself thrown off the property inside the first ten minutes.

"I'm just here to work, ma'am," he said.

"I'd like to know your opinion, all the same."

Just like a job interview. A character reference. Clearly she wanted exactly the right sort of person shoveling horse-shit for her.

"Mr. Reacher was a cop himself," Carmen said. "In the army."

Rusty nodded. "So what's your thinking, ex–army cop?"

Reacher shrugged. "Maybe there's an innocent explana-tion. Maybe he had a nervous breakdown and wandered off."

"Doesn't sound very likely. Now I see why they made you an ex-cop."

Silence for a long moment.

"Well, if there was trouble, maybe white folks made it," Reacher said.

"That's not going to be a popular view around here, son."

"It's not looking to be popular. It's looking to be right or wrong. And the population of Texas is three-quarters white, therefore I figure there's a three-in-four chance white folks were involved, assuming people are all the same as each other."

"That's a big assumption."

"Not in my experience."

Rusty bounced her gaze off the tabletop, back to Carmen.

"Well, no doubt you agree," she said. "With your new friend here."

Carmen took a breath.

"I never claim to be better than anyone else," she said. "So I don't see why I should agree I'm worse."

The room stayed quiet.

"Well, time will tell, I guess," Rusty said. "One or other of us is going to be eating humble pie."

She said it *paah*. The long syllable trailed into silence.

"Now, where's Sloop's little girl?" she asked, with an arti-ficial brightness in her voice, like the conversation had never happened. "You bring her back from school?"

Carmen swallowed and turned to face her. "She's in the barn, I think. She saw the sheriff and got worried her pony had been stolen."

"That's ridiculous. Who would steal her damn pony?"

"She's only a child," Carmen said.

"Well, the maid is ready to give the child its supper, so take it to the kitchen, and show Mr. Reacher to the bunkhouse on your way."

Carmen just nodded, like a servant with new instructions. Reacher followed her out of the parlor, back to the hallway. They went outside into the heat again and paused in the shadows on the porch.

"Ellie eats in the kitchen?" Reacher asked.

Carmen nodded.

"Rusty hates her," she said.

"Why? She's her granddaughter."

Carmen looked away.

"Her blood is tainted," she said. "Don't ask me to explain it. It's not rational. She hates her, is all I know."

"So why all the fuss if you took her away?"

"Because Sloop wants her here. She's his weapon against me. His instrument of torture. And his mother does what he wants."

"She make you eat in the kitchen, too?"

"No, she makes me eat with her," she said. "Because she knows I'd rather not."

He paused, at the edge of the shadow.

"You should have gotten out of here," he said. "We should be in Vegas by now."

"I was hopeful, for a second," she said. "About Al Eugene. I thought there might be a delay."

He nodded. "So was I. It would have been useful."

She nodded, tears in her eyes.

"I know," she said. "Too good to be true."

"So you should still think about running."

She wiped her eyes with the back of her hand. Shook her head.

"I won't run," she said. "I won't be a fugitive."

He said nothing.

"And you should have agreed with her," she said. "About the Mexicans. I'd have understood you were bluffing. I need her to keep you around."

"I couldn't."

"It was a risk."

She led him down the steps into the sun and across the yard. Beyond the motor barn was a horse barn. That structure was red like everything else, big as an aircraft hangar, with clerestory vents in the roof. There was a big door standing a foot open. There was a strong smell coming out of it.

"I'm not much of a country guy," he said.

"You'll get used to it," she said.

Behind the barn were four corrals boxed in with red fences. Two of them were covered in scrubby grass, and two of them had desert sand piled a foot thick. There were striped poles resting on oil drums to make jumping courses. Behind the corrals was another red building, long and low, with small windows high up under the eaves.

"The bunkhouse," she said.

She stood still for a moment, lost in thought. Then she shivered in the heat and came back, all business.

"The door is around the other side," she said. "You'll find two guys in there, Joshua and Billy. Don't trust either one of them. They've been here forever and they belong to the Greers. The maid will bring your meals down to you in about an hour, after Ellie eats, before we do."

"O.K.," he said.

"And Bobby will come down to check you out, sooner or later. Watch him carefully, Reacher, because he's a snake."

"O.K.," he said again.

"I'll see you later," she said.

"You going to be all right?"

She nodded once and walked away. He watched her until she was behind the horse barn, and then he walked around and found the door into the bunkhouse.

5

The boy filled a whole new page in his notebook. The men with the telescopes called out descriptions and the exact sequence of events. The arrival of the sheriff, the return of the beaner and the kid with the new guy in tow, the kid running off to the barn, the sheriff leaving, the beaner and the new guy entering the house, a long period of nothing doing, the emergence of the beaner and the new guy onto the porch, their walk together down toward the bunkhouse, her return alone.

"Who is he?" the boy asked.

"Hell should we know?" one of the men replied.

Very tall, heavy, not neatly dressed, shirt and pants, can't tell how old, the boy wrote. Then he added: *Not a wrangler, wrong shoes. Trouble?*

The grade fell away behind the bunkhouse and made it a two-story building. The lower floor had huge sliding doors, frozen open on broken tracks. There was another pick-up in there, and a couple of green tractors. At the far end to the right was a wooden staircase without a handrail leading upward through a rectangular hole in the ceiling. Reacher spent a minute on the ground floor looking at the vehicles. The pick-up had a gun rack in the rear window. The air was hot and heavy and smelled of gasoline and motor oil.

Then he used the staircase and came out on the second level. All the interior carpentry was painted red, walls, floor and roof beams alike. The air was hotter still up there, and stale. No air conditioning, and not much ventilation. There was a closed-off area at the far end, which he guessed was the bathroom. Apart from that the whole of the floor was one big open space, with sixteen beds facing each other eight to a side, with simple iron frames and thin striped mattresses and bedside cabinets and footlockers.

The two beds nearest the bathroom were occupied. Each had a small, wiry man lying half-dressed on top of the sheets. Both men wore blue jeans and fancy tooled boots and no shirts. Both had their hands folded behind their heads. They both turned toward the staircase as Reacher stepped up inside the room. They both unlaced their nearer arms to get a better look at him.

Reacher had done four years at West Point, and then thirteen years in the service, so he had a total seventeen years' experience of walking into a new dormitory and being stared at by its occupants. It wasn't a sensation that bothered him. There was a technique involved in handling it. An etiquette. The way to do it was to just walk in, select an unoccupied bed, and say absolutely nothing at all. Make somebody else speak first. That way, you could judge their disposition before you were forced to reveal your own.

He walked to a bed two places away from the head of the staircase, against the north wall, which he judged would be cooler than the south. In the past, in the army, he would have had a heavy canvas kit bag to dump on the bed as a symbol of possession. The kit bag would be stenciled with his name and his rank, and the number of restencilings on it would offer a rough guide to his biography. Kit bags saved a lot of talking time. But the best he could do in this new situation was take his folding toothbrush from his pocket and prop it on the bed-side cabinet. As a substitute gesture, it lacked physical impact. But it made the same point. It said *I live here now, same as you do. You got any kind of a comment to make about that?*

Both men kept on staring at him, saying nothing. Lying down, it was hard to judge their physiques with any degree of certainty, but they were both small. Maybe five-six or -seven each, maybe a hundred and fifty pounds. But they were wiry and muscular, like middleweight boxers. They had farmers' tans, deep brown on their arms and their faces and their necks, and milky white where T-shirts had covered their bodies. They had random knobs and old swellings here and there on their ribs and arms and collarbones. Reacher had seen marks like that before. Carmen had one. He had one or two himself. They were where old fractures had set and healed.

He walked past the two men to the bathroom. It had a door, but it was a communal facility inside, four of everything with no interior partitioning. Four toilets, four sinks, four shower heads in a single elongated stall. It was reasonably clean, and it smelled of warm water and cheap soap, like the two guys had recently showered, maybe ready for Friday evening off. There was a high window with a clogged insect screen and no glass. By standing tall he could see past the corner of the horse barn all the way up to the house. He could see half of the porch and a sliver of the front door.

He came back into the dormitory room. One of the guys had hauled himself upright and was sitting with his head turned, watching the bathroom door. His back was as pale as his front, and it had more healed fractures showing through the skin. The ribs, the right scapula. Either this guy spent a lot of time getting run over by trucks, or else he was a retired rodeo rider who had passed his career a little ways from the top of his trade.

"Storm coming," the guy said.

"What I heard," Reacher said.

"Inevitable, with a temperature like this."

Reacher said nothing.

"You hired on?" the guy asked.

"I guess," Reacher said.

"So you'll be working for us."

Reacher said nothing.

"I'm Billy," the guy said.

The other guy moved up on his elbows.

"Josh," he said.

Reacher nodded to them both.

"I'm Reacher," he said. "Pleased to meet you."

"You'll do the scut work for us," the guy called Billy said. "Shoveling shit and toting bales."

"Whatever."

"Because you sure don't look like much of a horse rider to me."

"I don't?"

Billy shook his head. "Too tall. Too heavy. Center of gravity way up there. No, my guess is you're not much of a horse rider at all."

"The Mexican woman bring you in?" Josh asked.

"Mrs. Greer," Reacher said.

"Mrs. Greer is Rusty," Billy said. "She didn't bring you in."

"Mrs. Carmen Greer," Reacher said.

Billy said nothing. The guy called Josh just smiled.

"We're heading out after supper," Billy said. "Bar, couple hours south of here. You could join us. Call it a get-to-know-you type of thing."

Reacher shook his head. "Maybe some other time, when I've earned something. I like to pay my own way, situation like that."

Billy thought about it and nodded.

"That's a righteous attitude," he said. "Maybe you'll fit right in."

The guy called Josh just smiled.

Reacher walked back to his bed and stretched himself out, keeping still, fighting the heat. He stared up at the red-painted rafters for a minute, and then he closed his eyes.

The maid brought supper forty minutes later. She was a middle-aged white woman who could have been a relative of Billy's. She greeted him with familiarity. Maybe a cousin.

Certainly she looked a little like him. Sounded like him. The same genes in there somewhere. She greeted Josh with ease and Reacher himself with coolness. Supper was a pail of pork and beans, which she served into metal bowls with a ladle taken from her apron pocket. She handed out forks and spoons, and empty metal cups.

"Water in the bathroom faucet," she said, for Reacher's benefit.

Then she went back down the stairs and Reacher turned his attention to the food. It was the first he had seen all day. He sat on his bed with the bowl on his knees and ate with the spoon. The beans were dark and soupy and mixed with a generous spoonful of molasses. The pork was tender and the fat was crisp. It must have been fried separately and mixed with the beans afterward.

"Hey, Reacher," Billy called over. "So what do you think?"

"Good enough for me," he said.

"Bullshit," Josh said. "More than a hundred degrees all day, and she brings us hot food? I showered already and now I'm sweating like a pig again."

"It's free," Billy said.

"Bullshit, it's free," Josh said back. "It's a part of our wages."

Reacher ignored them. Bitching about the food was a staple of dormitory life. And this food wasn't bad. Better than some he'd eaten. Better than what came out of most barracks cookhouses. He dumped his empty bowl on the cabinet next to his toothbrush and lay back down and felt his stomach go to work on the sugars and the fats. Across the room Billy and Josh finished up and wiped their mouths with their forearms and took clean shirts out of their footlockers. Shrugged them on and buttoned them on the run and combed through their hair with their fingertips.

"See you later," Billy called.

They clattered down the stairs and a moment later Reacher heard the sound of a gasoline engine starting up directly below. The pick-up, he guessed. He heard it back out through the doors and drive away. He stepped into the bathroom and saw it come around the corner and wind around the horse barn and bounce across the yard past the house.

He walked back through the dormitory and piled the three used bowls on top of each other, with the silverware in the topmost. Threaded the three cup handles onto his forefinger and walked down the stairs and outside. The sun was nearly below the horizon but the heat hadn't backed off at all. The air was impossibly hot. Almost suffocating. And it was getting humid. A warm damp breeze was coming in from somewhere. He walked up past the corrals, past the barn, through the yard. He skirted around the porch and looked for the kitchen door. Found it and knocked. The maid opened up.

"I brought these back," he said.

He held up the bowls and the cups.

"Well, that's kind of you," she said. "But I'd have come for them."

"Long walk," he said. "Hot night."

She nodded.

"I appreciate it," she said. "You had enough?"

"Plenty," he said. "It was very good."

She shrugged, a little bashful. "Just cowboy food."

She took the used dishes from him and carried them inside.

"Thanks again," she called.

It sounded like a dismissal. So he turned away and walked out to the road, with the low sun full on his face. He stopped under the wooden arch. Ahead of him to the west was nothing at all, just the empty eroded mesa he had seen on the way in. On the right, to the north, was a road sixty miles long with a few buildings at the end of it. A neighbor fifteen miles away. On the left, to the south, he had no idea. A bar two hours away, Billy had said. Could be a hundred miles. He turned around. To the east, Greer land for a stretch, and then somebody else's, and then somebody else's again, he guessed. Dry holes and dusty caliche and nothing much more all the way back to Austin, four hundred miles away.

New guy comes to gate and stares right at us, the boy wrote. *Then looks all around. Knows we're here? Trouble?*

He closed his book again and pressed himself tighter to the ground.

* * *

"Reacher," a voice called.

Reacher squinted right and saw Bobby Greer in the shadows on the porch. He was sitting in the swing set. Same denims, same dirty T-shirt. Same backward ball cap.

"Come here," he called.

Reacher paused a beat. Then he walked back past the kitchen and stopped at the bottom of the porch steps.

"I want a horse," Bobby said. "The big mare. Saddle her up and bring her out."

Reacher paused again. "You want that now?"

"When do you think? I want an evening ride."

Reacher said nothing.

"And we need a demonstration," Bobby said.

"Of what?"

"You want to hire on, you need to show us you know what you're doing."

Reacher paused again, longer.

"O.K.," he said.

"Five minutes," Bobby said.

He stood up and headed back inside the house. Closed the door. Reacher stood for a moment with the heat on his back and then headed down to the barn. Headed for the big door. The one with the bad smell coming out of it. A demonstration? *You're in deep shit now,* he thought. *More ways than one.*

There was a light switch inside the door, in a metal box screwed to the siding. He flicked it on and weak yellow bulbs lit the enormous space. The floor was beaten earth, and there was dirty straw everywhere. The center of the barn was divided into horse stalls, back to back, with a perimeter track lined with floor-to-ceiling hay bales inside the outer walls. He circled around the stalls. A total of five were occupied. Five horses. They were all tethered to the walls of their stalls with complicated rope constructions that fitted neatly over their heads.

He took a closer look at each of them. One of them was very small. A pony. Ellie's, presumably. *O.K., strike that.* Four to go. Two were slightly bigger than the other two. He bent down low and peered upward at them, one at a time. In principle he knew what a mare should look like, underneath. It should be easy enough to spot one. But in practice, it wasn't easy. The stalls were dark and the tails obscured the details. In the end he decided the first one he looked at wasn't a mare. Wasn't a stallion, either. Some parts were missing. *A gelding. Try the next.* He shuffled along and looked at the next. *O.K., that's a mare. Good.* The next one was a mare, too. The last one, another gelding.

He stepped back to where he could see both of the mares at once. They were huge shiny brown animals, huffing through their noses, moving slightly, making dull *clop* sounds with their feet on the straw. *No, their hoofs. Hooves?* Their necks were turned so they could watch him with one eye each. Which one was bigger? The one on the left, he decided. A little taller, a little heavier, a little wider in the shoulders. *O.K., that's the big mare. So far, so good.*

Now, the saddle. Each stall had a kind of a thick post coming horizontally out of the outside wall, right next to the gate, with a whole bunch of equipment piled on it. A saddle for sure, but also a lot of complicated straps and blankets and metal items. The straps are the reins, he guessed. The metal thing must be the bit. It goes in the horse's mouth. *The bit between her teeth, right?* He lifted the saddle off the post. It was very heavy. He carried it balanced on his left forearm. *Felt good.* Just like a regular cowboy. *Roy Rogers, eat your heart out.*

He stood in front of the stall gate. The big mare watched him with one eye. Her lips folded back like thick rolls of rubber, showing big square teeth underneath. They were yellow. *O.K., think. First principles.* Teeth like that, this thing is not a carnivore. It's not a biting animal. Well, it might try to nick you a little, but it's not a lion or a tiger. It eats grass. It's an herbivore. Herbivores are generally timid. Like antelope or wildebeests out there on the sweeping plains of Africa. So this thing's defense mechanism is to run away, not to attack. It gets scared, and it runs. But it's a herd animal, too. So it's looking for a leader. It will submit to a show of authority. *So be firm, but don't scare it.*

He opened the gate. The horse moved. Its ears went back and its head went up. Then down. Up and down, against the rope. It moved its back feet and swung its huge rear end toward him.

"Hey," he said, loud and clear and firm.

It kept on coming. He touched it on the side. It kept on coming. *Don't get behind it. Don't let it kick you.* That much, he knew. What was the phrase? *Like being kicked by a horse?* Had to mean something.

"Stand still," he said.

It was swinging sideways toward him. He met its flank with his right shoulder. Gave it a good solid shove, like he was aiming to bust down a door. The horse quieted. Stood still, huffing gently. He smiled. *I'm the boss, O.K.?* He put the back of his right hand up near its nose. It was something he had seen at the movies. *You rub the back of your hand on its nose, and it gets to know you. Some smell thing.* The skin on its nose felt soft and dry. Its breath was strong and hot. Its lips peeled back again and its tongue came out. It was huge and wet.

"O.K., good girl," he whispered.

He lifted the saddle two-handed and dumped it down on her back. Pushed and pulled at it until it felt solid. It wasn't easy. *Was it the right way around?* Had to be. It was shaped a little like a chair. There was a definite front and a back. There were broad straps hanging down on either side. Two long, two short. Two had buckles, two had holes. What were *they* for? To hold the saddle on, presumably. You bring the far ones around and buckle them at the side, up underneath where the rider's thigh would be. He ducked down and tried to grab the far straps, underneath the horse's belly. He could barely reach them. This was one wide animal, that was for damn sure. He stretched and caught the end of one strap in his fingertips and the saddle slipped sideways.

"Shit," he breathed.

He straightened up and leveled the saddle again. Ducked down and grabbed for the far straps. The horse moved and put them way out of his reach.

"Shit," he said again.

He stepped closer, crowding the horse against the wall. It didn't like that, and it leaned on him. He weighed two hundred and fifty pounds. The horse weighed half a ton. He staggered backward. The saddle slipped. The horse stopped moving. He straightened the saddle again and kept his right hand on it while he groped for the straps with his left.

"Not like *that*," a voice called from way above him.

He spun around and looked up. Ellie was lying on top of the stack of hay bales, up near the roof, her chin on her hands, looking down at him.

"You need the *blanket* first," she said.

"What blanket?"

"The saddle cloth," she said.

The horse moved again, crowding hard against him. He shoved it back. Its head came around and it looked at him. He looked back at it. It had huge dark eyes. Long eyelashes. He glared at it. *I'm not afraid of you, pal. Stand still or I'll shove you again.*

"Ellie, does anybody know you're in here?" he called.

She shook her head, solemnly.

"I'm hiding," she said. "I'm good at hiding."

"But does anybody know you hide in here?"

"I think my mommy knows I do sometimes, but the Greers don't."

"You know how to do this horse stuff?"

"Of course I do. I can do my pony all by myself."

"So help me out here, will you? Come and do this one for me."

"It's easy," she said.

"Just show me, O.K.?"

She stayed still for a second, making her usual lengthy decision, and then she scrambled down the pile of bales and jumped to the ground and joined him in the stall.

"Take the saddle off again," she said.

She took a cloth off of the equipment post and shook it out and threw it up over the mare's back. She was too short and Reacher had to straighten it one-handed.

"Now put the saddle on it," she said.

He dropped the saddle on top of it. Ellie ducked underneath the horse's belly and caught the straps. She barely needed to stoop. She threaded the ends together and pulled.

"You do it," she said. "They're stiff."

He lined the buckles up and pulled hard.

"Not too tight," Ellie said. "Not yet. Wait for her to swell up."

"She's going to *swell up*?"

Ellie nodded, gravely. "They don't like it. They swell their stomachs up to try to stop you. But they can't hold it, so they come down again."

He watched the horse's stomach. It was already the size of an oil drum. Then it blew out, bigger and bigger, fighting the straps. Then it subsided again. There was a long sigh of air through its nose. It shuffled around and gave up.

"Now do them tight," Ellie said.

He pulled them as tight as he could. The mare shuffled in place. Ellie had the reins in her hands, shaking them into some kind of coherent shape.

"Take the rope off of her," she said. "Just pull it down."

He pulled the rope down. The mare's ears folded forward and it slid down over them, over her nose, and off.

"Now hold this up." She handed him a tangle of straps. "It's called the bridle."

He turned it in his hands, until the shape made sense. He held it against the horse's head until it was in the right position. He tapped the metal part against the mare's lips. *The bit.* She kept her mouth firmly closed. He tried again. No result.

"How, Ellie?" he asked.

"Put your thumb in."

"My thumb? Where?"

"Where her teeth stop. At the side. There's a hole."

He traced the ball of his thumb sideways along the length of the mare's lips. He could feel the teeth passing underneath, one by one, like he was counting them. Then they stopped, and there was just gum.

"Poke it in," Ellie said.

"My *thumb*?"

She nodded. He pushed, and the lips parted, and his thumb slipped into a warm, gluey, greasy socket. And sure enough, the mare opened her mouth.

"Quick, put the bit in," Ellie said.

He pushed the metal into the mouth. The mare used her

massive tongue to get it comfortable, like she was helping him, too.

"Now pull the bridle up and buckle it."

He eased the leather straps up over the ears and found the buckles. There were three of them. One fastened flat against the slab of cheekbone. One went over her nose. The third was hanging down under her neck.

"Not too tight," Ellie said. "She's got to breathe."

He saw a worn mark on the strap, which he guessed indicated the usual length.

"Now loop the reins up over the horn."

There was a long strap coming off of the ends of the bit in a loop. He guessed that was the rein. And he guessed the horn was the upright thing at the front end of the saddle. Like a handle, for holding on with. Ellie was busy pulling the stirrups down into place, walking right under the mare's belly from one side to the other.

"Now lift me up," she said. "I need to check everything."

He held her under the arms and lifted her into the saddle. She felt tiny and weighed nothing at all. The horse was way too wide for her, and her legs came out more or less straight on each side. She lay down forward and stretched her arms out and checked all the buckles. Redid some of them. Tucked the loose ends away. Pulled the mane hair out neatly from under the straps. Gripped the saddle between her legs and jerked herself from side to side, checking for loose movement.

"It's O.K.," she said. "You did very good."

She put her arms out to him and he lifted her down. She was hot and damp.

"Now just lead her out," she said. "Hold her at the side of her mouth. If she won't come, give her a yank."

"Thanks a million, kid," he said. "Now go hide again, O.K.?"

She scrambled back up the stack of hay bales and he tugged at a strap coming off a metal ring at the side of the mouth. The mare didn't move. He clicked his tongue and pulled again. The mare lurched forward. He jumped ahead and she got herself into some kind of a rhythm behind him. *Clop, clop, clop.* He led her out of the stall and pulled her around the corner and headed for the door. Let her come ahead to his shoulder and stepped with her into the yard. She walked easily. He adjusted to her pace. His arm was neatly bent at the elbow and her head was rocking up and down a little and her shoulder was brushing gently against his. He walked her across the yard like he'd done it every day of his life. *Roy Rogers, eat your damn heart out.*

Bobby Greer was back on the porch steps, waiting. The mare walked right up to him and stopped. Reacher held the little leather strap while Bobby checked all of the same things Ellie had. He nodded.

"Not bad," he said.

Reacher said nothing.

"But you took longer than I expected."

Reacher shrugged. "I'm new to them. I always find it's better to go slow, the first time. Until they're familiar with me."

Bobby nodded again. "You surprise me. I would have bet the farm the nearest you'd ever gotten to a horse was watching the Preakness on cable."

"The what?"

"The Preakness. It's a horse race."

"I know it is. I was kidding."

"So maybe it's a double surprise," Bobby said. "Maybe my sister-in-law was actually telling the truth for once."

Reacher glanced at him. "Why wouldn't she be?"

"I don't know why. But she hardly ever does. You need to bear that in mind."

Reacher said nothing. Just waited.

"You can go now," Bobby said. "I'll put her away when I'm through."

Reacher nodded and walked away. He heard a crunch of leather behind him, which he assumed was Bobby getting up into the saddle. But he didn't look back. He just walked through the yard, down past the barn, past the corrals, and around the corner of the bunkhouse to the foot of the stairway. He intended to go straight up and take a long shower to get rid of the terrible animal smell that was clinging to him. But when he got up to the second story, he found Carmen sitting on his bed with a set of folded sheets on her knees. She was still in her cotton dress, and the sheets glowed white against the skin of her bare legs.

"I got you these," she said. "From the linen closet in the bathroom. You're going to need them. I didn't know if you would realize where they were."

He stopped at the head of the stairs, one foot inside the room, the other foot still on the last tread.

"Carmen, this is crazy," he said. "You should get out, right now. They're going to realize I'm a phony. I'm not going to last a day. I might not even be here on Monday."

"I've been thinking," she said. "All the way through supper."

"About what?"

"About Al Eugene. Suppose it's about whoever Sloop is going to rat out? Suppose they woke up and took some action? Suppose they grabbed Al to stop the deal?"

"Can't be. Why would they wait? They'd have done it a month ago."

"Yes, but suppose everybody *thought* it was."

He stepped all the way into the room.

"I don't follow," he said, although he did.

"Suppose you made Sloop disappear," she said. "The exact same way somebody made Al disappear. They'd think it was all connected somehow. They wouldn't suspect you. You'd be totally in the clear."

He shook his head. "We've been through this. I'm not an assassin."

She went quiet. Looked down at the sheets in her lap and began picking at a seam. The sheets were frayed and old. Cast-offs from the big house, Reacher thought. Maybe Rusty and her dead husband had slept under those same sheets. Maybe Bobby had. Maybe Sloop had. Maybe Sloop and Carmen, together.

"You should just get out, right now," he said again.

"I can't."

"You should stay somewhere inside of Texas, just temporarily. Fight it, legally. You'd get custody, in the circumstances."

"I don't have any money. It could cost a hundred thousand dollars."

"Carmen, you have to do *something*."

She nodded.

"I know what I'm going to do," she said. "I'm going to take a beating, Monday night. Then Tuesday morning, I'm going to come find you, wherever you are. Then you'll *see,* and maybe you'll change your mind."

He said nothing. She angled her face up into the fading light from the high windows. Her hair tumbled back on her shoulders.

"Take a good look," she said. "Come close."

He stepped nearer.

"I'll be all bruised," she said. "Maybe my nose will be broken. Maybe my lips will be split. Maybe I'll have teeth missing."

He said nothing.

"Touch my skin," she said. "Feel it."

He put the back of his forefinger on her cheek. Her skin was soft and smooth, like warm silk. He traced the wide arch of her cheekbone.

"Remember this," she said. "Compare it to what you feel Tuesday morning. Maybe it'll change your mind."

He took his finger away. Maybe it *would* change his mind. That was what she was counting on, and that was what he was afraid of. The difference between cold blood and hot blood. It was a big difference. For him, a crucial difference.

"Hold me," she said. "I can't remember how it feels to be held."

He sat down next to her and took her in his arms. She slid hers around his waist and buried her head in his chest.

"I'm scared," she said.

They sat like that for twenty minutes. Maybe thirty. Reacher lost all track of time. She was warm and fragrant, breathing steadily. Then she pulled away and stood up, with a bleak expression on her face.

"I have to go find Ellie," she said. "It's her bedtime."

"She's in the barn. She showed me how to put all that crap on the horse."

She nodded. "She's a good kid."

"That's for sure," he said. "Saved my bacon."

She handed the sheets to him.

"You want to come riding tomorrow?" she asked.

"I don't know how."

"I'll teach you."

"Could be a long process."

"It can't be. We have to get up on the mesa."

"Why?"

She looked away.

"Something you have to teach *me*," she said. "In case Tuesday doesn't change your mind. I need to know how to work my gun properly."

He said nothing.

"You can't deny me the right to defend myself," she said.

He said nothing. She went quietly down the stairs, leaving him sitting on the bed holding the folded sheets on his knees, exactly like he had found her.

He made up his bed. The old sheets were thin and worn, which he figured was O.K., in the circumstances. The temperature was still somewhere in the high nineties. Middle of the night, it might cool off to eighty-five. He wasn't going to be looking for a lot of warmth.

He went back down the stairs and stepped outside. Looking east, there was a black horizon. He stepped around the bunkhouse corner and faced the sunset in the west. It flamed against the red buildings. He stood still and watched it happen. This far south, the sun would drop away pretty quickly. Like a giant red ball. It flared briefly against the rim of the mesa and then disappeared and the sky lit up red above it.

He heard the sound of footsteps in the dust ahead of him. Squinted into the sunset glare and saw Ellie walking down toward him. Little short steps, stiff arms, the blue halter dress specked with pieces of straw. Her hair was lit from behind and glowed red and gold like an angel.

"I came to say good night," she said.

He remembered times in the past, being entertained in family quarters on a base somewhere, the melancholy notes of taps sounding faintly in the distance, polite army kids say-

ing a formal farewell to their fathers' brother officers. He remembered it well. You shook their little hands, and off they
went. He smiled at her.

"O.K., good night, Ellie," he said.

"I like you," she said.

"Well, I like you, too," he said.

"Are you hot?"

"Very."

"There'll be a storm soon."

"Everybody tells me that."

"I'm glad you're my mommy's friend."

He said nothing. Just put out his hand. She looked at it.

"You're supposed to give me a good-night kiss," she said.

"Am I?"

"Of *course* you are."

"O.K.," he said.

Her face was about level with his thigh. He started to bend
down.

"No, pick me up," she said.

She held up her arms, more or less vertical. He paused a
beat and then swung her in the air and settled her in the crook
of his elbow. Kissed her cheek, gently.

"Good night," he said again.

"Carry me," she said. "I'm tired."

He carried her past the corrals, past the horse barn, across
the yard to the house. Carmen was waiting on the porch,
leaning on a column, watching them approach.

"There you are," she said.

"Mommy, I want Mr. Reacher to come in and say good
night," Ellie said.

"Well, I don't know if he can."

"I only work here," Reacher said. "I don't live here."

"Nobody will *know*," Ellie said. "Come in through the
kitchen. There's only the maid in there. She works here, too.
And she's allowed in the house."

Carmen stood there, unsure.

"Mommy, *please*," Ellie said.

"Maybe if we all go in together," Carmen said.

"Through the kitchen," Ellie said. Then she changed her

voice to a fierce whisper that was probably louder than talking. "We don't want the *Greers* to see us."

Then she giggled, and rocked in Reacher's arms, and ducked her face down into his neck. Carmen glanced at him, a question in her face. He shrugged back. *What's the worst thing can happen?* He lowered Ellie to the ground and she took her mother's hand. They walked together to the kitchen door and Carmen pushed it open.

Sunset, the boy wrote, and noted the time. The two men crawled backward from the lip of the gulch and raised themselves up on their knees and stretched. *Off duty,* the boy wrote, and noted the time. Then they all three scrabbled around on their knees and pulled the rocks off the corners of the tarp hiding their pick-up. Folded it as neatly as they could without standing up and stowed it in the load bed. Repacked the cooler and collapsed the telescopes and climbed three-in-a-row into the cab. Drove out of the far side of the gulch and headed due west across the hardpan toward the red horizon.

Inside the kitchen the maid was loading a huge dishwashing machine. It was made of green enamel and had probably been the very latest thing around the time man first walked on the moon. She looked up and said nothing. Just kept on stacking plates. Reacher saw the three bowls he had brought her. They were rinsed and ready.

"This way," Ellie whispered.

She led them through a door that led to a back hallway. There was no window, and the air was suffocating. There were plain wooden stairs on one side, painted red, worn back to the wood in crescent shapes on each tread. She led them upward. The stairs creaked under Reacher's weight.

They finished inside a kind of closet on the second floor. Ellie pushed the door open and crossed a hallway and made a right into a narrow corridor. Everything was wooden, the walls, the floor, the ceiling. Everything was painted red. Ellie's room was at the end of the corridor. It was maybe twelve feet square, and red. And very hot. It faced south and must have been baking in the sun all afternoon. The drapes were closed, and had been all day, Reacher guessed, offering some meager protection from the heat.

"We'll go get washed up," Carmen said. "Mr. Reacher will wait here, O.K.?"

Ellie watched until she was sure he was staying. He sat down on the end of the bed to confirm it. To help her reach her conclusion. She turned slowly and followed her mother out to the bathroom.

The bed was narrow, maybe thirty inches wide. And short, appropriate for a kid. It had cotton sheets printed with small colored animals of uncertain genus. There was a night table, and a bookcase, and a small armoire. This furniture looked reasonably new. It was made of blond wood, first bleached and then hand-painted with cheerful designs. It looked nice. Probably bought in a cute little boutique and hauled over from Austin, he thought. Or maybe all the way from Santa Fe. Some of the bookshelves held books, and the others held stuffed animals all jumbled together and crammed into the spaces.

He could hear the old air conditioner running. It thumped and rattled, patiently. It was louder here. Must be mounted in the attic, he thought. It made a soothing sound. But it didn't do much about cooling the house. Up there in the trapped air of the second floor, it felt like a hundred and twenty degrees.

Ellie and Carmen came back into the room. Ellie was suddenly quiet and bashful, maybe because she was in her pajamas. They looked like regular cotton shorts and a T-shirt, but they were printed with little things that might have been rabbits. Her hair was damp and her skin was pink. The back of one hand was wedged in her mouth. She climbed onto the bed and curled up near the pillow, using about half the available length of the mattress, close to him but careful not to touch him.

"O.K., good night, kid," he said. "Sleep well."

"Kiss me," she said.

He paused a second, and then he bent down and kissed her forehead. It was warm and damp and smelled of soap. She curled up more and snuggled down into the pillow.

"Thank you for being our friend," she said.

He stood up and stepped toward the door. Glanced at Carmen. *Did you tell her to say that? Or is it for real?*

"Can you find your way back down?" Carmen asked him. He nodded.

"I'll see you tomorrow," she said.

She stayed in Ellie's bedroom and he found the closet with the back stairs in it. He went down to the inside hallway and through the kitchen. The maid was gone. The old dishwasher was humming away to itself. He stepped out into the night and paused in the darkness and silence of the yard. It was hotter than ever. He stepped toward the gate. Ahead of him the sunset had gone. The horizon was black. There was pressure in the air. A hundred miles away to the southwest he could see heat lightning flickering. Faint sheets and bolts of dry electricity discharging randomly, like a gigantic celestial camera taking pictures. He looked straight up. No rain. No clouds. He turned around and caught gleams of white in the darkness off to his right. A T-shirt. A face. A semicircle of forehead showing through the back of a ball cap. Bobby Greer, again.

"Bobby," he said. "Enjoy your ride?"

Bobby ignored the inquiry. "I was waiting for you."

"Why?"

"Just making sure you came back out again."

"Why wouldn't I?"

"You tell me. Why would you go in there at all? In the first place? All three of you, like a little family."

"You saw us?"

Bobby nodded. "I see everything."

"Everything?" Reacher repeated.

"Everything I need to."

Reacher shrugged.

"I kissed the kid good night," he said. "You got a problem with that?"

Bobby was quiet for a beat.

"Let me walk you back to the bunkhouse," he said. "I need to talk to you."

He didn't talk any on the way down through the yard. He just walked. Reacher kept pace and looked ahead at the night sky in the east. It was vast and black and filled with stars. Apart from dim windows in some of the Greer buildings there was absolute pitch darkness everywhere. It threw the stars into vivid relief, impossibly tiny and numerous points of light dusting backward through billions of cubic miles of space. Reacher liked peering out into the universe. He liked thinking about it. He used it for perspective. He was just a tiny insignificant speck briefly sparked to life in the middle of nowhere. So what really mattered? Maybe nothing at all. So maybe he should just go ahead and bust Sloop Greer's head and have done with it. *Why not?* In the context of the whole universe, how was that so very different from not busting it at all?

"My brother had a problem," Bobby said, awkwardly. "I guess you know that."

"I heard he cheated on his taxes," Reacher said.

Bobby nodded in the dark. "IRS snoops are everywhere."

"Is that how they found him? Snooping?"

"Well, how else would they?" Bobby asked.

He went quiet. Walked ahead a couple of paces.

"Anyway, Sloop went to jail," he said.

Reacher nodded. "Getting out Monday, I heard."

"That's right. So he's not going to be too happy finding you here, kissing his kid, getting friendly with his wife."

Reacher shrugged as he walked. "I'm just here to work."

"Right, as a wrangler. Not as a nursemaid."

"I get time off, right?"

"But you need to be careful how you spend it."

Reacher smiled. "You mean I need to know my place?"

"Right," Bobby said. "And your place ain't alongside my brother's wife, or getting cozy with his kid."

"A man can't choose his friends?"

"Sloop ain't going to be happy, he gets home and finds some outsider has chosen his wife and kid for his friends."

Reacher stopped walking. Stood still in the dark. "Thing is, Bobby, why would I give a rat's ass what makes your brother happy?"

Bobby stopped, too. "Because we're a family. Things get talked about. You need to get that through your head. Or you won't work here too long. You could get run right out of here."

"You think?"

"Yeah, I think."

Reacher smiled again. "Who you going to call? The sheriff with the secondhand car? Guy like that could get a heart attack, just thinking about it."

Bobby shook his head. "West Texas, we look after things personally. It's a tradition. Never had too big of a law enforcement thing around here, so we kind of accustomed ourselves."

Reacher took a step closer.

"So you going to do it?" he said. "You want to do it now?"

Bobby said nothing. Reacher nodded.

"Maybe you'd prefer to set the maid on me," he said. "Maybe she'll come after me with a skillet."

"Josh and Billy will do what they're told."

"The little guys? The maid might be better. Or you, even."

"Josh and Billy get in the ring with bulls that weigh a ton and a half. They ain't going to be too worried about you."

Reacher started walking again. "Whatever, Bobby. I only said good night to the kid. No reason to start World War Three over it. She's starved for company. So is her mother. What can I do about it?"

"You can get smart about it, is what," Bobby said. "I told you before, she lies about everything. So whatever big story she's been telling you, chances are it's bullshit. So don't go making a fool out of yourself, falling for it. You wouldn't be the first."

They turned the corner beyond the corrals and headed for the bunkhouse door.

"What does that mean?" Reacher asked.

"How dumb do you think I am? She's gone all day every day for the best part of a month, gone all night as often as she can get away with it, leaving the kid here for us to tend to. And she's gone where? Some motel up in Pecos, is where, screwing the brains out of whatever new guy she can get to believe her bullshit stories about how her husband doesn't understand her. Which is entirely her business, but it's *my* business if she thinks she can go ahead and bring the guy back here. Two days before her husband gets home? Passing you off as some stranger looking for ranch work? What kind of crap is that?"

"What did you mean, I wouldn't be the first?"

"Exactly what I said. Talk to Josh and Billy about it. They ran him off."

Reacher said nothing. Bobby smiled at him.

"Don't believe her," he said. "There are things she doesn't tell you, and what she does tell you is mostly lies."

"Why doesn't she have a key to the door?"

"She had a key to the damn door. She lost it, is all. It's never locked, anyway. Why the hell would it be locked? We're sixty miles from the nearest crossroads."

"So why does she have to knock?"

"She doesn't have to knock. She could walk right in. But she puts on a big thing about how we exclude her. But it's all bullshit. Like, how do we exclude her? Sloop *married* her, didn't he?"

Reacher said nothing.

"So you work if you want to," Bobby said. "But stay away from her and the kid. And I'm saying that for your sake, O.K.?"

"Can I ask you something?" Reacher said.

"What?"

"Did you know your hat is on backward?"

"My what?"

"Your cap," Reacher said. "It's on backward. I wondered if you knew that. Or if maybe it just kind of slipped around, accidentally."

Bobby stared at him.

"I like it this way," he said.

Reacher nodded again.

"Well, I guess it keeps the sun off of your neck," he said. "Keeps it from getting any redder."

"You watch your mouth," Bobby said. "You stay away from my brother's family, and watch your damn mouth."

Then he turned in the dark and headed back up to the house. Reacher stood and watched him walk away. Beyond him the lightning still danced on the far southwest horizon. Then he disappeared behind the barn and Reacher listened to the sound his boots made in the dust, until it faded away to nothing.

Reacher went right to bed, even though it was still early. *Sleep when you can, so you won't need to when you can't.* That was his rule. He had never worked regular hours. To him, there was no real difference between a Tuesday and a Sunday, or a Monday and a Friday, or night and day. He was happy to sleep twelve hours, and then work the next thirty-six. And if he didn't have to work the next thirty-six, then he'd sleep twelve hours again, and again, as often as he could, until something else cropped up.

The bed was short and the mattress was lumpy. The air in the room had settled like a thick hot soup on the thin sheet covering him. He could hear insects outside, clicking and whining loudly. There might have been a billion of them, separately audible if he concentrated hard enough, merging together into a single scream if he didn't. The sound of the night, far from anywhere. There were lonely guttural cries from cougars and coyotes way off in the distance. The horses heard them too, and he sensed restless movement over in the barn, quieting after a moment, starting up again after the next ghostly, plaintive yelp. He heard rustling air and imagined he felt changes in pressure as colonies of bats took flight. He imagined he could feel the beat of their leathery wings. He fell asleep watching the stars through a small window high above him.

The road from Pecos to El Paso is more than two hundred miles long, and is dotted on both sides with occasional clumps of motels and gas stations and fast food outlets. The killing crew drove an hour west, which took them seventy miles, and then stopped at the second place they saw. That was the woman's habit. Not the first place. Always the second place. And always arrive very late. It was close to a superstition, but she rationalized it as good security.

The second place had a gas station big enough for eighteen-wheelers to use and a two-story motel and a twenty-four-hour diner. The tall fair man went into the motel office and paid cash for two rooms. They weren't adjoining. One was on the first floor far from the office and the second was upstairs, halfway down the row. The woman took the upstairs room.

"Get some sleep," she told her partners. "We've still got work to do."

Reacher heard Josh and Billy come back at two in the morning. The air was still hot. The insects were still loud. He heard the pick-up engine a couple of miles south, growing nearer and louder, slowing, turning in at the gate. He heard the squeal of springs as it bounced across the yard. He heard it drive into the shed beneath him, and he heard the motor switch off. Then there was just tinkling and clicking as it cooled, and footsteps on the stairs. They were loud and clumsy. He stayed as deeply asleep as he could and tracked their sounds past him, over to the bathroom, back to their bunks. Their bedsprings creaked as they threw themselves down. Then there was nothing but the insects and the wet rhythmic breathing of men who had worked hard all day and drunk hard all night. It was a sound he was familiar with. He had spent seventeen years in dormitories, off and on.

The insect noise was completely gone when he woke. So were the stars. The high window showed luminous streaks of dawn in their place. Maybe six in the morning, he thought, summer, this far south. It was already hot. He lifted his arm and checked his watch. Ten past six, Saturday morning. He thought about Jodie, in London. It was ten past twelve in London. Six hours ahead. She would have been up for ages. Probably at a museum, looking at pictures. Maybe thinking about lunch, in some English tearoom. Then he thought about Carmen Greer, over in the main house, forty-eight hours away from waking up on the day Sloop came home. And then Ellie, maybe hot and restless on her tiny cot, innocently barreling on toward the day her little life would change again.

He threw back the crumpled sheet and walked naked to the bathroom, carrying his clothes balled in his hand. Josh and Billy were still deep asleep. They were both still dressed. Josh still had his boots on. They were snoring half-heartedly, sprawled out and inert. There was a vague smell of old beer in the air. The smell of hangovers.

He set the shower going warm until he had soaped the sweat off his body and then turned it to cold to wake himself up. The cold water was nearly as warm as the hot. He imagined it pumping out of the baked ground, picking up heat all the way. He filled a sink with water and soaked his clothes. It was a trick he'd picked up as a kid, long ago, somewhere out in the Pacific, from sentries on the midday watch. If you dress in wet clothes, you've got a built-in air conditioner that keeps you cool until they dry out. An evaporative principle, like a swamp cooler. He dressed with the clammy cotton snagging against his skin and headed down the stairs and outside into the dawn. The sun was over the horizon ahead of him. The sky was arching purple overhead. No trace of cloud. The dust under his feet was still hot from yesterday.

* * *

The watchers assembled piecemeal, like they had five times before. It was a familiar routine by then. One of the men drove the pick-up to the boy's place and found him outside and waiting. Then they drove together to the second man's place, where they found that the routine had changed.

"He just called me," the second man explained. "Some different plan. We got to go to someplace up on the Coyanosa Draw for new instructions, face to face."

"Face to face with who?" the first man said. "Not him, right?"

"No, some new people we're going to be working with."

The boy said nothing. The first man just shrugged.

"O.K. with me," he said.

"Plus, we're going to get paid," the second man said.

"Even better," the first man said.

The second man squeezed onto the bench seat and closed his door and the pick-up turned and headed north.

Reacher walked around the corner of the bunkhouse and past the corrals to the barn. He could hear no sound at all. The whole place felt stunned by the heat. He was suddenly curious about the horses. Did they lie down to sleep? He ducked in the big door and found the answer was no, they didn't. They were sleeping standing up, heads bowed, knees locked against their weight. The big old mare he'd tussled with the night before smelled him and opened an eye. Looked at him blankly and moved a front foot listlessly and closed her eye again.

He glanced around the barn, rehearsing the work he might be expected to perform. The horses would need feeding, presumably. So there must be a food store someplace. What did they eat? Hay, he guessed. There were bales of it all over the place. Or was that straw, for the floor? He found a separate corner room stacked with sacks of some kind of food supplement. Big waxed-paper bags, from some specialist feed supplier up in San Angelo. So probably the horses got mostly hay, with some of the supplement to make up the vitamins. They'd need water, too. There was a faucet in one corner, with a long hose attached to it. A trough in each stall.

He came out of the barn and walked up the track to the house. Peered in through the kitchen window. Nobody in there. No activity. It looked the same as it had when he left the night before. He walked on toward the road. Heard the front door open behind him and turned to see Bobby Greer stepping out on the porch. He was wearing the same T-shirt and the same ball cap, but now it was the right way around. The peak was low over his eyes. He was carrying a rifle in his right hand. One of the pieces from the rack in the hallway. A fine .22 bolt-action, modern and in good condition. He put it up on his shoulder and stopped short.

"I was on my way to get you up," he said. "I need a driver."

"Why?" Reacher asked. "Where are you going?"

"Hunting," Bobby said. "In the pick-up."

"You can't drive?"

"Of course I can drive. But it takes two. You drive while I shoot."

"You shoot from a truck?"

"I'll show you," Bobby said.

He walked across to the motor barn. Stopped next to the newer pick-up. It had a roll bar built into the load bed.

"You drive," he said. "Out on the range. I'm here in back, leaning on the bar. Gives me a three-hundred-sixty-degree field of fire."

"While we're moving?"

"That's the skill of it. It's fun. Sloop invented it. He was real good."

"What are you hunting?"

"Armadillo," Bobby said. He stepped sideways and pointed down the track into the desert. It was a narrow dirt road scuffed into the landscape, meandering left and right to avoid rock formations, taking the path of least resistance.

"Hunting country," he said. "It's pretty good, south of here. And they're all out there, good fat ones. 'Dillo chili, can't beat it for lunch."

Reacher said nothing.

"You·never ate armadillo?" Bobby asked.

Reacher shook his head.

"Good eating," Bobby said. "Back when my granddaddy was a boy, Depression times, it was about all the eating there was. Texas turkey, they called it. Or Hoover hog. Kept people alive. Now the tree-huggers have got it protected. But if it's on our land, it's ours to shoot. That's the way I see it."

"I don't think so," Reacher said. "I don't like hunting."

"Why not? It's a challenge."

"For you, maybe," Reacher said. "I already know I'm smarter than an armadillo."

"You work here, Reacher. You'll do what you're told."

"We need to discuss some formalities, before I work here."

"Like what?"

"Like wages."

"Two hundred a week," Bobby said. "Bed and three squares a day thrown in."

Reacher said nothing.

"O.K.?" Bobby asked. "You wanted work, right? Or is it just Carmen you want?"

Reacher shrugged. *Two hundred a week?* It was a long time since he'd worked for two hundred a week. But then, he wasn't there for the money.

"O.K.," he said.

"And you'll do whatever Josh and Billy tell you to."

"O.K.," Reacher said again. "But I won't take you hunting. Not now, not ever. Call it a matter of conscience."

Bobby was quiet for a long moment. "I'll find ways to keep you away from her, you know. Every day, I'll find something."

"I'll be in the barn," Reacher said, and walked away.

Ellie brought his breakfast to him there. She was wearing a miniature set of blue denim dungarees. Her hair was wet and loose. She was carrying a plate of scrambled eggs. She had silverware in her breast pocket, upright, like pens. She was concentrating on remembering a message.

"My mommy says, don't forget the riding lesson," she recited. "She wants you to meet her here in the barn after lunch."

Then she ran back toward the house without another word. He sat down on a bale and ate the eggs. Took the empty plate back to the kitchen and headed down to the bunkhouse. Josh and Billy weren't there to tell him to do anything. *Suits me,* he thought. He didn't go looking for them. Just lay down and dozed in the heat.

The Coyanosa Draw was a watercourse with a bed wide enough to carry the runoff from the Davis Mountains to the Pecos River, which took it to the Rio Grande all the way down on the border with Mexico. But runoff was seasonal and unreliable, so the region was sparsely populated. There were abandoned farmsteads built close to the dry riverbed, far from each other, far from anywhere. One of them had an old swaybacked house baked gray by the sun. In front of it was an empty barn. The barn had no doors, just an open wall facing west toward the house. The way the buildings were set in the landscape, the interior of the barn was invisible except from the yard right in front of it.

The Crown Victoria was waiting inside the barn, its engine idling to keep the air going. The barn had an exterior staircase leading up to a hayloft, with a small platform outside the door at the top. The woman was out in the heat, up on the platform, where she could survey the meandering approach road. She saw the watchers' pick-up two miles away. It was traveling fast and kicking up a plume of dust. She waited until she was sure it was unaccompanied and then she turned and walked down the stairs. Signaled to the others.

They got out of the car and stood waiting in the heat. They heard the pick-up on the road, and then it pulled around the corner of the barn and slowed in the yard. They directed it with hand signals, like traffic cops. They pointed into the barn. One of them led the truck on foot, gesturing like the guy on the airport apron. He brought it tight up to the rear wall, gesturing all the time, and then he gave a thumbs-up to

halt it. He stepped alongside the driver's window and his
partner stepped to the passenger door.

The driver shut off the motor and relaxed. Human nature.
The end of a fast drive to a secret rendezvous, the intrigue of
new instructions, the prospect of a big payday. He wound down
his window. On the passenger's side, the second man did the
same thing. Then they both died, shot in the side of the head
with nine-millimeter bullets. The boy in the middle lived exactly one second longer, both sides of his face splattered with
blood and brain tissue, his notebook clutched in his hands.
Then the small dark man leaned in and shot him twice in the
chest. The woman pushed him out of the way and adjusted the
window winders on both doors to leave the glass cracked open
about an inch. An inch would let insects in and keep scavengers
out. Insects would help with decomposition, but scavengers
could drag body parts away, which would risk visibility.

Reacher dozed a couple of hours before Josh and Billy got
back. They didn't give him any instructions. They just got
cleaned up for lunch. They told him they were invited inside
the house to eat. And he wasn't, because he had refused to
drive.

"Bobby told me you ran some guy off," he said.

Joshua just smiled.

"What guy?" Billy said.

"Some guy came down here with Carmen."

"The Mexican?"

"Some friend of hers."

Billy shook his head. "Don't know anything about it. We
never ran any guy off. What are we, cops?"

"You're the cop," Joshua said.

"Am I?"

Joshua nodded. "Bobby said so. You were a military cop."

"You been discussing me?"

Joshua shrugged and went quiet.

"Got to go," Billy said.

Twenty minutes later Carmen herself brought his armadillo lunch to him. It was in a covered dish and smelled

strongly of chili. She left, nervous and in a hurry, without saying a word. He tried the meal. The meat was halfway between sweet and ordinary. It had been shredded and chopped and mixed with beans and two-alarm sauce from a bottle. Then slightly overdone in a warm oven. He had eaten worse, and he was hungry, which helped. He took his time, and then carried the dish back to the kitchen. Bobby was standing out on the porch steps, like a sentry.

"Horses need more feed supplement," he called. "You'll go with Josh and Billy to pick it up. After siesta. Get as many bags as fit in the truck."

Reacher nodded and walked on to the kitchen. Gave the used dish to the maid, and thanked her for the meal. Then he walked down to the barn and went inside and sat on a bale of straw to wait. The horses turned around in their stalls to watch him do it. They were patient and listless in the heat. One of them was chewing slowly. There were hay stalks stuck to its lips.

Carmen came in ten minutes later. She had changed into faded blue jeans and a checked cotton shirt with no sleeves. She was carrying a straw hat and her pocketbook. She looked tiny and afraid.

"Bobby doesn't know you called the IRS," he said. "He thinks it was random snooping. So maybe Sloop does, too."

She shook her head. "Sloop knows."

"How?"

She shrugged. "Actually, he doesn't *know*. But he convinced himself it had to be me. He was looking for somebody to blame, and who else is there? No evidence or anything, but as it happens he's right. Ironic, isn't it?"

"But he didn't tell Bobby."

"He wouldn't. He's too stubborn to agree with them. They hate me, he hates me, he keeps it a secret, they keep it a secret. From him, I mean. They make sure I know it."

"You should get out. You've got forty-eight hours."

She nodded. "Forty-eight hours exactly, I think. They'll let him out at seven in the morning. They'll drive all night to be there for him. It's about seven hours. So he'll be back home this time on Monday. Just after lunch."

"So get out, right now."

"I can't."

"You should," he said. "This place is impossible. It's like the outside world doesn't exist."

She smiled, bitterly. "Tell me about it. I've lived here nearly seven years. My whole adult life, give or take."

She hung her hat and her pocketbook on a nail in the wall. Did all the saddling work herself, quickly and efficiently. She was lithe and deft. The slim muscles in her arms bunched and relaxed as she lifted the saddles. Her fingers were precise with the buckles. She readied two horses in a quarter of the time he had taken to do one.

"You're pretty good at this," he said.

"*Gracias, señor,*" she said. "I get a lot of practice."

"So how can they believe you keep falling off, regular as clockwork?"

"They think I'm clumsy."

He watched her lead his horse out of its stall. It was one of the geldings. She was tiny beside it. In the jeans, he could have spanned her waist with his hand.

"You sure don't look clumsy," he said.

She shrugged. "People believe what they need to."

He took the reins from her. The horse huffed through its nose and shifted its feet. Moved its head up and down, up and down. His hand went with it.

"Walk him out," she said.

"Shouldn't we have leather pants? And riding gloves?"

"Are you kidding? We never wear that stuff here. It's way too hot."

He waited for her. Her horse was the smaller mare. She wedged her hat on her head and took her pocketbook off the nail and put it in a saddlebag. Then she followed him, leading her mare confidently out into the yard, into the heat and the sun.

"O.K., like this," she said. She stood on the mare's left and put her left foot in the stirrup. Gripped the horn with her left hand and bounced twice on her right leg and jacked herself smoothly into the saddle. He tried it the same way. Put his left foot in the stirrup, grasped the horn, put all his weight on the stirrup foot and straightened his leg and pulled with his hand. Leaned his weight forward and right and suddenly he was up there in the seat. The horse felt very wide, and he was very high in the air. About the same as riding on an armored personnel carrier.

"Put your right foot in," she said.

He jammed his foot into the other stirrup and squirmed around until he was as comfortable as he was ever going to get. The horse waited patiently.

"Now bunch the reins on the horn, in your left hand."

That part was easy. It was just a question of imitating the movies. He let his right hand swing free, like he was carrying a Winchester repeater or a coil of rope.

"O.K., now just relax. And kick gently with your heels."

He kicked once and the horse lurched into a walk. He used his left hand on the horn to keep himself steady. After a couple of paces he began to understand the rhythm. The horse was moving him left and right and forward and back with every alternate step. He held tight to the horn and used pressure from his feet to keep his body still.

"Good," she said. "Now I'll go in front and he'll follow. He's pretty docile."

I would be, too, he thought, *a hundred ten degrees and two hundred fifty pounds on my back.* Carmen clicked her tongue and kicked her heels and her horse moved smoothly around his and led the way through the yard and past the house. She swayed easily in the saddle, the muscles in her thighs bunching and flexing as she kept her balance. Her hat was down over her eyes. Her left hand held the reins and her right was hanging loose at her side. He caught the blue flash of the fake diamond in the sun.

She led him out under the gate to the road and straight across without looking or stopping. He glanced left and right, south and north, and saw nothing at all except heat shimmer and distant silver mirages. On the far side of the road was a step about a foot high onto the limestone ledge. He leaned forward and let the horse climb it underneath him. Then the rock rose gently into the middle distance, reaching maybe fifty feet of elevation in the best part of a mile. There were deep fissures running east-west and washed-out holes the

size of shell craters. The horses picked their way between
them. They seemed pretty sure on their feet. So far, he hadn't
had to do any conscious steering. Which he was happy about,
because he wasn't exactly sure how to.

"Watch for rattlesnakes," Carmen called.

"Great," he called back.

"Horses get scared by anything that moves. They'll spook
and run. If that happens, just hang on tight and haul on the
reins."

"Great," he said again.

There were scrubby plants rooting desperately in cracks in
the rock. There were smaller holes, two or three feet across,
some of them with undercut sides. *Just right for a snake,* he
thought. He watched them carefully at first. Then he gave it
up, because the shadows were too harsh to see anything. And
the saddle was starting to wear on him.

"How far are we going?" he called.

She turned, like she had been waiting for the question.

"We need to get over the rise," she said. "Down into the
gulches."

The limestone smoothed out into broader unbroken
shelves and she slowed to let his horse move up alongside
hers. But it stayed just short of level, which kept him behind
her. Kept him from seeing her face.

"Bobby told me you had a key," he said.

"Did he?"

"He said you lost it."

"No, that's not true. They never gave me one."

He said nothing.

"They made a big point of not giving me one," she said.
"Like it was a symbol."

"So he was lying?"

She nodded, away from him. "I told you, don't believe
anything he says."

"He said the door's never locked, anyway."

"Sometimes it is, sometimes it isn't."

"He told me you don't have to knock, either."

"That's a lie, too," she said. "Since Sloop's been gone, if I
don't knock, they run and grab a rifle. Then they go, *oh sorry,*

but strangers prowling around the house make us nervous.
Like a big pretend show."

He said nothing.

"Bobby's a liar, Reacher," she said. "I told you that."

"I guess he is. Because he also told me you brought some
other guy down here, and he got Josh and Billy to run him
off. But Josh and Billy didn't know anything about any
guy."

She was quiet for a long moment.

"No, that was true," she said. "I met a man up in Pecos,
about a year ago. We had an affair. At first just at his place up
there. But he wanted more."

"So you brought him here?"

"It was his idea. He thought he could get work, and be
close to me. I thought it was crazy, but I went along with it.
That's where I got the idea to ask you to come. Because it actually worked for a spell. Two or three weeks. Then Bobby
caught us."

"And what happened?"

"That was the end of it. My friend left."

"So why would Josh and Billy deny it to me?"

"Maybe it wasn't Josh and Billy who ran him off. Maybe
they didn't know about it. Maybe Bobby did it himself. My
friend wasn't as big as you. He was a schoolteacher, out of
work."

"And he just disappeared?"

"I saw him again, just once, back in Pecos. He was scared.
Wouldn't talk to me."

"Did Bobby tell Sloop?"

"He promised he wouldn't. We had a deal."

"What kind of a deal?"

She went quiet again. Just rode on, sitting slackly on the
swaying horse.

"The usual kind," she said. "If I'd do something for him,
he'd keep quiet."

"What kind of something?"

She paused again.

"Something I really don't want to tell you about," she said.

"I see."

"Yes, you see."

"And did he keep quiet?"

"I really have no idea. He made me do it twice. It was disgusting. *He's* disgusting. But he promised faithfully. But he's a liar, so I'm assuming he told Sloop anyway. On one of his brotherly visits. I always knew it was a lose-lose gamble, but what could I do? What choice did I have?"

"Bobby figures that's why I'm here. He thinks we're having an affair, too."

She nodded. "That would be my guess. He doesn't know Sloop hits me. Even if he did, he wouldn't expect me to do anything about it."

Reacher was quiet for a spell. Another twenty yards, thirty, at the slow patient pace of a walking horse.

"You need to get out," he said. "How many times do you have to hear it?"

"I won't run," she answered.

They reached the top of the rise and she made a small sound and her horse stopped walking. His stopped, too, at her shoulder. They were about fifty feet above the plain. Ahead of them, to the west, the caliche sloped gently down again, pocked by dry gulches the size of ballparks. Behind them, to the east, the red house and the other buildings in the compound were spread out a mile away, flat on the baked land like a model. The road ran like a gray ribbon, north and south. Behind the tiny motor barn the dirt track wandered south and east through the desert, like a scar on burned and pockmarked skin. The air was dry and unnaturally clear all the way to both horizons, where it broke up into haze. The heat was a nightmare. The sun was fearsome. Reacher could feel his face burning.

"Take care as we go down," Carmen said. "Stay balanced."

She moved off ahead of him, letting her horse find its own way down the incline. He kicked with his heels and followed her. He lost the rhythm as his horse stepped short and he started bouncing uncomfortably.

"Follow me," she called.

She was moving to the right, toward a dry gulch with a flat floor, all stone and sand. He started trying to figure which rein he should pull on, but his horse turned anyway. Its feet crunched on gravel and slipped occasionally. Then it stepped right down into the gulch, which jerked him violently backward and forward. Ahead of him Carmen was slipping out of the saddle. Then she was standing on the ground, stretching, waiting for him. His horse stopped next to hers and he shook his right foot free of the stirrup and got off by doing the exact opposite of what had got him on a half hour before.

"So what do you think?" she asked.

"Well, I know why John Wayne walked funny."

She smiled briefly and led both horses together to the rim of the gulch and heaved a large stone over the free ends of both sets of reins. He could hear absolute silence, nothing at all behind the buzz and shimmer of the heat. She lifted the flap of her saddlebag and took out her pocketbook. Zipped it open and slipped her hand in and came out with a small chromium handgun.

"You promised you'd teach me," she said.

"Wait," he said.

"What?"

He said nothing. Stepped left, stepped right, crouched down, stood tall. Stared at the floor of the gulch, moving around, using the shadows from the sun to help him.

"What?" she said again.

"Somebody's been here," he said. "There are tracks. Three people, a vehicle driving in from the west."

"Tracks?" she said. "Where?"

He pointed. "Tire marks. Some kind of a truck. Stopped here. Three people, crawled up to the edge on their knees."

He put himself where the tracks ended at the rim of the gulch. Lay down on the hot grit and hauled himself forward on his elbows. Raised his head.

"Somebody was watching the house," he said.

"How do you know?"

"Nothing else to see from here."

She knelt alongside him, the chromium pistol in her hand.

"It's too far away," she said.

"Must have used field glasses. Telescopes, even."

"Are you sure?"

"You ever see reflections? The sun on glass? In the morn-ings, when the sun was in the east?"

She shuddered.

"No," she said. "Never."

"Tracks are fresh," he said. "Not more than a day or two old."

She shuddered again.

"Sloop," she said. "He thinks I'm going to take Ellie. Now I know he's getting out. He's having me watched."

Reacher stood up and walked back to the center of the bowl.

"Look at the tire tracks," he said. "They were here four or five times."

He pointed down. There were several overlapping sets of tracks in a complex network. At least four, maybe five. The tire treads were clearly pressed into the powdered sand. There was a lot of detail. The outside shoulder of the front right tire was nearly bald.

"But they're not here today," Carmen said. "Why not?"

"I don't know," Reacher said.

Carmen looked away. Held out the gun to him.

"Please show me how to use this," she said.

He moved his gaze from the tracks in the sand and looked at the gun. It was a Lorcin L-22 automatic, two-and-a-half-inch barrel, chrome frame, with plastic molded grips made to look like pink mother-of-pearl. Made in Mira Loma, Califor-nia, not too long ago, and probably never used since it left the factory.

"Is it a good one?" she asked.

"How much did you pay for it?"

"Over eighty dollars."

"Where?"

"In a gun store up in Pecos."

"Is it legal?"

She nodded. "I did all the proper paperwork. Is it any good?"

"I guess," he said. "As good as you'll get for eighty bucks, anyway."

"The man in the store said it was ideal."

"For what?"

"For a lady. I didn't tell him why I needed it."

He hefted it in his hand. It was tiny, but reasonably solid. Not light, not heavy. Not heavy enough to be loaded, anyway.

"Where are the bullets?" he asked.

She stepped back toward the horses. Took a small box out of her bag. Came back and handed it to him. It was neatly packed with tiny .22 shells. Maybe fifty of them.

"Show me how to load it," she said.

He shook his head.

"You should leave it out here," he said. "Just dump it and forget about it."

"But why?"

"Because this whole thing is crazy. Guns are dangerous, Carmen. You shouldn't keep one around Ellie. There might be an accident."

"I'll be very careful. And the house is full of guns anyway."

"Rifles are different. She's too small to reach the trigger and have it pointing at herself simultaneously."

"I keep it hidden. She hasn't found it yet."

"Only a matter of time."

She shook her head.

"My decision," she said. "She's my daughter."

He said nothing.

"She won't find it," she said. "I keep it by the bed, and she doesn't come in there."

"What happens to her if you decide to use it?"

She nodded. "I know. I think about that all the time. I just hope she's too young to really understand. And when she's old enough, maybe she'll see it was the lesser of two evils."

"No, what *happens* to her? There and then? When you're in jail?"

"They don't send you to jail for self-defense."

"Who says it's self-defense?"

"You *know* it would be self-defense."

"Doesn't matter what I know. I'm not the sheriff, I'm not the DA, I'm not the judge and jury."

She went quiet.

"Think about it, Carmen," he said. "They'll arrest you, you'll be charged with first-degree homicide. You've got no bail money. You've got no money for a lawyer either, so you'll get a public defender. You'll be arraigned, and you'll go to trial. Could be six or nine months down the road. Could be a year. Then let's say everything goes exactly your way from that point on. The public defender makes out it's self-defense, the jury buys it, the judge apologizes that a wronged woman has been put through all of that, and you're back on the street. But that's a year from now. At least. What's Ellie been doing all that time?"

She said nothing.

"She'll have spent a year with Rusty," he said. "On her own. Because that's where the court would leave her. The grandmother? Ideal solution."

"Not when they understood what the Greers are like."

"O.K., so partway through the year Family Services will arrive and haul her off to some foster home. Is that what you want for her?"

She winced. "Rusty would send her there anyway. She'd refuse to keep her, if Sloop wasn't around anymore."

"So leave the gun out here in the desert. It's not a good idea."

He handed it back to her. She took it and cradled it in her palms, like it was a precious object. She tumbled it from one hand to another, like a child's game. The fake pearl grips flashed in the sun.

"No," she said. "I want to learn to use it. For self-confidence. And that's a decision that's mine to make. You can't decide for me."

He was quiet for a beat. Then he shrugged.

"O.K.," he said. "Your life, your kid, your decision. But guns are serious business. So pay attention."

She passed it back. He laid it flat on his left palm. It reached from the ball of his thumb to the middle knuckle of his middle finger.

"Two warnings," he said. "This is a very, very short barrel. See that?" He traced his right index finger from the chamber to the muzzle. "Two and a half inches, is all. Did they explain that at the store?"

She nodded. "The guy said it would fit real easy in my bag."

"It makes it a very inaccurate weapon," he said. "The longer the barrel, the straighter it shoots. That's why rifles are three feet long. If you're going to use this thing, you need to get very, very close, O.K.? Inches away would be best. Right next to the target. *Touching* the target if you can. You try to use this thing across a room, you'll miss by miles."

"O.K.," she said.

"Second warning." He dug a bullet out of the box and held it up. "This thing is tiny. And slow. The pointy part is the bullet, and the rest of it is the powder in the shell case. Not a very big bullet, and not very much powder behind it. So it's not necessarily going to do a lot of damage. Worse than a bee sting, but one shot isn't going to be enough. So you need to get real close, and you need to keep on pulling the trigger until the gun is empty."

"O.K.," she said again.

"Now watch."

He clicked out the magazine and fed nine bullets into it. Clicked the magazine back in and jacked the first shell into the breech. Took out the magazine again and refilled the empty spot at the bottom. Clicked it back in and cocked the gun and left the safety catch on.

"Cocked and locked," he said. "You do two things. Push the safety catch, and pull the trigger ten times. It'll fire ten times before it's empty, because there's one already in the mechanism and nine more in the magazine."

He handed the gun to her.

"Don't point it at me," he said. "Never point a loaded gun at anything you don't *definitely* want to kill."

She took it and held it away from him, cautiously.

"Try it," he told her. "The safety, and the trigger."

She used her left hand to unlatch the safety. Then she pointed it in her right and closed her eyes and pulled the trigger. The gun twisted in her grip and pointed down. The blast

of the shot sounded quiet, out there in the emptiness. A chip
of rock and a spurt of dust kicked off the floor ten feet away.
There was a metallic ricochet *whang* and a muted ring as the
shell case ejected and the horses shuffled in place and then silence closed in again.

"Well, it works," she said.

"Put the safety back on," he said.

She clicked the catch and he turned to look at the horses.
He didn't want them to run. Didn't want to spend time chas-
ing them in the heat. But they were happy enough, standing
quietly, watching warily. He turned back and undid his top
button and slipped his shirt off over his head. Walked fifteen
feet south and laid the shirt on the rim of the gulch, hanging
it down and spreading it out to represent a man's torso. He
walked back and stood behind her.

"Now shoot my shirt," he said. "You always aim for the
body, because it's the biggest target, and the most vulnerable."

She raised the gun, and then lowered it again.

"I can't do this," she said. "You don't want holes in your
shirt."

"I figure there isn't much of a risk," he said. "Try it."

She forgot to release the safety catch. Just pulled on the
unyielding trigger. Twice, puzzled why it wouldn't work.
Then she remembered and clicked it off. Pointed the gun and
closed her eyes and fired. Reacher guessed she missed by
twenty feet, high and wide.

"Keep your eyes open," he said. "Pretend you're mad at
the shirt, you're standing there pointing your finger right at it,
like you're yelling."

She kept her eyes open. Squared her shoulders and pointed
with her right arm held level. She fired and missed again,
maybe six feet to the left, maybe a little low.

"Let me try," he said.

She passed him the gun. It was tiny in his hand. The trigger
guard was almost too small to fit his finger. He closed one
eye and sighted in.

"I'm aiming for where the pocket was," he said.

He fired a double-tap, two shots in quick succession, with

his hand rock-steady. The first hit the shirt in the armpit opposite the torn pocket. The second hit centrally but low down. He relaxed his stance and handed the gun back.

"Your turn again," he said.

She fired three more, all of them hopeless misses. High to the right, wide to the left. The last hit the dirt, maybe seven feet short of the target. She stared at the shirt and lowered the gun, disappointed.

"So what have you learned?" he asked.

"I need to get close," she said.

"Damn right," he said. "And it's not entirely your fault. A short-barrel handgun is a close-up weapon. See what I did? I missed by twelve inches, from fifteen feet. One bullet went left, and the other went down. They didn't even miss consistently. And I can shoot. I won competitions for pistol shooting in the army. Couple of years, I was the best there was."

"O.K.," she said.

He took the gun from her and squatted in the dust and reloaded it. One up the spout and nine in the magazine. He cocked it and locked it and laid it on the ground.

"Leave it there," he said. "Unless you're very, very sure. Could you do it?"

"I think so," she said.

"Thinking so isn't enough. You've got to *know* so. You've got to be prepared to get real close, jam it into his gut, and fire ten times. If you don't, or if you hesitate, he'll take it away from you, maybe turn it on you, maybe fire wildly and hit Ellie running in from her room."

She nodded, quietly. "Last resort."

"Believe it. You pull the gun, from that point on, it's all or nothing."

She nodded again.

"Your decision," he said. "But I suggest you leave it there."

She stood still for a long, long time. Then she bent down and picked up the gun. Slipped it back into her bag. He walked over and retrieved his shirt and slipped it over his head. Neither bullet hole showed. One was under his arm, and the other tucked in below the waistband of his pants. Then he tracked around the gulch and picked up all eight spent shell cases. It was an old habit, and good housekeeping. He jingled them together in his hand like small change and put them in his trouser pocket.

They talked about fear on the ride home. Carmen was quiet on the way back up the rise, and she stopped again at the peak. The Red House compound stretched below them in the distant haze, and she just sat and looked down at it, both hands clasped on the horn of her saddle, saying nothing, a faraway look in her eyes. Reacher's horse stopped as usual slightly behind hers, so he got the same view, but framed by the curve of her neck and her shoulder.

"Do you ever get afraid?" she asked.

"No," he said.

She was quiet again for a spell.

"But how is that possible?" she asked.

He looked at the sky. "It's something I learned, when I was a little boy."

"How?"

He looked at the ground. "I had a brother, older than me. So he was always ahead. But I wanted to be doing the same stuff as him. He had scary comics, and anywhere we had American television he'd be watching it. So I looked at the same comics and watched the same shows. There was one show about space adventures. I don't remember what it was called. We watched it in black-and-white somewhere. Maybe in Europe. They had a spaceship that looked like a little submarine with spider legs. They would land it somewhere and get out and go exploring. I remember one night they got chased by this scary creature. It was hairy, like an ape. Like Bigfoot. Long hairy arms and a big snarl. It chased them back to the spaceship, and they jumped in and slammed the hatch shut just as it was climbing in after them."

"And you were scared?"

He nodded, even though he was behind her. "I was about four, I think. I was terrified. That night I was certain the thing was under my bed. I had this high old bed, and I knew the thing was living under it. It was going to come out and get me. I could just about feel its paw reaching up for me. I couldn't sleep. If I went to sleep, it would come out and get me for sure. So I stayed awake for hours. I would call for my dad, but when he came in, I was too ashamed to tell him. It went on like that for days and days."

"And what happened?"

"I got mad. Not at myself for being afraid, because as far as I was concerned the thing was totally real and I *should* be afraid. I got mad at the thing for *making* me afraid. For threatening me. One night I just kind of exploded with fury. I yelled *O.K., come out and try it! Just damn well try it! I'll beat the shit right out of you!* I faced it down. I turned the fear into aggression."

"And that worked?"

"I've never been scared since. It's a habit. Those space explorers shouldn't have turned and run, Carmen. They should have stood there and faced the creature down. They should have stood and fought. You see something scary, you should stand up and step *toward* it, not away from it. Instinctively, reflexively, in a raging fury."

"Is that what you do?"

"Always."

"Is it what I should do? With Sloop?"

"I think it's what everybody should do."

She was quiet for a moment. Just staring down at the house, and then lifting her eyes to the horizon beyond it. She clicked her tongue, and both horses moved off together, down the long slow slope toward the road. She shifted in the saddle to keep her balance. Reacher imitated her posture and stayed safely aboard. But not comfortably. He figured horseback riding would be one of the things he tried once and didn't repeat.

"So what did Bobby say?" she asked. "About us?"

"He said you've been away most days for a month, and some nights, and he figured we've been up in a motel in Pecos together having an affair. Now he's all outraged that you've brought me down here, so close to Sloop getting back."

"I wish we had been," she said. "In a motel, having an affair. I wish that was all it was."

He said nothing. She paused a beat.

"Do you wish we had been, too?" she asked.

He watched her in the saddle. Lithe, slim, hips swaying gently against the patient gait of the horse. The dark honey skin of her arms was bright in the sun. Her hair hung to the middle of her back.

"I could think of worse things," he said.

It was very late in the afternoon when they got back. Josh and Billy were waiting. They were leaning side by side against the wall of the barn, in the harsh shadow below the eaves. Their pick-up was ready for the trip to the feed supplier. It was parked in the yard.

"It takes all three of you?" Carmen whispered.

"It's Bobby," Reacher said back. "He's trying to keep me away from you. Trying to spoil the fun we're supposed to be having."

She rolled her eyes.

"I'll put the horses away," she said. "I should brush them first."

They dismounted together in front of the barn door. Josh and Billy peeled off the wall, impatience in their body language.

"You ready?" Billy called.

"He should have been ready a half hour ago," Josh said.

For that, Reacher made them wait. He walked down to the bunkhouse, very slowly, because he wasn't going to let them hurry him, and because he was stiff from the saddle. He used the bathroom and rinsed dust off his face. Splashed cold water over his shirt. Walked slowly back. The pick-up had turned to face the gate and the engine was running. Carmen was brushing his horse. Thin clouds of dust were coming off its chestnut fur. *Hair? Coat?* Josh was sitting sideways in the driver's seat. Billy was standing next to the passenger door.

"So let's go," he called.

He put Reacher in the middle seat. Josh swung his feet in and slammed his door shut. Billy crowded in on the other side and Josh took off toward the gate. Paused at the road and then made a left, at which point Reacher knew the situation was a lot worse than he had guessed.

7

He had seen the feed bags in the storeroom. There were plenty of them, maybe forty, in head-high stacks. Big waxed-paper bags, probably thirty pounds to a bag. Altogether twelve hundred pounds of feed. About half a ton. How fast were four horses and a pony going to eat their way through all of that?

But he had always understood the trip was Bobby's idea of a diversion. Buying more feed before it was strictly necessary was as good a way as any of getting him out of Carmen's life for a spell. But they weren't buying more feed. Because they had turned left. The bags were all printed with a brand name and nutritional boasts and the name and the address of the feed supplier. The feed supplier was in San Angelo. He had seen it repeated forty times, once on each bag, in big clear letters. *San Angelo, San Angelo, San Angelo*. And San Angelo was north and east of Echo County. Way north and east. Not south and west. They should have turned right.

So, Bobby was planning to get him out of Carmen's life *permanently*. Josh and Billy had been told to get rid of him.

And Josh and Billy will do what they're told, Bobby had said. He smiled at the windshield. *Forewarned is forearmed.* They didn't know he'd seen the feed bags, didn't know he'd read the writing on them, and they didn't know he'd been looking at maps of Texas for most of the last week. They didn't know a left turn instead of a right would mean anything to him.

How would they aim to do it? Carmen had implied her out-of-work teacher friend had been scared off. Scared pretty badly, if he wouldn't even talk to her later, up in the relative safety of Pecos. So were they going to try to scare *him?* If so, they really had to be kidding. He felt the aggression building inside. He used it and controlled it like he had learned to. He used the adrenaline flow to ease the stiffness in his legs. He let it pump him up. He flexed his shoulders, leaning on Josh on one side, Billy on the other.

"How far is it?" he asked innocently.

"Couple hours," Billy said.

They were doing about sixty, heading south on the dead-straight road. The landscape was unchanging. Scrubby dry grassland on the left, sullen limestone caliche on the right, broken up into ledges and layers. All of it baking under the relentless sun. There was no traffic. The road looked like it saw one or two vehicles a day. Maybe all they had to do was get far enough away, pull over, throw him out, and he'd die slowly of thirst before anybody got to him. Or of exhaustion, walking back. Or of rattlesnake bites.

"No, less than a couple hours," Josh said. "Hundred miles is all."

So maybe they were headed to the bar they had mentioned yesterday. Maybe they had friends there. *They better had,* Reacher thought. *A pair of fifth-rate cowboys ain't going to do it for me.* Then he breathed out again. Relaxed. Struggled with a decision. The problem with the kind of undiluted raging aggression he had described to Carmen was it came out so all-or-nothing. He recalled his first day in high school. The summer after he finished his elementary education, the family moved back stateside for a six-month tour. He was enrolled in a big high school off-base, somewhere in New Jersey, somewhere near Fort Dix. And he was ready for it. In his usual serious earnest fashion he calculated that high school would be bigger and better than elementary school, in every way, including the seriousness of the locker-room scuffling. So he made his usual new-school first-day plan to jump on the very first guy who tried anything. That had always worked well for him. Hit hard, hit early, get your retaliation in first. It made a big impression. But this time, make an even bigger impression, hit harder than ever, because clearly high school was going to be a whole new kind of a deal.

So sure enough some hard kid shoved him the first morning, and ten minutes later the hard kid was on his way to the hospital for a three-week stay. Then Reacher discovered it was really a very genteel school, in a good neighborhood, and that he'd reacted way too drastically, and everybody was looking at him like he was some sort of a barbarian. And he felt like one. He felt a little ashamed. From then on, he'd become calmer. He'd learned to be certain what he was into before he did anything. And he'd learned to offer warnings, sometimes, in certain circumstances.

"We coming straight back?" he asked.

It was a smart tactical question. They couldn't say no, without alerting him. They couldn't say yes, if they weren't going there in the first place.

"We're going for a couple beers first," Billy said.

"Where?"

"Where we went yesterday."

"I'm broke," Reacher said. "I didn't get paid yet."

"We're buying," Josh said.

"The feed store open late? On a Saturday?"

"Big order, they'll accommodate us," Billy said.

Maybe it was a new supplier. Maybe they changed their source.

"I guess you use them a lot," he said.

"All the years we've been here," Josh said.

"Then we're going straight back?"

"Sure we are," Billy said. "You'll be back in time for your beauty sleep."

"That's good," Reacher said.

He paused.

"Because that's the way I like it," he said.

Mess with me now, you get what you get.

Billy said nothing. Josh just smiled and drove.

The scenery flattened very gradually as they headed south.
From his time with the maps he knew the Rio Grande was
curling around toward them from the west. They were entering the river basin, where wide prehistoric waters had
scoured the land. Josh kept the speed at a steady sixty. Billy
stared idly out of his window. The road remained straight and
featureless. Reacher rested his head on the gun rack behind
him and waited. Waiting was something he was accustomed
to. Many times in his career, frantic action had been preceded
by a long drive. It usually happened that way. The patient ac-
cumulation of evidence, the arrival at a conclusion, the identification of a suspect, the drive out to deal with him. Waiting
was a skill you learned fast, in the military.

The road got rougher the farther south they drove. The
truck labored over it. The load bed was empty, so the rear
wheels bounced and skipped. There were vultures on some of
the telephone poles. The sun was low in the west. There was
a sign on the shoulder. It said Echo 5 miles. It was pocked
with bullet holes.

"I thought Echo was north," Reacher said. "Where Ellie
goes to school."

"It's split," Billy said. "Half of it up there, half of it down
here. Hundred sixty miles of nothing in between."

"World's biggest town, end to end," Josh said. "Bigger
than Los Angeles."

He eased off the gas around a long slow curve and a clus-
ter of small buildings came into view in the distance, all of
them built low to the ground, all of them lit from behind by
the low sun. There were tin advertisements on the shoulder,
three miles out, announcing well in advance what the buildings were going to be. There was going to be another gas station, and a country store. And a bar, called the Longhorn
Lounge, owned and operated by somebody named Harley. It
had the last sign, but it was the first establishment they came

to. It was a hundred feet east of the shoulder of the road, built out of tarred boards under an iron roof, crouched low at an angle in the middle of two acres of parched earth. There were ten or twelve pick-up trucks parked nose-in to the building like airplanes at a terminal. And nearest the door was the sheriff's secondhand police car, just sitting there like it had been abandoned.

Josh bumped across the parking lot and put the truck in line with the others. The bar had neon beer signs in the windows, trapped between dirty glass and faded gingham drapes. Josh turned the motor off. Put the keys in his pocket. In the sudden quiet Reacher could hear bar noise, the roar of extractor fans and air conditioners, the thump of an overworked jukebox amplifier, the rumble of talking, the chink of bottles and glasses, the click of pool balls. Sounded like a reasonable crowd in there.

Josh and Billy opened their doors together and swung out. Reacher slid out through the passenger door and stood with his back to the sun. It was still hot. He could feel heat all over him, right from the back of his neck to the heels of his shoes.

"O.K.," Billy said. "We're buying."

There was an inside lobby with an old-fashioned pay phone and scrawled numbers and old messages creeping over the boards alongside it. Then there was a second door, with a yellow glass window in it, that led into the bar itself. Billy pushed it open.

For a military cop, walking into a bar is like a batter stepping to the plate. It's his place of business. Maybe ninety percent of low-grade trouble in the service happens in bars. Put a bunch of young men trained for aggression and reaction alongside a limitless supply of alcohol, add in unit rivalries, add in the presence of civilian women and their civilian husbands and boyfriends, and it becomes inevitable. So just like a batter walks warily from the on-deck circle, watching the infield, surveying the outfield, calculating angles and distances, a military cop is all eyes on the way into a bar. First, he counts the exits. There are usually three. The front door, the back door out beyond the rest rooms, and the private door from the office behind the bar. Reacher saw that the Longhorn Lounge had all three of them. The windows were too small to be useful to anybody.

Then the MP looks at the crowd. He looks for knots of trouble. Who falls silent and stares? Where are the challenges? Nowhere, in the Longhorn. There were maybe twenty or twenty-five people in the long low room, all men, all tanned and lean and dressed in denim, none of them paying any kind of attention beyond casual glances and nods of easy familiarity toward Billy and Josh. The sheriff was nowhere to be seen. But there was an unoccupied stool at the bar with a fresh bottle sitting on a used napkin in front of it. Maybe the place of honor.

Then the MP looks for weapons. There was an antique revolver above the bar, wired onto a wooden plaque with a message branded into it with a hot poker: We don't call 911. There would be a few modern handguns here and there in the room. There were long-neck bottles all over the place, but Reacher wasn't worried about them. Bottles are no real use as weapons. Except in the movies, where they make them out of spun sugar and print the labels on tissue paper. A real bottle won't break against a table top. The glass is too thick. They just make a loud banging noise. They have some marginal use as clubs, but the pool table worried him more. It sat in the middle of the room, all covered in hard celluloid balls, four guys with four cues using it, maybe a dozen more cues vertical in a long rack on the nearest wall. Short of a shotgun, a pool cue is the best barroom weapon ever invented. Short enough to be handy, long enough to be useful, made out of fine hardwood and nicely weighted with lead.

The air was unnaturally cold and thick with beer fumes and smoke and noise. The jukebox was near the pool table, and beyond it was an area with small round lounge tables surrounded by stools padded with red vinyl. Billy held up three fingers to the barman and got three cold bottles in exchange. He carried them laced between his fingers and led the way toward the tables. Reacher stepped ahead of him and got there first. He wanted his choice of seats. *Back to the wall* was his rule. *All three exits in view, if possible*. He threaded his way in and sat down. Josh sat to his half-right, and Billy sat half-left. Pushed a bottle across the scarred surface of the table. People had stubbed cigarettes on the wood. The sheriff came into the room from the rear, from the direction of the rest rooms, checking that his pants were zipped. He paused a second when he saw Reacher, nothing in his face, and then he moved on and sat down at the bar, on the unoccupied stool, his shoulders hunched, his back to the crowd.

Billy raised his bottle like a toast.

"Good luck," he said.

You're going to need it, pal, Reacher thought. He took a long pull from his own bottle. The beer was cold and gassy. It tasted strongly of hops.

"I need to make a phone call," Billy said.

He pushed back from the table and stood up again. Josh leaned to his right, trying to fill the new vacant space in front of Reacher. Billy made it through the crowd and went outside to the lobby. Reacher took another sip of his beer and estimated the passage of time. And counted the people in the room. There were twenty-three of them, excluding himself, including the barman, who he guessed was Harley. Billy came back inside two minutes and forty seconds. He bent and spoke into the sheriff's ear. The sheriff nodded. Billy spoke some more. The sheriff nodded again. Drained his bottle and pushed back from the bar and stood up. Turned to face the room. Glanced once in Reacher's direction and then stepped away and pushed out through the door. Billy stood and watched him go and then threaded his way back to the table.

"Sheriff's leaving," he said. "He remembered he had urgent business elsewhere."

Reacher said nothing.

"Did you make your call?" Josh asked, like it was rehearsed.

"Yes, I made my call," Billy said.

Then he sat down on his stool and picked up his bottle.

"Don't you want to know who I called?" he said, looking across at Reacher.

"Why would I give a rat's ass who you called?" Reacher said.

"I called for the ambulance," Billy said. "Best to do it

ahead of time, because it comes all the way from Presidio. It can take hours to get here."

"See, we got a confession to make," Josh said. "We lied to you before. There was a guy we ran off. He was knocking boots with the Mexican woman. Bobby didn't think that was appropriate behavior, in the circumstances, what with Sloop being in prison and all. So we got asked to take care of it. We brought him down here."

"Want to know what we did?" Billy asked.

"I thought we were going to the feed store," Reacher said.

"Feed store's up in San Angelo."

"So what are we doing all the way down here?"

"We're telling you, is what. This is where we brought the other guy."

"What's this other guy got to do with me?"

"Bobby figures you're in the same category, is what."

"He thinks I'm knocking boots with her too?"

Josh nodded. "He sure does."

"What do you think?"

"We agree with him. Why else would you come around? You're no horseman, that's for damn sure."

"Suppose I told you we're just good friends?"

"Bobby says you're more than that."

"And you believe him?"

Billy nodded. "Sure we do. She comes on to *him*. He told us that himself. So why should you be any different? And hey, we don't blame you. She's a good-looking piece of ass. I'd go there myself, except she's Sloop's. You got to respect family, even with beaners. That's the rule around here."

Reacher said nothing.

"Her other guy was a schoolteacher," Billy said. "Got way out of line. So we brought him down here, and we took him out back, in the yard, and we got us a hog butchering knife, and we got us a couple of guys to hold him, and we pulled his pants down, and we told him we were going to cut it off. He was all crying and whimpering and messing himself. Begging and whining. Promising he'd get himself lost. Pleading with us not to cut. But we cut just a little anyway. For the fun of it. There was blood everywhere. Then we let him go. But we told him if we ever saw his face again, we'd take it all the way off for real. And you know what? We never saw his face again."

"So it worked," Josh said. "It worked real good. Only problem was he nearly bled out, from the wound. We should have called ahead for the ambulance. We figured we should remember that, for the next time. Live and learn, that's what we always say. So this time, we did call ahead. Especially for you. So you should be grateful."

"You cut the guy?" Reacher asked.

"We sure did."

"Sounds like you're real proud of yourselves."

"We do what it takes. We look after the family."

"And you're admitting it to me?"

Josh nodded. "Why shouldn't we? Like, who the hell are you?"

Reacher shrugged. "Well, I'm not a schoolteacher."

"What's that supposed to mean?"

"It means you aim to cut me, it'll be you goes in the ambulance."

"You think?"

Reacher nodded. "That horse I was on shit more trouble than you guys are going to give me."

He looked at each of them in turn, openly and evenly. Serene self-confidence works wonders, in a situation like that. And he felt confident. It was confidence born of experience. It was a long, long time since he'd lost a two-on-one bar fight.

"Your choice," he said. "Quit now, or go to the hospital."

"Well, you know what?" Josh said, smiling. "I think we'll stay with the program. Because whatever the hell kind of a guy you think you are, we're the ones got a lot of friends in here. And you don't."

"I didn't inquire about your social situation," Reacher said.

But it was clearly true. They had friends in there. Some kind of a subliminal vibe was quieting the room, making people restless and watchful. They were glancing over, then glancing at each other. The atmosphere was building. The pool game was slowing down. Reacher could feel tension in

the air. The silences were starting. The challenges. Maybe it
was going to be worse than two-on-one. Maybe a lot worse.

Billy smiled.

"We don't scare easy," he said. "Call it a professional
thing."

They get in the ring with bulls that weigh a ton and a half,
Bobby had said. *They ain't going to be too worried about
you.* Reacher had never been to a rodeo. He knew nothing
about them, except for occasional passing impressions from
television or the movies. He guessed the riders sat on some
kind of a fence, near the pen, and they jumped on just as the
bull was released out into the ring. Then they had to stay on.
What was it, eight seconds? And if they didn't, they could get
kicked around pretty badly. They could get stomped. Or
gored, with the horns. So these guys had some kind of dumb
courage. And strength. And resilience. And they were accustomed to pain and injury. But they were also accustomed to
some kind of a *pattern*. Some kind of a structured buildup.
Some kind of a measured countdown, before the action suddenly started. He didn't know for sure how it went. Maybe
three, two, one, go. Maybe *ten, nine, eight.* Whatever, they
were accustomed to waiting, counting off the seconds, tensing up, breathing deeply, getting ready for it.

"So let's do it," he said. "Right now, in the yard."

He came out from behind the table and stepped past Josh
before he could react. Walked ahead, away from the jukebox,
to the right of the pool table, heading for the rest room exit.
Knots of people blocked him and then parted to let him
through. He heard Josh and Billy following right behind him.
He felt them counting down, tensing up, getting ready.
Maybe twenty paces to the exit, maybe thirty seconds to the
yard. *Twenty-nine, twenty-eight.* He kept his steps even,
building on the rhythm. *Twenty-seven, twenty-six.* Arms
loose by his side. *Twenty-five, twenty-four.*

He snatched the last pool cue from the rack and reversed it
in his hands and scythed a complete hundred-eighty-degree
turn and hit Billy as hard as he could in the side of the head,
one. There was a loud crunch of bone clearly audible over the
jukebox noise and a spray of blood and Billy went down like

he had been machine-gunned. He swung again, chopping full-force at Josh like a slugger swinging for the fences, *two*. Josh's hand came up to block the blow and his forearm broke clean in half. He screamed and Reacher swung again for the head, *three,* connecting hard, knocking him sideways. He jabbed for the face and punched out a couple of teeth, *four*. Backhanded the cue with all his strength against the upper arm and shattered the bone, *five*. Josh went down head-to-toe with Billy and Reacher stood over them both and swung again four more times, fast and hard, *six, seven, eight, nine,* against ribs and collarbones and knees and skulls. A total of nine swings, maybe six or seven seconds of furious explosive force. *Hit hard, hit early, get your retaliation in first*. While they're still waiting for the bell.

The other men in the bar had spun away from the action and now they were crowding back in again, slowly and war- ily. Reacher turned a menacing circle with the cue held ready. He bent and took the truck keys from Josh's pocket. Then he dropped the cue and let it clatter to the floor and barged his way through the crowd to the door, breathing hard, shoving people out of his way. Nobody seriously tried to stop him. Clearly friendship had its limits, down there in Echo County. He made it into the lot, still breathing fast. The heat broke him out in a sweat, instantly. He made it back to the truck. Slid inside and fired it up and backed away from the building and peeled away north. The bar door stayed firmly closed. Nobody came after him.

The sun set far away in the west an hour into his drive back and it was full dark when he turned in under the ranch gate. But every light in the Red House was burning. And there were two cars parked in the yard. One was the sheriff's secondhand cruiser. The other was a lime green Lincoln. The sheriff's car was flashing red and blue. The Lincoln was lit by the spill from the porch and the hot yellow light made it look the color of a dead man's skin. There were clouds of moths every- where, big papery insects crowding the bulbs above the porch like tiny individual snowstorms, forming and re-forming as they fluttered from one to the next. Behind them the chant of the night insects was already rhythmic and insistent.

The front door of the house was standing open and there was noise in the foyer. Loud excited conversation, from a small crowd of people. Reacher stepped up and looked into the room and saw the sheriff, and Rusty Greer, and Bobby, and then Carmen standing alone near the rack of rifles. She had changed out of her jeans and shirt. She was wearing a dress. It was red and black and had no sleeves. It finished at the knee. She looked numb. Conflicting emotions in her face made it blank and expressionless. There was a man in a suit at the opposite end of the room, standing near the red-framed mirror so Reacher could see the front and back of him at the same time. The Lincoln driver, obviously. He was sleek and slightly overweight, not short, not tall, dressed in pressed seersucker. Maybe thirty years old, with light-colored hair carefully combed and receding from a domed brow. He had a pale indoor face, red with sunburn on the upward-facing planes like he played golf in the early afternoon. The face was split into a huge politician's smile. He looked like he had been receiving fulsome accolades and pretending they were completely unnecessary.

Reacher paused on the porch and decided not to enter. But his weight put a loud creak into the boards and Bobby heard it. He glanced out into the night and did a perfect double-take. Stood completely still for a second and then came hurrying through the door. Took Reacher's elbow and pulled him into the lee of the wall, alongside the entrance, out of sight of the foyer.

"What are you doing here?" he asked.

"I work here," Reacher said. "Remember?"

"Where are Josh and Billy?"

"They quit."

Bobby stared at him. "They what?"

"They quit," Reacher said again.

"What does that mean?"

"It means they decided they didn't want to work here anymore."

"Why would they do that?"

Reacher shrugged. "How would I know? Maybe they were just exercising their prerogative inside a free labor market."

"What?"

Reacher said nothing. Bobby's absence and the voices on the porch had pulled people to the door. Rusty Greer was first out, followed by the sheriff and the guy in the seersucker suit. Carmen stayed inside, near the rifles, still looking numb. They all fell silent, looking at Reacher, Rusty like she had a social difficulty to deal with, the sheriff puzzled, the new guy in the suit wondering who the hell this stranger was.

"What's going on?" Rusty asked.

"This guy says Josh and Billy quit on us," Bobby said.

"They wouldn't do that," Rusty said. "Why would they do that?"

The guy in the suit was looming forward, like he expected to be introduced.

"Did they give a reason?" Rusty asked.

The sheriff was looking straight at Reacher, nothing in his face. Reacher made no reply. Just stood there, waiting.

"Well, I'm Hack Walker," the guy in the suit said, in a big honest voice, holding out his hand. "I'm the DA up in Pecos, and I'm a friend of the family."

"Sloop's oldest friend," Rusty said, absently.

Reacher nodded and took the guy's hand.

"Jack Reacher," he said. "I work here."

The guy held on to his hand in both of his own and beamed a subtle little smile that was partly genuine, partly *you-know-how-it-is* ironic. A perfect politician's smile.

"You registered to vote here yet?" he asked. "Because if so, I just want to point out I'm running for judge in November, and I'd surely like to count on your support."

Then he started up with a self-deprecating chuckle, a man secure among friends, amused about how the demands of democracy can intrude on good manners. *You know how it is.* Reacher took his hand back and nodded without speaking.

"Hack's worked so hard for us," Rusty said. "And now he's brought us the most delightful news."

"Al Eugene showed up?" Reacher asked.

"No, not yet," Rusty said. "Something else entirely."

"And nothing to do with the election," Hack said. "You folks all understand that, don't you? I agree, November time makes us want to do something for everybody, but you *know* I'd have done this for you anyhow."

"And *you* know we'd all vote for you anyhow, Hack," Rusty said.

Then everybody started beaming at everybody else. Reacher glanced beyond them at Carmen standing alone in the foyer. She wasn't beaming.

"You're getting Sloop out early," he said. "Tomorrow, I guess."

Hack Walker ducked his head, like Reacher had offered him a compliment.

"That's for sure," he said. "All along they claimed they couldn't do administration on the weekend, but I managed to change their minds. They said it would be the first Sunday release in the history of the system, but I just said hey, there's a first time for everything."

"Hack's going to drive us up there," Rusty said. "We're leaving soon. We're going to drive all night."

"We're going to be waiting on the sidewalk," Hack said. "Right outside the prison gate, seven o'clock in the morning. Old Sloop's going to get a big welcome."

"You all going?" Reacher asked.

"I'm not," Carmen said.

She had come out onto the porch, quietly, like a wraith. She was standing with her feet together, both hands on the railing, leaning forward from the waist, elbows locked, staring north at the black horizon.

"I have to stay and see to Ellie," she said.

"Plenty of room in the car," Hack said. "Ellie can come too."

Carmen shook her head. "I don't want her to see her father walking out of a prison door."

"Well, please yourself," Rusty said. "He's only your husband, after all."

Carmen made no reply. Just shivered slightly, like the night air was thirty degrees instead of ninety.

"Then I guess I'll stay too," Bobby said. "Keep an eye on things. Sloop will understand."

Reacher glanced at him. Carmen turned abruptly and walked back into the house. Rusty and Hack Walker drifted after her. The sheriff and Bobby stayed on the porch, each taking a half-step toward the other, to put a subliminal human barrier between Reacher and the door.

"So why did they quit?" Bobby asked.

Reacher glanced at them both and shrugged.

"Well, they didn't exactly quit," he said. "I was trying to sugar the pill, for the family, was all. Truth is we were in a bar, and they picked a fight with some guy. You saw us in the bar, right, Sheriff?"

The sheriff nodded, cautiously.

"It was after you left," Reacher said. "They picked a fight and lost."

"Who with?" Bobby asked. "What guy?"

"The wrong guy."

"But who was he?"

"Some big guy," Reacher said. "He smacked them around for a minute or two. I think somebody called the ambulance for them. They're probably in the hospital now. Maybe they're dead, for all I know. They lost, and they lost real bad."

Bobby stared. "Who was the guy?"

"Just some guy, minding his own business."

"Who?"

"Some stranger, I guess."

Bobby paused. "Was it you?"

"Me?" Reacher said. "Why would they pick a fight with me?"

Bobby said nothing.

"Why would they pick a fight with me, Bobby?" Reacher asked again. "What possible kind of a reason would they have for that?"

Bobby made no reply. Just stared and then turned and stalked into the house. Slammed the door loudly behind him. The sheriff stayed where he was.

"So they got hurt bad," he said.

Reacher nodded. "Seems that way. You should make some calls, check it out. Then start spreading the news. Tell people that's what happens, if they start picking fights with the wrong strangers."

The sheriff nodded again, still cautious.

"Maybe it's something you should bear in mind, too," Reacher said. "Bobby told me down here folks sort out their own differences. He told me they're reluctant to involve law enforcement people. He implied cops stay out of private disputes. He said it's some kind of a big old West Texas tradition."

The sheriff was quiet for a moment.

"I guess it might be," he said.

"Bobby said it definitely was. A definite tradition."

The sheriff turned away.

"Well, you could put it that way," he said. "And I'm a very traditional guy."

Reacher nodded.

"I'm very glad to hear it," he said.

The sheriff paused on the porch steps, and then moved on again without looking back. He slid into his car and killed the flashing lights and started the engine. Maneuvered carefully past the lime green Lincoln and headed out down the driveway and under the gate. His engine was running rich. Reacher could smell unburned gasoline in the air, and he could hear the muffler popping with tiny explosions. Then the car accelerated into the distance and he could hear nothing at all except the grasshoppers clicking and chattering.

He came down off the porch and walked around to the kitchen door. It was standing open, either for ventilation or so the maid could eavesdrop on the excitement. She was standing just inside the room, close to an insect screen made of plastic strips hanging down in the doorway.

"Hey," Reacher said. He had learned long ago to be friendly with the cookhouse detail. That way, you eat better. But she didn't answer him. She just stood there, warily.

"Let me guess," he said. "You only made two suppers for the bunkhouse."

She said nothing, which was as good as a yes.

"You were misinformed," he said. "Was it Bobby?"

She nodded. "He told me you weren't coming back."

"He was mistaken," he said. "It was Josh and Billy who didn't come back. So I guess I'll eat their dinners. Both of them. I'm hungry."

She paused. Then she shrugged.

"I'll bring them down," she said. "In a minute."

He shook his head.

"I'll eat them here," he said. "Save you the walk."

He parted the plastic strips with the backs of his hands and stepped inside the kitchen. It smelled of chili, left over from lunchtime.

"What did you make?" he asked.

"Steaks," she said.

"Good," he said. "I like bovines better than edentates."

"What?"

"I like beef better than I like armadillo."

"So do I," she said.

She used pot holders and took two plates out of a warming oven. Each held a medium-sized rib-eye steak, and a large mound of mashed potato and a smaller mound of fried onions. She put them side by side on the kitchen table, with a fork on the left of the left-hand plate and a knife all the way to the right. It looked like a double-barreled meal.

"Billy was my cousin," she said.

"He probably still is," Reacher said. "Josh got it worse."

"Josh was my cousin, too."

"Well, I'm sorry to hear that."

"Different branch of the family," she said. "More distant. And they were both fools."

Reacher nodded. "Not the sharpest chisels in the box."

"But the Greers are sharp," she said. "Whatever it is you're doing with the Mexican woman, you should remember that."

Then she left him alone to eat.

* * *

He rinsed both plates when he finished and left them stacked in the sink. Walked down to the horse barn and sat down to wait in the foul heat inside because he wanted to stay close to the house. He sat on a hay bale and kept his back to the horses. They were restless for a spell, and then they got used to his presence. He heard them fall asleep, one by one. The shuffling hooves stopped moving and he heard lazy huffs of breath.

Then he heard feet over on the boards of the porch, and then on the steps, and then the crunch of dry dust under them as they crossed the yard. He heard the Lincoln's doors open, then shut again. He heard the engine start, and the transmission engage. He stood up and stepped to the barn door and saw the Lincoln turning around in front of the house. It was lit from behind by the porch lights, and he could see Hack Walker silhouetted at the wheel, with Rusty Greer beside him. The porch lights turned her teased-up hair to cotton candy. He could see the shape of her skull underneath it.

The big car drove straight out under the gate and swooped right without pausing and accelerated away down the road. He watched the bright cone of its headlights through the picket fence, bouncing left to right through the darkness. Then it was gone and the sounds of the night insects came back and the big moths around the lights were all that was moving.

He waited just inside the barn door, trying to guess who would come for him first. Carmen, probably, he thought, but it was Bobby who stepped out on the porch, maybe five minutes after his mother had left to bring his brother home. He came straight down the steps and headed across the yard, down toward the path to the bunkhouse. He had his ball cap on again, reversed on his head. Reacher stepped out of the barn and cut him off.

"Horses need watering," Bobby said. "And I want their stalls cleaned out."

"You do it," Reacher said.

"What?"

"You heard."

Bobby stood still.

"I'm not doing it," he said.

"Then I'll make you do it."

"What the hell is this?"

"A change, is what," Reacher said. "Things just changed for you, Bobby, big time, believe me. Soon as you decided to set Josh and Billy on me, you crossed a line. Put yourself in a whole different situation. One where you do exactly what I tell you."

Bobby said nothing.

Reacher looked straight at him. "I tell you *jump,* you don't even ask how high. You just start jumping. That clear? I own you now."

Bobby stood still. Reacher swung his right hand, aiming a big slow roundhouse slap. Bobby ducked away from it, straight into Reacher's left, which pulled the ball cap off his head.

"So go look after the horses," Reacher said. "Then you can sleep in there with them. I see you again before breakfast time, I'll break your legs."

Bobby stood still.

"Who are you going to call, little brother?" Reacher asked him. "The maid, or the sheriff?"

Bobby said nothing. The vastness of the night closed in. Echo County, a hundred and fifty souls, most of them at least sixty or a hundred miles beyond the black horizons. The absolute definition of isolation.

"O.K.," Bobby said quietly.

He walked slowly toward the barn. Reacher dropped the ball cap in the dirt and strolled up to the house, with the porch lights shining in his eyes and the big papery moths swarming out to greet him.

Two-thirds of the killing crew saw him stroll. They were doing it better than the watchers had. The woman had checked the map and rejected the tactic of driving in from the west. For one thing, the Crown Vic wouldn't make it over the desert terrain. For another, to hide a mile away made no sense at all. Especially during the hours of darkness. Far better to

drive straight down the road and stop a hundred yards shy of
the house, long enough for two of the team to jump out, then
turn the car and head back north while the two on foot
ducked behind the nearest line of rocks and worked south toward the red gate and holed up in the small craters ten yards
from the blacktop.

It was the two men on foot. They had night-vision devices.
Nothing fancy, nothing military, just commercial equipment
bought from a sporting goods catalog and carried along with
everything else in the black nylon valise. They were binocu-
lars, with some kind of electronic enhancement inside. Some
kind of infrared capability. It picked up the night heat rising
off the ground, and made Reacher look like he was wobbling
and shimmering as he walked.

8

Reacher found Carmen in the parlor. The light was dim and the air was hot and thick. She was sitting alone at the red-painted table. Her back was perfectly straight and her forearms were resting lightly on the wooden surface and her gaze was blank and absolutely level, focused on a spot on the wall where there was nothing to see.

"Twice over," she said. "I feel cheated, twice over. First it was a year, and then it was nothing. Then it was forty-eight hours, but really it was only twenty-four."

"You can still get out," he said.

"Now it's less than twenty-four," she said. "It's sixteen hours, maybe. I'll have breakfast by myself, but he'll be back for lunch."

"Sixteen hours is enough," he said. "Sixteen hours, you could be anywhere."

"Ellie's fast asleep," she said. "I can't wake her up and bundle her in a car and run away and be chased by the cops forever."

Reacher said nothing.

"I'm going to try to face it," she said. "A fresh start. I'm planning to tell him, enough is enough. I'm planning to tell him, he lays a hand on me again, I'll divorce him. Whatever it takes. However long."

"Way to go," he said.

"Do you believe I can?" she asked.

"I believe anybody can do anything," he said. "If they want it enough."

"I want it," she said. "Believe me, I want it."

She went quiet. Reacher glanced around the silent room.

"Why did they paint everything red?" he asked.

"Because it was cheap," she said. "During the fifties, no-body down here wanted red anything, because of the Communists. So it was the cheapest color at the paint store."

"I thought they were rich, back then. With the oil."

"They were rich. They still are rich. Richer than you could ever imagine. But they're also mean."

He looked at the places where the fifty-year-old paint was worn back to the wood.

"Evidently," he said.

She nodded again. Said nothing.

"Last chance, Carmen," he said. "We could go, right now. There's nobody here to call the cops. By the time they get back, we could be anywhere you want."

"Bobby's here."

"He's going to stay in the barn."

"He'd hear the car."

"We could rip out the phones."

"He'd chase us. He could get to the sheriff inside two hours."

"We could fix the other cars so they wouldn't work."

"He'd hear us doing it."

"I could tie him up. I could drown him in a horse trough."

She smiled, bitterly. "But you won't drown Sloop."

He nodded. "Figure of speech, I guess."

She was quiet for a beat. Then she scraped back her chair and stood up.

"Come and see Ellie," she said. "She's so beautiful when she's asleep."

She passed close to him and took his hand in hers. Led him out through the kitchen and into the rear lobby and up the back stairs, toward the noise of the fan turning slowly. Down the long hot corridor to Ellie's door. She eased it open with her foot and maneuvered him so he could see inside the room.

There was a night-light plugged into an outlet low on the wall and its soft orange glow showed the child sprawled on her back, with her arms thrown up around her head. She had kicked off her sheet and the rabbit T-shirt had ridden up and was showing a band of plump pink skin at her waist. Her hair was tumbled over the pillow. Long dark eyelashes rested on her cheeks like fans. Her mouth was open a fraction.

"She's six and a half," Carmen whispered. "She needs this. She needs a bed of her own, in a place of her own. I can't make her live like a fugitive."

He said nothing.

"Do you see?" she whispered.

He shrugged. He didn't, really. At age six and a half, he had lived exactly like a fugitive. He had at every age, right from birth to yesterday. He had moved from one service base to another, all around the world, often with no notice at all. He recalled days when he got up for school and instead was driven to an airstrip and ended up on the other side of the planet thirty hours later. He recalled stumbling tired and bewildered into dank bungalow bedrooms and sleeping on unmade beds. The next morning, his mother would tell him which country they were in. Which continent they were on. If she knew yet. Sometimes she didn't. It hadn't done him any harm.

Or, maybe it had.

"It's your call, I guess," he said.

She pulled him back into the corridor and eased Ellie's door shut behind him.

"Now I'll show you where I hid the gun," she said. "You can tell me if you approve."

She walked ahead of him down the corridor. The air conditioner was loud. He passed under a vent and a breath of air played over him. It was warm. Carmen's dress swayed with every step. She was wearing heels and they put tension in the muscles of her legs. He could see tendons in the backs of her knees. Her hair hung down her back and merged with the black pattern on the red fabric of the dress. She turned left and then right and stepped through an archway. There was another staircase, leading down.

"Where are we going?" he asked.

"Separate wing," she said. "It was added. By Sloop's grandfather, I think."

The staircase led to a long narrow ground-floor hallway that led out of the main building to a master suite. It was as big as a small house. There was a dressing area, and a spacious bathroom, and a sitting room with a sofa and two armchairs. Beyond the sitting room was a broad archway. Beyond the archway, there was a bedroom.

"In here," she said.

She walked straight through the sitting room and led him to the bedroom.

"You see what I mean?" she said. "We're a long way from anywhere. Nobody hears anything. And I try to be quiet, anyway. If I scream, he hits me harder."

He nodded and looked around. There was a window, facing east, with insects loud beyond the screen. There was a king-size bed close to it, with side tables by the head, and a chest-high piece of furniture full of drawers opposite the foot. It looked like it had been made a hundred years ago, out of some kind of oak trees.

"Texas ironwood," she said. "It's what you get if you let the mesquite grow tall."

"You should have been a teacher," he said. "You're always explaining things."

She smiled, vaguely. "I thought about it, in college. It was a possibility, back then. In my other life."

She opened the drawer on the top right.

"I moved the gun," she said. "I listened to your advice. Bedside cabinet was too low. Ellie could have found it. This is too high for her."

He nodded again and moved closer. The drawer was a couple of feet wide, maybe eighteen inches deep. It was her underwear drawer. The pistol was lying on top of her things, which were neatly folded, and silky, and insubstantial, and fragrant. The mother-of-pearl plastic on the grips looked right at home there.

"You could have told me where it was," he said. "You didn't need to show me."

She was quiet for a beat.

"He'll want sex, won't he?" she said.

Reacher made no reply.

"He's been locked up a year and a half," she said. "But I'm going to refuse."

Reacher said nothing.

"It's a woman's right, isn't it?" she asked. "To say no?"

"Of course it is," he said.

"Even though the woman is married?"

"Most places," he said.

She was quiet for a beat.

"And it's also her right to say yes, isn't it?" she asked.

"Equally," he said.

"I'd say yes to you."

"I'm not asking."

She paused. "So is it O.K. for me to ask you?"

He looked straight at her. "Depends on why, I guess."

"Because I want to," she said. "I want to go to bed with you."

"Why?"

"Honestly?" she said. "Just because I want to."

"And?"

She shrugged. "And I want to hurt Sloop a little, I guess, in secret. In my heart."

He said nothing.

"Before he gets home," she said.

He said nothing.

"And because Bobby already thinks we're doing it," she said. "I figure, why get the blame without getting the fun?"

He said nothing.

"I just want a little fun," she said. "Before it all starts up again."

He said nothing.

"No strings attached," she said. "I'm not looking for it to change anything. About your decision, I mean. About Sloop."

He nodded.

"It wouldn't change anything," he said.

She looked away.

"So what's your answer?" she asked.

He watched her profile. Her face was blank. It was like all other possibilities were exhausted for her, and all that was left was instinct. Early in his service career, when the threat was still plausible, people talked about what they would do when the enemy missiles were airborne and incoming. This was absolutely the number-one pick, by a huge, huge margin. A universal instinct. And he could see it in her. She had heard the four-minute warning, and the sirens were sounding loud in her mind.

"No," he said.

She was quiet for a long moment.

"Will you at least stay with me?" she asked.

The killing crew moved fifty miles closer to Pecos in the middle of the night. They did it secretly, some hours after booking in for a second night at their first location. It was the woman's preferred method. Six false names, two overlapping sets of motel records, the confusion built fast enough to keep them safe.

They drove east on I-10 until they passed the I-20 interchange. They headed down toward Fort Stockton until they saw signs for the first group of motels serving the Balmorhea state recreation area. Those motels were far enough from the actual tourist attraction to make them cheap and anonymous. There wasn't going to be a lot of cutesy decor and personal service. But they would be clean and decent. And they would be full of people exactly like themselves. That was what the woman wanted. She was a chameleon. She had an instinct for the right type of place. She chose the second establishment they came to, and sent the small dark man to pay cash for two rooms.

Reacher woke up on Sloop Greer's sofa with the Sunday dawn. Beyond him, the bedroom window faced east and the night insects were gone and the sky was bright. The bed sheet looked damp and tangled. Carmen wasn't under it. He could hear the shower running in the bathroom. And he could smell coffee.

He got off the sofa and stretched. Wandered through the archway to the bedroom. He saw Carmen's dress on the floor. He went to the window and checked the weather. No change. The sky was hazed with heat. He wandered back to the sitting area. There was a credenza in one corner, set up with a small coffee machine. There were two upturned mugs beside it, with spoons, like a hotel. The bathroom door was closed. The shower sounded loud behind it. He filled a mug with coffee and wandered into the dressing area. There were two large closets there, parallel, one on each side. Not walk-ins, just long deep alcoves screened with sliding doors made out of mirrored glass.

He opened the left-hand closet. It was hers. It was full of dresses and pants on hangers. There were blouses. There was a rack of shoes. He closed it again and turned around and opened the other one. It was Sloop's. There were a dozen suits, and rows and rows of chinos and blue jeans. Cedar shelves stacked with T-shirts, and dress shirts folded into plastic wraps. A row of neckties. Belts, with fancy buckles. A long row of dusty shoes on the floor. The shoes looked to be about size eleven. He swapped his coffee cup into his other hand and nudged open a suit coat, looking for the label. It was a forty-four long. It would fit a guy about six feet two or three, maybe a hundred and ninety or two hundred pounds. So Sloop was not an especially big guy. Not a giant. But he was a foot taller and twice the weight of his wife. Not the world's fairest match-up.

There was a photograph frame face-down on top of a stack of shirts. He turned it over. There was a five-by-seven color print under a cream card mat glassed into a lacquered wooden surround. The print showed three guys, young, halfway between boyhood and manhood. Maybe seventeen years old, maybe eighteen. They were standing close together, leaning on the bulging fender of an old-fashioned pick-up truck. They were peering expectantly at the camera, like maybe it was perched close by on a rock and they were waiting for the self-timer to click in. They looked full of youthful energy and excitement. Their whole lives ahead of them, full of infinite possibilities. One of them was Hack Walker, a little slimmer, a little more muscular, a lot more hair. He guessed the other two were Al Eugene and Sloop Greer himself. Teen-aged buddies. Eugene was a head shorter than Sloop, and chubby. Sloop looked like a younger version of Bobby.

He heard the shower shut off and put the photograph back and closed the slider. Moved back to the sitting area. A moment later the bathroom door opened and Carmen came out in a cloud of steam. She was wrapped in two white towels, one around her body, the other bound like a turban around her hair. He looked at her and stayed quiet, unsure of what to say.

"Good morning," she said in the silence.

"To you, too," he said.

She unwrapped the turban and shook out her hair. It hung wet and straight.

"It isn't, though, is it?" she said. "A good morning? It's a bad morning."

"I guess," he said.

"He could be walking out the gate, this exact minute."

He checked his watch. It was almost seven.

"Any time now," he said.

"Use the shower if you want," she said. "I have to go and see to Ellie."

"O.K."

He stepped into the bathroom. It was huge, and made out of some kind of reconstituted marble with gold tones in it. It looked like a place he'd once stayed, in Vegas. He used the john and rinsed his mouth at the sink and stripped off his stale clothes and stepped into the shower stall. It was enclosed with bronze-tinted glass and it was enormous. There was a shower head the size of a hubcap above him, and tall pipes in each corner with additional water jets pointing directly at him. He turned the faucet and a huge roaring started up. Then a deluge of warm water hit him from all sides. It was like standing under Niagara Falls. The side jets started pulsing hot and cold and he couldn't hear himself think. He washed as quickly as he could and soaped his hair and rinsed off and shut it all down.

He took a fresh towel from a stack and dried off as well as he could in the humidity. Wrapped the towel around him and stepped back into the dressing area. Carmen was buttoning her shirt. It was white, and she had white pants on. Gold jewelry. Her skin looked dark against it and her hair was glossy and already curling in the heat.

"That was quick," she said.

"Hell of a shower," he said.

"Sloop chose it," she said. "I hate it. There's so much water, I can hardly breathe in there."

She slid her closet shut and twisted left and right to examine her reflection in the mirrored doors.

"You look good," he said.

"Do I look Mexican enough?" she asked. "With the white clothes?"

He said nothing.

"No jeans today," she said. "I'm sick of trying to look like I was born a cowgirl in Amarillo."

"You look good," he said again.

"Seven hours," she said. "Six and a half, if Hack drives fast."

He nodded. "I'm going to find Bobby."

She stretched tall and kissed him on the cheek.

"Thanks for staying," she said. "It helped me."

He said nothing.

"Join us for breakfast," she said. "Twenty minutes."

Then she walked slowly out of the room, on her way to wake her daughter.

Reacher dressed and found a different way back into the house. The whole place was a warren. He came out through a living room he hadn't seen before and into the foyer with the mirror and the rifles. He opened the front door and stepped out on the porch. It was already hot. The sun was coming from low on his right, and it was casting harsh early shadows. The shadows made the yard look pocked and lumpy.

He walked down to the barn and went in the door. The heat and the smell were as bad as ever, and the horses were awake and restless. But they were clean. They had water. Their feed troughs had been filled. He found Bobby asleep in an unoccupied stall, on a bed of clean straw.

"Rise and shine, little brother," he called.

Bobby stirred and sat up, confused as to where he was, and why. Then he remembered, and went tense with resentment. His clothes were dirty and hay stalks clung to him all over.

"Sleep well?" Reacher asked.

"They'll be back soon," Bobby said. "Then what do you think is going to happen?"

Reacher smiled. "You mean, am I going to tell them I made you clean out the barn and sleep in the straw?"

"You couldn't tell them."

"No, I guess I couldn't," Reacher said. "So are *you* going to tell them?"

Bobby said nothing. Reacher smiled again.

"No, I didn't think you would," he said. "So stay in here until noontime, then I'll let you in the house to get cleaned up for the main event."

"What about breakfast?"

"You don't get any."

"But I'm hungry."

"So eat the horse food. Turns out there's bags and bags of it, after all."

He went back to the kitchen and found the maid brewing coffee and heating a skillet.

"Pancakes," she said. "And that will have to do. They'll want a big lunch, so that's where my morning is going."

"Pancakes are fine," he said.

He walked on into the silent parlor and listened for sounds from above. Ellie and Carmen should be moving around somewhere. But he couldn't hear anything. He tried to map the house in his head, but the layout was too bizarre. Clearly it had started out a substantial ranch house, and then random additions had been made whenever necessary. Overall, there was no coherence to it.

The maid came in with a stack of plates. Four of them, with four sets of silverware and four paper napkins piled on top.

"I assume you're eating in here," she said.

Reacher nodded. "But Bobby isn't. He's staying in the barn."

"Why?"

"I think a horse is sick."

The maid dumped the stack of plates and slid one out, leaving three of everything.

"So I'll have to carry it down to him, I guess," she said, irritated.

"I'll take it," Reacher said. "You're very busy."

He followed her back to the kitchen and she piled the first four pancakes off the skillet onto a plate. Added a little butter and maple syrup. Reacher wrapped a knife and a fork into a napkin and picked up the plate and walked back out into the heat. He found Bobby where he had left him. He was sitting up, doing nothing.

"What's this?" he said.

"Breakfast," Reacher said. "I had a change of heart. Because you're going to do something for me."

"Yeah, what?"

"There's going to be some kind of a big lunch, for Sloop getting back."

Bobby nodded. "I expect so."

"You're going to invite me. As your guest. Like I'm you're big buddy."

"I am?"

"Sure you are. If you want these pancakes, and if you want to walk without sticks the rest of your life."

Bobby went quiet.

"Dinner, too," Reacher said. "You understand?"

"Her *husband*'s coming home, for God's sake," Bobby said. "It's *over*, right?"

"You're jumping to conclusions, Bobby. I've got no particular interest in Carmen. I just want to get next to Sloop. I need to talk to him."

"About what?"

"Just do it, O.K.?"

Bobby shrugged.

"Whatever," he said.

Reacher handed him the plate of pancakes and headed for the house again.

Carmen and Ellie were sitting side by side at the table. Ellie's hair was wet from the shower and she was in a yellow seersucker dress.

"My daddy's coming home today," she said. "He's on his way, right now."

Reacher nodded. "I heard that."

"I thought it was going to be tomorrow. But it's today."

Carmen was looking at the wall, saying nothing. The maid brought pancakes in on a platter. She served them out, two for the kid, three for Carmen, four for Reacher. Then she took the platter away and went back to the kitchen.

"I was going to stay home from school tomorrow," Ellie said. "Can I still?"

Carmen said nothing.

"Mom? Can I still?"

Carmen turned and looked at Reacher, like he had spoken. Her face was blank. It reminded him of a guy he had known who had gone to the eye doctor. He had been having trouble reading fine print. The eye doctor spotted a tumor in the retina. Made arrangements there and then for him to have the eye removed the next day. Then the guy had sat around knowing that tomorrow he was going into the hospital with two eyes and coming back out with one. The certainty had burned him up. The anticipation. The dread. Much worse than a split-second accident with the same result.

"Mommy? Can I?" Ellie asked again.

"I guess," Carmen said. "What?"

"Mommy, you're not *listening*. Are you excited too?"

"Yes," Carmen said.

"So can I?"

"Yes," Carmen said again.

Ellie turned to her food and ate it like she was starving. Reacher picked at his, watching Carmen. She ate nothing.

"I'm going to see my pony now," Ellie said.

She scrambled off her chair and ran out of the room like a miniature whirlwind. Reacher heard the front door open and close and the thump of her shoes on the porch steps. He finished his breakfast while Carmen held her fork in midair, like she was uncertain what to do with it, like she had never seen one before.

"Will you talk to him?" she asked.

"Sure," he said.

"I think he needs to know it's not a secret anymore."

"I agree."

"Will you look at him? When you're talking to him?"

"I guess so," he said.

"Good. You should. Because you've got gunfighter's eyes. Maybe like Clay Allison had. You should let him see them. Let him see what's coming."

"We've been through all of that," he said.

"I know," she answered.

Then she went off alone and Reacher set about killing time. It felt like waiting for an air raid. He walked out onto the porch and looked across the yard at the road where it came in from the north. He followed it with his eyes to where the red picket fence finished, and beyond that to where it disappeared over the curve of the earth. The air was still clear with morning and there was no mirage over the blacktop. It was just a dusty ribbon framed by the limestone ledge to the west and the power lines to the east.

He turned back and sat down on the porch swing. The chains creaked under his weight. He settled sideways, facing the ranch gate, one leg up and the other on the floor. Then he did what most soldiers do when they're waiting for action. He went to sleep.

* * *

Carmen woke him maybe an hour later. She touched him on the shoulder and he opened his eyes and saw her standing over him. She had changed her clothes. Now she was in pressed blue jeans and a checked shirt. She was wearing boots made out of lizard skin. A belt to match. Her hair was tied back and she had made up her face with pale powder and blue eye shadow.

"I changed my mind," she said. "I don't want you to talk to him. Not yet."

"Why not?"

"It might set him off. If he knows somebody else knows."

"You didn't think that before."

"I thought it over again. I think it might be worse, if we start out like that. It's better coming from me. At least at first."

"You sure?"

She nodded. "Let me talk to him, the first time."

"When?"

"Tonight," she said. "I'll tell you tomorrow how it went."

He sat up, with both feet on the ground.

"You were pretty sure you'd have a busted nose tomorrow," he said.

"I think this is best," she said.

"Why did you change your clothes?"

"These are better," she said. "I don't want to provoke him."

"You look like a cowgirl, born in Amarillo."

"He likes me like this."

"And dressing like who you are would provoke him?"

She made a face. A defeated face, he thought.

"Don't chicken out, Carmen," he said. "Stand and fight instead."

"I will," she said. "Tonight. I'll tell him I'm not going to take it anymore."

He said nothing.

"So don't talk to him today, O.K.?" she said.

He looked away.

"It's your call," he said.

"It's better this way."

She went back into the house. Reacher stared north at the

road. Sitting down, he could see a mile less of it. The heat was up, and the shimmer was starting.

She woke him again after another hour. The clothes were the same, but she had removed the makeup.

"You think I'm doing this wrong," she said.

He sat up and rubbed both hands over his face, like he was washing.

"I think it would be better out in the open," he said. "He should know somebody else knows. If not me, then his family, maybe."

"I can't tell them."

"No, I guess you can't."

"So what should I do?"

"You should let me talk to him."

"Not right away. It would be worse. Promise me you won't."

He nodded.

"It's your call," he said. "But you promise *me* something, O.K.? Talk to him yourself, tonight. For sure. And if he starts anything, get out of the room and just scream your head off until we all come running. Scream the place down. Demand the cops. Shout for help. It'll embarrass him. It'll change the dynamic."

"You think?"

"He can't pretend it isn't happening, not if everybody hears you."

"He'll deny it. He'll say I was just having a nightmare."

"But deep inside, he'll know we know."

She said nothing.

"Promise me, Carmen," he said. "Or I'll talk to him first."

She was quiet for a moment.

"O.K., I promise you," she said.

He settled back on the swing and tried to doze another hour. But his internal clock was telling him the time was getting near. The way he remembered the maps of Texas, Abi-

lene was probably less than seven hours from Echo County.
Probably nearer six, for a driver who was a DA and therefore
a part of the law enforcement community and therefore relatively unconcerned about speeding tickets. So assuming
Sloop got out at seven without any delay, they could be home
by one o'clock. And he probably would get out without any
delay, because a minimum-security federal facility wouldn't
have a whole lot of complicated procedures. They'd just
make a check mark on a clipboard and cut him loose.

He guessed it was nearly twelve and looked at his watch to
confirm it. It was one minute past. He saw Bobby come out
of the horse barn and start up the track past the car barn. He
was carrying his breakfast plate, blinking in the sun, walking
like his limbs were stiff. He crossed the yard and stepped up
on the porch. Said nothing. Just walked on into the house and
closed the door behind him.

About twelve-thirty, Ellie came wandering up from the direction of the corrals. Her yellow dress was all covered in dirt
and sand. Her hair was matted with it and her skin was
flushed from the heat.

"I've been jumping," she said. "I pretend I'm a horse and I
go around and around the jumps as fast as I can."

"Come here," Reacher said.

She stood close and he dusted her down, brushing the sand
and the dirt to the floor with his palm.

"Maybe you should go shower again," he said. "Get your
hair clean."

"Why?"

"So you look nice, for your daddy getting home."

She thought about it, with intense concentration.

"O.K.," she said.

"Be quick."

She looked at him for a moment, and then she turned and
ran into the house.

* * *

At a quarter to one, Bobby came outside. He was clean and dressed in fresh jeans and a new T-shirt. He had alligator boots on his feet. They had silver accents at the toe. He was wearing another red ball cap. It was backward on his head, and it had a flash on the side reading *Division Series 1999*.

"They lost, right?" Reacher said.

"Who?"

"The Texas Rangers. In the 1999 Division Series. To the Yankees."

"So?"

"So nothing, Bobby."

Then the door opened again and Carmen and Ellie came out together. Carmen was still in the cowgirl outfit. She had the makeup on again. Ellie was still in the yellow seersucker. Her hair was wet and tied back into a ponytail with a ribbon. Carmen was holding her hand and staggering slightly, like her knees were weak.

Reacher stood up and gestured that she should sit down. Ellie climbed up and sat next to her. Nobody spoke. Reacher stepped to the porch rail and watched the road. He could see all the way to where the power lines disappeared in the haze. Maybe five miles north. Maybe ten. It was hard to be certain.

He was deep in the shadow of the porch, and the world was hot and white in front of him. He saw the dust cloud right at the extremity of his vision. It smudged in the haze and hung and drifted east, like a faint desert breeze was catching it and pushing it over toward Greer land. It grew until he could make out its shape. It was a long yellow teardrop of dust, rising and falling, dodging left and right with the curves of the road. It grew to a mile long, and many generations of it bloomed and dissipated before it came close enough for him to see the lime green Lincoln at its head. It came up over a contour in the road and shimmered through the haze and slowed where the barbed wire gave way to the red picket fence. It looked dusty and tired and travel-stained. It braked hard close to the gate and the front end squatted as the suspension compressed. It turned in sharply. The cone of dust behind it drifted straight on south, like it had been outwitted by the abrupt change of direction.

There was a crunch of dirt and gravel and the sun flashed once in the windshield as the car came through its turn, and then three figures were clearly visible inside. Hack Walker was at the wheel. Rusty Greer was in the backseat. And there was a large pale man in the front. He had short fair hair and a plain blue shirt. He was craning his neck, looking around, smiling broadly. Sloop Greer, arriving home.

9

The Lincoln stopped next to the porch and the suspension settled and the engine died. Nobody inside the car moved for a moment. Then three doors opened up and all three people spilled out and Bobby and Ellie clattered down the porch steps toward them. Reacher moved back from the rail. Carmen stood up slowly and stepped forward and took his place there.

Sloop Greer left his door open and stretched in the sun like anyone would after a year and a half in a cell and six hours on the road. His face and hands were white with prison pallor and he was overweight from the starchy food, but he was Bobby's brother. There was no doubt about that. He had the same hair, the same face, the same bones, the same posture. Bobby stepped straight in front of him and held his arms wide and hugged him hard. Sloop hugged back and they staggered around and whooped and clapped each other on the back like they were on a lawn in front of a frat house and somebody had done something big in a game of college football.

Ellie froze and hung back, like she was suddenly confused by the noise and the commotion. Sloop let Bobby go and squatted down and held his arms out to her. Reacher turned and watched Carmen's face. It was locked up tight. Ellie stood in the dirt, shy and motionless, knuckles in her mouth, and then she made some kind of a mental connection and launched herself into Sloop's embrace. He whirled her up into the air and hugged her. Kissed her cheek. Danced her around and around in a circle. Carmen made a small sound in her throat and looked away.

Sloop set Ellie down on the ground and looked up into the porch and smiled triumphantly. Behind him Bobby was talking to his mother and Hack Walker. They were huddled together behind the car. Sloop was holding out his hand, beckoning to his wife. She backed away from the porch rail, deep into the shadow.

"Maybe you should talk to him after all," she whispered.

"Make your mind up," Reacher whispered back.

"Let me see how it goes," she said.

She took a deep breath and forced a smile and skipped down the steps. Took Sloop's hands and folded herself into his arms. They kissed, long enough that nobody would think they were brother and sister, but not long enough that anybody would think there was real passion there. Behind the car Bobby and his mother had detached themselves from Hack and were walking around the hood and heading for the porch. Bobby had a worried look on his face and Rusty was fanning herself with her hand and looking hard in Reacher's direction, all the way up the steps.

"I hear Bobby invited you to lunch," she said quietly, at the top.

"Very gracious of him," Reacher said.

"Yes, it was. Very gracious. But it's going to be a purely family thing today."

"Is it?" Reacher said.

"Not even Hack is staying," she added, like it was final proof of something.

Reacher said nothing.

"So I'm sorry," she said. "But the maid will bring your

meals down to the bunkhouse, in the usual way. You boys can get together again tomorrow."

Reacher was silent for a long moment. Then he nodded.

"O.K.," he said. "I wouldn't want to intrude."

Rusty smiled and Bobby avoided his eye. They walked into the house and Reacher went down the steps into the yard, out into the midday heat. It was like a furnace. Hack Walker was on his own next to the Lincoln, getting ready to leave.

"Hot enough for you?" he asked, with his politician's smile.

"I'll survive," Reacher said.

"Going to be a storm."

"So people say."

Walker nodded. "Reacher, right?"

Reacher nodded. "So everything went O.K. in Abilene, I guess."

"Like clockwork," Hack said. "But I'm tired, believe me. Texas is a big, big place. You can forget that, sometimes. You can drive forever. So I'm leaving these folks to their celebrations and hitting the rack. Gratefully, let me tell you."

Reacher nodded again. "So I'll see you around, maybe."

"Don't forget to vote in November," Hack replied. "For me, preferably."

He used the same bashful expression he had used the night before. Then he paused at the car door and waved across the roof to Sloop. Sloop made a gun with his fingers and leveled it at Hack and pursed his lips like he was supplying the sound of the shot. Hack slid into the car and fired it up and backed into a turn and headed for the gate. He paused a second and made a right and accelerated away and a moment later Reacher was watching a new cone of dust drifting north along the road.

Then he turned back and saw Sloop strolling up across the yard, holding Ellie's hand in his right and Carmen's in his left. His eyes were screwed tight against the sun. Carmen was saying nothing and Ellie was saying a lot. They all walked straight past him and up the steps, three abreast. They paused at the door and Sloop turned his right shoulder to allow Ellie

in ahead of him. He followed her across the threshold and
then turned his shoulder the other way to pull Carmen in after
him. The door closed on them hard enough to raise a puff of
hot dust off the porch floorboards.

Reacher saw nobody except the maid for nearly three
hours. He stayed inside the bunkhouse and she brought him
lunch and then came back to collect the plate an hour later.
Time to time he would watch the house from the high bathroom window, but it was closed up tight and he saw nothing
at all. Then late in the afternoon he heard voices behind the
horse barn and walked up there and found Sloop and Carmen
and Ellie out and about, taking the air. It was still very hot.
Maybe hotter than ever. Sloop looked restless. He was sweating. He was scuffing his shoes through the dirt. Carmen
looked very nervous. Her face was slightly red. Maybe tension, maybe strain. Maybe the fearsome heat. But it wasn't
impossible she'd been slapped a couple of times, either.

"Ellie, come with me to see your pony," she said.

"I saw him this morning, Mommy," Ellie said.

Carmen held out her hand. "But I didn't. So let's go see
him again."

Ellie looked mystified for a second, and then she took Carmen's hand. They stepped behind Sloop and set off slowly
for the front of the barn. Carmen turned her head and
mouthed *talk to him* as she walked. Sloop turned around and
watched them go. Turned back and looked at Reacher, like he
was seeing him for the first time.

"Sloop Greer," he said, and held out his hand.

Up close, he was an older, wiser version of Bobby. A little
older, maybe a lot wiser. There was intelligence in his eyes.
Not necessarily a pleasant sort of intelligence. It wasn't hard
to imagine some cruelty there. Reacher shook his hand. It
was big-boned, but soft. It was a bully's hand, not a fighter's.

"Jack Reacher," he said. "How was prison?"

There was a split-second flash of surprise in the eyes. Then
it was replaced by instant calm. *Good self-control,* Reacher
thought.

"It was pretty awful," Sloop said. "You been in yourself?" *Quick, too.*

"On the other side of the bars from you," Reacher said.

Sloop nodded. "Bobby told me you were a cop. Now you're an itinerant worker."

"I have to be. I didn't have a rich daddy."

Sloop paused a beat. "You were military, right? In the army?"

"Right, the army."

"I never cared much for the military, myself."

"So I gathered."

"Yeah, how?"

"Well, I hear you opted out of paying for it."

Another flash in the eyes, quickly gone. *Not easy to rile,* Reacher thought. *But a spell in prison teaches anybody to keep things well below the surface.*

"Shame you spoiled it by crying uncle and getting out early."

"You think?"

Reacher nodded. "If you can't do the time, then don't do the crime."

"You got out of the army. So maybe you couldn't do the time either."

Reacher smiled. *Thanks for the opening,* he thought.

"I had no choice," he said. "Fact is, they threw me out."

"Yeah, why?"

"I broke the law, too."

"Yeah, how?"

"Some scumbag of a colonel was beating up on his wife. Nice young woman. He was a furtive type of a guy, did it all in secret. So I couldn't prove it. But I wasn't about to let him get away with it. That wouldn't have been right. Because I don't like men who hit women. So one night, I caught him on his own. No witnesses. He's in a wheelchair now. Drinks through a straw. Wears a bib, because he drools all the time."

Sloop said nothing. He was so silent, the skin at the inside corners of his eyes turned dark purple. *Walk away now,* Reacher thought, *and you're confessing it to me.* But Sloop stayed exactly where he was, very still, staring into space,

seeing nothing. Then he recovered. The eyes came back into
focus. Not quickly, but not too slowly, either. A smart guy.

"Well, that makes me feel better," he said. "About with-
holding my taxes. They might have ended up in your pocket."

"You don't approve?"

"No, I don't," Sloop said.

"Of who?"

"Either of you," Sloop said. "You, or the other guy."

Then he turned and walked away.

Reacher went back to the bunkhouse. The maid brought
him dinner and came back for the plate. Full darkness fell
outside and the night insects started up with their crazy chant.
He lay down on his bed and sweated. The temperature stayed
rock-steady around a hundred degrees. He heard isolated
coyote howls again, and cougar screams, and the invisible
beating of bats' wings.

Then he heard a light tread on the bunkhouse stair. He sat
up in time to see Carmen come up into the room. She had one
hand pressed flat on her chest, like she was out of breath, or
panicking, or both.

"Sloop talked to Bobby," she said. "For ages."

"Did he hit you?" Reacher asked.

Her hand went up to her cheek.

"No," she said.

"Did he?"

She looked away.

"Well, just once," she said. "Not hard."

"I should go break his arms."

"He called the sheriff."

"Who did?"

"Sloop."

"When?"

"Just now. He talked to Bobby, and then he called."

"About me?"

She nodded. "He wants you out of here."

"It's O.K.," Reacher said. "The sheriff won't do anything."

"You think?"

Reacher nodded. "I squared him away, before."

She paused a beat. "I've got to get back now. He thinks I'm with Ellie."

"You want me to come with you?"

"Not yet. Let me talk to him first."

"Don't let him hit you again, Carmen. Come get me, soon as you need me. Or make noise, O.K.? Scream and shout."

She started back down the stairs.

"I will," she said. "I promise. You sure about the sheriff?"

"Don't worry," he said. "The sheriff won't do a thing."

But the sheriff did one thing. He passed the problem to the state police. Reacher found that out ninety minutes later, when a Texas Ranger cruiser turned in under the gate, looking for him. Somebody directed it all the way down past the barns and in behind the bunkhouse. He heard its motor and the sound of its tires crushing the dust on the track. He got off of his bed and went down the stairs and when he got to the bottom he was lit up by the spotlight mounted in front of its windshield. It shone in past the parked farm tractors and picked him out in a bright cone of light. The car doors opened and two Rangers got out.

They were not similar to the sheriff. Not in any way. They were in a different class altogether. They were young and fit and professional. Both of them were medium height, both of them were halfway between lean and muscled. Both had military-style buzz cuts. Both had immaculate uniforms. One was a sergeant and the other was a trooper. The trooper was Hispanic. He was holding a shotgun.

"What?" Reacher called.

"Step to the hood of the car," the sergeant called back.

Reacher kept his hands clear of his body and walked to the car.

"Assume the position," the sergeant said.

Reacher put his palms on the fender and leaned down. The sheet metal was hot from the engine. The trooper covered him with the shotgun and the sergeant patted him down.

"O.K., get in the car," he said.

Reacher didn't move.

"What's this about?" he asked.

"A request from a property owner to remove a trespasser."

"I'm not a trespasser. I work here."

"Well, I guess they just terminated you. So now you're a trespasser. And we're going to remove you."

"That's a state police job?"

"Small community like this, we're on call to help the local guys, their days off, or serious crimes."

"Trespassing is a serious crime?"

"No, Sunday is the Echo sheriff's day off."

The moths had found the spotlight. They fluttered in and crowded the lens, landing and taking off again when the heat of the bulb got to them. They batted against Reacher's right arm. They felt dry and papery and surprisingly heavy.

"O.K., I'll leave," he said. "I'll walk out to the road."

"Then you'll be a vagrant on a county highway. That's against the law, too, around here, especially during the hours of darkness."

"So where are we going?"

"You have to leave the county. We'll let you out in Pecos."

"They owe me money. I never got paid."

"So get in the car. We'll stop at the house."

Reacher glanced left at the trooper, and the shotgun. Both of them looked businesslike. He glanced right, at the sergeant. He had his hand on the butt of his gun. He saw in his mind the two Greer boys, two versions of the same face, both of them grinning, smug and triumphant. But it was Rusty he saw mouthing *checkmate* at him.

"There's a problem here," he said. "The daughter-in-law is getting smacked around by her husband. It's an ongoing situation. He just got out of prison today."

"She made a complaint?"

"She's scared to. The sheriff's a good old boy and she's a Hispanic woman from California."

"Nothing we can do without a complaint."

Reacher glanced the other way at the trooper, who just shrugged.

"Like the man told you," he said. "Nothing we can do without we hear about it."

"You're hearing about it now," Reacher said. "I'm telling you."

The trooper shook his head. "Needs to come from the victim."

"Get in the car," the sergeant said.

"You don't have to do this."

"Yes, we do."

"I need to be here. For the woman's sake."

"Listen, pal, we were informed you're trespassing. So all we got is a question of whether you're wanted here, or whether you're not. And apparently, you're not."

"The woman wants me here. Like her bodyguard."

"Is she the property owner?"

"No, she isn't."

"Are you employed by her? Like officially?"

Reacher shrugged. "More or less."

"She paying you? You got a contract we can see?"

Reacher said nothing.

"So get in the car."

"She's in danger."

"We get a call, we'll come running."

"She can't call. Or if she does, the sheriff won't pass it on."

"Then there's nothing we can do. Now get in the car."

Reacher said nothing. The sergeant opened the rear door. Then he paused.

"You could come back tomorrow," he said, quietly. "No law says a man can't try to get himself rehired."

Reacher took a second look at the shotgun. It was a big handsome Ithaca with a muzzle wide enough to stick his thumb in. He took a second look at the sergeant's handgun. It was a Glock, secured into an oiled leather holster by a strap that would take about half a second to unfasten.

"But right now, get in the car."

Checkmate.

"O.K.," Reacher said. "But I'm not happy."

"Very few of our passengers are," the sergeant said back.

He used his hand on the top of Reacher's head and folded

him into the back seat. It was cold in there. There was a
heavy wire barrier in front of him. Either side, the door handles and the window winders had been removed. Small
squares of aluminum had been riveted over the holes in the
trim. The seat was vinyl. There was a smell of disinfectant
and a heavy stink from an air freshener shaped like a pine
tree hanging from the mirror in front. There was a radar device built up on top of the dash and quiet radio chatter coming from a unit underneath it.

The sergeant and the trooper swung in together in front and
drove him up to the house. All the Greers except Ellie were on
the porch to see him go. They were standing in a line at the
rail, first Rusty, then Bobby, then Sloop and Carmen. They
were all smiling. All except Carmen. The sergeant stopped the
car at the foot of the steps and buzzed his window down.

"This guy says you owe him wages," he called.

There was silence for a second. Just the sound of the insects.

"So tell him to sue us," Bobby called back.

Reacher leaned forward to the metal grille.

"¡Carmen!" he shouted. "¡Si hay un problema, llama di-
rectamente a estos hombres!"

The sergeant turned his head. "What?"

"Nothing."

"So what do you want to do?" the sergeant asked. "About
your money?"

"Forget about it," Reacher said.

The sergeant buzzed his window up again and pulled out toward the gate. Reacher craned his neck and saw them all turn to
watch him go, all except for Carmen, who stood absolutely still
and stared rigidly ahead at the spot where the car had just been.
The sergeant made a right onto the road and Reacher turned his
head the other way and saw them all filing back into the house.
Then the sergeant accelerated hard and they were lost to sight.

"What was that you called out to them?" he asked.

Reacher said nothing. The trooper answered for him.

"It was Spanish," he said. "For the woman. It meant 'Carmen, if there's trouble, call these guys direct.' Terrible accent."

Reacher said nothing.

* * *

They drove the same sixty miles he had covered the other way in the white Cadillac, back to the crossroads hamlet with Ellie's school and the gas station and the old diner. The sergeant stuck to a lazy fifty-five all the way, and it took an hour and five minutes. When they got there, everything was closed up tight. There were lights burning in two of the houses, and nothing else. Then they drove the stretch where Carmen had chased the school bus. Nobody talked. Reacher sprawled sideways on the vinyl bench and watched the darkness. Another twenty minutes north he saw the turn where Carmen had come down out of the hills. They didn't take it. They just kept on going, heading for the main highway, and then Pecos beyond it.

They never got there. The radio call came in a mile short of the county line. An hour and thirty-five minutes into the ride. The call was bored and laconic and loud with static. A woman dispatcher's voice.

"Blue Five, Blue Five," it said.

The trooper unhooked the microphone and stretched the cord and clicked the switch.

"Blue Five, copy, over," he said.

"Required at the Red House Ranch immediately, sixty miles south of north Echo crossroads, domestic disturbance reported, over."

"Copy, nature of incident, over?"

"Unclear at this time, believed violent, over."

"Well, shit," the sergeant said.

"Copy, on our way, out," the trooper said. He replaced the microphone. Turned around. "So she understood your Spanish. I guess your accent wasn't too far off, after all."

Reacher said nothing. The sergeant turned his head.

"Look on the bright side, pal," he said. "Now we can do something about it."

"I warned you," Reacher said. "And you should have damn well listened to me. So if she's hurt bad, it's on you. Pal."

The sergeant said nothing to that. Just jammed on the

brakes and pulled a wide slow turn across the whole of the road, shoulder to shoulder. Got it pointing straight south again and hustled. He got it up to a hundred on the straightaways, kept it at ninety on the curves. He didn't use the lights or the siren. Didn't even slow at the crossroads. He didn't need to. The chances of meeting traffic on that road were worse than winning the lottery.

They were back again exactly two hours and thirty minutes after they left. Ninety-five minutes north, fifty-five minutes south. First thing they saw was the sheriff's secondhand cruiser, dumped at an angle in the yard, door open, light bar flashing. The sergeant slewed through the dirt and jammed to a stop right behind it.

"Hell's he doing here?" he said. "It's his day off."

There was nobody in sight. The trooper opened his door. The sergeant shut down the motor and did the same.

"Let me out," Reacher said.

"No dice, pal," the sergeant said back. "You stay right there."

They got out and walked together to the porch steps. They went up. Across the boards. They pushed the door. It was open. They went inside. The door swung shut behind them. Reacher waited. Five minutes. Seven. Ten. The car grew warm. Then hot. There was silence. No sound at all beyond random static from the radio and the ticking of the insects.

The trooper came out alone after about twelve minutes. Walked slowly back to his side of the car and opened his door and leaned in for the microphone.

"Is she O.K.?" Reacher asked.

The guy nodded, sourly.

"She's fine," he said. "At least physically. But she's in a shitload of trouble."

"Why?"

"Because the call wasn't about *him* attacking *her*. It was the other way around. She shot him. He's dead. So we just arrested her."

10

The trooper clicked the microphone and called in for backup and an ambulance. Then he dictated an interim report to the dispatcher. He used the words *gunshot wounds* twice and *homicide* three times.

"Hey," Reacher called to him. "Stop calling it homicide on the radio."

"Why?"

"Because it was self-defense. He was beating her. We all need to get that straight, from the start."

"Not for me to say. You, either."

Reacher shook his head. "It *is* for you to say. Because what you say now counts for something, later. You put it in people's heads it's a homicide, it'll be tough for her. Better that everybody's real clear from the start about what it is."

"I don't have that kind of influence."

"Yes, you do."

"How would *you* know what kind of influence I have?"

"Because I *was* you, once upon a time. I was a cop, in the military. I called things in. I know how it works."

The trooper said nothing.

"She's got a kid," Reacher said. "You should remember that. So she needs minimum bail, and she needs it tonight. You can influence that for her."

"She shot him," the trooper said. "She should have thought about all that before."

"The guy was beating up on her. It was self-defense."

The trooper said nothing.

"Give her a break, O.K.? Don't make her a victim twice over."

"*She's* the victim? Her husband is the one lying there dead."

"You should have sympathy. You must know how it is for her."

"Why? What's the connection between her and me?"

Now it was Reacher who said nothing.

"You think I should cut her a break just because I'm Hispanic and she is too?"

"You wouldn't be cutting her a break," Reacher said. "You'd be being accurate, is all. She needs your help."

The trooper hung up the microphone.

"Now you're offending me," he said.

He backed out of the car and slammed the door. Walked away, up to the house again. Reacher glanced through the window to his right, toward the rocky land west of the compound, full of regret. *I knew how it would be,* he thought. *I should have made her leave the damn gun up there on the mesa. Or I should have taken care of the whole thing myself.*

The state cops stayed inside the house and Reacher saw nothing until the backup arrived more than an hour later. It was an identical cruiser with another trooper driving and another sergeant riding alongside him. This time the trooper was white and the sergeant was Hispanic. They got out of their car and walked straight into the house. The heat and the quiet came back. There were animal howls in the far distance and the whisper of insects and the beating of invisible wings. Lights came on in some of the house windows and then snapped off again. After twenty minutes, the Echo sheriff left. He came out of the house and stumbled down the porch steps to his car. He looked tired and disoriented. His shirt was dark with sweat. He maneuvered his cruiser out from behind the tangle of police vehicles and drove away.

Another hour later, the ambulance came. It had its emergency lights on. Reacher saw the night pulsing red far to the south and then bright headlight beams and a boxy vehicle painted red and gold and white lurching in through the gate. It was marked Presidio Fire Department. Maybe it was the same truck Billy had called the night before. It turned a slow circle in the yard and backed up to the porch steps. The crew got out lazily and stretched and yawned in the dark. They knew they weren't about to be called on for their paramedic skills.

They opened the rear doors and took out a rolling gurney and the backup sergeant met them on the steps and led them inside. Reacher was sweating inside the car. It was airless and hot. He traced in his mind the medics walking through the interior hallways to the bedroom. Attending to the corpse. Lifting it onto the gurney. Rolling the gurney out. It was going to be difficult to handle. There were narrow stairs and tight corners.

But they came back out about as fast as was feasible and lifted the gurney down the porch steps. Sloop Greer was just a large heavy shape on it, wound into a white sheet. The medics lined up the gurney with the rear of the ambulance and pushed. The wheels folded up and the gurney slid inside and the medics closed the doors on it.

Then they stood around in a group with three of the cops. The trooper who Reacher had offended wasn't there. He must have been guarding Carmen, somewhere inside the house. The three cops out in the yard were slow and relaxed. The excitement was over. The deal was done. So they were standing there a little deflated, and maybe a little disappointed, like cops often get, like something had happened they were supposed to prevent from happening. Reacher knew exactly how they felt.

They talked for a couple of minutes and then the ambu-

lance crew climbed back into their cab and bounced their vehicle across the yard to the gate. It paused there for a second
and turned right and headed slowly north. The cops watched
it until it was gone and then they turned together and headed
back inside the house. Five minutes later they came out
again, all four of them, and this time they brought Carmen
with them.

She was dressed in the same jeans and shirt. Her hair was
heavy with water. Her hands were cuffed behind her back. Her
head was down and her face was pale and filmed with sweat
and her eyes were blank. The backup cops held an elbow
each. They brought her down the steps slowly and clumsily,
three people moving out of step. They stopped and regrouped
in the dirt and walked her over to their cruiser. The trooper
opened the rear door and the sergeant placed a hand on the top
of her head and folded her inside. She offered no resistance.
She was completely passive. Reacher saw her shuffle sideways on the seat, looking awkward and uncomfortable with
her hands trapped behind her. Then she hitched her feet in after her, pointing her toes, suddenly looking elegant again. The
trooper waited a beat and closed the door on her and Rusty
and Bobby came out on the porch to watch her go.

Rusty's hair was a mess, like she'd been to bed and gotten
up again. She was wearing a short satin robe that shone in the
porch lights. It was white, and below it her legs were as pale
as the fabric. Bobby was behind her. He was in jeans and a T-
shirt, and he was barefoot. They pressed up against the porch
rail. Both of their faces were pale and stunned. Their eyes
were wide and blank and staring.

The backup cops climbed into their cruiser and started it
up. The first two slid into the front of Reacher's car and did
the same. They waited for the backup to ease ahead and then
followed it out to the gate. Reacher turned his head and saw
Rusty and Bobby craning to watch them go. The cars paused
and turned right together and accelerated north. Reacher
turned his head the other way and the last thing he saw was
Ellie stumbling out onto the porch. She was in her rabbit pajamas and was carrying a small bear in her left hand and had
the knuckles of her right pressed hard into her mouth.

* * *

The inside of the cop car cooled right down after about a mile. There was an aperture in the wire grille in front of him and if he sat in the middle of the seat and ducked his head he could line it up with the view through the windshield above the radar unit and below the mirror. It was like watching a movie unfold in front of him. The backup car swayed in the headlight beams, close and vivid and unreal in the intense dusty blackness all around it. He couldn't see Carmen. Maybe she was slumped down in the seat and her head was hidden behind the police lights stacked along the rear shelf, behind the glass.

"Where are they taking her?" he called.

The sergeant shifted in his seat. Answered a hundred yards later.

"Pecos," he said. "County jail."

"But this is Echo," Reacher said. "Not Pecos."

"There are a hundred and fifty people in Echo County. You think they operate a separate jurisdiction just for them? With jails and all? And courthouses?"

"So how does it work?"

"Pecos picks it up, that's how it works. For all the little counties, around and about. All the administrative functions."

Reacher was quiet for a beat.

"Well, that's going to be a real big problem," he said.

"Why?"

"Because Hack Walker is the Pecos DA. And he was Sloop Greer's best buddy. So he'll be prosecuting the person who shot his friend."

"Worried about a conflict of interest?"

"Aren't you?"

"Not really," the sergeant said. "We know Hack. He's not a fool. He sees some defense counsel about to nail him for an impropriety, he'll pass on it. He'll have to. What's the word, excuse himself?"

"Recuse," Reacher said.

"Whatever. He'll give it to an assistant. And I think both

the Pecos ADAs are women, actually. So the self-defense thing will get some sympathy."

"It doesn't need sympathy," Reacher said. "It's plain as day."

"And Hack's running for judge in November," the sergeant said. "Bear that in mind. Lots of Mexican votes in Pecos County. He won't let anybody do anything that'll give her lawyer a chance to make him look bad in the newspaper. So she's lucky, really. A Mexican woman shoots a white man in Echo, gets tried for it by a woman ADA in Pecos, couldn't be better for her."

"She's from California," Reacher said. "She's not Mexican."

"But she looks Mexican," the sergeant said. "That's what's important to a guy who needs votes in Pecos County."

The two state police cruisers drove on in convoy. They caught and passed the ambulance just short of the school and the gas station and the diner at the crossroads. Left it lumbering north in their wake.

"The morgue's in Pecos, too," the sergeant said. "One of the oldest institutions in town, I guess. They needed it right from the get-go. Pecos was that kind of a place."

Reacher nodded, behind him.

"Carmen told me," he said. "It was the real Wild West."

"You going to stick around?"

"I guess so. I need to see she's O.K. She told me there's a museum in town. Things to see. Somebody's grave."

"Clay Allison's," the sergeant said. "Some old gunslinger."

"Never killed a man who didn't need killing."

The sergeant nodded in the mirror. "That could be her position, right? She could call it the Clay Allison defense."

"Why not?" Reacher said. "It was justifiable homicide, any way you cut it."

The sergeant said nothing to that.

"Should be enough to make bail, at least," Reacher said. "She's got a kid back there. She needs bail, like tomorrow."

The sergeant glanced in the mirror again.

"Tomorrow could be tough," he said. "There's a dead guy in the picture, after all. Who's her lawyer?"

"Hasn't got one."

"She got money for one?"

"No."

"Well, shit," the sergeant said.

"What?" Reacher asked.

"How old is the kid?"

"Six and a half."

The sergeant went quiet.

"What?" Reacher asked again.

"Having no lawyer is a big problem, is what. Kid's going to be seven and a half before mom even gets a bail *hearing*."

"She'll get a lawyer, right?"

"Sure, Constitution says so. But the question is, when? This is Texas."

"You ask for a lawyer, you don't get one right away?"

"Not right away. You wait a long, long time. You get one when the indictment comes back. And that's how old Hack Walker is going to avoid his little conflict problem, isn't it? He'll just lock her up and forget about her. He'd be a fool not to. She's got no lawyer, who's to know? Could be Christmas before they get around to indicting her. By which time old Hack will be a judge, most likely, not a prosecutor. He'll be long gone. No more conflict of interest. Unless he happens to pull the case later, whereupon he'd have to excuse himself anyway."

"Recuse."

"Whatever, not having her own lawyer changes everything."

The trooper in the passenger seat turned and spoke for the first time in an hour.

"See?" he said. "Didn't matter what I called it on the radio."

"So don't you spend your time at the museum," the sergeant said. "You want to help her, you go find her a lawyer. You go beg, borrow or steal her one."

Nobody spoke the rest of the way into Pecos County. They crossed under Interstate 10 and followed the backup car

across more empty blackness all the way to Interstate 20,
about a hundred miles west of where Reacher had forced his
way out of Carmen's Cadillac sixty hours previously. The
sergeant slowed the car and let the backup disappear ahead
into the darkness. He braked and pulled off onto the shoulder
a hundred yards short of the cloverleaf.

"We're back on patrol from here," he said. "Time to let you
out."

"Can't you drive me to the jail?"

"You're not going to jail. You haven't done anything. And
we're not a taxicab company."

"So where am I?"

The sergeant pointed straight ahead.

"Downtown Pecos," he said. "Couple miles, that way."

"Where's the jail?"

"Crossroads before the railroad. In the courthouse basement."

The sergeant opened his door and slid out and stretched.
Stepped back and opened Reacher's door with a flourish.
Reacher slid out feet first and stood up. It was still hot. Haze hid
the stars. Lonely vehicles whined by on the highway bridge,
few enough in number that absolute silence descended between
each one. The shoulder was sandy, and stunted velvet mesquite
and wild indigo struggled at its margin. The cruiser's headlights
picked out old dented beer cans tangled among the stalks.

"You take care now," the sergeant said.

He climbed back into his seat and slammed his door. The
car crunched its way back to the blacktop and curved to the
right, onto the cloverleaf, up onto the highway. Reacher
stood and watched its taillights disappear in the east. Then he
set off walking north, under the overpass, toward the neon
glow of Pecos.

He walked through one pool of light after another, along a
strip of motels that got smarter and more expensive the farther he moved away from the highway. Then there was a
rodeo arena set back from the street with posters still in place
from a big event a month ago. *There's a rodeo there in July,*

Carmen had said. *But you've missed it for this year.* He walked in the road because the sidewalks had long tables set up on them, like outdoor market stalls. They were all empty. But he could smell cantaloupe on the hot night air. *The sweetest in the whole of Texas,* she had said. *Therefore in their opinion, in the whole of the world.* He guessed an hour before dawn old trucks would roll in loaded with ripe fruit from the fields, maybe hosed down with irrigation water to make it look dewy and fresh and attractive. Maybe the old trucks would have whole families crammed in the cabs ready to unload and sell all day and find out whether their winter was going to be good or bad, lean or prosperous. But really he knew nothing at all about agriculture. All his ideas came from the movies. Maybe it was all different in reality. Maybe there were government subsidies involved, or giant corporations.

Beyond the cantaloupe market was a pair of eating places. There was a doughnut shop, and a pizza parlor. Both of them were dark and closed up tight. Sunday, the middle of the night, miles from anywhere. At the end of the strip was a crossroads, with a sign showing the museum was straight across. But before the turn, on the right, was the courthouse. It was a nice enough building, but he didn't spend any time looking at it. Just ducked around the side to the back. No jail he had ever seen had an entrance on the street. There was a lit doorway in the back wall at semi-basement level with two cement steps leading down from a parking area. There was a dusty four-cylinder Chevrolet in one corner. The lot was fenced with razor wire and hung with large notices warning unauthorized parkers their cars would be towed. There were yellow lightbulbs mounted on the fence posts. Clouds of silent insects crowded each of them. The blacktop was still hot under his feet. No cooling breezes back there. The jail door was scarred steel and had No Admittance stenciled across it in faded paint. Above it was a small video camera angled down, with a red diode glowing above the lens.

He went down the steps and knocked hard on the door. Stepped back a pace so the camera could pick him up. Nothing happened for a long moment. He stepped forward and knocked again. There was the click of a lock and a woman opened the door. She was dressed in a court bailiff's uniform. She was white, maybe fifty, with gray hair dyed the color of sand. She had a wide belt loaded with a gun and a nightstick and a can of pepper spray. She was heavy and slow, but she looked awake and on the ball.

"Yes?" she said.

"You got Carmen Greer in here?"

"Yes."

"Can I see her?"

"No."

"Not even for a minute?"

"Not even."

"So when can I?"

"You family?"

"I'm a friend."

"Not a lawyer, right?"

"No."

"Then Saturday," the woman said. "Visiting is Saturday, two to four."

Almost a week.

"Can you write that down for me?" he said. He wanted to get inside. "Maybe give me a list of what I'm allowed to bring her?"

The bailiff shrugged and turned and stepped inside. Reacher followed her into the dry chill of an air conditioner running on high. There was a lobby. The bailiff had a high desk, like a lectern. Like a barrier. Behind it were cubbyholes covering the back wall. He saw Carmen's lizard-skin belt rolled into one of them. There was a small Ziploc bag with the fake ring in it. Off to the right was a barred door. A tiled corridor beyond.

"How is she?" he asked.

The bailiff shrugged again. "She ain't happy."

"About what?"

"About the cavity search, mainly. She was screaming fit to burst. But rules are rules. And what, she thinks I enjoy it either?"

She pulled a mimeographed sheet from a stack. Slid it across the top of the desk.

"Saturday, two to four," she said. "Like I told you. And don't bring her anything that's not on the list, or we won't let you in."

"Where's the DA's office?"

She pointed at the ceiling. "Second floor. Go in the front."

"When does it open?"

"About eight-thirty."

"You got bail bondsmen in the neighborhood?"

She smiled. "Ever see a courthouse that didn't? Turn left at the crossroads."

"What about lawyers?"

"Cheap lawyers or expensive lawyers?"

"Free lawyers."

She smiled again.

"Same street," she said. "That's all it is, bondsmen and community lawyers."

"Sure I can't see her?"

"Saturday, you can see her all you want."

"Not now? Not even for a minute?"

"Not even."

"She's got a daughter," Reacher said, irrelevantly.

"Breaks my heart," the woman said back.

"When will you see her?"

"Every fifteen minutes, whether she likes it or not. Suicide watch, although I don't think your friend is the type. You can tell pretty easy. And she's a tough cookie. That's my estimation. But rules are rules, right?"

"Tell her Reacher was here."

"Who?"

"Reacher. Tell her I'll stick around."

The woman nodded, like she'd seen it all, which she probably had.

"I'm sure she'll be thrilled," she said.

Then Reacher walked back to the motel strip, remembering all the jailhouse duty he'd pulled early in his career, wishing he could put his hand on his heart and say he'd acted a whole lot better than the woman he'd just met.

He walked almost all the way back to the highway, until the prices ducked under thirty bucks. Picked a place and woke the night clerk and bought the key to a room near the end of the

row. It was worn and faded and crusted with the kind of dirt
that shows the staff isn't all the way committed to excellence.
The bedding was limp and the air smelled dank and hot, like
they saved power by turning the air conditioning off when the
room wasn't rented. But it was serviceable. One advantage of
being ex-military was almost any place was serviceable.
There was always somewhere worse to compare it with.

He slept restlessly until seven in the morning and showered in tepid water and went out for breakfast at the doughnut
shop halfway back to the courthouse. It was open early and
advertised Texas-sized doughnuts. They were larger than
normal, and more expensive. He ate two with three cups of
coffee. Then he went looking for clothes. Since he ended his
brief flirtation with owning a house he had gone back to his
preferred system of buying cheap items and junking them instead of laundering them. It worked well for him. It kept the
permanence monkey off his back, literally.

He found a cheap store that had already been open an hour.
It sold a little bit of everything, from bales of cheap toilet paper to work boots. He found a rack of chinos with the brand
labels cut out. Maybe they were flawed. Maybe they were
stolen. He found the right size and paired them with a khaki
shirt. It was thin and cut loose like something from Hawaii,
but it was plain, and it cost less than a Texas-sized doughnut.
He found white underwear. The store had no fitting rooms. It
wasn't that kind of a place. He talked the clerk into letting
him use the staff bathroom. He put on the new gear and transferred his stuff from pocket to pocket. He still had the eight
shell cases from Carmen's Lorcin, rattling around like loose
change. He weighed them in his hand and then dropped them
in his new pants pocket.

He balled up the old clothes and stuffed them in the bathroom trash. Went back out to the register and paid thirty
bucks in cash. He might get three days out of it. Ten bucks a
day, just for clothes, made no sense at all until you figured a
washing machine cost four hundred and a dryer another three
and the basement to put them in implied a house, which cost
at least a hundred grand to buy and then tens of thousands a
year in taxes and maintenance and insurance and associated

bullshit. Then ten bucks a day for clothes suddenly made all the sense in the world.

He waited on the sidewalk until eight o'clock, leaning against a wall under an awning to stay out of the sun. He figured the bailiffs would change shifts at eight. That would be normal. And sure enough at five minutes past he saw the heavy woman drive herself out of the lot in the dusty four-cylinder Chevrolet. She made a left and drove right past him. He crossed the street and walked down the side of the courthouse again. *If the night shift won't help you, maybe the day shift will.* Night workers are always tougher. Less regular contact with the public, less immediate supervision, makes them think they're king of the castle.

But the day worker was just as bad. He was a man, a little younger, a little thinner, but otherwise the exact equivalent of his opposite number. The conversation was just the same. *Can I see her? No. When, then? Saturday. Is she O.K.? As well as can be expected.* It sounded like something you would hear in front of a hospital, from a cautious spokesperson. The guy confirmed that only lawyers were allowed unrestricted access to the prisoners. So Reacher came back up the steps and went out looking for a lawyer.

It was clear that the events of the previous night had left the red house stunned and quiet. And depopulated, which suited the killing crew just fine. The ranch hands weren't there, the tall stranger was gone, and Carmen Greer was gone. And her husband, obviously. That left just the old woman, the second son, and the granddaughter. Three of them, all at home. It was Monday, but the kid hadn't gone to school. The bus came and went without her. She just hung around, in and out of the barn. She looked confused and listless. They all did. Which made them easier to watch. Better targets.

The two men were behind a rock, opposite the ranch gate, well hidden and elevated about twenty feet up the slope. Their view was good enough. The woman had dropped them three hundred yards north and driven back toward Pecos.

"When do we do this?" they had asked her.
"When I say," she had replied.

Reacher turned left at the crossroads in the center of Pecos
and followed a street that ran parallel with the railroad tracks.
He passed the bus depot and hit a strip that might have started
out as anything but now was made up entirely of low-rent operations serving the courthouse population, bail bondsmen
and storefront legal missions, like the night shift woman had
said. The legal missions all had rows of desks facing the store
windows with customer chairs in front of them and waiting
areas inside the doors. All of them were grimy and undeco-
rated and messy, with piles of files everywhere, and notes and
memos taped and tacked to the walls next to the desks.
Twenty past eight in the morning, they were all busy. They all
had patient knots of people waiting inside and anxious clients
perched on the customer chairs. Some of the clients were on
their own, but most of them were in family groups, some of
them with a bunch of children. All of them were Hispanic. So
were some of the lawyers, but overall they were a mixed
bunch. Men, women, young, old, bright, defeated. The only
thing they had in common was they all looked harassed to the
breaking point.

He chose the only establishment that had an empty chair in
front of a lawyer. It was halfway down the street and the chair
was way in back of the store and the lawyer was a young
white woman of maybe twenty-five with thick dark hair cut
short. She had a good tan and was wearing a white sports bra
instead of a shirt and there was a leather jacket slung over the
back of her chair. She was nearly hidden behind two tall
stacks of files. She was on the phone, and she was at the point
of tears.

He approached her desk and waited for a *sit down* gesture.
He didn't get one, but he sat down anyway. She glanced at
him and glanced away. Kept on talking into the phone. She
had dark eyes and white teeth. She was talking slow Spanish
with an East Coast accent, haltingly enough that he could follow most of it. She was saying *yes, we won.* Then *but he*

won't pay. He simply won't. He just refuses. Time to time she would stop and listen to whoever was on the other end. Then she would repeat herself. *We won, but he still won't pay.* Then she listened again. The question must have been *so what do we do now,* because she said *we go back to court, to enforce the judgment.* Then the question was obviously *how long does that take* because she went very quiet and said *a year. Maybe two.* Reacher heard clear silence at the other end and watched the woman's face. She was upset and embarrassed and humiliated. Blinking back tears of bitter frustration. She said, *"Llamaré de nuevo más tarde"* and hung up. *I'll call again soon.*

Then she faced front and closed her eyes and breathed deeply through her nose, in and out, in and out. She rested her hands palms-down on the desk. Breathed some more. Maybe it was a relaxation technique they taught you in law school. But it didn't seem to be working. She opened her eyes and dropped a file into a drawer and focused between the piles of paper across the desk at Reacher.

"Problem?" he asked her.

She shrugged and nodded all at the same time. An all-purpose expression of misery.

"Winning the case is only half the battle," she said. "Sometimes, a lot less than half, believe me."

"So what happened?"

She shook her head. "We don't need to go into it."

"Some guy won't pay up?" Reacher said.

She shrugged and nodded again.

"A rancher," she said. "Crashed his car into my client's truck. Injured my client and his wife and two of his children. It was early in the morning. He was on his way back from a party, drunk. They were on their way to market. It was harvest time and they couldn't work the fields and they lost their whole crop."

"Cantaloupe?"

"Bell peppers, actually. Rotted on the vine. We sued and won twenty thousand dollars. But the guy won't pay. He just refuses. He's waiting them out. He plans to starve them back to Mexico, and he will, because if we have to go back to court it'll take at least another year and they can't live another whole year on fresh air, can they?"

"They didn't have insurance?"

"Premiums are way too expensive. These people are barely scratching a living. All we could do was proceed directly against the rancher. Solid case, well presented, and we won. But the old guy is sitting tight, with a big smirk on his damn face."

"Tough break," Reacher said.

"Unbelievable," she said. "The things these people go through, you just wouldn't believe it. This family I'm telling you about, the border patrol killed their eldest son."

"They did?"

She nodded. "Twelve years ago. They were illegals. Paid their life savings to some guide to get them here, and he just abandoned them in the desert. No food, no water, they're holing up in the daytime and walking north at night, and a patrol chases them in the dark with rifles and kills their eldest boy. They bury him and walk on."

"Anything get done about it?"

"Are you kidding? They were illegals. They couldn't do anything. It happened all the time. Everybody's got a story like that. And now they're settled and been through the immigration amnesty, we try to get them to trust the law, and then something like this happens. I feel like such a fool."

"Not your fault."

"It is my fault. I should know better. *Trust us,* I tell them."

She went quiet and Reacher watched her try to recover.

"Anyway," she said, and then nothing more. She looked away. She was a good-looking woman. It was very hot. There was a single air conditioner stuck in the fanlight over the door, a big old thing, a long way away. It was doing its best.

"Anyway," she said again. Looked at him. "How can I help you?"

"Not me," Reacher said. "A woman I know."

"She needs a lawyer?"

"She shot her husband. He was abusing her."

"When?"

"Last night. She's across the street, in jail."

"Is he dead?"

Reacher nodded. "As a doornail."

Her shoulders sagged. She opened a drawer and took out a yellow pad.

"What's your name?" she asked.

"My name?"

"You're the one talking to me."

"Reacher," he said. "What's your name?"

She wrote "Reacher" on the pad, first line.

"Alice," she said. "Alice Amanda Aaron."

"You should go into private practice. You'd be first in the Yellow Pages."

She smiled, just a little.

"One day, I will," she said. "This is a five-year bargain with my conscience."

"Paying your dues?"

"Atoning," she said. "For my good fortune. For going to Harvard Law. For coming from a family where twenty thousand dollars is a month's common charge on the Park Avenue co-op instead of life or death during the winter in Texas."

"Good for you, Alice," he said.

"So tell me about your woman friend."

"She's of Mexican heritage and her husband was white. Her name is Carmen Greer and her husband was Sloop Greer."

"Sloop?"

"Like a boat."

"O.K.," Alice said, and wrote it all down.

"The abuse stopped for the last year and a half because he was in prison for tax evasion. He got out yesterday and started it up again and she shot him."

"O.K."

"Evidence and witnesses are going to be hard to find. The abuse was covert."

"Injuries?"

"Fairly severe. But she always passed them off as accidental, to do with horses."

"Horses?"

"Like she fell off of them."

"Why?"

Reacher shrugged. "I don't know. Family dynamic, coercion, shame, fear, embarrassment, maybe."

"But there's no doubt the abuse happened?"

"Not in my mind."

Alice stopped writing. Stared down at the yellow paper.

"Well, it's not going to be easy," she said. "Texas law isn't *too* far behind the times on spousal abuse, but I'd prefer lots of clear evidence. But his spell in prison helps us. Not a model citizen, is he? We could plead it down to involuntary manslaughter. Maybe settle for time served, with probation. If we work hard, we stand a chance."

"It was justifiable homicide, not manslaughter."

"I'm sure it was, but it's a question of what will work, and what won't."

"And she needs bail," Reacher said. "Today."

Alice looked up from the paper and stared at him.

"Bail?" she repeated, like it was a foreign word. "Today? Forget about it."

"She's got a kid. A little girl, six and a half."

She wrote it down.

"Doesn't help," she said. "Everybody's got kids."

She ran her fingers up and down the tall stacks of files.

"They've all got kids," she said again. "Six and a half, one and a half, two kids, six, seven, ten."

"She's called Ellie," Reacher said. "She needs her mother."

Alice wrote "Ellie" on the pad, and connected it with an arrow to "Carmen Greer."

"Only two ways to get bail in a case like this," she said. "First way is we stage essentially the whole trial at the bail hearing. And we're not ready to do that. It'll be months before I can even *start* working on it. My calendar is totally full. And even when I *can* start, it'll take months to prepare, in these circumstances."

"What circumstances?"

"Her word against a dead man's reputation. If we've got no eyewitnesses, we'll have to subpoena her medical records and find experts who can testify her injuries weren't caused by falling off horses. And clearly she's got no money, or you wouldn't be in here on her behalf, so we're going to have to find some experts who'll appear for free. Which isn't impossible, but it can't be done in a hurry."

"So what can be done in a hurry?"

"I can run over to the jail and say 'Hi, I'm your lawyer, I'll see you again in a year.' That's about all can be done in a hurry."

Reacher glanced around the room. It was teeming with people.

"Nobody else will be faster," Alice said. "I'm relatively new here. I've got less of a backlog."

It seemed to be true. She had just two head-high stacks of files on her desk. The others all had three or four or five.

"What's the second way?"

"Of what?"

"Getting bail. You said there were two ways."

She nodded. "Second way is we convince the DA not to oppose it. If we stand up and ask for bail and he stands up and says he has no objection, then all that matters is whether the judge thinks it's appropriate. And the judge will be influenced by the DA's position, probably."

"Hack Walker was Sloop Greer's oldest buddy."

Alice's shoulder's sagged again.

"Great," she said. "He'll recuse himself, obviously. But his staff will go to bat for him. So forget bail. It isn't going to happen."

"But will you take the case?"

"Sure I will. That's what we do here. We take cases. So I'll call Hack's office, and I'll go see Carmen. But that's all I can do right now. You understand? Apart from that, right now taking the case is the same thing as not taking the case."

Reacher sat still for a second. Then he shook his head.

"Not good enough, Alice," he said. "I want you to get to work right now. Make something happen."

"I can't," she said. "Not for months. I told you that."

She went quiet and he watched her for a second more.

"You interested in a deal?" he asked.

"A deal?"

"Like I help you, you help me."

"How can you help me?"

"There are things I could do for you. Like, I could recover the twenty grand for your pepper growers. Today. And then you could start work for Carmen Greer. Today."

"What are you, a debt collector?"

"No, but I'm a quick learner. It's probably not rocket science."

"I can't let you do that. It's probably illegal. Unless you're registered somewhere."

"Just suppose the next time you saw me I was walking back in here with a check for twenty grand in my pocket?"

"How would you do that?"

He shrugged. "I'd just go ask the guy for it."

"And that would work?"

"It might," he said.

She shook her head. "It would be unethical."

"As opposed to what?"

She didn't answer for a long time. Just stared off somewhere behind his head. But then he saw her glance down at the phone. He saw her rehearsing the good news call in her mind.

"Who's the rancher?" he asked.

She glanced at the drawer. Shook her head again.

"I can't tell you," she said. "I'm worried about the ethics."

"I'm offering," he said. "You're not asking."

She sat still.

"I'm volunteering," he said. "Like a paralegal assistant."

She looked straight at him.

"I have to go to the bathroom," she said.

She stood up suddenly and walked away. She was wearing denim shorts, and she was taller than he had guessed. Short shorts, long legs. A fine tan. Walking, she looked pretty good from the back. She went through a door in the rear wall of the old store. He stood up and leaned over the desk and pulled open the drawer. Lifted the top file out and reversed it so he could read it. It was full of legal paper. He shuffled through to some kind of a deposition printed on a single sheet. There was a name and address typed neatly in a box labeled "Defendant." He folded the paper into quarters and put it in his shirt pocket. Closed the file and dropped it back in the drawer. Hooked the drawer shut and sat down again. A moment later Alice Amanda Aaron came out through the rear door and walked back to the desk. She looked pretty good from the front, too.

"Any place around here I can borrow a car?" he asked her.

"You don't have one?"

He shook his head.

"Well, you can borrow mine, I guess," she said. "It's in the lot, behind the building."

She fiddled in her jacket pocket, behind her. Came out with a set of keys.

"It's a VW," she said.

He took the keys from her.

"There are maps in the glove compartment," she said. "You know, in case a person isn't familiar with the area."

He pushed back from the desk.

"Maybe I'll catch you later," he said.

She said nothing. He stood up and walked through the quiet crowd of people and out into the sun.

11

Alice's car was the only VW in the lot behind the building. It was baking in the sun right in the center, a new-shape Beetle, bright yellow in color, New York plates, about a year and a half old, and there was more than a bunch of maps in the glove compartment. There was a handgun in there, too.

It was a beautiful nickel-finished Heckler & Koch P7M10, four-inch barrel, ten .40 caliber shells. In Reacher's day the army had wanted the same thing in the 9mm blued-steel version, but the defense department had balked at the cost, which must have been about sixteen times the price of Carmen Greer's eighty-dollar Lorcin. It was a fine, fine piece. One of the best available. Maybe it was a gift from the family back on Park Avenue. Maybe the car was, too. He could just imagine it. The VW was an easy choice. The perfect graduation present. But the gun might have caused some consternation. The parents would have been sitting up there on their high floor in New York, worrying about it. *She's going to work where? With poor people? She'll need protection, surely.* So they would have researched the whole matter thoroughly and gone out and bought her the best on the market, like they would have bought her a Rolex if she had needed a watch.

Out of habit he took it apart and checked the action and re-assembled it. It was new, but it had been fired and cleaned maybe four or five times. It spoke of conscientious hours put in at the practice range. Maybe some exclusive Manhattan basement. He smiled. Slotted it back in the glove compartment under the maps. Then he racked the seat all the way back and fiddled with the key and fired the engine up and started the air running. He took the maps out of the glove compartment and spread them on the empty seat beside him. Took the folded paper from his shirt pocket and checked the maps for the rancher's address. It seemed to be somewhere north and east of town, maybe an hour away if he hustled hard.

The VW had a manual transmission with a sharp clutch and he stalled out twice before he got the hang of driving it. He felt awkward and conspicuous. The ride was firm and there was some kind of a bud vase attached to the dash, loaded with a little pink bloom that was reviving steadily as the car got colder. There was subtle perfume in the air. He had learned to drive nearly twenty-five years before, under-age and illegally, in a Marine Corps deuce-and-a-half with the driving seat six feet off the ground, and he felt about as far away from that experience as it was possible to get.

The map showed seven ways out of Pecos. He had come in on the southernmost, and it didn't have what he was looking for. So he had six to cover. His instinct led him west. The town's center of gravity seemed to be lumped to the east of the crossroads, therefore east would be definitely wrong. So he drove away from the lawyers and the bondsmen in the di-rection of El Paso and followed a slight right-hand curve and found exactly what he wanted, all spread out in front of him and receding into the distance. Every town of any size has a strip of auto dealers clustered together on one of the ap-proaches, and Pecos was no different.

He cruised up the strip and turned around and cruised back, looking for the right kind of place. There were two pos-

sibilities. Both of them had gaudy signs offering Foreign Car
Service. Both of them offered Free Loaners. He chose the
place farther out of town. It had a used car business in front
with a dozen clunkers decked with flags and low prices on
their windshields. An office in a trailer. Behind the sales lot
was a long low shed with hydraulic hoists. The floor of the
shed was oil-stained earth. There were four mechanics visible. One of them was halfway underneath a British sports car.
The other three were unoccupied. A slow start to a hot Monday morning.

He drove the yellow VW right into the shed. The three unoccupied mechanics drifted over to it. One of them looked
like a foreman. Reacher asked him to adjust the VW's clutch
so its action would be softer. The guy looked happy to be offered the work. He said it would cost forty bucks. Reacher
agreed to the price and asked for a loaner. The guy led him
behind the shed and pointed to an ancient Chrysler LeBaron
convertible. It had been white once, but now it was khaki
with age and sunlight. Reacher took Alice's gun with him,
wrapped up in her maps like a store-bought package. He
placed it on the Chrysler's passenger seat. Then he asked the
mechanic for a tow rope.

"What you want to tow?" the guy asked.

"Nothing," Reacher said. "I just want the rope, is all."

"You want a rope, but you don't want to tow anything?"

"You got it," Reacher said.

The guy shrugged and walked away. Came back with a coil
of rope. Reacher put it in the passenger footwell. Then he
drove the LeBaron back into town and out again heading north
and east, feeling a whole lot better about the day. Only a fool
would try unlicensed debt-collecting in the wilds of Texas in a
bright yellow car with New York plates and a bud vase on the
dash.

He stopped once in empty country, to unscrew the
Chrysler's plates with a penny from his pocket. He stored
them on the floor on the passenger's side, next to the coil of
rope. Put the bolts in the glove compartment. Then he drove

on, looking for his destination. He was maybe three hours
north of the Greer place, and the land looked pretty much the
same, except it was better irrigated. Grass was growing. The
mesquite had been burned back. There were cultivated acres,
with green bushes all over them. Peppers, maybe. Or cantaloupe. He had no idea. There was wild indigo on the shoulders of the road. An occasional prickly pear. No people. The
sun was high and the horizons were shimmering.

The rancher's name was listed on the legal paper as Lyndon J. Brewer. His address was just a route number, which
Alice's map showed was a stretch of road that ran about forty
miles before it disappeared into New Mexico. It was the same
sort of road as the drag heading south out of Echo down to
the Greer place, a dusty blacktop ribbon and a string of
drooping power lines punctuated by big ranch gates about
every fifteen miles. The ranches had names, which weren't
necessarily going to be the names of the owners, like the Red
House had nowhere been labeled Greer. So finding Lyndon J.
Brewer in person wasn't necessarily going to be easy.

But then it was, because the road was crossed by another
and the resulting crossroads had a line of mailboxes laid out
along a gray weathered plank and the mailboxes had people's
names and ranch names on them together. Brewer was
painted freehand in black on a white box, and Big Hat Ranch
was painted right below it.

He found the entrance to the Big Hat Ranch fifteen miles
to the north. There was a fancy iron arch, painted white, like
something you might see holding up a conservatory roof in
Charleston or New Orleans. He drove right past it and
stopped on the shoulder of the road at the foot of the next
power line pole. Got out of the car and looked straight up.
There was a big transformer can at the top of the pole where
the line split off in a T and ran away at a right angle toward
where the ranch house must be. And, looping parallel all the
way, about a foot lower down, the telephone line ran with it.

He took Alice's gun from under the maps on the passenger
seat and the rope from the footwell. Tied one end of the rope
into the trigger guard with a single neat knot. Passed twenty
feet of rope through his hands and swung the gun like a

weight. Then he clamped the rope with his left hand and
threw the gun with his right, aiming to slot it between the
phone line and the electricity supply above it. The first time,
he missed. The gun fell about a foot short and he caught it
coming down. The second time he threw a little harder and
hit it just right. The gun sailed through the gap and fell and
snagged the rope over the wire. He played the rope out over
his left palm and lowered the gun back down to himself. Un-
tied it and tossed it back into the car and clamped the looped
rope in both hands and pulled sharply. The phone line broke
at the junction box and snaked down to the ground, all the
way up to the next pole a hundred yards away.

He coiled the rope again and dropped it back in the
footwell. Got in the car and backed up and turned in under
the white-painted gate. Drove the best part of a mile down a
private driveway to a white-painted house that should have
been in a historical movie. It had four massive columns at the
front, holding up a second-story balcony. There were broad
steps leading up to a double front door. There was a tended
lawn. A parking area made from raked gravel.

He stopped the car on the gravel at the bottom of the steps
and shut off the motor. Tucked his shirt tight into the waistband of his pants. Some girl who worked as a personal trainer
had told him it made his upper body look more triangular. He
slipped the gun into his right hip pocket. Its shape showed
through nicely. Then he rolled the sleeves of his new shirt all
the way up to the shoulders. Gripped the LeBaron's wheel
and squeezed until it started to give and the veins in his biceps were standing out big and obvious. When you've got
arms bigger than most people's legs, sometimes you need to
exploit what nature has given you.

He got out of the car and went up the steps. Used a bell he
found to the right of the doors. Heard a chime somewhere
deep inside the mansion. Then he waited. He was about to
use the bell again when the left-hand door opened. There was
a maid standing there, about half the height of the door. She
was dressed in a gray uniform and looked like she came from
the Philippines.

"I'm here to see Lyndon Brewer," Reacher said.

"Do you have an appointment?" the maid said. Her English was very good.

"Yes, I do."

"He didn't tell me."

"He probably forgot," Reacher said. "I understand he's a bit of an asshole."

Her face tensed. Not with shock. She was fighting a smile.

"Who shall I announce?"

"Rutherford B. Hayes," Reacher said.

The maid paused and then smiled, finally.

"He was the nineteenth President," she said. "The one after Ulysses S. Grant. Born 1822 in Ohio. Served from 1877 until 1881. One of seven presidents from Ohio. The middle one of three consecutive."

"He's my ancestor," Reacher said. "I'm from Ohio, too. But I've got no interest in politics. Tell Mr. Brewer I work for a bank in San Antonio and we just discovered stock in his grandfather's name worth about a million dollars."

"He'll be excited about that," the maid said.

She walked away and Reacher stepped through the door in time to see her climbing a wide staircase in back of the entrance foyer. She moved neatly, without apparent effort, one hand on the rail all the way. The foyer was the size of a basketball court, and it was hushed and cool, paneled in golden hardwood polished to a deep luster by generations of maids. There was a grandfather clock taller than Reacher, ticking softly to itself once a second. An antique chaise like you see society women perched on in oil-painted portraits. Reacher wondered if it would break in the middle if he put his weight on it. He pressed on the velvet with his hand. Felt horsehair padding under it. Then the maid came back down the stairs the same way she had gone up, gliding, her body perfectly still and her hand just grazing the rail.

"He'll see you now," she said. "He's on the balcony, at the back of the house."

There was an upstairs foyer with the same dimensions and the same decor. French doors let out onto the rear balcony, which ran the whole width of the house and looked out over acres of hot grassland. It was roofed and fans turned lazily near the ceiling. There was heavy wicker furniture painted white and arranged in a group. A man sat in a chair with a small table at his right hand. The table held a pitcher and a glass filled with what looked like lemonade, but it could have been anything. The man was a bull-necked guy of about sixty. He was softened and faded from a peak that might have been impressive twenty years ago. He had plenty of white hair and a red face burned into lines and crags by the sun. He was dressed all in white. White pants, white shirt, white shoes. It looked like he was ready to go lawn bowling at some fancy country club.

"Mr. Hayes?" he called.

Reacher walked over and sat down without waiting for an invitation.

"You got children?" he asked.

"I have three sons," Brewer replied.

"Any of them at home?"

"They're all away, working."

"Your wife?"

"She's in Houston, visiting."

"So it's just you and the maid today?"

"Why do you ask?" He was impatient and puzzled, but polite, like people are when you're about to give them a million dollars.

"I'm a banker," Reacher said. "I have to ask."

"Tell me about the stock," Brewer said.

"There is no stock. I lied about that."

Brewer looked surprised. Then disappointed. Then irritated.

"Then why are you here?" he asked.

"It's a technique we use," Reacher said. "I'm really a loan officer. A person needs to borrow money, maybe he doesn't want his domestic staff to know."

"But I don't need to borrow money, Mr. Hayes."

"You sure about that?"

"Very."

"That's not what we heard."

"I'm a rich man. I lend. I don't borrow."

"Really? We heard you had problems meeting your obligations."

Brewer made the connection slowly. Shock traveled through his body to his face. He stiffened and grew redder and glanced down at the shape of the gun in Reacher's pocket, like he was seeing it for the first time. Then he put his hand down to the table and came back with a small silver bell. He shook it hard and it made a small tinkling sound.

"Maria!" he called, shaking the bell. "Maria!"

The maid came out of the same door Reacher had used. She walked soundlessly along the boards of the balcony.

"Call the police," Brewer ordered. "Dial 911. I want this man arrested."

She hesitated.

"Go ahead," Reacher said. "Make the call."

She ducked past them and into the room directly behind Brewer's chair. It was some kind of a private study, dark and masculine. Reacher heard the sound of a phone being picked up. Then the sound of rapid clicking, as she tried to make it work.

"The phones are out," she called.

"Go wait downstairs," Reacher called back.

"What do you want?" Brewer asked.

"I want you to meet your legal obligation."

"You're not a banker."

"That's a triumph of deduction."

"So what are you?"

"A guy who wants a check," Reacher said. "For twenty thousand dollars."

"You represent those . . . *people?*"

He started to stand up. Reacher put his arm out straight and shoved him back in his chair, hard enough to hurt.

"Sit still," he said.

"Why are you doing this?"

"Because I'm a compassionate guy," Reacher said. "That's why. There's a family in trouble here. They're going to be upset and worried all winter long. Disaster staring them in the face. Never knowing which day is going to bring everything

crashing down around them. I don't like to see people living
that way, whoever they are."

"They don't like it, they should get back to Mexico, where
they belong."

Reacher glanced at him, surprised.

"I'm not talking about *them,*" he said. "I'm talking about
you. Your family."

"My family?"

Reacher nodded. "I stay mad at you, they'll all suffer. A
car wreck here, a mugging there. You might fall down the
stairs, break your leg. Or your wife might. The house might
catch on fire. Lots of accidents, one after the other. You'll
never know when the next one is coming. It'll drive you
crazy."

"You couldn't get away with it."

"I'm getting away with it right now. I could start today.
With you."

Brewer said nothing.

"Give me that pitcher," Reacher said.

Brewer hesitated a moment. Then he picked it up and held
it out, like an automaton. Reacher took it. It was fancy crystal
with a cut pattern, maybe Waterford, maybe imported all the
way from Ireland. It held a quart and probably cost a thousand bucks. He balanced it on his palm and sniffed its contents. Lemonade. Then he tossed it over the edge of the
balcony. Yellow liquid arced out through the air and a second
later there was a loud crash from the patio below.

"Oops," he said.

"I'll have you arrested," Brewer said. "That's criminal
damage."

"Maybe I'll start with one of your sons," Reacher said. "Pick
one out at random and throw him off the balcony, just like that."

"I'll have you arrested," Brewer said again.

"Why? According to you, what the legal system says
doesn't matter. Or does that only apply to you? Maybe you
think you're something special."

Brewer said nothing. Reacher stood up and picked up his
chair and threw it over the rail. It crashed and splintered on
the stone below.

"Give me the check," he said. "You can afford it. You're a rich man. You just got through telling me."

"It's a matter of principle," Brewer said. "They shouldn't be here."

"And you should? Why? They were here first."

"They lost. To us."

"And now you're losing. To me. What goes around, comes around."

He bent down and picked up the silver bell from the table. It was probably an antique. Maybe French. The cup part was engraved with filigree patterns. Maybe two and a half inches in diameter. He held it with his thumb on one side and all four fingers on the other. Squeezed hard and crushed it out of shape. Then he transferred it into his palm and squashed the metal flat. Leaned over and shoved it in Brewer's shirt pocket.

"I could do that to your head," he said.

Brewer made no reply.

"Give me the check," Reacher said, quietly. "Before I lose my damn temper."

Brewer paused. Five seconds. Ten. Then he sighed.

"O.K.," he said. He led the way into the study and over to the desk. Reacher stood behind him. He didn't want any revolvers appearing suddenly out of drawers.

"Make it out to cash," he said.

Brewer wrote the check. He got the date right, he got the amount right, and he signed it.

"It better not bounce," Reacher said.

"It won't," Brewer said.

"It does, you do, too. Off the patio."

"I hope you rot in hell."

Reacher folded the check into his pocket and found the way out to the upstairs foyer. Went down the stairs and walked over to the grandfather clock. Tilted it forward until it overbalanced. It fell like a tree and smashed on the floor and stopped ticking.

The two men exfiltrated after nearly three hours. The heat was too brutal to stay longer. And they didn't really need to.

Nobody was going anywhere. That was clear. The old woman and her son stayed mostly in the house. The kid was hanging around in the barn, coming out now and then until the sun drove her back inside, once walking slowly back to the house when the maid called her to come and eat. So they gave it up and crawled north in the lee of the rocks and came out to wait on the dusty shoulder as soon as they were out of sight of the house. The woman in the Crown Vic turned up right on time. She had the air blasting and water in bottles. They drank the water and made their report.

"O.K.," the woman said. "So I guess we're ready to make our move."

"I guess we are," the dark man said.

"Sooner the better," the fair man agreed. "Let's get it done."

Reacher put the plates back on the old LeBaron as soon as he was out of sight of the Brewer house. Then he drove straight back to Pecos and reclaimed Alice Aaron's VW from the mechanics. He paid them their forty bucks without complaint, but afterward he wasn't really sure they'd done anything to the car. The clutch felt just as sharp as it had before. He stalled out twice on the way back to the legal mission.

He left it in the lot behind the building with the maps and the handgun in the glove compartment where he had found them. Entered the old store from the front and found Alice at her desk in back. She was on the phone and busy with clients. There was a whole family group in front of her. Three generations of quiet, anxious people. She had changed her clothes. Now she was wearing black high-waisted pants made out of some kind of thin cotton or linen, and a black jacket to match. The jacket made the white sports bra look like a shirt. The whole thing looked very formal. Instant attorney.

She saw him and put her hand over the phone and excused herself from her clients. She twisted away from them and he leaned down next to her.

"We've got big problems," she said quietly. "Hack Walker wants to see you."

"Me?" he said. "Why?"

"Better you hear it from him."

"Hear what? Did you meet with him?"

She nodded. "I went right over. We talked for a half hour."

"And? What did he say?"

"Better you hear it from him," she said again. "We can talk about it later, O.K.?"

There was worry in her voice. He looked at her. She turned back to the phone. The family in front of her desk leaned forward to catch her words. He took the twenty-thousand-dollar check out of his pocket and unfolded it and smoothed it on the desktop. She saw it and stopped talking. Put her hand over the phone again. Took a deep breath.

"Thanks," she said.

Now there was embarrassment in her voice. Like maybe she had reconsidered her end of the bargain. He dropped her car keys on the desk and walked back out to the sidewalk. Turned right and headed for the courthouse.

The Pecos County District Attorney's office occupied the whole of the courthouse's second floor. There was an entry door from the stairwell that led to a narrow passage that passed through a wooden gate into an open area used as a secretarial pen. Beyond that were three doors leading into three offices, one for the DA and one for each of the assistants. All the interior walls separating the offices from the pen and from each other were glass from the waist up. They had old-fashioned venetian blinds covering the glass, with wide wooden slats and cotton tapes. The whole place looked cramped and out-of-date. There were air conditioners in every external window. They were all set on high and their motors put a deep booming tone into the structure of the walls.

The secretarial pen had two cluttered desks, both of them occupied, the farther one by a middle-aged woman who looked like she belonged there, the nearer one by a young man who could have been an intern working his summer vacation from college. Clearly he doubled as the office receptionist, because he looked up with a bright *how may we help you* expression on his face.

"Hack Walker wants to see me," Reacher said.

"Mr. Reacher?" the kid asked.

Reacher nodded and the kid pointed to the corner office.

"He's expecting you," he said.

Reacher threaded his way through the cluttered space to the corner office. The door had a window with an acetate plaque below it. The plaque read Henry F. W. Walker, District Attorney. The window was covered on the inside by a closed blind. Reacher knocked once and went in without waiting for a reply.

The office had a window on each wall and a mess of filing cabinets and a big desk piled with paper and a computer and three telephones. Walker was in his chair behind it, leaning back, holding a photograph frame in both hands. It was a small wooden thing with a fiberboard tongue on the back that would prop it upright on a desk or a shelf. He was staring at the front of it. Some kind of serious distress on his face.

"What can I do for you?" Reacher asked.

Walker transferred his gaze from the photograph.

"Sit down," he said. "Please."

The hearty politician's boom had gone from his voice. He sounded tired and ordinary. There was a client chair in front of the desk. Reacher picked it up and turned it sideways to give himself some legroom.

"What can I do for you?" he asked again.

"You ever had your life turned upside down overnight?"

Reacher nodded. "Now and then."

Walker propped the photograph on the desk, sideways, so it was visible to both of them. It was the same color shot he had seen in Sloop Greer's closet. The three young men leaning on the old pick-up's fender, good friends, intoxicated with youth, on the cusp of infinite possibilities.

"Me and Sloop and Al Eugene," he said. "Now Al's a missing person and Sloop is dead."

"No word on Eugene?"

Walker shook his head. "Not a thing."

Reacher said nothing.

"We were such a threesome," Walker said. "And you know

how that goes. Isolated place like this, you get to be more than friends. It was us against the world."

"Was Sloop his real name?"

Walker looked up. "Why do you ask?"

"Because I thought yours was Hack. But I see from the sign on your door it's Henry."

Walker nodded, and smiled a tired smile. "It's Henry on my birth certificate. My folks call me Hank. Always did. But I couldn't say it as a youngster, when I was learning to talk. It came out *Hack*. It kind of stuck."

"But Sloop was for real?"

Walker nodded again. "It was Sloop Greer, plain and simple."

"So what can I do for you?" Reacher asked for the third time.

"I don't know, really," Walker said. "Maybe just listen awhile, maybe clarify some things for me."

"What kind of things?"

"I don't know, really," Walker said again. "Like, when you look at me, what do you see?"

"A district attorney."

"And?"

"I'm not sure."

Walker was quiet for a spell.

"You like what you see?" he asked.

Reacher shrugged. "Less and less, to be honest."

"Why?"

"Because I come in here and find you getting all misty-eyed over your boyhood friendship with a crooked lawyer and a wife-beater."

Walker looked away. "You certainly come straight to the point."

"Life's too short not to."

There was silence for a second. Just the dull roar of all the air conditioner motors, rising and falling as they slipped in and out of phase with each other.

"Actually I'm three things," Walker said. "I'm a man, I'm a DA, and I'm running for judge."

"So?"

"Al Eugene isn't a crooked lawyer. Far from it. He's a good man. He's a campaigner. And he needs to be. Fact is, structurally, the state of Texas is not big on protecting the rights of the accused. The *indigent* accused, even worse. You know that, because you had to find a lawyer for Carmen yourself, and that can only be because you were told she wouldn't get a court appointment for months. And the lawyer you found must have told you she's still looking at months and months of delay. It's a bad system, and I'm aware of it, and Al is aware of it. The Constitution guarantees access to counsel, and Al takes that promise very seriously. He makes himself available to anybody who can find his door. He gives them fair representation, whoever they are. Inevitably some of them are bad guys, but don't forget the Constitution applies to bad guys too. But most of his clients are O.K. Most of them are just poor, is all, black or white or Hispanic."

Reacher said nothing.

"So let me take a guess," Walker said. "I don't know where you heard Al called crooked, but a buck gets ten it was from an older white person with money or position."

It was Rusty Greer, Reacher thought.

"Don't tell me who," Walker said. "But ten gets a hundred I'm right. A person like that sees a lawyer sticking up for poor people or colored people, and they regard it as a nuisance, or as an unpleasantness, and then as some kind of treachery against their race or their class, and from there on it's a pretty easy jump to calling it crooked."

"O.K.," Reacher said. "Maybe I'm wrong about Eugene."

"I guarantee you're wrong about him. I guarantee you could go back to the very day he passed the bar exam and not find any crooked behavior, anywhere at all."

He placed his fingernail on the photograph, just below Al Eugene's chin.

"He's my friend," he said. "And I'm happy about that. As a man, and as a DA."

"What about Sloop Greer?"

Walker nodded. "We'll get to that. But first let me tell you about being a DA."

"What's to tell?"

"Same kind of stuff. I'm like Al. I believe in the Constitution, and the rule of law, and impartiality, and fairness. I can absolutely guarantee you could turn this office upside down and never find one single case where I've been less than fair and impartial. I've been tough, sure, and I've sent lots of people to prison, and some of them to death row, but I've never done anything if I wasn't absolutely convinced it was right."

"Sounds like a stump speech," Reacher said. "But I'm not registered to vote."

"I know," Walker said. "I checked, finally. That's why I'm talking like this. If this was politics, it would be too hokey for words. But this is for real. I want to be a judge, because I could do some good. You familiar with how things work in Texas?"

"Not really."

"Judges in Texas are all elected. They have a lot of power. And it's a weird state. A lot of rich people, but a lot of poor people, too. The poor people need court-appointed lawyers, obviously. But there's no public defender system in Texas. So the judges choose the poor people's lawyers for them. They just pick them out, from any old law firm they want. They're in control of the whole process. They determine the fees, too. It's patronage, pure and simple. So who is the judge going to appoint? He's going to appoint somebody who contributed to his election campaign. It's about cronyism, not fitness or talent. The judge hands out ten thousand dollars of taxpayer money to some favored law firm, the law firm assigns some incompetent lackey who puts in a hundred dollars' worth of work, the net result being nine thousand nine hundred dollars unearned profit for the law firm and some poor guy in jail for something he maybe didn't do. Most defense lawyers meet their clients for the first time at the start of the trial, right there in the courtroom. We've had drunk lawyers and lawyers who fall asleep at the defense table. They don't do any work. They don't check anything. Like, the year before I got here, some guy was on trial for the rape of a child. He was convicted and went to prison for life. Then some pro-bono operation like you went and proved the guy had actually been in jail at the time the rape happened. In *jail*, Reacher. Fifty miles away. Awaiting trial for stealing a car. There was paperwork from here to there, proving it beyond any doubt, all of it in black and white in the public record. His first lawyer never even checked."

"Not too good," Reacher said.

"So I do two things," Walker said. "First, I aim to become a judge, so I can help to put things right in the future. Second, right now, right here in the DA's office, we act out both sides. Every single time, one of us assembles the prosecution case, and another of us does the defense's work and tries to tear it down. We work real hard at it, because we know nobody else will, and I couldn't sleep nights if we didn't."

"Carmen Greer's defense is rock solid," Reacher said.

Hack Walker looked down at the desk.

"No, the Greer situation is a nightmare," he said. "It's a total disaster, all ways around. For me personally, as a man, as a DA, and as a candidate for a judgeship."

"You have to recuse yourself."

Walker looked up. "Of course I'll recuse myself. No doubt about that. But it's still personal to me. And I'm still in overall charge. Whatever happens, it's still my *office*. And that'll have repercussions for me."

"You want to tell me what your problem is?"

"Don't you see? Sloop was my friend. And I'm an honest prosecutor. So in my heart and in my head, I want to see justice done. But I'm looking at sending a Hispanic *woman* to *death row*. I do that, I can forget about the election, can't I? This county is heavily Hispanic. But I want to be a judge. Because I could do some good. And asking for the death penalty against a minority woman *now* will stop me dead. Not just here. It will be headline news *everywhere*. Can you imagine? What's *The New York Times* going to say? They already think we're dumb redneck barbarians who marry our own cousins. It'll follow me the rest of my life."

"So don't prosecute her. It wouldn't be justice, anyhow. Because it was self-defense, pure and simple."

"She got you convinced of that?"

"It's obvious."

"I wish it *was* obvious. I'd give my right arm. For the first time in my career, I'd twist and turn to make this go away."

Reacher stared at him. "You don't need to twist and turn. Do you?"

"Let's talk it through," Walker said. "Step by step, right from the beginning. The spousal-abuse defense can work, but it has to be white-heat, spur-of-the-moment stuff. You understand? That's the law. There can't be premeditation. And Carmen premeditated like crazy. That's a fact, and it won't go away. She bought the gun more or less immediately when she heard he was coming home. The paperwork comes through this office eventually, so I know that's true. She was ready and waiting to ambush him."

Reacher said nothing.

"I know her," Walker said. "Obviously, I know her. Sloop was my friend, so I've known her as long as he did, near enough."

"And?"

Walker shrugged, miserably. "There are problems."

"What problems?"

He shook his head. "I don't know how much I should say, legitimately. So I'm just going to take a few guesses, O.K.? And I don't want you to respond at all. Not a word. It might put you in a difficult position."

"Difficult how?"

"You'll see, later. She probably told you she comes from a rich wine-growing family north of San Francisco, right?"

Reacher said nothing.

"She told you she met Sloop at UCLA, where they were students together."

Reacher said nothing.

"She told you Sloop got her pregnant and they had to get married and as a consequence her parents cut her off."

Reacher said nothing.

"She told you Sloop hit her from the time she was pregnant. She said there were serious injuries that Sloop made her pass off as riding accidents."

Reacher said nothing.

"She claimed it was her who tipped off the IRS, which made her all the more frantic about Sloop coming home."

Reacher said nothing.

"O.K.," Walker said. "Now strictly speaking, anything she told you is merely hearsay and is inadmissible in court. Even though they were spontaneous statements that indicated how acute her anguish was. So in a situation like this, her lawyer will try hard to get the hearsay admitted, because it goes to her state of mind. And there *are* provisions that might allow it. Obviously most DAs would fight it, but this office wouldn't. We'd tend to allow it, because we know marital abuse can be covert. My instinct would be to allow *anything* that gets us nearer to the truth. So let's say you or a person like you were allowed to testify. You'd paint a pretty horrible picture, and in the circumstances, what with his return home looming over her and all, the jury might tend to be sympathetic. They might overlook the element of premeditation. She might get a not guilty verdict."

"So where's the problem?"

"Problem is, if you testified, you'd be cross-examined, too."

"So?"

Walker looked down at the desk again. "Let me take a couple more guesses. Don't respond. And please, if I'm guessing wrong, don't be offended. If I'm wrong, I apologize most sincerely in advance. O.K.?"

"O.K."

"My guess is the premeditation was extensive. My guess is she thought about it and then she tried to recruit you to do it for her."

Reacher said nothing.

"My guess is she didn't pick you up by accident. She selected you in some way and tried hard to persuade you."

Reacher said nothing. Walker swallowed.

"Another guess," he said. "She offered you sex as a bribe."

Reacher said nothing.

"Another guess," Walker said. "She didn't give up. At some stage, she tried again to get you into bed."

Reacher said nothing.

"You see?" Walker said. "If I'm right, and I think I am, because I *know* this woman, all that stuff would come out too, under cross-examination. Evidence of thorough preparation. Unless you were to lie on the stand. Or unless we didn't ask the right questions. But assuming we asked the right questions and you told us the truth, the whole premeditation issue would be damaged. Very seriously. Probably fatally."

Reacher said nothing.

"And it gets worse, I'm afraid," Walker said. "Much worse. Because if she's told you things, what matters then is her *credibility,* right? Specifically, was she telling you the truth about the abuse, or was she not? We'd test that by asking you questions we *do* know the answers to. So under cross-examination, we'd ask you innocent stuff first, like who she is and where she's from, and you'd tell us what she told you."

"And?"

"And her credibility would fall apart. Next stop, death by lethal injection."

"Why?"

"Because I *know* this woman, and she makes things up."

"What things?"

"Everything. I've heard her stories, over and over. Did she in fact tell you she's from a rich wine-growing family?"

Reacher nodded. "More or less. She said she's from a thousand acres in the Napa Valley. Isn't she?"

Walker shook his head. "She's from some barrio in South Central L.A. Nobody knows anything about her parents. She probably doesn't, either."

Reacher was quiet for a moment. Then he shrugged. "Disguising a humble background isn't a crime."

"She was never a student at UCLA. She was a stripper. She was a whore, Reacher. She serviced the UCLA frat parties, among other things. Sloop met her when she was performing. Part of her repertoire was an interesting little trick with a long-neck beer bottle. He fell for her, somehow. You know, *let me take you away from all this* sort of thing. I guess I can understand it. She's cute now. She was stunning then. And smart. She looked at Sloop and saw a rich man's son from Texas, with a big fat wallet. She saw a meal ticket. She went to live with him. Came off the pill and lied about it and got herself pregnant. Whereupon Sloop did the decent thing, because he was like that, in a gentlemanly way. She suckered him, and he let her."

"I don't believe you."

Walker shrugged. "Doesn't matter if you do or if you don't, and I'll tell you exactly why in a moment. But it's all true, I'm afraid. She had brains. She knew what happens to whores when they get old. It goes right downhill, and it doesn't start very high, does it? She wanted a way out, and Sloop was it. She bled him for years, diamonds, horses, everything."

"I don't believe you," Reacher said again.

Walker nodded. "She's very convincing. Can't argue with that."

"Even if it *is* true, does it justify him hitting her?"

Walker paused a beat.

"No, of course not," he said. "But here's the big problem. The thing is, he didn't hit her. Never, Reacher. He wasn't violent with her. Not ever. I *knew* Sloop. He was a lot of things, and to be absolutely honest about it, not all of them were good. He was lazy, he was a little casual in business. A little dishonest, to be truthful. I'm not wearing rose-colored spectacles. But all his faults came from the feeling he was a Texan gentleman. I'm very aware of that, because I was a poor boy by comparison. Practically trash. He had the big ranch and the money. It made him a little arrogant and superior, hence the laziness and the impatience with strict principle. But part of being a gentleman in Texas is you would *never, ever* hit a woman. Whoever the woman was. Not ever. So, she's making all that up, too. I know it. He never hit her. I promise you that."

Reacher shook his head. "What *you* promise me doesn't prove a damn thing. I mean, what else would you say? You were his friend."

Walker nodded again. "I take your point. But there's nothing else to go on. There's just nothing there. Absolutely no evidence, no witnesses, no nothing. We were close. I was with them a thousand times. I heard about the horseback riding accidents as they happened. There weren't *that* many, and they seemed genuine. We'll ask for the medical records, of course, but I don't hold out much hope they'll be ambiguous."

"You said it yourself, abuse can be covert."

"That covert? I'm a DA, Reacher. I've seen everything. Some lone couple in a trailer park, maybe. But Sloop and Carmen lived with family, and they saw friends every day. And before you told the story to Alice Aaron, nobody in the whole of Texas had ever heard the faintest whiff of a rumor about violence between them. Not me, not Al, nobody. So do you understand what I mean? There's no evidence. All we've got is her word. And you're the *only other person* who ever heard it. But if you take the stand to back her up, then her trial is over before it's begun, because the *other* stuff you'll have to say will prove she's a pathological liar. Like, *did* she say she'd tipped off the IRS?"

"Yes, she did. She said she called them. Some special unit."

Walker shook his head. "They caught him through bank records. It was just a purely accidental by-product of an audit on somebody else. She knew nothing about it. I know that *for sure,* for an absolute fact, because Sloop went straight to Al Eugene and Al came straight to me for advice. I saw the indictment. Black and white. Carmen is a liar, Reacher, pure and simple. Or maybe not pure and simple. Maybe there are some very complicated reasons behind it."

Reacher paused a long moment.

"Maybe she is a liar," he said. "But liars can still get abused, same as anybody else. And abuse can be covert. You don't *know* it wasn't happening."

Walker nodded. "I agree. I don't *know.* But I would bet my life it wasn't."

"She convinced me."

"She probably convinced herself. She lives in a fantasy world. I *know* her, Reacher. She's a liar, is all, and she's guilty of first-degree homicide."

"So why are we talking?"

Walker paused.

"Can I trust you?" he asked.

"Does it matter?" Reacher said.

Walker went very quiet. Just stared at his office wall, a whole minute, then another. And another. The boom of the air conditioners crowded into the silence.

"Yes, it matters," he said. "It matters plenty. To Carmen, and to me. Because right now you're reading me completely wrong. I'm not an angry friend trying to protect my old buddy's reputation. Fact is, I *want* to find a defense for Carmen, don't you see that? Even *invent* one. You know, maybe just *pretend* the abuse happened and back-pedal like crazy on the premeditation. I'm seriously tempted. Because then I don't need to charge her at all and I can probably save my shot at the judgeship."

The silence came back. Nothing but the air conditioner motors and telephones ringing faintly outside the office door. The distant chatter of a fax machine.

"I want to go see her," Reacher said.

Walker shook his head. "Can't let you. You're not her lawyer."

"You could bend the rules."

Walker sighed again and dropped his head into his hands. "Please, don't tempt me. Right now I'm thinking about throwing the rules off the top of the building."

Reacher said nothing. Walker stared into space, his eyes jumping with strain.

"I want to figure out her real motive," he said finally. "Because if it was something real cold, like money, I don't have a choice. She has to go down."

Reacher said nothing.

"But if it wasn't, I want you to help me," Walker said. "If her medical records are remotely plausible, I want to try to save her with the abuse thing."

Reacher said nothing.

"O.K., what I really mean is I want to try to save myself," Walker said. "Try to save my chances in the election. Or both things, O.K.? Her *and* me. Ellie, too. She's a great kid. Sloop loved her."

"So what would you want from me?"

"If we go down that road."

Reacher nodded. "If," he said.

"I'd want you to lie on the stand," Walker said. "I'd want you to repeat what she told you about the beatings, and modify what she told you about everything else, in order to preserve her credibility."

Reacher said nothing.

"That's why I need to trust you," Walker said. "And that's why I needed to lay everything out for you. So you know exactly what you're getting into with her."

"I've never done that sort of a thing before."

"Neither have I," Walker said. "It's killing me just to talk about it."

Reacher was quiet for a long moment.

"Why do you assume I'd want to?" he asked.

"I think you like her," Walker said. "I think you feel sorry for her. I think you want to help her. Therefore indirectly you could help me."

"How would you work it?"

Walker shrugged. "I'll be withdrawn from the case from the start, so one of my assistants will be handling it. I'll find out exactly what she can prove for sure, and I'll coach you on it so you don't get tripped up. That's why I can't let you go see Carmen now. They keep a record downstairs. It would look like prior collusion."

"I don't know," Reacher said.

"I don't, either. But maybe it won't have to go all the way to trial. If the medical evidence is a little flexible, and we take a deposition from Carmen, and one from you, then maybe dropping the charges altogether would be justified."

"Lying in a deposition would be just as bad."

"Think about Ellie."

"And your judgeship."

Walker nodded. "I'm not hiding that from you. I want to get elected, no doubt about it. But it's for an honest reason. I want to make things better, Reacher. It's always been my ambition. Work my way up, improve things from the inside. It's the only way. For a person like me, anyway. I've got no influence as a lobbyist. I'm not a politician, really. I find all that stuff embarrassing. I don't have the skills."

Reacher said nothing.

"Let me think it over," Walker said. "A day or two. I'll take it from there."

"You sure?"

Walker sighed again. "No, of course I'm not *sure*. I hate this whole thing. But what the hell, Sloop's dead. Nothing's going to change that. Nothing's going to bring him back. It'll trash his memory, of course. But it would save Carmen. And he loved her, Reacher. In a way nobody else could ever understand. The disapproval he brought down on himself was unbelievable. From his family, from polite society. He'd be happy to exchange his reputation for her life, I think. *His* life for *her* life, effectively. He'd exchange mine, or Al's, or anybody's, probably. He loved her."

There was silence again.

"She needs bail," Reacher said.

"Please," Walker said. "It's out of the question."

"Ellie needs her."

"That's a bigger issue than bail," Walker said. "Ellie can stand a couple of days with her grandmother. It's the rest of her life we need to worry about. Give me time to work this out."

Reacher shrugged and stood up.

"This is all in strict confidence, right?" Walker said. "I guess I should have made that clear right from the start."

Reacher nodded.

"Get back to me," he said.

Then he stood up and walked out the room.

12

"One simple question," Alice said. "Is it plausible that domestic abuse could be so covert that close friends are totally
unaware of it?"

"I don't know," Reacher said. "I don't have much experience."

"Neither do I."

They were on opposite sides of Alice's desk in the back of
the legal mission. It was the middle of the day, and the heat
was so brutal it was enforcing a *de facto* siesta on the whole
town. Nobody was out and about who didn't desperately
need to be. The mission was largely deserted. Just Alice and
Reacher and one other lawyer twenty feet away. The inside
temperature was easily over a hundred and ten degrees. The
humidity was rising. The ancient air conditioner above the
door was making no difference at all. Alice had changed into
shorts again. She was leaning back in her chair, arms above
her head, her back arched off the sticky vinyl. She was slick
with sweat from head to foot. Over the tan it made her skin

look oiled. Reacher's shirt was soaked. He was reconsidering its projected three-day life span.

"It's a catch-22," Alice said. "Abuse you *know* about isn't covert. *Really* covert abuse, you might assume it isn't happening. Like, I assume my dad isn't beating my mom. But maybe he is. Who would know? What about yours?"

Reacher smiled. "I doubt it. He was a U.S. Marine. Big guy, not especially genteel. But then, you should have seen my mother. Maybe she was beating *him.*"

"So yes or no about Carmen and Sloop?"

"She convinced me," Reacher said. "No doubt about it."

"Despite everything?"

"She convinced me," he said again. "Maybe she's all kinds of a liar about other things, but he was beating her. That's my belief."

Alice looked at him, a lawyer's question in her eyes.

"No doubt at all?" she asked.

"No doubt at all," he said.

"O.K., but a difficult case just got a lot harder. And I hate it when that happens."

"Me too," he said. "But hard is not the same thing as impossible."

"You understand the exact legalities here?"

He nodded. "It's not rocket science. She's in deep shit, whichever way you cut it. If there *was* abuse, she's blown it anyway by being so premeditated. If there *wasn't,* then it's murder one, pure and simple. And whatever, she has zero credibility because she lies and exaggerates. Ballgame over, if Walker didn't want to be judge so bad."

"Exactly," Alice said.

"You happy about riding that kind of luck?"

"No."

"Neither am I."

"Not morally, not practically," Alice said. "Anything could happen here. Maybe Hack's got a love child somewhere, and it'll come out and he'll have to withdraw anyway. Maybe he likes to have sex with armadillos. It's a long time until November. Counting on him to stay electable no matter what would be foolish. So his tactical problem with Carmen could disappear at any time. So she needs a properly structured defense."

Reacher smiled again. "You're even smarter than I figured."

"I thought you were going to say than I *looked.*"

"I think more lawyers should dress that way."

"You need to stay off the stand," she said. "Much safer for her. No deposition, either. Without you, the gun is the only thing that suggests premeditation. And we should be able to argue that *buying* the gun and actually *using* it weren't necessarily closely connected. Maybe she bought it for another reason."

Reacher said nothing.

"They're testing it now," she said. "Over at the lab. Ballistics and fingerprints. Two sets of prints, they say. Hers, I guess, maybe his, too. Maybe they struggled over it. Maybe the whole thing was an accident."

Reacher shook his head. "The second set must be mine. She asked me to teach her how to shoot. We went up on the mesa and practiced."

"When?"

"Saturday. The day before he got home."

She stared at him.

"Christ, Reacher," she said. "You *definitely* stay off the stand, O.K.?"

"I plan to."

"What about if things change and they subpoena you?"

"Then I'll lie, I guess."

"Can you?"

"I was a cop of sorts for thirteen years. It wouldn't be a totally radical concept."

"What would you say about your prints on the gun?"

"I'd say I found it dumped somewhere. Innocently gave it back to her. Make it look like she had reconsidered after buying it."

"You comfortable with saying stuff like that?"

"If the ends justify the means, I am. And I think they do here. She's given herself a problem proving it, is all. You?"

She nodded. "A case like this, I guess so. I don't care about the lies about her background. People do stuff like that, all the time, all kinds of reasons. So all that's left is the premeditation thing. And most other states, premeditation wouldn't be an issue. They recognize the reality. A battered woman can't necessarily be effective on the spur of the moment. Sometimes she needs to wait until he's drunk, or asleep. You know, bide her time. There are lots of cases like that in other jurisdictions."

"So where do we start?"

"Where we're forced to," Alice said. "Which is a pretty bad place. The circumstantial evidence is overwhelming. *Res ipsa loquitur,* they call it. The thing speaks for itself. Her bedroom, her gun, her husband lying there dead on the floor. That's murder one. We leave it like that, they'll convict her on the first vote."

"So?"

"So we back-pedal on the premeditation and then we prove the abuse through the medical records. I already started the paperwork. We joined with the DA's office for a common-cause subpoena. All Texas hospitals, and all neighboring states. Domestic violence, that's standard procedure, because people sometimes drive all over to hide it. The hospitals generally react pretty fast, so we should get the records overnight. Then it's *res ipsa loquitur* again. If the injuries *were* caused by violence, then the records will at least show they *could have* been. That's just common sense. Then she takes the stand and she talks about the abuse. She'll have to take it on the chin about the bullshit stories about her past. But if we present it right, she could even look quite good. No shame in being an ex-hooker trying to reform. We could build up some sympathy there."

"You sound like a pretty good lawyer."

She smiled. "For one so young?"

"Well, what are you, two years out of school?"

"Six months," she said. "But you learn fast down here."

"Evidently."

"Whatever, with careful jury selection, we'll get at least half and half don't-knows and not-guiltys. The not-guiltys will wear down the don't-knows within a couple of days. Especially if it's this hot."

Reacher pulled the soaked fabric of his shirt off his skin. "Can't stay this hot much longer, can it?"

"Hey, I'm talking about *next* summer," Alice said. "That's if she's lucky. Could be the summer after that."

He stared at her. "You're kidding."

She shook her head. "The record around here is four years in jail between arrest and trial."

"What about Ellie?"

She shrugged. "Just pray the medical records look real good. If they do, we've got a shot at getting Hack to drop the charges altogether. He's got a lot of latitude."

"He wouldn't need much pushing," Reacher said. "The mood he's in."

"So look on the bright side. This whole thing could be over in a couple of days."

"When are you going to go see her?"

"Later this afternoon. First I'm going to the bank to cash a twenty-thousand-dollar check. Then I'm going to put the money in a grocery bag and drive out and deliver it to some very happy people."

"O.K.," Reacher said.

"I don't want to know what you did to get it."

"I just asked for it."

"I don't want to know," she said again. "But you should come with me and meet them. And be my bodyguard. Not every day I carry twenty thousand dollars around the Wild West in a grocery bag. And it'll be cool in the car."

"O.K.," Reacher said again.

The bank showed no particular excitement about forking over twenty grand in mixed bills. The teller treated it like a completely routine part of her day. She just counted the money three times and stacked it carefully in a brown-paper grocery bag Alice provided for the purpose. Reacher carried it back to the parking lot for her. But she didn't need him to.

There was no danger of getting mugged. The fearsome heat had just about cleared the streets, and what few people remained were moving slowly and listlessly.

The interior of the VW had heated up to the point where they couldn't get in right away. Alice started the air going and left the doors open until the blowers took thirty degrees off it. It was probably still over a hundred when they slid inside. But it felt cool. All things are relative. Alice drove, heading north and east. She was good. Better than him. She didn't stall out a single time.

"There'll be a storm," she said.

"Everybody tells me that," he said. "But I don't see it coming."

"You ever felt heat like this before?"

"Maybe," he said. "Once or twice. Saudi Arabia, the Pacific. But Saudi is drier and the Pacific is wetter. So, not exactly."

The sky ahead of them was light blue, so hot it looked white. The sun was a diffuse glare, like it was located everywhere. There was no cloud at all. He was squinting so much the muscles in his face were hurting.

"It's new to me," she said. "That's for sure. I figured it would be hot here, but this is completely unbelievable."

Then she asked him when he'd been in the Middle East and the Pacific islands, and he responded with the expanded ten-minute version of his autobiography because he found he was enjoying her company. The first thirty-six years were easy enough, as always. They made a nicely linear tale of childhood and adulthood, accomplishment and progress, punctuated and underlined in the military fashion with promotions and medals. The last few years were harder, as usual. The aimlessness, the drifting. He saw them as a triumph of disengagement, but he knew other people didn't. So as always he just told the story and answered the awkward questions and let her think whatever she wanted.

Then she responded in turn with an autobiography of her own. It was more or less the same as his, in an oblique way. He was the son of a soldier, she was the daughter of a lawyer. She had never really considered straying away from the family trade, just like he hadn't. All her life she had seen people talk the talk and walk the walk and then she had set about following after them, just like he had. She spent seven years at Harvard where he spent four at West Point. Now she was twenty-five and the rough equivalent of an ambitious lieutenant in the law business. He had been an ambitious lieutenant at twenty-five, too, and he could remember exactly how it felt.

"So what's next?" he asked.

"After this?" she said. "Back to New York, I guess. Maybe Washington, D.C. I'm getting interested in policy."

"You won't miss this down-and-dirty stuff?"

"I will, probably. And I won't give it up completely. Maybe I'll volunteer a few weeks a year. Certainly I'll try to fund it. That's where all our money comes from, you know. Big firms in the big cities, with a conscience."

"I'm glad to hear it. Somebody needs to do something."

"That's for sure."

"What about Hack Walker?" he asked. "Will he make a difference?"

She shrugged at the wheel. "I don't know him very well. But his reputation is good. And he can't make things any worse, can he? It's a really screwed-up system. I mean, I'm a democrat, big D *and* little d, so theoretically to elect your judges is perfectly fine with me. Theoretically. But in practice, it's totally out of hand. I mean, what does it cost to run a campaign down here?"

"No idea."

"Well, figure it out. We're talking about Pecos County, basically, because that's where the bulk of the electorate is. A bunch of posters, some newspaper ads, half a dozen homemade commercials on the local TV channels. A market like this, you'd have to work really hard to spend more than five figures. But these guys are all picking up contributions running to hundreds and hundreds and *hundreds* of thousands of dollars. Millions, maybe. And the law says if you don't get around to spending it, you don't have to give it back. You just keep it, for miscellaneous future expenses. So what it amounts to is they're all picking up their bribes in advance.

The law firms and the oil people and the special interests are paying *now* for future help. You can get seriously rich, running for judge in Texas. And if you get elected and do the right things all your years on the bench, you retire straight into some big law partnership and you get asked onto the boards of a half-dozen big companies. So it's not really about trying to get elected a *judge*. It's about trying to get elected a *prince*. Like turning into royalty overnight."

"So will Walker make a difference?" he asked again.

"He will if he wants to. Simple as that. And right now, he'll make a difference to Carmen Greer. That's what we need to focus on."

He nodded. She slowed the car, hunting a turn. They were back up in ranch country. Somewhere near the Brewer place, he guessed, although he didn't recognize any specific features of the landscape. It was laid out in front of him, so dry and so hot it seemed the parched vegetation could burst into flames at any moment.

"Does it bother you she told all those lies?" Alice asked.

He shrugged. "Yes and no. Nobody likes to be lied to, I guess. But look at it from her point of view. She reached the conclusion he had to be gotten rid of, so she set about achieving it."

"So there *was* extensive premeditation?"

"Should I be telling you this?"

"I'm on her side."

He nodded. "She had it all planned. She said she looked at a hundred guys and sounded out a dozen before she picked on me."

Alice nodded back. "Actually that makes me feel better somehow, you know? Kind of proves how bad it was. Surely *nobody* would do that without some kind of really urgent necessity."

"Me too," he said. "I feel the same way."

She slowed again and turned the car onto a farm track. After ten yards the track passed under a poor imitation of the older ranch gates he had seen elsewhere. It was just a rectangle of unpainted two-by-fours nailed together, leaning slightly to the left. The crossbar had a name written on it. It was indecipherable, scorched and faded to nothing by the sun. Beyond it were a few acres of cultivated ground. There were straight rows of turned dirt and an irrigation system pieced together from improvised parts. There were piles of fieldstone here and there. Neat wooden frames to carry wires to support the bushes that no longer grew. Everything was dry and crisp and fallow. The whole picture spoke of agonizing months of back-breaking manual labor in the fearsome heat, followed by tragic disappointment.

There was a house a hundred yards beyond the last row of turned earth. It wasn't a bad place. It was small and low, wood-framed, painted dull white with a finish that had cracked and crazed in the sun. There was a windmill behind it. There was a barn, with an irrigation pump venting through the roof and a damaged three-quarter-ton truck standing idle. The house had a closed front door. Alice parked the VW right next to it.

"They're called García," she said. "I'm sure they're home."

Twenty thousand dollars in a grocery bag had an effect like he'd never seen before. It was literally a gift of life. There were five Garcías, two generations, two in the older and three in the younger. They were all small and scrappy people. The parents were maybe in their late forties and the eldest child was a girl of maybe twenty-four. The younger offspring were both boys and could have been twenty-two and twenty. They all stood quietly together inside the doorway. Alice said a bright hello and walked straight past them and spilled the money on their kitchen table.

"He changed his mind," she said, in Spanish. "He decided to pay up, after all."

The Garcías formed a semicircle around the table, silent, looking at the money, like it represented such a stunning reversal of fortune that no reaction was possible. They didn't ask any questions. Just accepted it had finally happened and then paused a second and burst out with a long list of plans. First, they would get the telephone reconnected so they wouldn't have to walk eight miles to their neighbor's place.

Then the electricity. Then they would pay back what they had borrowed from friends. Then they would buy diesel fuel, so the irrigation pump could run again. Then they would get their truck fixed and drive it to town for seed and fertilizer. They went quiet again when it dawned on them they could get a whole crop grown and harvested and sold before the winter came.

Reacher hung back and looked around the room. It was an eat-in, live-in kitchen, opening to a front parlor. The parlor was hot and airless and had a yard-long encyclopedia set and a bunch of religious statuettes on a low shelf. A single picture on the wall. The picture was a photograph of a boy. It was a studio portrait. The boy was maybe fourteen, with a precocious smudge of mustache above his lip. He was wearing a white confirmation robe and smiling shyly. The picture was in a black frame and had a dusty square of black fabric hung around it.

"My eldest son," a voice said. "That picture was made just before we left our village in Mexico."

Reacher turned and found the mother standing behind him.

"He was killed, on the journey here," she said.

Reacher nodded. "I know. I heard. The border patrol. I'm very sorry."

"It was twelve years ago. His name was Raoul García."

The way she said his name was like a small act of remembrance.

"What happened?" Reacher asked.

The woman was silent for a second.

"It was awful," she said. "They hunted us for three hours in the night. We were walking and running, they had a truck with bright lights. We got split up. Divided, in the dark. Raoul was with his sister. He was protecting her. She was twelve. He sent her one way and walked the other way, into the lights. He knew it was worse, if they captured girls. He gave himself up to save his sister. But they didn't try to arrest him or anything. Didn't even ask him any questions. They just shot him down and drove away. They came near where I was hiding. They were laughing. I heard them. Like it was a sport."

"I'm very sorry," Reacher said again.

The woman shrugged. "It was very common then. It was a bad time, and a bad area. We found that out, later. Either our guide didn't know, or didn't care. We found out that there were more than twenty people killed on that route in a year. For fun. Some of them in horrible ways. Raoul was lucky, just to be shot. Some of them, their screams could be heard for miles, across the desert, in the darkness. Some of the girls were carried away and never seen again."

Reacher said nothing. The woman gazed at the picture for a moment longer. Then she turned away with an immense physical effort and forced a smile and gestured that Reacher should rejoin the party in the kitchen.

"We have tequila," she said quietly. "Saved especially for this day."

There were shot glasses on the table, and the daughter was filling them from a bottle. The girl that Raoul had saved, all grown up. The younger son passed the glasses around. Reacher took his and waited. The García father motioned for quiet and raised his drink toward Alice in a toast.

"To our lawyer," he said. "For proving the great Frenchman Honoré de Balzac wrong when he wrote, 'Laws are spider webs through which the big flies pass and the little ones get caught.'"

Alice blushed a little. García smiled at her and turned to Reacher. "And to you, sir, for your generous assistance in our time of need."

"De nada," Reacher said. *"No hay de que."*

The tequila was rough and Raoul's memory was everywhere, so they refused a second shot and left the Garcías alone with their celebrations. They had to wait again until the air conditioner made the VW's interior bearable. Then they headed back to Pecos.

"I enjoyed that," Alice said. "Felt like I finally made a difference."

"You did make a difference."

"Even though it was you made it happen."

"You did the skilled labor," he said.

"Nevertheless, thanks."

"Did the border patrol ever get investigated?" he asked.

She nodded. "Thoroughly, according to the record. There was enough noise made. Nothing specific, of course, but enough general rumors to make it inevitable."

"And?"

"And nothing. It was a whitewash. Nobody was even indicted."

"But did it stop?"

She nodded again. "As suddenly as it started. So obviously they got the message."

"That's how it works," he said. "I've seen it before, different places, different situations. The investigation isn't really an investigation, as such. It's more like a message. Like a coded warning. Like saying, you can't get away with this anymore, so you better stop doing it, whoever you are."

"But justice wasn't done, Reacher. Twenty-some people died. Some of them gruesomely. It was like a pogrom, a year long. Somebody should have paid."

"Did you recognize that Balzac quotation?" he asked.

"Sure," she said. "I went to Harvard, after all."

"Remember Herbert Marcuse, too?"

"He was later, right? A philosopher, not a novelist."

He nodded. "Born ninety-nine years after Balzac. A social and political philosopher. He said, 'Law and order are everywhere the law and order which protect the established hierarchy.'"

"That stinks."

"Of course it does," he said. "But that's the way it is."

They made it back to Pecos inside an hour. She parked on the street right outside the legal mission so they only had to walk ten feet through the heat. But ten feet was enough. It was like walking ten feet through a blast furnace with a hot towel wrapped around your head. They made it inside and found Alice's desk covered in little handwritten notes stuck randomly to its surface. She peeled them off and scooped them up and read them through, one by one. Then she dropped them all in a drawer.

"I'm going to check in with Carmen at the jail," she said. "But the prints and the ballistics are back from the lab. Hack Walker wants to see you about them. Sounds like he's got a problem."

"I'm sure he has," Reacher said.

They walked to the door and paused a second before braving the sidewalk again. Then they split up in front of the courthouse. Alice walked on toward the jailhouse entrance and Reacher went up the front steps and inside. The public areas and the staircase had no air-conditioning. Making it up just one floor soaked him in sweat. The intern at the desk pointed silently to Hack Walker's door. Reacher went straight in and found Walker studying a technical report. He had the look of a man who thinks if he reads a thing often enough, maybe it will change what it says.

"She killed him," he said. "Everything matches. The ballistics are perfect."

Reacher sat down in front of the desk.

"Your prints were on the gun, too," Walker said.

Reacher made no reply. If he was going to lie, he was going to save it for when it would count for something.

"You're in the national fingerprint database," Walker said. "You know that?"

Reacher nodded. "All military personnel are."

"So maybe you found the gun discarded," Walker said. "Maybe you handled it because you were worried about a family with a kid having a stray firearm around. Maybe you picked it up and put it away in a place of safety."

"Maybe," Reacher said.

Walker turned a page in the file.

"But it's worse than that, isn't it?" he said.

"Is it?"

"You a praying man?"

"No," Reacher said.

"You damn well should be. You should get on your knees and thank somebody."

"Like who?"

"Maybe the state cops. Maybe old Sloop himself for calling the sheriff."

"Why?"

"Because they just saved your life."

"How?"

"Because you were on the road in a squad car when this went down. If they'd left you in the bunkhouse, you'd be our number-one suspect."

"Why?"

Walker turned another page.

"Your prints were on the gun," he said again. "*And* on every one of the shell cases. *And* on the magazine. *And* on the ammunition box. You loaded that gun, Reacher. Probably test-fired it too, they think, then reloaded it ready for action. She bought it, so it was technically *her* possession, but it looks from the fingerprint evidence that it was effectively *your* weapon."

Reacher said nothing.

"So you see?" Walker asked. "You should set up a little shrine to the state police and give thanks every morning you wake up alive and free. Because the obvious thing for me to do would be come right after *you*. You could have crept up from the bunkhouse to the bedroom, easy as anything. Because you knew where the bedroom was, didn't you? I talked to Bobby. He told me you spent the previous night in there. Did you really think he'd just sit quiet in the barn? He probably watched you two going at it, through the window."

"I didn't sleep with her," Reacher said. "I was on the sofa."

Walker smiled. "Think a jury would believe you? Or an ex-whore? I don't. So we could easily prove some kind of a sexual jealousy motive. The next night you could have crept up there and got the gun out of the drawer and shot Sloop dead, and then crept back again. Only you couldn't have, because you were in the back of a police car at the time. So you're a lucky man, Reacher. Because right now a white male shooter would be worth his weight in gold to me. You could go integrate death row single-handed. A big WASP like you, in among all the blacks and the Hispanics, I'd look like the fairest prosecutor in Texas. The election would be over before it started."

Reacher said nothing. Walker sighed.

"But you didn't do it, unfortunately," he said. "She did it. So *now* what have I got? The premeditation thing is going from bad to worse. It's just about shot to hell now. Clearly she thought, and she thought, even to the extent of hooking up with some ex-army guy to give her weapons training. We got your record, after we got your prints. You were a pistol-shooting champ two straight years. You did a spell as an instructor, for Christ's sake. You loaded her gun for her. What the hell am I going to do?"

"What you planned," Reacher said. "Wait for the medical reports."

Walker went quiet. Then he sighed again. Then he nodded.

"We'll have them tomorrow," he said. "And you know what I did? I hired a defense expert to take a look at them. You know there are experts who only appear for the defense? Normally we wouldn't go near them. Normally we want to know how *much* we can get out of a thing, not how little. But I hired a defense guy, the exact same guy Alice Aaron would hire if she could afford him. Because I want somebody who can persuade me there's a faint possibility Carmen's telling the truth, so I can let her go without looking like I'm crazy."

"So relax," Reacher said. "It'll be over tomorrow."

"I hope so," Walker said. "And it might be. Al Eugene's office is sending over some financial stuff. Al did all that kind of work for Sloop. So if there's no financial motive, and the medical reports are good, maybe I *can* relax."

"She had no money at all," Reacher said. "It was one of her big problems."

Walker nodded. "Good," he said. "Because *her* big problems solve *my* big problems."

The office went quiet underneath the drone of the air conditioners. The back of Reacher's neck felt cold and wet.

"You should be more proactive," he said. "With the election."

"Yeah, how?"

"Do something popular."

"Like what?"

"Like reopen something about the border patrol. People

would like that. I just met a family whose son was murdered by them."

Walker went quiet again for a second, then just shook his head.

"Ancient history," he said.

"Not to those families," Reacher said. "There were twenty-some homicides in a year. Most of the survivors live around here, probably. And most of them will be voters by now."

"The border patrol was investigated," Walker said. "Before my time, but it was pretty damn thorough. I went through the files years ago."

"You have the files?"

"Sure. Mostly happened down in Echo, and all that stuff comes here. It was clearly a bunch of rogue officers on a jag of their own, and the investigation most likely served to warn them off. They probably quit. Border patrol has a pretty good turnover of staff. The bad guys could be anywhere by now, literally. Probably left the state altogether. It's not just the im-migrants who flow north."

"It would make you look good."

Walker shrugged. "I'm sure it would. A lot of things would make me look good. But I do have *some* standards, Reacher. It would be a total waste of public money. Grandstanding, pure and simple. It wouldn't get anywhere. Nowhere at all. They're long gone. It's ancient history."

"Twelve years ago isn't ancient history."

"It is around here. Things change fast. Right now I'm con-centrating on what happened in Echo last night, not twelve years ago."

"O.K.," Reacher said. "Your decision."

"I'll call Alice in the morning. When we get the material we need. Could be all over by lunchtime."

"Let's hope so."

"Yeah, let's," Walker said.

Reacher went out through the hot trapped air in the stair-well and stepped outside. It was hotter still on the sidewalk.

So hot, it was difficult to breathe properly. It felt like all the oxygen molecules had been burned out of the air. He made it across the street and down to the mission with sweat running into his eyes. He pushed in through the door and found Alice sitting alone at her desk.

"You back already?" he asked, surprised.

She just nodded.

"Did you see her?"

She nodded again.

"What did she say?"

"Nothing at all," Alice said. "Except she doesn't want me to represent her."

"What do you mean?"

"What I said. Literally the only words I got out of her were, and I quote, 'I refuse to be represented by you.'"

"Why?"

"She didn't say. She said nothing at all. I just told you that. Except she doesn't want me on the case."

"Why the hell not?"

Alice just shrugged and said nothing.

"Has this kind of a thing ever happened before?"

Alice shook her head. "Not to me. Not to anybody within living memory in this place. Normally they can't make their minds up whether to bite your hand off or smother you with hugs and kisses."

"So what the hell happened?"

"I don't know. She was fairly calm, fairly rational."

"Did you try to persuade her?"

"Of course I did. To a point. But I wanted to get out of there before she lost it and started hollering. A witness hears her say it, I lose all standing. And then she's really in trouble. I plan to go back and try again later."

"Did you tell her I sent you?"

"Sure I did. I used your name. Reacher this, Reacher that. Made no difference. All she said was she refused representation. Over and over again, three or four times. Then she gave me the silent treatment."

"Can you think of a reason?"

Alice shrugged. "Not really, in the circumstances. I mean, I'm not exactly Perry Mason. Maybe I don't inspire much confidence. I go in there half-naked and sweating like a pig, and if this was Wall Street or somewhere I could understand somebody taking one look and thinking *wow, like, forget about it*. But this isn't Wall Street. This is Pecos County jail, and she's Hispanic, and I'm a lawyer with a pulse, so she should have been dancing with joy I came at all."

"So why?"

"It's inexplicable."

"What happens now?"

"Now it's a balancing act. I have to get her to accept representation before anybody hears her refuse it."

"And if she still doesn't?"

"Then I go about my business and she's completely on her own. Until six months from now when the indictment's in and some crony of the judge's sends some useless jerk to see her."

Reacher was quiet for a moment. "I'm sorry, Alice. I had no idea this would happen."

"Not your fault."

"Go back about seven, O.K.?" he said. "When the upstairs offices are empty and before the night shift woman comes on. She struck me as nosier than the day guy. He probably won't pay too much attention. So you can press her some. Let her holler if she wants to."

"O.K.," she said. "Seven o'clock it is. Hell of a day. Up and down, like a roller coaster."

"Like life itself," Reacher said.

She smiled, briefly. "Where will I find you?"

"I'm in the last motel before the highway."

"You like traffic noise?"

"I like cheap. Room eleven, name of Millard Fillmore."

"Why?"

"Habit," he said. "I like aliases. I like anonymity."

"So who is Millard Fillmore?"

"President, two before Abraham Lincoln. From New York."

She was quiet for a moment. "Should I dress up like a lawyer for her? You think that might make a difference?"

Reacher shrugged. "I doubt it. Look at me. I look like a scarecrow, and she never said anything about it."

Alice smiled again. "You do a little, you know. I saw you come in this morning and I thought *you* were the client. Some kind of homeless guy in trouble."

"This is a new outfit," Reacher said. "Fresh today."

She looked him over again and said nothing. He left her with paperwork to do and walked as far as the pizza parlor south of the courthouse. It was nearly full with people and had a huge air conditioner over the door spilling a continuous stream of moisture on the sidewalk. Clearly it was the coldest place in town, and therefore right then the most popular. He went in and got the last table and drank ice water as fast as the busboy could refill his glass. Then he ordered an anchovy pizza, heavy on the fish. He figured his body needed to replace salt.

As he ate it a new description was being passed by phone to the killing crew. The call was carefully rerouted through Dallas and Las Vegas to a motel room a hundred miles from Pecos. The call was made by a man, speaking quietly but clearly. It contained a detailed identification of a new target, a male, starting with his full name and his age, and accompanied by an exact rundown of his physical appearance and all of his likely destinations within the next forty-eight hours.

The information was taken by the woman, because she had sent her partners out to eat. She made no notes. She was naturally cautious about leaving written evidence, and she had an excellent memory. It had been honed by constant practice. She listened carefully until the caller stopped talking and then she decided the crew's price. She wasn't reluctant to speak on the phone. She was talking through an electronic device bought in the Valley that made her sound like a robot with a head cold. So she named the price and then listened to the silence on the other end. Listened to the guy deciding whether to negotiate the cost. But he didn't. Just said O.K. and hung up. The woman smiled. *Smart guy,* she thought. Her crew didn't work for cheapskates. A parsimonious attitude about money betrayed all kinds of other negative possibilities.

Reacher had ice cream after the pizza, and more water, and then coffee. He lingered over it as long as was reasonable and then he paid his check and walked back to his motel room. The heat felt worse than ever after being cold and dry for an hour. He took a long shower in tepid water and rinsed his clothes in the sink. Shook them hard to eliminate the wrinkles and arranged them on a chair to dry. Then he turned the room air to high and lay down on the bed to wait for Alice. Checked his watch. He figured if she got there anytime after eight o'clock it would be a good sign, because if Carmen decided to get serious they would need to talk for at least an hour. He closed his eyes and tried to sleep.

13

She got there at seven-twenty. He woke from a feverish overheated doze and heard a tentative knock at his door. Rolled off the bed and wrapped a damp towel around his waist and padded barefoot across the dirty carpet and opened up. Alice was standing there. He looked at her. She just shook her head. He stared out at the dusk light for a second. Her yellow car was parked in the lot. He turned and stepped back into the room. She followed him inside.

"I tried everything," she said.

She had changed back into her lawyer outfit. The black pants and the jacket. The pants had a very high waistband, so high it almost met the bottom edge of the sports bra. There was an inch of tanned midriff showing. Apart from that, she looked exactly like the real deal. And he couldn't see how an inch of skin would be significant to a woman in Carmen's position.

"I asked her, was it me?" Alice said. "Did she want somebody different? Older? A man? A Hispanic person?"

"What did she say?"

"She said she didn't want anybody at all."

"That's crazy."

"Yes, it is," Alice said. "I described her predicament. You know, in case she wasn't seeing it clearly. It made no difference."

"Tell me everything she said."

"I already have."

Reacher was uncomfortable in the towel. It was too small.

"Let me put my pants on," he said.

He scooped them off the chair and ducked into the bathroom. The pants were wet and clammy. He pulled them on and zipped them up. Came back out. Alice had taken her jacket off and laid it on the chair, next to his wet shirt. She was sitting on the bed with her elbows on her knees.

"I tried everything," she said again. "I said, show me your arm. She said, what for? I said, I want to see how good your veins are. Because that's where the lethal injection will go. I told her she'd be strapped down on the gurney, I described the drugs she'd get. I told her about the people behind the glass, there to watch her die."

"And?"

"It made no difference at all. Like talking to the wall."

"How hard did you push?"

"I shouted a little. But she waited me out and just repeated herself. She's refusing representation, Reacher. We better face it."

"Is that kosher?"

"Of course it is. No law says you *have* to have counsel. Just that you have to be *offered* counsel."

"Isn't it evidence of insanity or something?"

She shook her head.

"Not in itself," she said. "Otherwise every murderer would just refuse to have a lawyer and automatically get off with an incapacity defense."

"She's not a murderer."

"She doesn't seem very anxious to prove it."

"Did anybody hear her?"

"Not yet. But I'm worried. Logically her next move is to put it in writing. Then I can't even get in the door. Nor can anybody else."

"So what do we do?"

"We have to finesse her. That's all we *can* do. We just have to ignore her completely and keep on dealing with Walker behind her back. On her behalf. If we can get him to drop the charges, then we've set her free whether she wants us to or not."

He shrugged. "Then that's what we'll do. But it's completely bizarre, isn't it?"

"It sure is," Alice said. "I never heard of such a thing before."

A hundred miles away, the two male members of the killing crew returned to their motel after eating dinner. They had chosen pizza, too, but with pitchers of cold beer instead of water and coffee. They found their woman partner waiting for them inside their room. She was alert and pacing, which they recognized as a sign of news.

"What?" the tall man asked.

"A supplementary job," she said.

"Where?"

"Pecos."

"Is that smart?"

She nodded. "Pecos is still safe enough."

"You think?" the dark man asked.

"Wait until you hear what he's paying."

"When?"

"Depends on the prior commitment."

"O.K.," the tall man said. "Who's the target?"

"Just some guy," the woman said. "I'll give you the details when we've done the other thing."

She walked to the door.

"Stay inside now," she said. "Get to bed, get some sleep. We've got a very busy day coming up."

"This is a crummy room," Alice said.

Reacher glanced around. "You think?"

"It's awful."

"I've had worse."

She paused a beat. "You want dinner?"

He was full of pizza and ice cream, but the inch of midriff was attractive. So was the corresponding inch of her back. There was a deep cleft there. The waistband of the pants spanned it like a tiny bridge.

"Sure," he said. "Where?"

She paused again.

"My place?" she said. "It's difficult for me to eat out around here. I'm a vegetarian. So usually I cook for myself."

"A vegetarian in Texas," he said. "You're a long way from home."

"Sure feels like it," she said. "So how about it? And I've got better air conditioning than this."

He smiled. "Woman-cooked food *and* better air? Sounds good to me."

"You eat vegetarian?"

"I eat anything."

"So let's go."

He shrugged his damp shirt on. She picked up her jacket. He found his shoes. Locked up the room and followed her over to the car.

She drove a couple of miles west to a low-rise residential complex built on a square of scrubby land trapped between two four-lane roads. The buildings had stucco walls painted the color of sand with dark-stained wooden beams stuck all over the place for accents. There were maybe forty rental units and they all looked halfhearted and beaten down by the heat. Hers was right in the center, like a small city town house sandwiched between two others. She parked outside her door on a fractured concrete pad. There were parched desert weeds wilting in the cracks.

But it was gloriously cool inside the house. There was central air running hard. He could feel the pressure it was creating. There was a narrow living room with a kitchen area in back. A staircase on the left. Cheap rented furniture and a lot of books. No television.

"I'm going to shower," she said. "Make yourself at home."

She disappeared up the stairs. He took a look around. The

books were mostly law texts. The civil and criminal codes of Texas. Some constitutional commentaries. There was a phone on a side table with four speed dials programmed. Top slot was labeled *Work*. Second was *J Home*. Third was *J Work*. Fourth was *M & D*. On one of the bookshelves there was a photograph in a silver frame, showing a handsome couple who could have been in their middle fifties. It was a casual outdoors shot, in a city, probably New York. The man had gray hair and a long patrician face. The woman looked a little like an older version of Alice herself. Same hair, minus the color and the youthful bounce. The Park Avenue parents, no doubt. Mom and Dad, M & D. They looked O.K. He figured *J* was probably a boyfriend. He checked, but there was no photograph of him. Maybe his picture was upstairs, next to her bed.

He sat in a chair and she came back down within ten minutes. Her hair was wet and combed, and she was wearing shorts again with a T-shirt that probably said *Harvard Soccer* except it had been washed so many times the writing was nearly illegible. The shorts were short and the T-shirt was thin and tight. She had dispensed with the sports bra. That was clear. She was barefoot and looked altogether sensational.

"You played soccer?" he asked.

"My partner did," she said.

He smiled at the warning. "Does he still?"

"He's a she. Judith. I'm gay. And yes, she still plays."

"She any good?"

"As a partner?"

"As a soccer player."

"She's pretty good. Does it bother you?"

"That she's pretty good at soccer?"

"No, that I'm gay."

"Why would it?"

Alice shrugged. "It bothers some people."

"Not this one."

"I'm Jewish, too."

Reacher smiled. "Did your folks buy you the handgun?"

She glanced at him. "You found that?"

"Sure," he said. "Nice piece."

She nodded. "A gay Jewish vegetarian woman from New York, they figured I should have it."

Reacher smiled again. "I'm surprised they didn't get you a machine gun or a grenade launcher."

She smiled back. "I'm sure they thought about it."

"You obviously take your atoning seriously. You must feel like I did walking around in the Lebanon."

She laughed. "Actually, it's not so bad here. Texas is a pretty nice place, overall. Some great people, really."

"What does Judith do?"

"She's a lawyer, too. She's in Mississippi right now."

"Same reasons?"

Alice nodded. "A five-year plan."

"There's hope for the legal profession yet."

"So it doesn't bother you?" she said. "That it's just a meal with a new friend and then back to the motel on your own?"

"I never thought it would be anything else," he lied.

The meal was excellent. It had to be, because he wasn't hungry. It was some kind of a homemade dark chewy confection made out of crushed nuts bound together with cheese and onions. Probably full of protein. Maybe some vitamins, too. They drank a little wine and a lot of water with it. He helped her clear up and then they talked until eleven.

"I'll drive you back," she said.

But she was barefoot and comfortable, so he shook his head.

"I'll walk," he said. "Couple of miles will do me good."

"It's still hot," she said.

"Don't worry. I'll be O.K."

She didn't put up much of a protest. He arranged to meet her at the mission in the morning and said goodnight. The outside air was as thick as soup. The walk took forty minutes and his shirt was soaked again when he got back to the motel.

He woke early in the morning and rinsed his clothes and put them on wet. They were dry by the time he reached the law offices. The humidity had gone and the hot desert air sucked the moisture right out of them and left them as stiff as new canvas. The sky was blue and completely empty.

Alice was already at her usual desk in a black A-line dress
with no sleeves. A Mexican guy was occupying one of her
client chairs. He was talking quietly to her. She was writing
on a yellow pad. The young intern from Hack Walker's office
was waiting patiently behind the Mexican guy's shoulder. He
was holding a thin orange and purple FedEx packet in his
hand. Reacher took a place right behind him. Alice was suddenly aware of the gathering crowd and looked up. Sketched
a surprised *just a minute* gesture in the air and turned back to
her client. Eventually put her pencil down and spoke quietly
in Spanish. The guy responded with stoic blank-faced pa-
tience and stood up and shuffled away. The intern moved forward and laid the FedEx packet on the desk.

"Carmen Greer's medical reports," he said. "These are the
originals. Mr. Walker took copies. He wants a conference at
nine-thirty."

"We'll be there," Alice said.

She pulled the packet slowly toward her. The intern followed the Mexican guy out. Reacher sat down in the client
chair. Alice glanced at him, her fingers resting on the packet,
a puzzled expression on her face. He shrugged. The packet
was a lot thinner than he had expected, too.

She unfolded the flap and pressed the edges of the packet
inward so it opened like a mouth. Held it up and spilled the
contents on the desk. There were four separate reports
packed loose in individual green covers. Each cover was
marked with Carmen's name and her Social Security number
and a patient reference. There were dates on all of them. The
dates ranged back more than six years. The older the date, the
paler the cover, like the green color had faded out with age.
Reacher slid his chair around the desk and put it next to Alice's. She stacked the four reports in date order, with the oldest at the top of the pile. She opened it up and nudged it left,
so it was exactly between them. Then she moved her chair a
fraction, so her shoulder was touching his.

"O.K.," she said. "So let's see."

The first report was about Ellie's birth. The whole thing
was timed in hours and minutes. There was a lot of gynecol-
ogical stuff about dilation and contractions. Fetal monitors

had been attached. An epidural anesthetic had been administered at thirteen minutes past four in the morning. It had been judged fully effective by four-twenty. There had been a delivery-room shift change at six. Labor had continued until the following lunchtime. Accelerants had been used. An episiotomy had been performed at one o'clock. Ellie had been born at twenty-five minutes past. No complications. Normal delivery of the placenta. The episiotomy had been stitched immediately. The baby was pronounced viable in every respect.

There was no mention of facial bruising, or a split lip, or loosened teeth.

The second report concerned two cracked ribs. It was dated in the spring, fifteen months after childbirth. There was an X-ray film attached. It showed the whole left side of her upper torso. The ribs were bright white. Two of them had tiny gray cracks. Her left breast was a neat dark shape. The attending physician had noted that the patient reported being thrown from a horse and landing hard against the top rail of a section of ranch fencing. As was usual with rib injuries, there was nothing much to be done except bind them tight and recommend plenty of physical rest.

"What do you think?" Alice asked.

"Could be something," Reacher said.

The third report was dated six months later, at the end of the summer. It concerned severe bruising to Carmen's lower right leg. The same physician noted she reported falling from a horse while jumping and landing with her shin against the pole that constituted the obstacle the horse was attempting. There was a long technical description of the contusion, with measurements vertically and laterally. The affected area was a tilted oval, four inches wide and five long. X rays had been taken. The bone was not fractured. Painkillers had been prescribed and the first day's supply provided from the emergency room pharmacy.

The fourth report was dated two and a half years later, which was maybe nine months before Sloop went to prison. It showed a broken collarbone on the right side. All the names in the file were new. It seemed like the whole ER staff had turned over. There was a new name for the attending physician, and she made no comment about Carmen's claim to have fallen off her horse onto the rocks of the mesa. There were extensive detailed notes about the injury. They were very thorough. There was an X-ray film. It showed the curve of her neck and her shoulder. The collarbone was cleanly snapped in the middle.

Alice squared all four reports together, upside down on the desk.

"Well?" she said.

Reacher made no reply. Just shook his head.

"Well?" she said again.

"Maybe she sometimes went to another hospital," he said.

"No, we'd have picked it up. I told you, we ask at all of them. Matter of routine."

"Maybe they drove out of state."

"We checked," she said. "Domestic violence, we cover all neighboring states. I told you that, too. Routine guidelines."

"Maybe she used another name."

"They're logged by Social Security number."

He nodded. "This isn't enough, Alice. She told me about more than this. We've got the ribs and we've got the collarbone, but she claimed he broke her arm, too. Also her jaw. She said she'd had three teeth reimplanted."

Alice said nothing. He closed his eyes. Tried to think about it like he would have in the old days, an experienced investigator with a suspicious mind and thirteen years of hard time behind him.

"Two possibilities," he said. "One, the hospital records system screwed up."

Alice shook her head. "Very unlikely."

He nodded again. "Agreed. So two, she *was* lying."

Alice was quiet for a long moment.

"Exaggerating, maybe," she said. "You know, to lock you in. To make sure of your help."

He nodded again, vaguely. Checked his watch. It was twenty past nine. He leaned sideways and slipped the stacked reports back into the FedEx packet.

"Let's go see what Hack thinks," he said.

Two thirds of the killing crew rolled south out of Pecos, uncharacteristically quiet. The third member waited in the motel room, pensive. They were taking risks now. Twelve years in the business, and they had never worked one area so long. It had always seemed too dangerous. In and out, quick and clean, had been their preferred method. Now they were departing from it. Radically. So there had been no conversation that morning. No jokes, no banter. No pre-mission excitement. Just a lot of nervous preoccupation with private thoughts.

But they had readied the car on schedule, and assembled the things they would need. Then they had half-eaten breakfast, and sat quiet, checking their watches.

"Nine-twenty," the woman said eventually. "It's time."

There was a visitor already seated in Walker's office. He was a man of maybe seventy, overweight and florid, and he was suffering badly in the heat. The air conditioners were going so hard that the rush of air was audible over the drone of the motors and papers were lifting off the desk. But the indoor temperature was still somewhere in the middle nineties. The visitor was mopping his brow with a large white handkerchief. Walker himself had his jacket off and was sitting absolutely still in his chair with his head in his hands. He had copies of the medical reports laid side by side on his desk and he was staring at them like they were written in a foreign language. He looked up blankly, and then he made a vague gesture toward the stranger.

"This is Cowan Black," he said. "Eminent professor of forensic medicine, lots of other things, too. The renowned defense expert. This is probably the first time he's ever been in a DA's office."

Alice stepped over and shook the guy's hand.

"I'm very pleased to meet you, sir," she said. "I've heard a lot about you."

Cowan Black said nothing. Alice introduced Reacher and they all shuffled their chairs into an approximate semicircle around the desk.

"The reports came in first thing this morning," Walker said. "Everything on file from Texas, which was one hospital only. There was nothing at all from New Mexico, Oklahoma,

Arkansas, or Louisiana. I personally photocopied everything and immediately sent the originals over to you. Dr. Black arrived a half hour ago and has studied the copies. He wants to see the X rays. Those, I couldn't copy."

Reacher passed the FedEx packet to Black, who spilled the contents the same way Alice had and extracted the three X-ray films. The ribs, the leg, the collarbone. He held them up against the light from the window and studied them, one by one, for minutes each. Then he slipped them back in their appropriate folders, neatly, like he was a man accustomed to order and precision.

Walker sat forward. "So, Dr. Black, are you able to offer us a preliminary opinion?"

He sounded tense, and very formal, like he was already in court. Black picked up the first folder. The oldest, the palest, the one about Ellie's birth.

"This is nothing at all," he said. His voice was deep and dark and rotund, like a favorite uncle in an old movie. A perfect voice for the witness stand. "This is purely routine obstetrics. Interesting only in that a rural Texas hospital was operating at a level that would have been considered state-of-the-art a decade or so earlier."

"Nothing untoward?"

"Nothing at all. One assumes the husband caused the pregnancy, but aside from that there's no evidence he did anything to her."

"The others?"

Black switched files, to the damaged ribs. Pulled the X-ray film out and held it ready.

"Ribs are there for a purpose," he said. "They form a hard, bony, protective cage to protect the vulnerable internal organs from damage. But not a *rigid* cage. That would be foolish, and evolution isn't a foolish process. No, the rib cage is a sophisticated structure. If it *were* rigid, the bones would shatter under any kind of severe blow. But there's complex ligament suspension involved at each of the bone terminations, so the cage's first response is to yield and distort, in order to spread the force of the impact."

He held up the X-ray film and pointed here and there on it.

"And that's exactly what happened here," he said. "There is obvious stretching and tearing of the ligaments all over the place. This was a heavy diffuse blow with a broad, blunt instrument. The force was dissipated by the flexibility of the rib cage, but even so was sufficient to crack two of the bones."

"What kind of a blunt instrument?" Walker asked.

"Something long and hard and rounded, maybe five or six inches in diameter. Something exactly like a fencing rail, I would think."

"It couldn't have been a kick?"

Black shook his head.

"Emphatically, no," he said. "A kick transfers a lot of energy through a tiny contact area. The welt at the toe of a boot is what? Maybe an inch and a half by a quarter inch? That's essentially a *sharp* object, not a blunt object. It would be too sudden and too concentrated for the yielding effect to operate. We would see the cracked bones, for sure, but we wouldn't see the ligament stretching at all."

"What about a knee?"

"A knee in the ribs? That's similar to a punch. Blunt, but an essentially circular impact site. The ligament stretching would show a completely different pattern."

Walker drummed his fingers on his desk. He was starting to sweat.

"Any way a person could have done it?" he asked.

Black shrugged. "If he were some kind of contortionist, maybe. If he could hold his whole leg completely rigid and somehow jump up and hit her in the side with it. Like it was a fence railing. I would say it was completely impossible."

Walker went quiet for a second.

"What about the bruised shin?" he asked.

Black swapped the third file into his hand. Opened it and read through the description of the contusion again. Then he shook his head.

"The shape of the bruise is crucial," he said. "Again, it's what you'd get from the impact of a long hard rounded object. Like a fence rail again, or maybe a sewer pipe, striking against the front of the shin at an oblique angle."

"Could he have hit her with a length of pipe?"

Black shrugged again.

"Theoretically, I suppose," he said. "If he was standing almost behind her, and somehow could reach over her, and he swung a hard downward blow, and struck her almost but not quite parallel with her leg. He'd have to do it two-handed, because nobody can hold a six-inch diameter pipe one-handed. Probably he'd have to stand on a chair, and position her very carefully in front of it. It's not very likely, is it?"

"But is it possible?"

"No," Black said. "It isn't possible. I say that now, and I'd certainly have to say it under oath."

Walker was quiet again.

"What about the collarbone?" he asked.

Black picked up the last report.

"These are very detailed notes," he said. "Clearly an excellent physician."

"But what do they tell you?"

"It's a classic injury," Black said. "The collarbone is like a circuit breaker. A person falls, and they try to break their fall by throwing out their hand. Their whole body weight is turned into a severe physical impact that travels upward as a shock wave through their rigid arm, through their rigid shoulder joint, and onward. Now, if it wasn't for the collarbone, that force would travel into the neck, and probably break it, causing paralysis. Or into the brain pan, causing unconsciousness, maybe a chronic comatose state. But evolution is smart, and it chooses the least of all the evils. The collarbone snaps, thereby dissipating the force. Inconvenient and painful, to be sure, but not life-threatening. A mechanical circuit breaker, and generations of bicyclists and inline skaters and horseback riders have very good reason to be grateful for it."

"Falling can't be the only way," Walker said.

"It's the *main* way," Black said. "And almost always the only way. But occasionally I've seen it happen other ways, too. A downward blow with a baseball bat aimed at the head might miss and break the collarbone. Falling beams in a burning building might impact against the top of the shoulder. I've seen that with firefighters."

"Carmen Greer wasn't a firefighter," Walker said. "And

there's no evidence a baseball bat was involved any other time."

Nobody spoke. The roar of the air conditioners filled the silence.

"O.K.," Walker said. "Let me put it this way. I need evidence that there was violent physical abuse against this woman. Is there any here?"

Black went quiet for a spell. Then he simply shook his head.

"No," he said. "Not within the bounds of reasonable likelihood."

"None at all? Not even a shred?"

"No, I'm afraid not."

"Stretching the bounds of reasonable likelihood?"

"There's nothing there."

"Stretching the bounds all the way until they break?"

"Still nothing. She had a normal pregnancy and she was an unlucky horseback rider. That's all I see here."

"No reasonable doubt?" Walker said. "That's all I need. Just a shred will do."

"It's not there."

Walker paused a beat. "Doctor, please let me say this with the greatest possible respect, O.K.? From a DA's point of view, you've been a pain in the rear end many more times than I can remember, to me and my colleagues throughout the state. There have been times when we're not sure what you've been smoking. You've always been capable of coming up with the most bizarre explanations for almost anything. So I'm asking you. Please. Is there any way *at all* you could interpret this stuff differently?"

Black didn't answer.

"I'm sorry," Walker said. "I offended you."

"Not in the way you think you did," Black said. "The fact is, I've never offered a bizarre explanation of anything. If I see possible exoneration, I speak up in court, sure. But what you clearly fail to understand is if I *don't* see possible exoneration, then I don't speak up *at all*. What your colleagues and I have clashed over in the past is merely the tip of the iceberg. Cases that have no merit don't get to trial, because I advise the defense to plead them out and hope for mercy. And I see many, many cases that have no merit."

"Cases like this one?"

Black nodded. "I'm afraid so. If I had been retained by Ms. Aaron directly, I would tell her that her client's word is not to be trusted. And you're right, I say that very reluctantly, with a long and honorable record of preferring to take the defense's side. Which is a record I have always maintained, despite the attendant risk of annoying our districts' attorneys. And which is a record I always aim to continue, for as long as I am spared. Which might not be much longer, if this damn heat keeps up."

He paused a second and looked around.

"For which reason I must take my leave of you now," he said. "I'm very sorry I was unable to help you, Mr. Walker. Really. It would have been enormously satisfying."

He squared the reports together and slipped them back into the FedEx packet. Handed it to Reacher, who was nearest. Then he stood up and headed for the door.

"But there has to be something," Walker said. "I don't believe this. The one time in my life I *want* Cowan Black to come up with something, and he can't."

Black shook his head. "I learned a long time ago, sometimes they're just guilty."

He sketched a brief gesture that was half-wave, half-salute, and walked slowly out of the office. The breeze from the air conditioners caught the door and crashed it shut behind him. Alice and Reacher said nothing. Just watched Walker at his desk. Walker dropped his head into his hands and closed his eyes.

"Go away," he said. "Just get the hell out of here and leave me alone."

The air in the stairwell was hot, and it was worse still out on the sidewalk. Reacher swapped the FedEx packet into his left hand and caught Alice's arm with his right. Stopped her at the curb.

"Is there a good jeweler in town?" he asked.

"I guess," she said. "Why?"

"I want you to sign out her personal property. You're still her lawyer, as far as anybody knows. We'll get her ring appraised. Then we'll find out if she's telling the truth about *anything*."

"You still got doubts?"

"I'm from the army. First we check, then we double-check."

"O.K.," she said. "If you want." They turned around and walked down the alley and she took possession of Carmen's lizard skin belt and her ring by signing a form that specified both items as material evidence. Then they went looking for a jeweler. They walked away from the cheap streets and found one ten minutes later in a row of upmarket boutiques. The window display was too crowded to be called elegant, but judging by the price tags the owner had a feel for quality. Or for blind optimism.

"So how do we do this?" Alice asked.

"Make out it's an estate sale," Reacher said. "Maybe it belonged to your grandmother."

The guy in the store was old and stooped. He might have looked pretty sharp forty years ago. But he still acted sharp. Reacher saw a flash in his eyes. *Cops?* Then he saw him answer his own question in the negative. Alice didn't look like a cop. Neither did Reacher, which was a mistaken impression he'd traded on for years. Then the guy went into an assessment of how smart these new customers might be. It was transparent, at least to Reacher. He was accustomed to watching people make furtive calculations. He saw him decide to proceed with caution. Alice produced the ring and told him she'd inherited it from family. Told him she was thinking of selling it, if the price was right.

The guy held it under a desk lamp and put a loupe in his eye.

"Color, clarity, cut and carat," he said. "The four Cs. That's what we look for."

He turned the stone left and right. It flashed in the light. He picked up a slip of stiff card that had circular holes punched through it. They started small and got bigger. He fitted the stone in the holes until he found one that fit exactly.

"Two and a quarter carats," he said. "Cut is real handsome. Color is good, maybe *just* on the yellow side of truly excellent. Clarity isn't flawless, but it's not very far off. This stone ain't bad. Not bad at all. How much do you want for it?"

"Whatever it's worth," Alice said.

"I could give you twenty," the guy said.

"Twenty what?"

"Thousand dollars," the guy said.

"Twenty thousand dollars?"

The guy put up his hands, palms out, defensively.

"I know, I know," he said. "Someone probably told you it's worth more. And maybe it is, retail, some big fancy store, Dallas or somewhere. But this is Pecos, and you're selling, not buying. And I have to make my profit."

"I'll think about it," Alice said.

"Twenty-five?" the guy said.

"Twenty-*five* thousand dollars?"

The guy nodded. "That's about as high as I can go, being fair to myself. I got to eat, after all."

"Let me think about it," Alice said.

"Well, don't think too long," the guy said. "The market might change. And I'm the only game in town. Piece like this, it'll scare anybody else."

They stopped together on the sidewalk right outside the store. Alice was holding the ring like it was red hot. Then she opened her pocketbook and put it in a zippered compartment. Used her fingertips to push it all the way down.

"Guy like that says twenty-five, it's got to be worth sixty," Reacher said. "Maybe more. Maybe a lot more. My guess is he's not the Better Business Bureau's poster boy."

"A lot more than thirty dollars, anyway," Alice said. "A fake? Cubic zirconium? She's playing us for fools."

He nodded, vaguely. He knew she meant *playing you for a fool*. He knew she was too polite to say it.

"Let's go," he said.

They walked west through the heat, back to the cheap part of town, beyond the courthouse, next to the railroad tracks. It was about a mile, and they spent thirty minutes on it. It was too hot to hurry. He didn't speak the whole way. Just fought his usual interior battle about exactly when to give up on a lost cause.

He stopped her again at the door to the mission.

"I want to try one last thing," he said.

"Why?" she asked.

"Because I'm from the army," he said. "First we double-check, then we triple-check."

She sighed. A little impatience there. "What do you want to do?"

"You need to drive me."

"Where?"

"There's an eyewitness we can talk to."

"An *eyewitness?* Where?"

"In school, down in Echo."

"The *kid?*"

He nodded. "Ellie. She's sharp as a tack."

"She's six years old."

"If it was happening, I'll bet she knows."

Alice stood completely still for a second. Then she glanced in through the windows. The place was crowded with customers. They looked listless from the heat and beaten down by life.

"It's not fair to *them,*" she said. "I need to move on."

"Just this one last thing."

"I'll lend you the car again. You can go alone."

He shook his head. "I need your opinion. You're the lawyer. And I won't get in the schoolhouse without you. You've got status. I haven't."

"I can't do it. It'll take all day."

"How long would it have taken to get the money from the rancher? How many billable hours?"

"We don't bill."

"You know what I mean."

She was quiet for a moment.

"O.K.," she said. "A deal's a deal, I guess."

"This is the last thing, I promise."

"Why, exactly?" she asked.

They were in the yellow VW, heading south on the empty road out of Pecos. He recognized none of the landmarks. It had been dark when he came the other way in the back of the police cruiser.

"Because I was an investigator," he said.

"O.K.," she said. "Investigators investigate. That, I can follow. But don't they *stop* investigating? I mean, ever? When they *know* already?"

"Investigators never know," he said. "They feel, and they guess."

"I thought they dealt in facts."

"Not really," he said. "I mean, eventually they do, I suppose. But ninety-nine percent of the time it's ninety-nine percent about what you *feel*. About people. A good investigator is a person with a feel for people."

"Feeling doesn't change black into white."

He nodded. "No, it doesn't."

"Weren't you ever wrong before?"

"Of course I was. Lots of times."

"But?"

"But I don't think I'm wrong now."

"So why, exactly?" she asked again.

"Because I know things about people, Alice."

"So do I," she said. "Like, I know Carmen Greer suckered you, too."

He said nothing more. Just watched her drive, and looked at the view ahead. He could see mountains in the distance, where Carmen had chased the school bus. He had the FedEx packet on his knees. He fanned himself with it. Balanced it on his fingers. Turned it over and over, aimlessly. Stared down at the front and the back, at the orange and purple logo, at the label, at the meaningless little words all over it, sender, addressee, *extremely urgent,* commodity description, dimensions in inches, twelve-by-nine, weight in pounds, two-point-six, payment, recipient's contact information, overnight, no post office box number, shipper must check: *this shipment does not contain dangerous goods*. He shook his head and pitched it behind him, onto the backseat.

"She had no money with her," he said.

Alice said nothing back. Just drove on, piloting the tiny car fast and economically. He could feel her pitying him. It was suddenly coming off her in waves.

"What?" he said.

"We should turn around," she said. "This is a complete waste of time."

"Why?"

"Because exactly what is Ellie going to tell us? I mean, I can follow your thinking. If Carmen really *did* get a broken arm, then she must have been wearing a plaster cast for six weeks. And Ellie's a smart kid, so she'll recall it. Same for the jaw thing. Broken jaw, you're all wired up for a spell. Certainly a kid would remember *that*. *If* any of this really happened, and *if* it happened recently enough that she can remember anything at all."

"But?"

"But we *know* she was never in a cast. We *know* she never had her jaw wired. We've got her medical records, remember? They're right here in the car with us. Everything she ever went to the hospital for. Or do you think setting bones is a do-it-yourself activity? You think the blacksmith did it in the barn? So the very best Ellie can do is confirm what we already know. And most likely she won't remember anything anyway, because she's just a kid. So this trip is a *double* waste of time."

"Let's do it anyway," he said. "We're halfway there already. She might recall something useful. And I want to see her again. She's a great kid."

"I'm sure she is," Alice said. "But spare yourself, O.K.? Because what are you going to do? Adopt her? She's the one with the raw end of this deal, so you might as well accept it and forget all about her."

They didn't speak again until they arrived at the crossroads with the diner and the school and the gas station. Alice parked exactly where Carmen had and they got out together into the heat.

"I better come with you," Reacher said. "She knows me. We can bring her out and talk in the car."

They went through the wire gate into the yard. Then through the main door into the schoolhouse itself, into the school smell. They were out again a minute later. Ellie Greer wasn't there, and she hadn't been there the day before, either.

"Understandable, I guess," Alice said. "Traumatic time for her."

Reacher nodded. "So let's go. It's only another hour south."

"Great," Alice said.

They got back in the VW and drove the next sixty miles of parched emptiness without talking. It took a little less than an hour, because Alice drove faster than Carmen had wanted to. Reacher recognized the landmarks. He saw the old oil field, on the distant horizon off to the left. Greer Three.

"It's coming up," he said.

Alice slowed. The red-painted picket fence replaced the wire and the gate swam into view through the haze. Alice braked and turned in under it. The small car bounced uncomfortably across the yard. She stopped it close to the bottom of the familiar porch steps and turned off the motor. The whole place was silent. No activity. But people were home, because all the cars were lined up in the vehicle barn. The white Cadillac was there, and the Jeep Cherokee, and the new pick-up, and the old pick-up. They were all crouched there in the shadows.

They got out of the car and stood for a second behind the open doors, like they offered protection from something. The air was very still, and hotter than ever. Easily a hundred and ten degrees, maybe more. He led her up the porch steps into the shadow of the roof and knocked on the door. It opened almost immediately. Rusty Greer was standing there. She was holding a .22 rifle, one-handed. She stayed silent for a long moment, just looking him over. Then she spoke.

"It's you," she said. "I thought it might be Bobby."

"You lost him?" Reacher said.

Rusty shrugged. "He went out. He isn't back yet."

Reacher glanced back at the motor barn.

"All the cars are here," he said.

"Somebody picked him up," Rusty said. "I was upstairs. Didn't see them. Just heard them."

Reacher said nothing.

"Anyway," Rusty said. "I didn't expect to see you again, ever."

"This is Carmen's lawyer," Reacher said.

Rusty turned and glanced at Alice. "This is the best she could do?"

"We need to see Ellie."

"What for?"

"We're interviewing witnesses."

"A child can't be a witness."

"I'll decide that," Alice said.

Rusty just smiled at her.

"Ellie's not here," she said.

"Well, where is she?" Reacher said. "She's not in school."

Rusty said nothing.

"Mrs. Greer, we need to know where Ellie is," Alice said.

Rusty smiled again. "I don't know where she is, lawyer girl."

"Why not?" Alice asked.

"Because Family Services took her, that's why not."

"When?"

"This morning. They came for her."

"And you let them take her?" Reacher said.

"Why wouldn't I? I don't want her. Now that Sloop is gone."

Reacher stared at her. "But she's your granddaughter."

Rusty made a dismissive gesture. The rifle moved in her hand.

"That's a fact I was never thrilled about," she said.

"Where did they take her?"

"An orphanage, I guess," Rusty said. "And then she'll get adopted, if anybody wants her. Which they probably won't. I understand half-breeds are very difficult to place. Decent folk generally don't want beaner trash."

There was silence. Just the tiny sounds of dry earth baking in the heat.

"I hope you get a tumor," Reacher said.

He turned around and walked back to the car without waiting for Alice. Got in and slammed the door and sat staring forward with his face burning and his massive hands clenching and unclenching. She got in beside him and fired up the motor.

"Get me out of here," he said. She took off in a cloud of dust. Neither of them spoke a single word, all the way north to Pecos.

It was three in the afternoon when they got back, and the legal mission was half empty because of the heat. There was the usual thicket of messages on Alice's desk. Five of them were from Hack Walker. They made a neat little sequence, each of them more urgent than the last.

"Shall we go?" Alice asked.

"Don't tell him about the diamond," Reacher said.

"It's over now, don't you see?"

And it was. Reacher saw it right away in Walker's face. There was relaxation there. Some kind of finality. Closure. Some kind of peace. He was sitting behind his desk. His desk was all covered with papers. They were arranged in two piles. One was taller than the other.

"What?" Reacher asked.

Walker ignored him and handed a single sheet to Alice.

"Waiver of her Miranda rights," he said. "Read it carefully. She's declining legal representation, and she's declaring that it's entirely voluntary. And she adds that she refused *your* representation from the very start."

"I doubted her competence," Alice said.

Walker nodded. "I'll give you the benefit of the doubt. But there's no doubt now. So you're here purely as a courtesy, O.K.? Both of you."

Then he handed over the smaller pile of papers. Alice took them and fanned them out and Reacher leaned to his right to look at them. They were computer printouts. They were all covered in figures and dates. They were bank records. Balance statements and transaction listings. Credits and debits. There seemed to be five separate accounts. Two were regular checking accounts. Three were money-market deposits. They were titled *Greer Non-Discretionary Trust,* numbers one through five. The balances were healthy. Very healthy. There was a composite total somewhere near two million dollars.

"Al Eugene's people messengered them over," Walker said. "Now look at the bottom sheets."

Alice riffed through. The bottom sheets were paper-clipped together. Reacher read over her shoulder. There was a lot of legal text. It added up to the formal minutes of a trust agreement. There was a notarized deed attached. It stated in relatively straightforward language that for the time being a single trustee was in absolute sole control of all Sloop

Greer's funds. That single trustee was identified as Sloop Greer's legal wife, Carmen.

"She had two million bucks in the bank," Walker said. "All hers, effectively."

Reacher glanced at Alice. She nodded.

"He's right," she said.

"Now look at the last clause of the minutes," Walker said.

Alice turned the page. The last clause concerned reversion. The trusts would become discretionary once again and return the funds to Sloop's own control at a future date to be specified by him. Unless he first became irreversibly mentally incapacitated. Or died. Whereupon all existing balances would become Carmen's sole property, in the first instance as a matter of prior agreement, and in the second, as a matter of inheritance.

"Is all of that clear?" Walker asked.

Reacher said nothing, but Alice nodded.

Then Walker passed her the taller pile.

"Now read this," he said.

"What is it?" she asked.

"A transcript," Walker said. "Of her confession."

There was silence.

"She confessed?" Alice said.

"We videotaped it," Walker said.

"When?"

"Noon today. My assistant went to see her as soon as the financial stuff came in. We tried to find you first, but we couldn't. Then she told us she didn't want a lawyer anyway. So we had her sign the waiver. Then she spilled her guts. We brought her up here and videotaped the whole thing over again. It's not pretty."

Reacher was half-listening, half-reading. It wasn't pretty. That was for damn sure. It started out with all the usual assurances about free will and absolute absence of coercion. She stated her name. Went all the way back to her L.A. days. She had been an illegitimate child. She had been a hooker. *Street stroller,* she called it. Some odd barrio expression, Reacher assumed. Then she came off the streets and started stripping, and changed her title to *sex worker*. She had latched onto Sloop, just like Walker had claimed. *My meal ticket,* she called him. Then it became a story of impatience. She was bored witless in Texas. She wanted out, but she wanted money in her pocket. The more money the better. Sloop's IRS trouble was a godsend. The trusts were tempting. She tried to have him killed in prison, which she knew from her peers was possible, but she found out that a federal minimum-security facility wasn't that sort of a place. So she waited. As soon as she heard he was getting out, she bought the gun and went recruiting. She planned to leverage her marks with invented stories about domestic violence. Reacher's name was mentioned as the last pick. He had refused, so she did it herself. Having already fabricated the abuse claims, she intended to use them to get off with self-defense, or diminished responsibility, or whatever else she could manage. But then she realized her hospital records would come up blank, so she was confessing and throwing herself on the mercy of the prosecutor. Her signature was scrawled on the bottom of every page.

Alice was a slow reader. She came to the end a full minute after him.

"I'm sorry, Reacher," she said.

There was silence for a moment.

"What about the election?" Reacher asked. The last hope.

Walker shrugged. "Texas code says it's a capital crime. Murder for remuneration. We've got enough evidence to choke a pig. And I can't ignore a voluntary confession, can I? So, couple hours ago I was pretty down. But then I got to thinking about it. Fact is, a voluntary confession helps me out. A confession and a guilty plea, saves the taxpayer the cost of a trial. Justifies me asking for a life sentence instead. The way I see it, with a story like that, she's going to look very, very bad, whoever you are. So if I back off the death penalty, I'll look magnanimous in comparison. Generous, even. The whites will fret a little, but the Mexicans will eat it up with a spoon. See what I mean? The whole thing is reversed now. She was the good guy, I was the heavy hand. But now she's the heavy hand, and I'm the good guy. So I think I'm O.K."

Nobody spoke for another minute. There was just the omnipresent roar of the air conditioners.

"I've got her property," Alice said. "A belt and a ring."

"Take them to storage," Walker said. "We'll be moving her, later."

"Where?"

"The penitentiary. We can't keep her here anymore."

"No, where's storage?"

"Same building as the morgue. Make sure you get a receipt."

Reacher walked with her over to the morgue. He wasn't aware of taking a single step. Wasn't aware of the heat, or the dust, or the noise, or the traffic, or the smells of the street. He felt like he was floating an inch above the sidewalk, insulated inside some kind of sensory-deprivation suit. Alice was talking to him, time to time, but he was hearing nothing that she said. All he could hear was a small voice inside his head that was saying *you were wrong. Completely wrong.* It was a voice he had heard before, but that didn't make it any easier to hear again, because he had built his whole career on hearing it fewer times than the next guy. It was like a box score in his mind, and his average had just taken some serious damage. Which upset him. Not because of vanity. It upset him because he was a professional who was supposed to get things right.

"Reacher?" Alice was saying. "You're not listening, are you?"

"What?" he said.

"I asked you, do you want to get a meal?"

"No," he said. "I want to get a ride."

She stopped walking. "What now? Quadruple-check?"

"No, I mean out of here. I want to go somewhere else. A long way away. I hear Antarctica is nice, this time of year."

"The bus depot is on the way back to the office."

"Good. I'll take a bus. Because I'm all done hitchhiking. You never know who's going to pick you up."

The morgue was a low industrial shed in a paved yard behind the street. It could have been a brake shop or a tire depot. It had metal siding and a roll-up vehicle door. There was a personnel entrance at the far end of the building. It had two steps up to it, framed by handrails fabricated from steel pipe. Inside, it was very cold. There were industrial-strength air conditioners running full blast. It felt like a meat store. Which it was, in a way. To the left of the foyer was a double door that gave directly onto the morgue operation. It was standing open, and Reacher could see the autopsy tables. There was plenty of stainless steel and white tile and fluorescent light in there.

Alice put the lizard skin belt on the reception counter and dug in her pocketbook for the ring. She told the attendant they were for *Texas* vs. *Carmen Greer*. He went away and came back with the evidence box.

"No, it's personal property," she said. "Not evidence. I'm sorry."

The guy gave her a *why didn't you say so* look and turned around.

"Wait," Reacher called. "Let me see that."

The guy paused, and then he turned back and slid the box across the counter. It had no lid, so it was really just a cardboard tray maybe three inches deep. Somebody had written *Greer* on the front edge with a marker pen. The Lorcin was in a plastic bag with an evidence number. Two brass shell cases were in a separate bag. Two tiny .22 bullets were in a bag each. They were gray and very slightly distorted. One bag was marked *Intercranial #1* and the other was marked *Intercranial #2*. They had reference numbers, and signatures.

"Is the pathologist here?" Reacher asked.

"Sure," the counter guy said. "He's always here."

"I need to see him," Reacher said. "Right now."

He was expecting objections, but the guy just pointed to the double doors.

"In there," he said.

Alice hung back, but Reacher went through. At first he thought the room was empty, but then he saw a glass door in the far corner. Behind it was an office, with a man in green scrubs at a desk. He was doing paperwork. Reacher knocked on the glass. The man looked up. Mouthed *come in*. Reacher went in.

"Help you?" the guy said.

"Only two bullets in Sloop Greer?" Reacher said.

"Who are you?"

"I'm with the perp's lawyer," Reacher said. "She's outside."

"The perp?"

"No, the lawyer."

"O.K.," the guy said. "What about the bullets?"

"How many were there?"

"Two," the guy said. "Hell of a time getting them out."

"Can I see the body?"

"Why?"

"I'm worried about a miscarriage of justice."

It's a line that usually works with pathologists. They figure there's going to be a trial, they figure they'll be called on for evidence, the last thing they want is to be humiliated by the defense on cross-examination. It's bad for their scientific image. And their egos. So they prefer to get any doubts squared away beforehand.

"O.K.," he said. "It's in the freezer."

He had another door in back of his office which led to a dim corridor. At the end of the corridor was an insulated steel door, like a meat locker.

"Cold in there," he said.

Reacher nodded. "I'm glad somewhere is."

The guy operated the handle and they went inside. The light was bright. There were fluorescent tubes all over the ceiling. There was a bank of twenty-seven stainless steel drawers on the far wall, nine across, three high. Eight of them were occupied. They had tags slipped into little receptacles on the front, the sort of thing you see on office filing cabinets. The air in the room was frosty. Reacher's breath clouded in front of him. The pathologist checked the tags and slid a drawer. It came out easily, on cantilevered runners.

"Had to take the back of his head off," he said. "Practically had to scoop his brains out with a soup ladle, before I found them."

Sloop Greer was on his back and naked. He looked small and collapsed in death. His skin was gray, like unfired clay. It was hard with cold. His eyes were open, blank and staring. He had two bullet holes in his forehead, about three inches apart. They were neat holes, blue and ridged at the edges, like they had been carefully drilled there by a craftsman.

"Classic .22 gunshot wounds," the pathologist said. "The

bullets go in O.K., but they don't come out again. Too slow. Not enough power. They just rattle around in there. But they get the job done."

Reacher closed his eyes. Then he smiled. A big, broad grin.

"That's for sure," he said. "They get the job done."

There was a knock at the open door. A low sound, like soft knuckles against hard steel. Reacher opened his eyes again. Alice was standing there, shivering.

"What are you doing?" she called to him.

"What comes after quadruple-check?" he called back.

His breath hung in the air in front of him, like a shaped cloud.

"Quintuple-check," she said. "Why?"

"And after that?"

"Sextuple," she said. "Why?"

"Because we're going to be doing a whole lot of checking now."

"Why?"

"Because there's something seriously wrong here, Alice. Come take a look."

14

Alice walked slowly across the tile.

"What's wrong?" she asked.

"Tell me what you see," Reacher said.

She dropped her eyes toward the corpse like it required a physical effort.

"Shot in the head," she said. "Twice."

"How far apart are the holes?"

"Maybe three inches."

"What else do you see?"

"Nothing," she said.

He nodded. "Exactly."

"So?"

"Look closer. The holes are clean, right?"

She took a step nearer the drawer. Bent slightly from the waist.

"They look clean," she said.

"That has implications," he said. "It means they're not contact wounds. A contact wound is where you put the muzzle of the gun directly against the forehead. You know what happens when you do that?"

She shook her head. Said nothing.

"First thing out of a gun barrel is an explosion of hot gas. If the muzzle was tight against the forehead, the gas punches in under the skin and then can't go anyplace, because of the bone. So it punches right back out again. It tears itself a big star-shaped hole. Looks like a starfish. Right, doc?"

The pathologist nodded.

"Star-burst splitting, we call it," he said.

"That's absent here," Reacher said. "So it wasn't a contact shot. Next thing out of the barrel is flame. If it was a real close shot, two or three inches, but not a contact shot, we'd see burning of the skin. In a small ring shape."

"Burn rim," the pathologist said.

"That's absent, too," Reacher said. "Next thing out is soot. Soft, smudgy black stuff. So if it was a shot from six or eight inches, we'd see soot smudging on his forehead. Maybe a patch a couple inches wide. That's not here, either."

"So?" Alice asked.

"Next thing out is gunpowder particles," Reacher said. "Little bits of unburned carbon. No gunpowder is perfect. Some of it doesn't burn. It just blasts out, in a spray. It hammers in under the skin. Tiny black dots. Tattooing, it's called. If it was a shot from a foot away, maybe a foot and a half, we'd see it. You see it?"

"No," Alice said.

"Right. All we see is the bullet holes. Nothing else. No evidence at all to suggest they were from close range. Depends on the exact powder in the shells, but they look to me like shots from three or four feet away, absolute minimum."

"Eight feet six inches," the pathologist said. "That's my estimation."

Reacher glanced at him. "You tested the powder?"

The guy shook his head. "Crime scene diagrams. He was on the far side of the bed. The bed was near the window, gave him an alley two feet six inches wide on his side. He was

found near the bedside table, up near the head, against the
window wall. We know she wasn't next to him there, or we'd
have found all that close-range stuff you just mentioned. So
the nearest she *could* have been was on the other side of the
bed. At the foot end, probably. Firing across it, diagonally,
according to the trajectories. He was probably retreating as
far as he could get. It was a king-size bed, so my best guess is
eight feet six inches, to allow for the diagonal."

"Excellent," Reacher said. "You prepared to say so on the
stand?"

"Sure. And that's only the theoretical minimum. Could
have been more."

"But what does it mean?" Alice asked.

"Means Carmen didn't do it," Reacher said.

"Why not?"

"How big is a man's forehead? Five inches across and two
high?"

"So?"

"No way she could have hit a target that small from eight
feet plus."

"How do you know?"

"Because I saw her shoot, the day before. First time she
pulled a trigger in her life. She was hopeless. Literally hopeless. She couldn't have hit the side of a barn from eight feet
plus. I told her she'd have to jam the gun in his gut and empty
the magazine."

"You're digging her grave," Alice said. "That sort of testimony shouldn't be volunteered."

"She didn't do it, Alice. She couldn't have."

"She could have gotten lucky."

"Sure, once. But not twice. Twice means they were aimed
shots. And they're close together, horizontally. He'd have
started falling after the first one. Which means it was a fast
double-tap. *Bang bang,* like that, no hesitation. That's skillful
shooting."

Alice was quiet for a second.

"She could have been faking," she said. "You know, before. About needing to learn. She lied about everything else.
Maybe she was really an expert shot, but she claimed not to

be. Because she wanted you to do it for her. For other reasons."

Reacher shook his head.

"She wasn't faking," he said. "All my life I've seen people
shoot. Either you can or you can't. And if you can, it shows.
You can't hide it. You can't unlearn it."

Alice said nothing.

"It wasn't Carmen," Reacher said. "Even *I* couldn't have
done it. Not with that piece of junk she bought. Not from that
distance. A fast double-tap to the head? Whoever did this is a
better shooter than me."

Alice smiled, faintly. "And that's rare?"

"Very," he said, unselfconsciously.

"But she confessed to it. Why would she do that?"

"I have no idea."

Ellie wasn't sure she understood completely. She had hidden on the stairs above the foyer when her grandmother
talked to the strangers. She had heard the words *new family*.
She understood what they meant. And she already knew she
needed a new family. The Greers had told her that her daddy
had died and her mommy had gone far away and wasn't ever
coming back. And they had told her they didn't want to keep
her with them. Which was O.K. with her. She didn't want to
stay with them, either. They were mean. They had already
sold her pony, and all the other horses, too. A big truck had
come for them, very early that morning. She didn't cry. She
just somehow knew it all went together. No more Daddy, no
more Mommy, no more pony, no more horses. Everything
had changed. So she went with the strangers, because she
didn't know what else to do.

Then the strangers had let her talk to her mommy on the
phone. Her mommy had cried, and at the end she said *be
happy with your new family*. But the thing was, she wasn't
sure if these strangers *were* her new family, or if they were
just *taking* her to her new family. And she was afraid to ask.
So she just kept quiet. The back of her hand was sore, where
she put it in her mouth.

* * *

"It's a can of worms," Hack Walker said. "You know what I mean? Best not to open it at all. Things could get out of hand, real quick."

They were back in Walker's office. It was easily fifty degrees hotter than the interior of the morgue building. They were both sweating heavily.

"You understand?" Walker asked. "It makes things worse again."

"You think?" Alice said.

Walker nodded. "It muddies the waters. Let's say Reacher is right, which is a stretch, frankly, because all he's got is a highly subjective opinion here. He's guessing, basically. And his guess is based on what, exactly? It's based on an impression she chose to give him beforehand, that she couldn't shoot, and we already know every *other* impression she chose to give him beforehand was total bullshit from beginning to end. But let's say he's right, just for the sake of argument. What does that give us?"

"What?"

"A conspiracy, is what. We know she tried to rope Reacher in. Now you've got her roping somebody else in. She gets ahold of somebody else, she tells them to come to the house, she tells them where and when, she tells them where her gun is concealed, they show up, get the gun, do the deed. If it happened that way, she's instigated a conspiracy to commit murder for remuneration. Hired a killer, cold-blooded as hell. We go down that road, she's headed for the lethal injection again. Because *that* looks a whole lot worse than a solo shot, believe me. In comparison, a solo shot looks almost benign. It looks like a crime of the moment, you know? We leave it exactly the way we got it, along with the guilty plea, I'm happy asking for a life sentence. But we start talking conspiracy, that's real evil, and we're back on track for death row."

Alice said nothing.

"So you see what I mean?" Walker said. "There's no net benefit. Absolutely the opposite effect. It makes things much worse for her. Plus, she already said she did it herself. Which

I think is true. But if it isn't, then her confession was a calculated lie, designed to cover her ass, because she knew a conspiracy would look worse. And we'd have to react to that. We couldn't let that go. It would make us look like fools."

Alice said nothing. Reacher just shrugged.

"So leave it alone," Walker said. "That's my suggestion. If it would help her, I'd look at it. But it won't. So we should leave it alone. For her sake."

"And for your judgeship's sake," Reacher said.

Walker nodded. "I'm not hiding that from you."

"You happy to leave it alone?" Alice asked. "As a prosecutor? Somebody could be getting clean away with something."

Walker shook his head. *"If* it happened the way Reacher thinks. If, if, if. *If* is a very big word. I got to say I think it's highly unlikely. Believe me, I'm a real enthusiastic prosecutor, but I wouldn't build a case and waste a jury's time on one person's purely subjective opinion about how well another person could shoot. Especially when that other person is as accomplished a liar as Carmen is. All we know, she's been shooting every day since she was a kid. A rough kid from some barrio in L.A., certainly a rural Texas jury wouldn't see any problem in swallowing that."

Reacher said nothing. Alice nodded again.

"O.K.," she said. "I'm not her lawyer, anyway."

"What would you do if you were?"

She shrugged. "I'd leave it, probably. Like you say, blundering into a conspiracy rap wouldn't help her any."

She stood up, slowly, like it was an effort in the heat. She tapped Reacher on the shoulder. Gave him a *what can we do?* look and headed for the door. He stood up and followed her. Walker said nothing. Just watched them partway out of the room and then dropped his eyes to the old photograph of the three boys leaning on the pick-up's fender.

They crossed the street together and walked as far as the bus depot. It was fifty yards from the courthouse, fifty yards from the legal mission. It was a small, sleepy depot. No buses in it. Just an expanse of diesel-stained blacktop ringed with

benches shaded from the afternoon sun by small white fiber-
glass roofs. There was a tiny office hut papered on the outside
with schedules. It had a through-the-wall air conditioner running hard. There was a woman in it, sitting on a high stool,
reading a magazine.

"Walker's right, you know," Alice said. "He's doing her a
favor. It's a lost cause."

Reacher said nothing.

"So where will you head?" she asked.

"First bus out," he said. "That's my rule."

They stood together and read the schedules. Next departure was to Topeka, Kansas, via Oklahoma City. It was due in
from Phoenix, Arizona, in a half hour. It was making a long
slow counterclockwise loop.

"Been to Topeka before?" Alice asked.

"I've been to Leavenworth," he said. "It's not far."

He tapped on the glass and the woman sold him a one-way
ticket. He put it in his pocket.

"Good luck, Alice," he said. "Four and a half years from
now, I'll look for you in the Yellow Pages."

She smiled.

"Take care, Reacher," she said.

She stood still for a second, like she was debating whether
to hug him or kiss him on the cheek, or just walk away. Then
she smiled again, and just walked away. He watched her go
until she was lost to sight. Then he found the shadiest bench
and sat down to wait.

She still wasn't sure. They had taken her to a very nice
place, like a house, with beds and everything. So maybe this
was her new family. But they didn't *look* like a family. They
were very busy. She thought they looked a bit like doctors.
They were kind to her, but busy too, with stuff she didn't understand. Like at the doctor's office. Maybe they were doctors. Maybe they knew she was upset, and they were going to
make her better. She thought about it for a long time, and
then she asked.

"Are you doctors?" she said.

"No," they answered.

"Are you my new family?"

"No," they said. "You'll go to your new family soon."

"When?"

"A few days, O.K.? But right now you stay with us."

She thought they all looked very busy.

The bus rolled in more or less on time. It was a big Greyhound, dirty from the road, wrapped in a diesel cloud, with heat shimmering visibly from its air conditioner grilles. It stopped twenty feet from him and the driver held the engine at a loud shuddering idle. The door opened and three people got off. Reacher stood up and walked over and got on. He was the only departing passenger. The driver took his ticket.

"Two minutes, O.K.?" the guy said. "I need a comfort stop."

Reacher nodded and said nothing. Just shuffled down the aisle and found a double seat empty. It was on the left, which would face the evening sun all the way after they turned north at Abilene. But the windows were tinted dark blue and the air was cold, so he figured he'd be O.K. He sat down sideways. Stretched out and rested his head against the glass. The eight spent shells in his pocket were uncomfortable against the muscle of his thigh. He hitched up and moved them through the cotton. Then he took them out and held them in his palm. Rolled them together like dice. They were warm, and they made dull metallic sounds.

Abilene, he thought.

The driver climbed back in and hung off the step and looked both ways, like an old railroad guy. Then he slid into his seat and the door wheezed shut behind him.

"Wait," Reacher called.

He stood up and shuffled forward again, all the way down the aisle.

"I changed my mind," he said. "I'm getting off."

"I already canceled your ticket," the driver said. "You want a refund, you'll have to mail a claim."

"I don't want a refund," Reacher said. "Just let me out, O.K.?"

The driver looked blank, but he operated the mechanism anyway and the doors wheezed open again. Reacher stepped down into the heat and walked away. He heard the bus leave behind him. It turned right where he had turned left and he heard its noise fade and die into the distance. He walked on to the law office. Working hours elsewhere were over and it was crowded again with groups of quiet worried people, some of them talking to lawyers, some of them waiting to. Alice was at her desk in back, talking to a woman with a baby on her knee. She looked up, surprised.

"Bus didn't come?" she asked.

"I need to ask you a legal question," he said.

"Is it quick?"

He nodded. "Civilian law, if some guy tells an attorney about a crime, how far can the cops press the attorney for the details?"

"It would be privileged information," Alice said. "Between lawyer and client. The cops couldn't press at all."

"Can I use your phone?"

She paused a moment, puzzled. Then she shrugged.

"Sure," she said. "Squeeze in."

He took a spare client chair and put it next to hers, behind the desk.

"Got phone books for Abilene?" he asked.

"Bottom drawer," she said. "All of Texas."

She turned back to the woman with the baby and restarted their discussion in Spanish. He opened the drawer and found the right book. There was an information page near the front, with all the emergency services laid out in big letters. He dialed the state police, Abilene office. A woman answered and asked how she could help him.

"I have information," he said. "About a crime."

The woman put him on hold. Maybe thirty seconds later the call was picked up elsewhere. Sounded like a squad room. Other phones were ringing in the background and there was faint people noise all around.

"Sergeant Rodríguez," a voice said.

"I have information about a crime," Reacher said again.

"Your name, sir?"

"Chester A. Arthur," Reacher said. "I'm a lawyer in Pecos County."

"O.K., Mr. Arthur, go ahead."

"You guys found an abandoned automobile south of Abilene on Friday. A Mercedes Benz belonging to a lawyer called Al Eugene. He's currently listed as a missing person."

There was the sound of a keyboard pattering.

"O.K.," Rodríguez said. "What can you tell me?"

"I have a client here who says Eugene was abducted from his car and killed very near the scene."

"What's your client's name, sir?"

"Can't tell you that," Reacher said. "Privileged information. And the fact is I'm not sure I even believe him. I need you to check his story from your end. If he's making sense, then maybe I can persuade him to come forward."

"What is he telling you?"

"He says Eugene was flagged down and put in another car. He was driven north to a concealed location on the left-hand side of the road, and then he was shot and his body was hidden."

Alice had stopped her conversation and was staring sideways at him.

"So I want you to search the area," Reacher said.

"We already searched the area."

"What kind of a radius?"

"Immediate surroundings."

"No, my guy says a mile or two north. You need to look under vegetation, in the cracks in the rock, pumping houses, anything there is. Some spot near where a vehicle could have pulled off the road."

"A mile or two north of the abandoned car?"

"My guy says not less than one, not more than two."

"On the left?"

"He's pretty sure," Reacher said.

"You got a phone number?"

"I'll call you back," Reacher said. "An hour from now."

He hung up. The woman with the baby was gone. Alice was still staring at him.

"What?" she said.

"We should have focused on Eugene before."

"Why?"

"Because what's the one solid fact we've got here?"

"What?"

"Carmen didn't shoot Sloop, that's what."

"That's an opinion, not a fact."

"No, it's a fact, Alice. Believe me, I *know* these things."

She shrugged. "O.K., so?"

"So somebody else shot him. Which raises the question, why? We know Eugene is missing, and we know Sloop is dead. They were connected, lawyer and client. So let's assume Eugene is dead, too, not just missing. For the sake of argument. They were working together on a deal that sprung Sloop from jail. Some kind of a big deal, because that isn't easy. They don't hand out remissions like candy. So it must have involved some heavy-duty information. Something valuable. Big trouble for somebody. Suppose that somebody took them *both* out, for revenge, or to stop the flow of information?"

"Where did you get this idea?"

"From Carmen, actually," he said. "She suggested that's how I should do it. Off Sloop and make like stopping the deal was the pretext."

"So Carmen took her own advice."

"No, Carmen's parallel," Reacher said. "She hated him, she had a motive, she's all kinds of a liar, but she didn't kill him. Somebody else did."

"Yes, *for* her."

"No," Reacher said. "It didn't happen that way. She just got lucky. It was a parallel event. Like he was run over by a truck someplace else. Maybe she's thrilled with the result, but she didn't *cause* it."

"How sure are you?"

"Very sure. Any other way is ridiculous. Think about it, Alice. Anybody who shoots that well is a professional. Professionals plan ahead, at least a few days. And if she had hired a professional a few days ahead, why would she trawl around Texas looking for guys like me hitching rides? And why would she allow Sloop to be killed in her own bedroom, where she would be the number-one suspect? With her own gun?"

"So what do you think happened?"

"I think some hit team took Eugene out on Friday and covered their ass by hiding the body so it won't be found until the trail is completely cold. Then they took Sloop out on Sunday and covered their ass by making it look like Carmen did it. In her bedroom, with her own gun."

"But she was with him. Wouldn't she have *noticed?* Wouldn't she have *said?*"

He paused. "Maybe she was with Ellie at the time. Maybe she walked back into the bedroom and found it done. Or maybe she was in the shower. Her hair was wet when they arrested her."

"Then she'd have heard the shots."

"Not with that shower. It's like Niagara Falls. And a .22 pistol is quiet."

"How do you know where they'll find Eugene's body? Assuming you're right?"

"I thought about how I would do it. They obviously had a vehicle of their own, out there in the middle of nowhere. So maybe they staged a breakdown or a flat. Flagged him down, forced him into their vehicle, drove him away. But they wouldn't want to keep him in there long. Too risky. Two or three minutes maximum, I figure, which is a mile or two from a standing start."

"Why north? Why on the left side?"

"I'd have driven way north first. Turned back and scouted the nearside shoulder. Picked my place and measured a couple of miles backward, turned around again and set up and waited for him."

"Conceivable," she said. "But the Sloop thing? That's impossible. They went down to that house? In Echo, in the middle of nowhere? Hid out and crept in? While she was in the shower?"

"I could have done it," he said. "And I'm assuming they're as good as me. Maybe they're better than me. They certainly shoot better."

"You're crazy," she said.

"Maybe," he said.

"No, for sure," she said. "Because she *confessed* to it. Why would she do that? If it was really nothing at all to do with her?"

"We'll figure that out later. First, we wait an hour."

He left Alice with work to do and went back out into the heat. Decided he'd finally take a look at the Wild West museum. When he got there, it was closed. Too late in the day. But he could see an alley leading to an open area in back. There was a locked gate, low enough for him to step over. Behind the buildings was a collection of rebuilt artifacts from the old days. There was a small one-cell jailhouse, and a replica of Judge Roy Bean's courthouse, and a hanging tree. The three displays made a nice direct sequence. Arrest, trial, sentence. Then there was Clay Allison's grave. It was well tended, and the headstone was handsome. Clay was his middle name. His first name was Robert. Robert Clay Allison, born 1840, died 1887. *Never killed a man that did not need killing.* Reacher had no middle name. It was Jack Reacher, plain and simple. Born 1960, not dead yet. He wondered what his headstone would look like. Probably wouldn't have one. There was nobody to arrange it.

He strolled back up the alley and stepped over the gate again. Facing him was a long low concrete building, two stories. Retail operations on the first floor, offices above. One of them had Albert E. Eugene, Attorney at Law painted on the window in old-fashioned gold letters. There were two other law firms in the building. The building was within sight of the courthouse. These were the cheap lawyers, Reacher guessed. Separated geographically from the free lawyers in Alice's row and the expensive lawyers who must be on some other street. Although Eugene had driven a Mercedes Benz. Maybe he did a lot of volume. Or maybe he was just vain and had been struggling with a heavy lease payment.

He paused at the crossroads. The sun was dropping low in the west and there were clouds stacking up on the southern horizon. There was a warm breeze on his face. It was gusting strong enough to tug at his clothes and stir dust on the sidewalk. He stood for a second and let it flatten the fabric of his shirt against his stomach. Then it died and the dull heat came back. But the clouds were still there in the south, like ragged stains on the sky.

He walked back to Alice's office. She was still at her desk. Still facing an endless stream of problems. There were people in her client chairs. A middle-aged Mexican couple. They had patient, trusting expressions on their faces. Her stack of paperwork had grown. She pointed vaguely at his chair, which was still placed next to hers. He squeezed in and sat down. Picked up the phone and dialed the Abilene number from memory. He gave his name as Chester Arthur and asked for Sergeant Rodríguez.

He was on hold a whole minute. Then Rodríguez picked up and Reacher knew right away they had found Eugene's body. There was a lot of urgency in the guy's voice.

"We need your client's name, Mr. Arthur," Rodriguez said.

"What did your people find?" Reacher asked.

"Exactly what you said, sir. Mile and a half north, on the left, in a deep limestone crevasse. Shot once through the right eye."

"Was it a .22?"

"No way. Not according to what I'm hearing. Nine millimeter, at least. Some big messy cannon. Most of his head is gone."

"You got an estimated time of death?"

"Tough question, in this heat. And they say the coyotes got to him, ate up some of the parts the pathologist likes to work with. But if somebody said Friday, I don't think we'd argue any."

Reacher said nothing.

"I need some names," Rodríguez said.

"My guy's not the doer," Reacher said. "I'll talk to him and maybe he'll call you."

Then he hung up before Rodríguez could start arguing. Alice was staring at him again. So were her clients. Clearly they spoke enough English to follow the conversation.

"Which president was Chester Arthur?" Alice asked.

"After Garfield, before Grover Cleveland," Reacher replied. "One of two from Vermont."

"Who was the other?"

"Calvin Coolidge."

"So they found Eugene," she said.

"Sure did."

"So now what?"

"Now we go warn Hack Walker."

"Warn him?"

Reacher nodded. "Think about it, Alice. Maybe what we've got here is two out of two, but I think it's more likely to be two out of three. They were a threesome, Hack and Al and Sloop. Carmen said they all worked together on the deal. She said Hack brokered it with the feds. So Hack knew what they knew, for sure. So he could be next."

Alice turned to her clients.

"Sorry, got to go," she said, in English.

Hack Walker was packing up for the day. He was on his feet with his jacket on and he was latching his briefcase closed. It was after six o'clock and his office windows were growing dim with dusk. They told him that Eugene was dead and watched the color drain out of his face. His skin literally contracted and puckered under a mask of sweat. He clawed his way around his desk and dumped himself down in his chair. He said nothing for a long moment. Then he nodded slowly.

"I guess I always knew," he said. "But I was, you know, hoping."

He turned to look down at the photograph.

"I'm very sorry," Reacher said.

"Do they know why?" Walker asked. "Or who?"

"Not yet."

Walker paused again. "Why did they tell you about it before me?"

"Reacher figured out where they should look," Alice said. *"He* told *them,* effectively."

Then she went straight into his two-for-three theory. The deal, the dangerous knowledge. The warning. Walker sat still and listened to it. His color came back, slowly. He stayed quiet, thinking hard. Then he shook his head.

"Can't be right," he said. "Because the deal was really nothing at all. Sloop caved in and undertook to pay the taxes and the penalties. That was all. Nothing more. He got desperate, couldn't stand the jail time. It happens a lot. Al contacted the IRS, made the offer, they didn't bat an eye. It's routine. It was handled at a branch office. By junior-grade personnel. That's how routine it was. The federal prosecutor needed to sign off on it, which is where I came in. I hustled it through, is all, a little faster than it might have gone without me. You know, the old boys' club. It was a routine IRS matter. And believe me, nobody gets killed over a routine IRS matter."

He shook his head again. Then he opened his eyes wide and went very still.

"I want you to leave now," he said.

Alice nodded. "We're very sorry for your loss. We know you were friends."

But Walker just looked confused, like that wasn't what he was worrying about.

"What?" Reacher said.

"We shouldn't talk anymore, is what," Walker said.

"Why not?"

"Because we're going around in a circle, and we're finishing up in a place where we don't want to be."

"We are?"

"Think about it, guys. Nobody gets killed over a routine IRS matter. Or do they? Sloop and Al were fixing to take the trust money away from Carmen and give most of it to the government. Now Sloop and Al are dead. Two plus two makes four. Her motive is getting bigger and better all the time. We keep talking like this, I've *got* to think conspiracy. Two deaths, not one. No choice, I've got to. And I don't want to do that."

"There was no conspiracy," Reacher said. "If she'd already hired people, why did she pick me up?"

Walker shrugged. "To confuse the issue? Distance herself?"

"Is she *that* smart?"

"I think she is."

"So prove it. Show us she hired somebody."

"I can't do that."

"Yes, you can. You've got her bank records. Show us the payment."

"The payment?"

"You think these people work for free?"

Walker made a face. Took keys from his pocket and unlocked a drawer in his desk. Lifted out the pile of financial information. *Greer Non-Discretionary Trust,* numbers 1 through 5. Reacher held his breath. Walker went through them, page by page. Then he squared them together again and reversed them on the desk. His face was blank.

Alice leaned forward and picked them up. Leafed through, scanning the fourth column from the left, which was the debit column. There were plenty of debits. But they were all small and random. Nothing bigger than two hundred and ninety-seven dollars. Several below a hundred.

"Add up the last month," Reacher said.

She scanned back.

"Nine hundred, round figures," she said.

Reacher nodded. "Even if she hoarded it, nine hundred bucks doesn't buy you much. Certainly doesn't buy you somebody who can operate the way we've seen."

Walker said nothing.

"We need to go talk to her," Reacher said.

"We can't," Walker said. "She's on the road, headed for the penitentiary."

"She didn't do it," Reacher said. "She didn't do anything. She's completely innocent."

"So why did she confess?"

Reacher closed his eyes. Sat still for a moment.

"She was forced to," he said. "Somebody got to her."

"Who?"

Reacher opened his eyes.

"I don't know who," he said. "But we can find out. Get the bailiff's log from downstairs. See who came to visit her."

Walker's face was still blank and sweaty. But he picked up the phone and dialed an internal number. Asked for the visitor's log to be brought up immediately. Then they waited in silence. Three minutes later they heard the sound of heavy footsteps in the secretarial pen and the bailiff came in through the office door. It was the day guy. He was breathing hard after running up the stairs. He was carrying a thick book in his hand.

Walker took it from him and opened it up. Scanned through it quickly and reversed it on the desk. Used his finger to point. Carmen Greer was logged in during the early hours of Monday morning. She was logged out two hours ago, into the custody of the Texas Department of Correction. In between she had received one visitor, twice. Nine o'clock on Monday morning and again on Tuesday at noon, the same assistant DA had gone down to see her.

"Preliminary interview, and then the confession," Walker said.

There were no other entries at all.

"Is this right?" Reacher asked.

The bailiff nodded.

"Guaranteed," he said.

Reacher looked at the log again. The first ADA interview had lasted two minutes. Clearly Carmen had refused to say a word. The second interview had lasted twelve minutes. After that she had been escorted upstairs for the videotape.

"Nobody else?" he asked.

"There were phone calls," the bailiff said.

"When?"

"All day Monday, and Tuesday morning."

"Who was calling her?"

"Her lawyer."

"Her *lawyer?*" Alice said.

The guy nodded.

"It was a big pain in the ass," he said. "I had to keep bringing her in and out to the phone."

"Who was the lawyer?" Alice asked.

"We're not allowed to ask, ma'am. It's a confidentiality thing. Lawyer discussions are secret."

"Man or woman?"

"It was a man."

"Hispanic?"

"I don't think so. He sounded like a regular guy. His voice was a little muffled. I think it was a bad phone line."

"Same guy every time?"

"I think so."

There was silence in the office. Walker nodded vaguely and the bailiff took it for a dismissal. They heard him walk out through the secretarial pen. They heard the lobby door close behind him.

"She didn't tell us she was represented," Walker said. "She told us she didn't *want* representation."

"She told me the same thing," Alice said.

"We need to know who this person was," Reacher said. "We need to get the phone company to trace the calls."

Walker shook his head. "Can't do it. Legal discussions are privileged."

Reacher stared at him. "You really think it was a *lawyer?*"

"Don't you?"

"Of course not. It was some guy, threatening her, forcing her to lie. Think about it, Walker. First time your ADA saw her, she wouldn't say a word. Twenty-seven hours later, she's confessing. Only thing that happened in between was a bunch of calls from this guy."

"But what kind of threat could make her say that?"

The killing crew was uneasy in its new role as baby-sitter. Each member felt exactly the same way, each for the exact same reasons. Holding a child hostage was not a normal part of their expertise. Taking her in the first place had been. That was a fairly standard operation, based as always on lure and deception. The woman and the tall fair man had gone to the Red House as a pair, because they figured that would match the public's perception of how social workers operate. They had arrived in the big official-looking sedan and used a brisk professional manner. They had mixed it with a generous helping of pious do-gooder sanctimony, like they were desperately concerned with the child's welfare above all else. They had a thick wad of bogus papers to display. The papers looked exactly like Family Services warrants and relevant authorizations from state agencies. But the grandmother hardly even looked at them. She offered no resistance at all. It struck them as unnatural. She just handed the kid over, like she was real glad about it.

The kid put up no resistance, either. She was very earnest and silent about the whole thing. Like she was trying to be on her best behavior. Like she was trying to please these new adults. So they just put her in the car and drove her away. No tears, no screaming, no tantrums. It went well, all things considered. Very well. About as effortless as the Al Eugene operation.

But then they departed from the usual. Radically. Standard practice would have been to drive straight to a scouted location and pull the triggers. Conceal the body and then get the hell out. But this task was different. They had to keep her hidden. And alive and unharmed. At least for a spell. Maybe days and days. It was something they had never done before. And professionals get uneasy with things they've never done before. They always do. That's the nature of professionalism. Professionals feel best when they stick to what they know.

"Call Family Services," Reacher said. "Right now."

Hack Walker just stared at him.

"You asked the question," Reacher said. "What kind of a threat could make her confess to something she didn't do? Don't you see? They must have gotten her kid."

Walker stared a beat longer, frozen. Then he wrestled himself into action and unlocked another drawer and rattled it open. Lifted out a heavy black binder. Opened it up and thumbed through and grabbed his phone and dialed a number. There was no answer. He dabbed the cradle and dialed another. Some kind of an evening emergency contact. It was picked up and he asked the question, using Ellie's full name, Mary Ellen Greer. There was a long pause. Then an answer. Walker listened. Said nothing. Just put the phone down, very slowly and carefully, like it was made out of glass.

"They never heard of her," he said.

Silence. Walker closed his eyes, and then opened them again.

"O.K.," he said. "Resources are going to be a problem. State police, of course. And the FBI, because this is a kidnap. But we've got to move immediately. Speed is absolutely paramount here. It always is, with kidnap cases. They could be taking her anywhere. So I want you two to go down to Echo right now, get the full story from Rusty. Descriptions and everything."

"Rusty won't talk to us," Reacher said. "She's too hostile. What about the Echo sheriff?"

"That guy is useless. He's probably drunk right now. You'll have to do it."

"Waste of time," Reacher said.

Walker opened another drawer and took two chromium stars from a box. Tossed them onto the desk.

"Raise your right hands," he said. "Repeat after me."

He mumbled his way through some kind of an oath. Reacher and Alice repeated it back, as far as they could catch it. Walker nodded.

"Now you're sheriff's deputies," he said. "Valid through-out Echo County. Rusty will *have* to talk to you."

Reacher just stared at him.

"What?" Walker said.

"You can still do that here? Deputize people?"

"Sure I can," Walker said. "Just like the Wild West. Now get going, O.K.? I've got a million calls to make."

Reacher took his chromium star and stood up, an accredited law enforcement official again for the first time in four and a quarter years. Alice stood up alongside him.

"Meet back here directly," Walker called. "And good luck."

Eight minutes later they were in the yellow VW again, heading south toward the Red House for the second time that day.

The woman took the call. She let the phone ring four times while she got the voice-altering device out of her bag and switched it on. But she didn't need it. She didn't need to talk at all. She just listened, because it was a one-sided message, long and complex but basically clear and concise and unambiguous, and the whole thing was repeated twice. When it was over, she hung up the phone and put the electronics back in her bag.

"It's tonight," she said.

"What is?" the tall man asked.

"The supplementary job," she said. "The Pecos thing. Seems like the situation up there is unraveling slightly. They found Eugene's body."

"Already?"

"Shit," the dark man said.

"Yes, shit," the woman said. "So we move on the supplementary right away, tonight, before things get any worse."

"Who's the target?" the tall man asked.

"His name is Jack Reacher. Some drifter, ex-military. I've got a description. There's a girl lawyer in the picture, too. She'll need attention as well."

"We do them simultaneous with this baby-sitting gig?"

The woman shrugged. "Like we always said, we keep the baby-sitting going as long as possible, but we reserve the right to terminate when necessary."

The men looked at each other. Ellie watched them from the bed.

15

Reacher was not good company on the ride south. He didn't talk at all for the first hour and a half. Evening dark had fallen fast and he kept the VW's dome light on and studied the maps from the glove compartment. In particular he concentrated on a large-scale topographical sheet that showed the southern part of Echo County. The county boundary was a completely straight line running east to west. At its closest point, it was fifty miles from the Rio Grande. That made no sense to him.

"I don't understand why she lied about the diamond," he said.

Alice shrugged. She was pushing the little car as fast as it was willing to go.

"She lied about everything," she said.

"The ring was different," he said.

"Different how?"

"A different sort of lie. Like apples are different from oranges."

"I don't follow."

"The ring is the only thing I can't explain to myself."

"The *only* thing?"

"Everything else is coherent, but the ring is a problem."

She drove on, another mile. The power line poles came and went, flashing through the headlight beams for a split second each.

"You know what's going on, don't you?" she said.

"You ever done computer-aided design?" he asked.

"No," she said.

"Me neither."

"So?"

"Do you know what it is?"

She shrugged again. "Vaguely, I guess."

"They can build a whole house or car or whatever, right there on the computer screen. They can paint it, decorate it, look at it. If it's a house, they can go *in* it, walk around. They can rotate it, look at the front, look at the back. If it's a car, they can see how it looks in daylight and in the dark. They can tilt it up and down, spin it around, examine it from every angle. They can crash it and see how it holds up. It's like a real thing, except it isn't. I guess it's a *virtual* thing."

"So?" she said again.

"I can see this whole situation in my mind, like a computer design. Inside and out, up and down. From every angle. Except for the ring. The ring screws it up."

"You want to explain that?"

"No point," he said. "Until I figure it out."

"Is Ellie going to be O.K.?"

"I hope so. That's why we're making this trip."

"You think the grandmother can help us?"

He shrugged. "I doubt it."

"So how is this trip helping Ellie?"

He said nothing. Just opened the glove compartment and put the maps back. Took out the Heckler & Koch handgun. Clicked out the magazine and checked the load. *Never assume.* But it still held its full complement of ten shells. He put the magazine back in and jacked the first round into the chamber. Then he cocked the pistol and locked it. Eased up off the passenger seat and slipped it into his pocket.

"You think we're going to need that?" she asked.

"Sooner or later," he said. "You got more ammo in your bag?"

She shook her head. "I never thought I'd actually *use* it."

He said nothing.

"You O.K.?" she asked.

"Feeling good," he said. "Maybe like you did during that big trial, before the guy refused to pay."

She nodded at the wheel. "It was a good feeling."

"That's your thing, right?"

"I guess it is."

"This is my thing," he said. "This is what I'm built for. The thrill of the chase. I'm an investigator, Alice, always was, always will be. I'm a *hunter*. And when Walker gave me that badge my head started working."

"You know what's going on, don't you?" she asked again.

"Aside from the diamond ring."

"Tell me."

He said nothing.

"Tell me," she said again.

"Did you ever ride a horse?"

"No," she said. "I'm a city girl. Openest space I ever saw was the median strip in the middle of Park Avenue."

"I just rode one with Carmen. First time ever."

"So?"

"They're very tall. You're way up there in the air."

"So?" she said again.

"You ever ride a bike?"

"In New York City?"

"Inline skating?"

"A little, back when it was cool."

"You ever fall?"

"Once, pretty badly."

He nodded. "Tell me about that meal you made for me."

"What about it?"

"Homemade, right?"

"Sure."

"You weighed out the ingredients?"

"You have to."

"So you've got a scale in your kitchen?"

"Sure," she said again.

"The scales of justice," he said.

"Reacher, what the hell are you talking about?"

He glanced to his left. The red picket fence was racing backward through the edge of her headlight beams.

"We're here," he said. "I'll tell you later."

She slowed and turned in under the gate and bumped across the yard.

"Face it toward the motor barn," he said. "And leave the headlights on. I want to take a look at that old pick-up truck."

"O.K.," she said.

She coasted a yard or two and hauled on the steering wheel until the headlight beams washed into the right-hand end of the barn. They lit up half of the new pick-up, half of the Jeep Cherokee, and all of the old pick-up between them.

"Stay close to me," he said.

They got out of the car. The night air felt suddenly hot and damp. Different than before. It was cloudy and there were disturbed insects floating everywhere. But the yard was quiet. No sound. They walked over together for a better look at the abandoned truck. It was some kind of a Chevrolet, maybe twenty years old, but still a recognizable ancestor of the newer truck alongside it. It had bulbous fenders and dulled paint and a roll bar built into the load bed. It must have had a million miles on it. Probably hadn't been started in a decade. The springs sagged and the tires were flat and the rubber was perished by the relentless heat.

"So?" Alice said.

"I think it's the truck in the photograph," Reacher said. "The one in Walker's office? Him and Sloop and Eugene leaning on the fender?"

"Trucks all look the same to me," she said.

"Sloop had the same photograph."

"Is that significant?"

He shrugged. "They were good friends."

They turned away. Alice ducked back into the VW and killed the lights. Then he led her to the foot of the porch steps. Up to the main entrance. He knocked. Waited. Bobby Greer opened the door. Stood there, surprised.

"So you came home," Reacher said.

Bobby scowled, like he had already heard it.

"My buddies took me out," he said. "To help with the grieving process."

Reacher opened his palm to show off the chromium star. *The badge flip*. It felt good. Not quite as good as flashing a United States Army Criminal Investigation Division credential, but it had an effect on Bobby. It stopped him closing the door again.

"Police," Reacher said. "We need to see your mother."

"Police? You?"

"Hack Walker just deputized us. Valid throughout Echo County. Where's your mother?"

Bobby paused a beat. Leaned forward and glanced up at the night sky and literally sniffed the air.

"Storm's rolling in," he said. "It's coming now. From the south."

"Where's your mother, Bobby?"

Bobby paused again.

"Inside," he said.

Reacher led Alice past Bobby into the red foyer with the rifles and the mirror. It was a degree or two cooler inside the house. The old air conditioner was running hard. It thumped and rattled patiently, somewhere upstairs. They walked through the foyer and into the parlor in back. Rusty Greer was sitting at the table in the same chair as the first time he had seen her. She was wearing the same style of clothes. Tight jeans and a fringed blouse. Her hair was lacquered up into a halo as hard as a helmet.

"We're here on official business, Mrs. Greer," Reacher said. He showed her the badge in his palm. "We need some answers."

"Or what, big man?" Rusty said. "You going to arrest me?"

Reacher pulled out a chair and sat opposite her. Just looked at her.

"I've done nothing wrong," she said.

Reacher shook his head. "As a matter of fact, you've done everything wrong."

"Like what?"

"Like, my grandmother would have died before she let her grandchildren get taken away. Literally. Over her dead body, she'd have said, and she'd have damn well meant every word."

Silence for a second. Just the endless tick of the fan.

"It was for the child's own good," Rusty said. "And I had no choice. They had papers."

"You given grandchildren away before?"

"No."

"So how do you know they were the *right* papers?"

Rusty just shrugged. Said nothing.

"Did you check?"

"How could I?" Rusty said. "And they looked right. All full of big words, aforementioned, hereinafter, the State of Texas."

"They were fakes," Reacher said. "It was a kidnap, Mrs. Greer. It was coercion. They took your granddaughter to threaten your daughter-in-law with."

He watched her face, for dawning realization, for guilt or shame or fear or remorse. There was some expression there. He wasn't exactly sure what it was.

"So we need descriptions," he said. "How many were there?"

She said nothing.

"How many people, Mrs. Greer?"

"Two people. A man and a woman."

"White?"

"Yes."

"What did they look like?"

Rusty shrugged again.

"Ordinary," she said. "Normal. Like you would expect. Like social workers. From a city. They had a big car."

"Hair? Eyes? Clothes?"

"Fair hair, I think. Both of them. Cheap suits. The woman wore a skirt. Blue eyes, I think. The man was tall."

"What about their car?"

"I don't know about cars. It was a big sedan. But kind of ordinary. Not a Cadillac."

"Color?"

"Gray or blue, maybe. Not dark."

"You got any humble pie in the kitchen?"

"Why?"

"Because I should cram it down your throat until it chokes you. Those fair-haired white people with the blue eyes are the ones who killed Al Eugene. And you gave your own grand-daughter to them."

She stared at him. "Killed? Al is dead?"

"Two minutes after they took him out of his car."

She went pale and her mouth started working. She said *what about,* and then stopped. And again, *what about.* She couldn't add the word *Ellie*.

"Not yet," Reacher said. "That's my guess. And my hope. Ought to be *your* hope, too, because if they hurt her, you know what I'm going to do?"

She didn't answer. Just clamped her lips and shook her head from side to side.

"I'm going to come back down here and break your spine. I'm going to stand you up and snap it like a rotten twig."

They made her take a bath, which was awful, because one of the men watched her do it. He was quite short and had black hair on his head and his arms. He stood inside the bathroom door and watched her all the time she was in the tub. Her mommy had told her, *never let anybody see you undressed, especially not a man*. And he was right there watching her. And she had no pajamas to put on afterward. She hadn't brought any. She hadn't brought *anything*.

"You don't need pajamas," the man said. "It's too hot for pajamas."

He stood there by the door, watching her. She dried herself with a small white towel. She needed to pee, but she wasn't going to let him watch her do *that*. She had to squeeze very near him to get out of the room. Then the other two watched her all the way to the bed. The other man, and the woman. They were horrible. They were *all* horrible. She got into the bed and pulled the covers up over her head and tried hard not to cry.

"What now?" Alice asked.

"Back to Pecos," Reacher said. "I want to keep on the move. And we've got a lot of stuff to do tonight. But go slow, O.K.? I need time to think."

She drove out to the gate and turned north into the darkness. Switched the fan on high to blow the night heat away.

"Think about what?" Alice asked.

"About where Ellie is."

"Why do you think it was the same people as killed Eugene?"

"It's a deployment issue," he said. "I can't see anybody using a separate hit team and kidnap team. Not down here in the middle of nowhere. So I think it's one team. Either a hit team moonlighting on the kidnap, or a kidnap team moonlighting on the hits. Probably the former, because the way they did Eugene was pretty expert. If that was moonlighting, I'd hate to see them do what they're *really* good at."

"All they did was shoot him. Anybody could do that."

"No, they couldn't. They got him to stop the car, they talked him into theirs. They kept him quiet throughout. That's really good technique, Alice. Harder than you can imagine. Then they shot him through the eye. That means something, too."

"What?"

He shrugged. "It's a tiny target. And in a situation like that, it's a snap shot. You raise the gun, you fire. *One, two.* No rational reason to pick such a tiny target. It's a kind of exuberance. Not exactly showing off, as such. More like just celebrating your own skill and precision. Like reveling in it. It's a joy thing."

Silence in the car. Just the hum of the motor and the whine of the tires.

"And now they've got the kid," Alice said.

"And they're uneasy about it, because they're moonlighting. They're used to each other alone. They're accustomed to

their normal procedures. Having a live kid around makes
them worried about being static and visible."

"They'll look like a family. A man, a woman, a little girl."

"No, I think there's more than two of them."

"Why?"

"Because if it was me, I'd want three. In the service, we
used three. Basically a driver, a shooter and a back-watcher."

"You shot people? The military police?"

He shrugged. "Sometimes. You know, things better not
brought to trial."

She was quiet for a long moment. He saw her debating
whether to hitch an inch farther away from him. Then he saw
her decide to stay where she was.

"So why didn't you do it for Carmen?" she asked. "If
you've done it before?"

"She asked me the same question. My answer is, I really
don't know."

She was quiet again, another mile.

"Why are they holding Ellie?" she said. "I mean, *still* holding her? They already coerced the confession. So what's still
to gain?"

"You're the lawyer," he said. "You have to figure that one
out. When does it become set in stone? You know, irrevoca-
ble?"

"Never, really. A confession can be retracted anytime. But
in practice, I guess if she answered *nolo contendere* to the
grand jury indictment, that would be regarded as a mile-
stone."

"And how soon could that happen?"

"Tomorrow, easily. Grand jury sits more or less permanently. It would take ten minutes, maybe a quarter of an hour."

"I thought justice ground real slow in Texas."

"Only if you plead not guilty."

Silence again, for many miles. They passed through the
crossroads hamlet with the school and the gas station and the
diner. It whipped backward through the headlight beams,
three short seconds end to end. The sky up ahead was still
clear. The stars were still visible. But the clouds were building fast behind them, in the south.

"So maybe tomorrow they'll let her go," Alice said.

"And maybe tomorrow they won't. They'll be worried she could make the ID. She's a smart kid. She sits quiet, watching and thinking all the time."

"So what do we do?"

"We try to figure out where she is."

He opened the glove compartment and took out the maps again. Found a large-scale plan of Pecos County and spread it on his knee. Reached up and clicked on the dome light.

"How?" Alice asked. "I mean, where do you start?"

"I've done this before," Reacher said. "Years and years, I hunted deserters and AWOLs. You train yourself to think like them, and you usually find them."

"That easy?"

"Sometimes," he said.

Silence in the speeding car.

"But they could be anywhere," Alice said. "I mean, there must be a million hide-outs. Abandoned farmsteads, ruined buildings."

"No, I think they're using motels," Reacher said.

"Why?"

"Because appearances are very important to them. Part of their technique. They suckered Al Eugene somehow, and they looked plausible to Rusty Greer, not that she cared too much. So they need running water and showers and closets and working electricity for hairdryers and shavers."

"There are hundreds of motels here," she said. "Thousands, probably."

He nodded. "And they're moving around, almost certainly. A different place every day. Basic security."

"So how do we find the right one tonight?"

He held the map where it caught the light.

"We find it in our heads. Think like them, figure out what *we'd* do. Then that should be the same thing as what *they'd* do."

"Hell of a gamble."

"Maybe, maybe not."

"So are we going to start now?"

"No, we're going back to your office now."

"Why?"

"Because I don't like frontal assaults. Not against people this good, not with a kid in the crossfire."

"So what do we do?"

"We divide and rule. We lure two of them out. Maybe we capture a tongue."

"A tongue? What's that?"

"An enemy prisoner who'll talk."

"How do we do that?"

"We decoy them. They're already aware we know about them. So they'll come for us, try a little damage control."

"They *know* we know? But how?"

"Somebody just told them."

"Who?"

Reacher didn't reply. Just stared down at the map. Looked at the faint red lines that represented roads meandering across thousands of empty miles. Closed his eyes and tried hard to imagine what they looked like in reality.

Alice parked in the lot behind the law offices. She had a key to the rear door. There were a lot of shadows, and Reacher was very vigilant as they walked. But they made it inside O.K. The old store was deserted and dusty and silent and hot. The air conditioner had been turned off at the end of the day. Reacher stood still and listened for the inaudible quiver of people waiting. It's a primeval sensation, received and understood far back in the brain. It wasn't there.

"Call Walker and give him an update," he said. "Tell him we're here."

He made her sit back-to-back with him at somebody else's desk in the center of the room, so he could watch the front entrance while she watched the rear. He rested the pistol in his lap with the safety off. Then he dialed Sergeant Rodríguez's number in Abilene. Rodríguez was still on duty, and he sounded unhappy about it.

"We checked with the bar association," he said. "There are no lawyers licensed in Texas called Chester A. Arthur."

"I'm from Vermont," Reacher said. "I'm volunteering down here, pro bono."

"Like hell you are."

The line went quiet.

"I'll deal," Reacher said. "Names, in exchange for conversation."

"With who?"

"With you, maybe. How long have you been a Ranger?"

"Seventeen years."

"How much do you know about the border patrol?"

"Enough, I guess."

"You prepared to give me a straight yes-no answer? No comebacks?"

"What's the question?"

"You recall the border patrol investigation twelve years ago?"

"Maybe."

"Was it a whitewash?"

Rodríguez paused a long moment, and then he answered, with a single word.

"I'll call you back," Reacher said.

He hung up and turned and spoke over his shoulder to Alice.

"You get Walker?" he asked.

"He's up to speed," she said. "He wants us to wait for him here, for when he's through with the FBI."

Reacher shook his head. "Can't wait here. Too obvious. We need to stay on the move. We'll go to him, and then we'll get back on the road."

She paused a beat. "Are we in serious danger?"

"Nothing we can't handle," he said.

She said nothing.

"You worried?" he asked.

"A little," she said. "A lot, actually."

"You can't be," he said. "I'm going to need your help."

"Why was the lie about the ring different?"

"Because everything else is hearsay. But I found out for myself the ring wasn't a fake. Direct personal discovery, not hearsay. Feels very different."

"I don't see how it's important."

"It's important because I've got a whole big theory going and the lie about the ring screws it up like crazy."

"Why do you want to believe her so much?"

"Because she had no money with her."

"What's the big theory?"

"Remember that Balzac quotation? And Marcuse?"

Alice nodded.

"I've got another one," Reacher said. "Something Ben Franklin once wrote."

"What are you, a walking encyclopedia?"

"I remember stuff I read, is all. And I remember something Bobby Greer said, too, about armadillos."

She just looked at him.

"You're crazy," she said.

He nodded. "It's only a theory. It needs to be tested. But we can do that."

"How?"

"We just wait and see who comes for us."

She said nothing.

"Let's go check in with Walker," he said.

They walked through the heat to the courthouse building. There was a breeze again, blowing in from the south. It felt damp and urgent. Walker was on his own in his office, looking very tired. His desk was a mess of phone books and paper.

"Well, it's started," he said. "Biggest thing you ever saw. FBI and state police, roadblocks everywhere, helicopters in the air, more than a hundred and fifty people on the ground. But there's a storm coming in, which ain't going to help."

"Reacher thinks they're holed up in a motel," Alice said.

Walker nodded, grimly. "If they are, they'll find them. Manhunt like this, it's going to be pretty relentless."

"You need us anymore?" Reacher asked.

Walker shook his head. "We should leave it to the professionals now. I'm going home, grab a couple hours rest."

Reacher looked around the office. The door, the floor, the windows, the desk, the filing cabinets.

"I guess we'll do the same thing," he said. "We'll go to Alice's place. Call us if you need us. Or if you get any news, O.K.?"

Walker nodded.

"I will," he said. "I promise."

"We'll go as FBI again," the woman said. "It's a no-brainer."

"All of us?" the driver asked. "What about the kid?"

The woman paused. She had to go, because she was the shooter. And if she had to split the team two and one, she wanted the tall guy with her, not the driver.

"You stay with the kid," she said.

There was a moment's silence.

"Abort horizon?" the driver asked.

It was their standard operating procedure. Whenever the team was split, the woman set an abort horizon. Which meant that you waited until the time had passed, and then, if the team wasn't together again, you got the hell out, every man for himself.

"Four hours, O.K.?" the woman said. "Done and dusted."

She stared at him a second longer, eyebrows raised, to make sure he understood the implication of her point. Then she knelt and unzipped the heavy valise.

"So let's do it," she said.

They did the exact same things they had done for Al Eugene, except they did them a whole lot faster because the Crown Vic was parked in the motel's lot, not hidden in a dusty turnout miles from anywhere. The lot was dimly lit and mostly empty, and there was nobody around, but it still wasn't a secure feeling. They pulled the wheel covers off and threw them in the trunk. They attached the communications antennas to the rear window and the trunk lid. They zipped blue jackets over their shirts. They loaded up with spare ammunition clips. They squared the souvenir ballcaps on their heads. They checked the loads in their nine-millimeter pistols and racked the slides and clicked the safety catches and jammed the guns in their pockets. The tall fair man slipped into the driver's seat. The woman paused outside the motel room door.

"Four hours," she said again. "Done and dusted."

The driver nodded and closed the door behind her.

Glanced over at the kid in the bed. *Done and dusted* meant *leave nothing at all behind, especially live witnesses*.

Reacher took the Heckler & Koch and the maps of Texas and the FedEx packet out of the VW and carried them into Alice's house, straight through the living room and into the kitchen area. It was still and cool inside. And dry. The central air was running hard. He wondered for a second what her utility bills must be like.

"Where's the scale?" he asked.

She pushed past him and squatted down and opened a cupboard. Used two hands and lifted a kitchen scale onto the countertop. It was a big piece of equipment. It was new, but it looked old. A retro design. It had a big white upright face the size of a china plate, like the speedometer on an old-fashioned sedan. It was faced with a bulbous plastic window with a chromium bezel. There was a red pointer behind the window and large numbers around the circumference. A manufacturer's name and a printed warning: *Not Legal For Trade*.

"Is it accurate?" he asked.

Alice shrugged.

"I think so," she said. "The nut roast comes out O.K."

There was a chromium bowl resting in a cradle above the dial. He tapped on it with his finger and the pointer bounced up to a pound and then back down to zero. He took the magazine out of the Heckler & Koch and laid the empty gun in the bowl. It made a light metallic sound. The pointer spun up to two pounds and six ounces. Not an especially light weapon. About right, he figured. His memory told him the catalog weight was in the region of forty-three ounces, with an empty magazine.

He put the gun back together and opened cupboards until he found a store of food. He lifted out an unopened bag of granulated sugar. It was in a gaudy yellow packet that said *5 lbs.* on the side.

"What are you doing?" Alice asked.

"Weighing things," he said.

He stood the sugar upright in the chromium bowl. The

pointer spun up to five pounds exactly. He put the sugar back in the cupboard and tried a cellophane-wrapped packet of chopped nuts. The pointer read two pounds. He looked at the label on the packet and saw *2 lbs*.

"Good enough," he said.

He folded the maps and laid them across the top of the bowl. They weighed one pound and three ounces. He took them off and put the nuts back on. Still two pounds. He put the nuts back in the cupboard and tried the FedEx packet. It weighed one pound and one ounce. He added the maps and the pointer inched up to two pounds and four ounces. Added the loaded gun on top and the pointer jerked around to five pounds and three ounces. If he had wanted to, he could have calculated the weight of the bullets.

"O.K., let's go," he said. "But we need gas. Long ride ahead. And maybe you should get out of that dress. You got something more active?"

"I guess," she said, and headed for the stairs.

"You got a screwdriver?" he called after her.

"Under the sink," she called back.

He bent down and found a brightly colored toolbox in the cupboard. It was made out of plastic and looked like a lunch pail. He clicked it open and selected a medium-sized screwdriver with a clear yellow handle. A minute later Alice came back down the stairs wearing baggy khaki cargo pants and a black T-shirt with the sleeves torn off at the shoulder seams.

"O.K.?" she asked.

"Me and Judith," he said. "Got a lot in common."

She smiled and said nothing.

"I'm assuming your car is insured," he said. "It could get damaged tonight."

She said nothing. Just locked up her door and followed him out to the VW. She drove out of her complex, with Reacher craning his neck, watching the shadows. She got gas at a neon-bright all-night station out on the El Paso road. Reacher paid for it.

"O.K., back to the courthouse," he said. "Something I want from there."

She said nothing. Just turned the car and headed east.

Parked in the lot behind the building. They walked around
and tried the street door. It was locked up tight.

"So what now?" she asked.

It was hot on the sidewalk. Still up there around ninety degrees, and damp. The breeze had died again. There were
clouds filling the sky.

"I'm going to kick it in," he said.

"There's probably an alarm."

"There's definitely an alarm. I checked."

"So?"

"So I'm going to set it off."

"Then the cops will come."

"I'm counting on it."

"You want to get us arrested?"

"They won't come right away. We've got three or four
minutes, maybe."

He took two paces back and launched forward and smashed
the flat of his sole above the handle. The wood splintered and
sagged open a half inch, but held. He kicked again and the
door crashed back and bounced off the corridor wall. A blue
strobe high up outside started flashing and an urgent electric
bell started ringing. It was about as loud as he had expected.

"Go get the car," he said. "Get it started and wait for me in
the alley."

He ran up the stairs two at a time and kicked in the outer
office door without breaking stride. Jinked through the secretarial pen like a running back and steadied himself and
kicked in Walker's door. It smashed back and the venetian
blind jerked sideways and the glass pane behind it shattered
and the shards rained down like ice in winter. He went
straight for the bank of filing cabinets. The lights were off
and the office was hot and dark and he had to peer close to
read the labels. It was an odd filing system. It was arranged
partly in date order and partly by the alphabet. That was going to be a minor problem. He found a cabinet marked *B* and
jammed the tip of the screwdriver into the keyhole and hammered it in with the heel of his hand. Turned it sharp and hard
and broke the lock. Pulled the drawer and raked through the
files with his fingers.

The files all had tiny labels encased in plastic tabs arranged so they made a neat diagonal from left to right. The labels were all typed with words starting with *B*. But the contents of the files were way too recent. Nothing more than four years old. He stepped two paces sideways and skipped the next *B* drawer and went to the next-but-one. The air was hot and still and the bell was ringing loud and the glare of the flashing blue strobe pulsed in through the windows. It was just about keeping time with his heartbeat.

He broke the lock and slid the drawer. Checked the labels. No good. Everything was either six or seven years old. He had been inside the building two minutes and thirty seconds. He could hear a distant siren under the noise of the bell. He stepped sideways again and attacked the next *B* drawer. He checked the dates on the tabs and walked his fingers backward. Two minutes and fifty seconds. The bell seemed louder and the strobe seemed brighter. The siren was closer. He found what he was looking for three-quarters of the way back through the drawer. It was a two-inch-thick collection of paperwork in a heavy paper sling. He lifted the whole thing out and tucked it under his arm. Left the drawer all the way open and kicked all the others shut. Ran through the secretarial pen and down the stairs. Checked the street from the lobby and when he was certain it was clear he ducked around into the alley and straight into the VW.

"Go," he said.

He was a little breathless, and that surprised him.

"Where?" Alice asked.

"South," he said. "To the Red House."

"Why? What's there?"

"Everything," he said.

She took off fast and fifty yards later Reacher saw red lights pulsing in the distance behind them. The Pecos Police Department, arriving at the courthouse just a minute too late. He smiled in the dark and turned his head in time to catch a split-second glimpse of a big sedan nosing left two hundred yards ahead of them into the road that led down to Alice's place. It flashed through the yellow wash of a streetlight and disappeared. It looked like a police-spec Crown Victoria,

plain steel wheels and four VHF antennas on the back. He
stared into the darkness that had swallowed it and turned his
head as they passed.

"Fast as you can," he said to Alice.

Then he laid the captured paperwork on his knees and
reached up and clicked on the dome light so he could read it.

The *B* was for "border patrol," and the file summarized the
crimes committed by it twelve years ago and the measures
taken in response. It made for unpleasant reading.

The border between Mexico and Texas was very long,
and for an accumulated total of about half its length there
were roads and towns near enough on the American side to
make it worth guarding pretty closely. Theory was if illegals penetrated there, they could slip away into the interior
fast and easily. Other sectors had nothing to offer except
fifty or a hundred miles of empty parched desert. Those
sectors weren't really guarded at all. Standard practice was
to ignore the border itself and conduct random vehicle
sweeps behind the line by day or night to pick the migrants
up at some point during their hopeless three- or four-day
trudge north across the wastelands. It was a practice that
worked well. After the first thirty or so miles on foot
through the heat the migrants became pretty passive. Often
they surrendered willingly. Often the vehicle sweeps turned
into first-aid mercy missions, because the walkers were sick
and dehydrated and exhausted because they had no food or
water.

They had no food or water because they had been cheated.
Usually they would pay their life savings to some operator on
the Mexican side who was offering them a fully accompanied
one-way trip to paradise. Vans and minibuses would take
them from their villages to the border, and then the guide
would crouch and point across a deserted footbridge to a distant sandhill and swear that more vans and minibuses were
waiting behind it, full of supplies and ready to go. The migrants would take a deep breath and sprint across, only to
find nothing behind the distant sandhill. Too hopeful and too

afraid to turn back, they would just blindly walk ahead into exhaustion.

Sometimes there *would* be a vehicle waiting, but its driver would demand a separate substantial payment. The migrants had nothing left to offer, except maybe some small items of personal value. The new driver would laugh and call them worthless. Then he would take them anyway and offer to see what cash he could raise on them up ahead. He would drive off in a cloud of hot dust and never be seen again. The migrants would eventually realize they had been duped, and they would start stumbling north on foot. Then it became a simple question of endurance. The weather was key. In a hot summer, the mortality rate was very high. That was why the border patrol's random sweeps were often seen as mercy missions.

Then that suddenly changed.

For a whole year, the roving vehicles were as likely to bring sudden death as arrest or aid. At unpredictable intervals, always at night, rifles would fire and a truck would roar in and swoop and maneuver until one lone runner was winnowed out from the pack. Then the lone runner would be hunted for a mile or so and shot down. Then the truck would disappear into the dark again, engine roaring, headlights bouncing, dust trailing, and stunned silence would descend.

Sometimes it wasn't so clean.

Some victims were wounded and dragged away and tortured. The corpse of one teenage boy was found tied to a cactus stump with barbed wire. He had been partially flayed. Some were burned alive or beheaded or mutilated. Three teenage girls were captured over a period of four months. Their autopsy details were gruesome.

None of the survivor families made official complaints. They all shared the illegal's basic fear of involvement with bureaucracy. But stories began to circulate around the community of legal relatives and their support groups. Lawyers and rights advocates started compiling files. Eventually the subject was broached at the appropriate level. A low-level inquiry was started. Evidence was gathered, anonymously. A provable total of seventeen homicides was established.

Added to that was an extrapolated figure of eight more, to represent cases where bodies had never been found or where they had been buried by the survivors themselves. Young Raoul García's name was included in the second total.

There was a map in the file. Most of the ambushes had taken place inside a pear-shaped pocket of territory enclosing maybe a hundred square miles. It was marked on the map like a stain. It was centered on a long north-south axis with the southerly bulge sitting mostly inside the Echo County line. That meant the victims had already made it fifty miles or more. By then they would be weak and tired and in no shape to resist.

Border patrol brass launched a full-scale investigation one August, eleven months after the first vague rumors surfaced. There was one more attack at the end of that month, and then nothing ever again. Denied an ongoing forensic basis for examination, the investigation got nowhere at all. There were preventive measures enforced, like strict accounting of ammunition and increased frequency of radio checks. But no conclusions were reached. It was a thorough job, and to their credit the brass kept hard at it, but a retrospective investigation into a closed paramilitary world where the only witnesses denied ever having been near the border in the first place was hopeless. The matter wound down. Time passed. The homicides had stopped, the survivors were building new lives, the immigration amnesties had insulated the outrage. The tempo of investigation slowed to a halt. The files were sealed four years later.

"So?" Alice said.

Reacher butted the papers together with the heel of his hand. Closed the file. Pitched it behind him into the rear seat.

"Now I know why she lied about the ring," he said.

"Why?"

"She didn't lie. She was telling the truth."

"She said it was a fake worth thirty bucks."

"And she thought that was the truth. Because some jeweler in Pecos laughed at her and *told* her it was a fake worth thirty bucks. And she believed him. But he was trying to rip her off, was all, trying to buy it for thirty bucks and sell it again for sixty thousand. Oldest scam in the world. Exact same thing happened to some of these immigrants in the file. Their first experience of America."

"The *jeweler* lied?"

He nodded. "I should have figured it before, because it's obvious. Probably the exact same guy we went to. I figured he didn't look like the Better Business Bureau's poster boy."

"He didn't try to rip *us* off."

"No, Alice, he didn't. Because you're a sharp-looking white lawyer and I'm a big tough-looking white guy. She was a small Mexican woman, all alone and desperate and scared. He saw an opportunity with her that he didn't see with us."

Alice was quiet for a second.

"So what does it mean?" she asked.

Reacher clicked off the dome light. Smiled in the dark and stretched. Put his palms on the dash in front of him and flexed his massive shoulders against the pressure.

"It means we're good to go," he said. "It means all our ducks are in a neat little row. And it means you should drive faster, because right now we're maybe twenty minutes ahead of the bad guys, and I want to keep it that way as long as I can."

She blew straight through the sleeping crossroads hamlet once again and made the remaining sixty miles in forty-three minutes, which Reacher figured was pretty good for a yellow four-cylinder import with a bud vase next to the steering wheel. She made the turn in under the gate and braked hard and stopped at the foot of the porch steps. The porch lights were on and the VW's dust fogged up around them in a khaki cloud. It was close to two o'clock in the morning.

"Leave it running," Reacher said.

He led her up to the door. Hammered hard on it and got no reply. Tried the handle. It was unlocked. *Why would it be locked? We're sixty miles from the nearest crossroads.* He swung it open and they stepped straight into the red-painted foyer.

"Hold your arms out," he said.

He unloaded all six .22 hunting rifles out of the rack on the wall and laid them in her arms, alternately muzzle to stock so they would balance. She staggered slightly under the weight.

"Go put them in the car," he said.

There was the sound of footsteps overhead, then creaking from the stairs, and Bobby Greer came out of the parlor door, rubbing sleep out of his eyes. He was barefoot and wearing boxers and a T-shirt and staring at the empty gun rack.

"Hell you think you're doing?" he said.

"I want the others," Reacher said. "I'm commandeering your weapons. On behalf of the Echo County sheriff. I'm a deputy, remember?"

"There aren't any others."

"Yes, there are, Bobby. No self-respecting redneck like you is going to be satisfied with a bunch of .22 popguns. Where's the heavy metal?"

Bobby said nothing.

"Don't mess with me, Bobby," Reacher said. "It's way too late for that."

Bobby paused. Then he shrugged.

"O.K.," he said.

He padded barefoot across the foyer and pushed open a door that led into a small dark space that could have been a study. He flicked on a light and Reacher saw black-and-white pictures of oil wells on the walls. There was a desk and a chair and another gun rack filled with four 30–30 Winchesters. Seven-shot lever-action repeaters, big handsome weapons, oiled wood, twenty-inch barrels, beautifully kept. *Wyatt Earp, eat your heart out.*

"Ammunition?" Reacher asked.

Bobby opened a drawer in the gun rack's pedestal. Took out a cardboard box of Winchester cartridges.

"I've got some special loads, too," he said. Took out another box.

"What are they?"

"I made them myself. Extra power."

Reacher nodded. "Take them all out to the car, O.K.?"

He took the four rifles out of the rack and followed Bobby

out of the house. Alice was sitting in the car. The six .22s were
piled on the seat behind her. Bobby leaned in and placed the
ammunition next to them. Reacher stacked the Winchesters upright behind the passenger seat. Then he turned back to Bobby.

"I'm going to borrow your Jeep," he said.

Bobby shrugged, barefoot on the hot dirt.

"Keys are in it," he said.

"You and your mother stay in the house now," Reacher
said. "Anybody seen out and about will be considered hostile,
O.K.?"

Bobby nodded. Turned and walked to the foot of the steps.
Glanced back once and went inside the house. Reacher
leaned into the VW to talk to Alice.

"What are we doing?" she said.

"Getting ready."

"For what?"

"For whatever comes our way."

"Why do we need ten rifles?"

"We don't. We need one. I don't want to give the bad guys
the other nine, is all."

"They're coming here?"

"They're about ten minutes behind us."

"So what do we do?"

"We're all going out in the desert."

"Is there going to be shooting?"

"Probably."

"Is that smart? You said yourself, they're good shots."

"With handguns. Best way to defend against handguns is
hide a long way off and shoot back with the biggest rifle you
can find."

She shook her head. "I can't be a part of this, Reacher. It's
not right. And I've never even held a rifle."

"You don't have to shoot," he said. "But you have to be a
witness. You have to identify exactly who comes for us. I'm
relying on you. It's vital."

"How will I see? It's dark out there."

"We'll fix that."

"It's going to rain."

"That'll help us."

"This is not right," she said again. "The police should handle this. Or the FBI. You can't just shoot at people."

The air was heavy with storm. The breeze was blowing again and he could smell pressure and voltage building in the sky.

"Rules of engagement, Alice," he said. "I'll wait for an overtly hostile act before I do anything. Just like the U.S. Army. O.K.?"

"We'll be killed."

"You'll be hiding far away."

"Then *you'll* be killed. You said it yourself, they're good at this."

"They're good at walking up to somebody and shooting them in the head. What they're like out in the open in the dark against incoming rifle fire is anybody's guess."

"You're crazy."

"Seven minutes," he said.

She glanced backward at the road from the north. Then she shook her head and shoved the gearstick into first and held her foot on the clutch. He leaned in and squeezed her shoulder.

"Follow me close, O.K.?" he said.

He ran down to the motor barn and got into the Greer family's Cherokee. Racked the seat back and started the engine and switched on the headlights. Reversed into the yard and straightened up and looped around the motor barn and headed straight down the dirt track into open country. Checked the mirror and saw the VW right there behind him. Looked ahead again and saw the first raindrop hit his windshield. It was as big as a silver dollar.

16

They drove in convoy for five fast miles through the dark.
There was no moonlight. No starlight. Cloud cover was low
and thick but it held the rain to nothing more than occasional
splattering drops, ten whole seconds between each of them,
maybe six in every minute. They exploded against the windshield into wet patches the size of saucers. Reacher swatted
each of them separately with the windshield wipers. He held
steady around forty miles an hour and followed the track
through the brush. It turned randomly left and right, heading
basically south toward the storm. The ground was very
rough. The Jeep was bouncing and jarring. The VW was
struggling to keep pace behind him. Its headlights were
swinging and jumping in his mirrors.

Five miles from the house the rain was still holding and the
mesquite and the fractured limestone began to narrow the
track. The terrain was changing under their wheels. They had
started out across a broad desert plain that might have been
cultivated grassland a century ago. Now the ground was rising slowly and shading into mesa. Rocky outcrops rose left

and right in the headlight beams, channeling them roughly south and east. Taller stands of mesquite crowded in and funneled them tighter. Soon there was nothing more than a pair of deep ruts worn through the hardpan. Ledges and sinkholes and dense patches of thorny low brush meant they had no choice but to follow them. They curved and twisted and felt like a riverbed.

Then the track bumped upward and straightened and ran like a highway across a miniature limestone mesa. The stone was a raised pan as big as a football field, maybe a hundred twenty yards long and eighty wide, roughly oval in shape. There was no vegetation growing on it. Reacher swung the Jeep in a wide circle and used the headlights on bright to check the perimeter. All around the edges the ground fell away a couple of feet into rocky soil. Stunted bushes crowded anyplace they could find to put their roots. He drove a second circle, wider, and he liked what he saw. The miniature mesa was as bare as a dinner plate laid on a dead lawn. He smiled to himself. Timed out in his head what they needed to do. Liked the answer he came up with.

He drove all the way to the far end of the rock table and stopped where the track bumped down off it and disappeared onward. Alice pulled the VW alongside him. He jumped out of the Jeep and ducked down to her window. The night air was still hot. Still damp. The urgent breeze was back. Big raindrops fell lazily and vertically. He felt like he could have dodged each one of them individually. Alice used a switch and buzzed the window down.

"You O.K.?" he asked her.

"So far," she said.

"Turn it around and back it up to the edge," he said. "All the way back. Block the mouth of the track."

She maneuvered the car like she was parking on a city street and ran it backward until it was centered in the mouth of the track and the rear wheels were tight against the drop. She left the front facing exactly north, the way they had come. He nosed the Jeep next to her and opened the tailgate.

"Kill the motor and the lights," he called. "Get the rifles."

She passed him the big Winchesters, one at a time. He laid

them sideways in the Jeep's load space. She passed him the .22s, and he pitched them away into the brush, as far as he could throw them. She passed him the two boxes of 30–30 ammunition. Winchester's own, and Bobby Greer's hand-loads. He laid them alongside the rifles. Ducked around to the driver's door and switched the engine off. The lumpy six-cylinder idle died. Silence fell. He listened hard and scanned the northern horizon. The mesquite sighed faintly in the wind. Unseen insects buzzed and chattered. Infrequent rain-drops hit his shoulders. That was all. Nothing else. Absolute blackness and silence everywhere.

He came back to the tailgate and opened the ammunition boxes. They were both packed tight with cartridges standing on their firing pins, points upward. The factory shells were new and bright. Bobby's were a little scuffed. Recycled brass. He took one out and held it up to the Jeep's interior light and looked hard at it. *I made them myself,* Bobby had said. *Extra power.* Which was logical. Why else would a jerk like Bobby hand-load his own cartridges? Not for *less* power, that was for sure. Like, why do people tune hot-rod motors? Not to make them milder than stock. It's a boy thing. So Bobby had probably packed and tamped a whole lot of extra powder into each one, maybe thirty or forty extra grains. And maybe he had used hotter powder than normal. Which would give him a couple hundred extra foot-pounds of muzzle energy, and maybe a hundred miles an hour extra velocity. And which would give him the muzzle flash from hell, and which would ruin his breech castings and warp his barrels inside a couple of weeks. But Reacher smiled and took ten more of the shells out of the box anyway. They weren't his guns, and he had just decided muzzle flash was exactly what he was looking for.

He loaded the first Winchester with a single sample of Bobby's hand-loads. The second, he filled with seven more. The third, he loaded alternately one stock round, one of Bobby's, another stock round, until it was full with four stock and three hand-loads. The fourth rifle he filled entirely with factory ammo. He laid the guns left to right in sequence across the Jeep's load space and closed the tailgate on them.

"I thought we only needed one," Alice said.

"I changed the plan," he said.

He stepped around to the driver's seat and Alice climbed in beside him.

"Where are we going now?" she asked.

He started the engine and backed away from the parked VW.

"Think of this mesa like a clock face," he said. "We came in at the six o'clock position. Right now your car is parked at the twelve, facing backward. You're going to be hiding on the rim at the eight. On foot. Your job is to fire a rifle, one shot, and then scoot down to the seven."

"You said I wouldn't have to shoot."

"I changed the plan," he said again.

"But I told you, I can't fire a rifle."

"Yes, you can. You just pull the trigger. It's easy. Don't worry about aiming or anything. All I want is the sound and the flash."

"Then what?"

"Then you scoot down to the seven and watch. I'm going to be busy shooting. I need you to ID exactly who I'm shooting at."

"This isn't right."

"It isn't wrong, either."

"You think?"

"You ever seen Clay Allison's grave?"

She rolled her eyes. "You need to read the history books, Reacher. Clay Allison was a total psychopath. He once killed a guy bunking with him, just because he snored. He was an amoral maniac, plain and simple. Nothing too noble about that."

Reacher shrugged. "Well, we can't back out now."

"Two wrongs don't make a right, you know?"

"It's a choice, Alice. Either we ambush them, or get ambushed *by* them."

She shook her head.

"Great," she said.

He said nothing.

"It's dark," she said. "How will I see anything?"

"I'll take care of that."

"How will I know when to fire?"

"You'll know."

He pulled the Jeep close to the edge of the limestone table and stopped. Opened the tailgate and took out the first rifle. Checked his bearings and ran to the fractured rock lip and laid the gun on the ground with the butt hanging over the edge and the barrel pointing at the emptiness twenty feet in front of the distant VW. He leaned down and racked the lever. It moved precisely with a sweet metallic *slick-slick*. A fine weapon.

"It's ready to fire," he said. "And this is the eight o'clock spot. Stay down below the lip, fire the gun, and then move to the seven. Crouch low all the way. And then watch, real careful. They might fire in your direction, but I guarantee they'll miss, O.K.?"

She said nothing.

"I promise," he said. "Don't worry about it."

"Are you sure?"

"Superman couldn't hit anything with a handgun in the dark at this distance."

"They might get lucky."

"No, Alice, tonight they're not going to get lucky. Believe me."

"But when do I fire?"

"Fire when ready," he said.

He watched her hide below the lip of the rock, an arm's length from her rifle.

"Good luck," he said. "I'll see you later."

"Great," she said again.

He climbed back into the Jeep and hustled it straight across the mesa to the four o'clock position. Spun the wheel and reversed the car and backed it straight off the rock. It bumped down two feet and came to a shuddering stop in the undergrowth. He killed the engine and the lights. Took the fourth rifle and propped it upright against the passenger door. Carried the second and third with him and climbed back onto the ledge and ran in the open to what he estimated was the two o'clock spot. Laid the third rifle carefully on the lip of the rock and ran the rest of the way to the parked VW.

Ducked inside and unscrewed the dome light. Eased the driver's door back to three inches from closed and left it. Measured twenty feet clockwise and laid the second rifle on the ground, on the rim of the ledge, somewhere between the twelve and the one. Twelve-thirty, maybe. *No, about twelve-seventeen, to be pedantic,* he thought. Then he crawled back and lay facedown on the ground, tight up against the VW, with his right shoulder tucked under the little running board and the right side of his face pressed against the sidewall of the front tire. He was breathing deeply. The tire smelled like rubber. His left shoulder was out in the weather. Big ponderous raindrops hit it at infrequent intervals. He hitched in closer and settled down to wait. *Eight minutes, perhaps,* he thought. *Maybe nine.*

It was eleven minutes. They were a little slower than he expected. He saw a flash in the north and at first thought it was lightning, but then it happened again and he saw it was headlight beams bouncing across rough terrain and catching the low gray cloud overhead. A vehicle was pitching and rolling its way through the darkness. It was heading his way, which he knew it would, because the landscape gave it no other choice but to stay on the track. Its lights flared and died as the nose rose and fell. He was sweating. The air around him was hotter then ever. He could feel pressure and electricity in the sky above. The raindrops were falling harder and a little faster. It felt like a fuse was burning and the storm was set to explode. *Not yet,* he thought. *Please, give me five minutes more.*

Thirty seconds later he could hear an engine. A gasoline engine, running hard. Eight cylinders. The sound rose and fell as the driven wheels gripped the dirt and then bounced and lost traction. *Hard suspension,* he thought. *Load-carrying suspension. Bobby's pick-up, probably. The one he used to hunt the armadillo.*

He tucked himself tighter against the underside of the VW. The engine noise grew louder. It rose and fell. The lights bounced and swerved. They lit the northern horizon with a

dull glow. Then they were near enough to make out as separate twin beams spearing through the mesquite. They threw
harsh shadows and flicked left and right as the vehicle turned.
Then the truck burst into sight. It bounced up onto the mesa
traveling fast. The engine screamed like all four wheels were
off the ground. The headlights flared high and then dipped
low as it crashed back to earth. It landed slightly off course
and the lights swept the perimeter for a second before they
straightened ahead. It accelerated on the flatter terrain. The
engine was loud. It came on and on, straight at him. Faster
and faster. Forty miles an hour, fifty. Seventy yards away.
Fifty. Forty. It came straight at him until the bouncing headlights washed over the stationary VW directly ahead of it.
The yellow paint above Reacher's shoulder glowed impossibly bright. Then the truck jammed to a panic stop. All four
wheels locked hard on the limestone grit and there was a
howl of rubber and the truck slewed slightly left and came to
rest facing eleven o'clock, maybe thirty yards in front of him.
The far edge of the headlight beams washed over him. He
forced himself tighter under the VW.

He could smell the raindrops in the dust.

Nothing happened for a second.

Then the pick-up driver killed his lights. They faded to
weak orange filaments and died to nothing and total darkness
came back. The insects went silent. No sound at all beyond
the truck engine idling against the brake. Reacher thought:
did they see me?

Nothing happened.

Now, Alice, Reacher thought.

Nothing happened.

Shoot, Alice, he thought. *Shoot now, for God's sake.*

Nothing happened.

Shoot the damn gun, Alice. Just pull the damn trigger.

Nothing happened.

He closed his eyes and paused another whole endless second and braced himself to launch outward anyway. Opened
his eyes and took a breath and started moving.

Then Alice fired.

There was a monstrous muzzle flash easily ten feet long

far away to his right and the buzzing whine of a supersonic bullet high in the air and a split second later an enormous barking crash clapped across the landscape. He rolled out from under the VW and reached in through the driver's door and flicked the headlights on. Jumped backward into the mesquite and kept rolling and came up into a low crouch six feet away to see the pick-up caught perfectly in the cone of bright light. Three people in it. A driver in the cab. Two figures crouching in the load bed, holding the roll bar one-handed. All three of them with their heads turned abruptly on their shoulders, rigid and frozen and staring backward at the spot Alice had fired from.

They were immobile a split second longer, and then they reacted. The driver flicked his own lights back on. The pick-up and the VW glared at each other like it was a contest. Reacher was dazzled by the light but he saw the figures in the load bed were wearing caps and blue jackets. One figure was smaller than the other. *A woman,* he thought. He fixed her position carefully in his mind. *Shoot the women first.* That was the standard counterterrorist doctrine. The experts figured they were more fanatical. And suddenly he knew she was the shooter. She had to be. Small hands, neat fingers. Carmen's Lorcin could have been built for her. She was crouched low alongside her partner on his left.

They both had handguns. They both stared sideways a half-second longer and then snapped forward into the glare and leaned on the pick-up's roof and started shooting at the VW's lights. *Their caps said FBI on the front.* He froze. *What the hell?* Then he relaxed. *Beautiful.* Fake apparel, fake ID, a tricked-up Crown Vic. *They just went to Alice's place in it. And that's how they stopped Al Eugene on Friday.* They were shooting continuously. He heard the flat dull thumps of powerful nine-millimeter pistols firing fast. He heard spent shells clattering out onto the pick-up's roof. He saw the VW's windshield explode and heard bullets punching through sheet metal and the tinkling of glass and then the VW's lights were gone and he could see nothing at all behind the dazzle of the pick-up's own lights. He sensed the pistols turning back to where they had Alice's firing position fixed in their memories. He saw tiny oblique muzzle flashes and heard bullets whining away from him. The left-hand gun stopped. *The woman. Reloading already. Only thirteen shots,* his subconscious mind told him. *Has to be a SIG Sauer P228 or a Browning Hi-Power.*

He crawled forward to the rim of the mesa and tracked fifteen feet left and found the rifle he had placed at twelve-seventeen. Winchester number two, full of Bobby Greer's hand-loads. He fired without aiming and the recoil almost knocked him off his knees. A tremendous flame leapt out of the muzzle. It was like the strobe on a camera. He had no idea where the bullet went. He racked the lever *slick-slick* and hustled right, toward the wrecked VW. Fired again. Two huge visible flashes, moving progressively counterclockwise. From the pick-up's vantage point it would look like a person traversing right-to-left. A smart shooter would fire ahead of the last flash and hope to hit the moving target. *Deflection shooting.* They went for it. He heard bullets whining off the rock near the car. Heard one hit it.

But by then he was on the move in the opposite direction, clockwise again. He dropped the rifle and bent low and ran for the next one. It was there at two o'clock. The third Winchester, the one with the sequenced load. The first shot was a factory bullet. Worth some care. He steadied himself on the lip of the ledge and aimed into the blackness eight feet behind the pick-up's headlights and four feet above them. Fired once. *Now they think there are three riflemen out here, one behind them on the left, two ahead on the right.* There was ringing in his ears and he couldn't see where his bullet went but he heard the woman's voice shout a faint command and the pick-up's headlights promptly died. He fired again at the same spot with the next shell, which was a hand-load. The gout of flame spat out and lit up the mesa and he jinked five feet right. Tracked the frozen visual target in his mind and fired the next. The second factory bullet, neat and straight and true. He heard a sharp scream. Danced one pace to his right and fired the next hand-load. The muzzle flash showed him a body falling headfirst out of the pick-up bed. It was caught entirely motionless in midair. *One down. But the wrong one*. It was too big. It was the man. *Factory round next*. He concentrated hard and aimed again slightly left of the place the guy had fallen from. Racked the lever. It moved a quarter-inch and jammed solid on the worn cartridge case from the last hand-load.

Then two things happened. First the pick-up moved. It lurched forward and peeled away fast in a tight desperate circle and headed back north, the way it had come. Then a handgun started firing close to the VW. *The woman was out of the truck. She was on foot in the dark.* She was firing fast. A hail of bullets. They were missing him by three or four feet. The truck raced away. Its lights flicked on again. He tracked them in the corner of his eye. They jerked and bounced and swerved and grew smaller. Then they disappeared off the end of the mesa. The truck just thumped down off the edge of the rock table and hurtled back toward the Red House. Its noise faded to nothing and its lights dimmed to a distant glow moving on the far black horizon. The handgun stopped firing. *Reloading again*. There was sudden total silence. Total darkness. A second later the insect chant swam back into focus. It sounded softer than usual. Less frantic. He realized the rain had changed. The heavy drops had stopped and in their place was an insistent patter of drizzle. He held his hand palm-up and felt it building. It grew perceptibly harder and harder within seconds like he was standing in a shower stall and an unseen hand was opening the faucet wider and wider.

He wiped water off his forehead to keep it out of his eyes and laid the jammed rifle quietly in the dust. The dust was already wet under his fingers. It was turning to mud. He moved left, tracking back toward the hidden Jeep. It was maybe forty yards away. The rain got harder. It built and built like there was going to be no limit to its power. It hissed and roared on the mesquite bushes all around him. *Good news and bad news*. The good news was it took making noise out of the equation. He wouldn't have backed himself to move as quietly as the woman could. Not through desert vegetation at night. A frame six feet five in height and two hundred fifty pounds in weight was good for a lot of things, but not for silent progress through unseen thorny plants. The noise of the

rain would help him more than her. That was the good news.
The bad news was visibility was soon going to be worse than
zero. They could bump into each other back-to-back before
either of them knew the other was there.

So a lever-action repeater was not going to be the weapon
of choice. Too slow for a snap shot. Too cumbersome to maneuver. And a Winchester throws the spent shell out of the
top, not out of the side. Which means in a heavy rainstorm it
can let water in through the ejection port. And this was going
to be a heavy rainstorm. He could sense it. It was going to try
to compensate for ten years of drought in a single night.

He made it back to the Jeep at the four o'clock position.
Found the fourth rifle propped against its door, full of factory
shells. It was already soaked. He shook it off and aimed
obliquely across the mesa toward the eleven. Pulled the trigger. It fired. It still worked fine. He fired four more spaced
shots, at the twelve, the one, the two, the three. Fan fire. *A
gamble*. The upside was he might get lucky and hit the
woman. Downside was it would tell her he was on his own.
One guy, more than one rifle. That was now an easy deduction. And it would tell her where he was. If she was counting
it would suggest to her he was waiting there with the last two
shells still in the magazine.

So he slid the gun under the Jeep and waded west through
the brush until he was forty feet from the edge of the rock.
Pulled Alice's Heckler & Koch out of his pocket and knocked
the safety off. Knelt down and smeared mud over his hands
and arms and face and waited for lightning to strike. Summer
storms he had witnessed before in hot parts of the world always featured lightning. Gigantic thunderheads rubbed and
jostled overhead and the voltage built to an unbearable level.
Five more minutes, he guessed. Then lightning would fire in
bolts or sheets and the landscape would flash with brightness.
He was in khaki clothes and had smeared khaki mud on his
skin. He doubted that she had.

He worked south, away from the Jeep, back toward the
wrecked VW, keeping forty feet in the undergrowth. The
darkness was total. The rain was building relentlessly. It built
to the point where it was absolutely impossible that it could

build any harder, and then it just kept on building. The limestone sinkholes were already full of water. Rain was lashing
their surfaces. Small rivers were running around his feet, gur-
gling into bottomless crevasses all around. The noise was as-
tonishing. The rain was roaring against the ground so hard
that it was impossible to imagine a louder sound. Then it fell
harder and the sound got louder.

He realized the camouflage mud had rinsed straight off his
skin. Impossible for it not to. Carmen's shower was like a
grudging trickle in comparison. He began to worry about
breathing. How could there be air to breathe, with so much
water? It was running down his face in solid streams and running straight into his mouth. He put his hand over his jaw and
sucked air through his fingers and spat and spluttered the
rainwater away.

He was opposite the two o'clock position and thirty feet
from the ledge when the lightning started. Far to the south a
ragged bolt exploded from the sky and hit the earth five miles
away. It was pure intense white and shaped like a bare tree
hurled upside down by a hurricane. He fell to a crouch and
stared straight ahead, looking for peripheral vision. Saw
nothing. The thunder followed the lightning five seconds
later, a ragged tearing rumble. *Where is she? Does she think
she's smarter than she thinks I am? In which case she'll be
behind me.* But he didn't turn around. Life is always about
guessing and gambling, and he had her pegged as a slick operator, for sure. *In her world.* Put her out on the street face-to-
face with Al Eugene, and she's got the smarts to charm the
birds out of the trees. *But put her down all alone in open
combat territory at night in a storm, and she's struggling.
I'm good at this. She's not. She's in front of me, clinging to
the edge of the mesa somewhere, scared like she's never been
scared before. She's mine.*

The storm was moving. The second lightning strike came
three minutes later and a mile north and east of the first one.
It was a jagged sheet that flickered insanely for eight or ten
seconds before dying into darkness. Reacher craned upward
and scanned ahead and right. Saw nothing. Turned and
scanned left. Saw the woman seventy feet away, crouched in

the lee of the ledge. He could see the white writing on her cap. *FBI*. Big letters. She was looking straight at him and her gun was rigid in her hand and her arm was fully extended from the shoulder. He saw the muzzle flash as she fired at him. It was a tiny dull spark completely overwhelmed by the storm.

The storm drifted slowly north and east and pushed the leading edge of rain ahead of it. It reached the motel building and built steadily and quickly from a whisper to a patter to a hard relentless drumming on the roof. It was a metal roof and within thirty seconds the noise was very loud. It woke Ellie from a restless troubled sleep. She opened her eyes wide and saw the small dark man with hair on his arms. He was sitting very still in a chair near the bed, watching her.

"Hi, kid," he said.

Ellie said nothing.

"Can't sleep?"

Ellie looked up at the ceiling.

"Raining," she said. "It's noisy."

The man nodded, and checked his watch.

She missed him. Impossible to tell by how much. The lightning died and plunged the world back into absolute darkness. Reacher fired once at the remembered target and listened hard. Nothing. *Probably a miss. Seventy feet in heavy rain, not an easy shot.* Then the thunderclap came. It was a shuddering bass boom that rocked the ground and rolled slowly away. He crouched again. He had nine bullets left. Then he threw the double-bluff dice. *She'll think I'll move, so I won't.* He stayed right where he was. Waited for the next lightning bolt. It would tell him how good she was. An amateur would move away from him. A good pro would move closer. A *really* good pro would double-bluff the double-bluff and stay exactly where she was.

By then the rain was as heavy as it was going to get. That was his guess. He had once been caught in a jungle storm in

Central America and gotten wet faster than falling fully
clothed into the sea. That was the hardest rain imaginable and
this was easily comparable. He was completely soaked to the
skin. *Beyond* soaked. Water was running in continuous tor-
rents under his shirt. Pouring off him, not dripping. It sluiced
out of his buttonholes like jets. He was cold. The temperature
had plummeted twenty or thirty degrees in less than twenty
minutes. As much water was bouncing upward around him as
was lashing down. The noise was unbearable. Leaves and
stalks were tearing off the bushes. They were flowing and ed-
dying away and building tiny beaver dams against every rock
on the ground. The hard hot grit had washed into slushy mud
six inches deep. His feet were sinking in it. His gun was
soaked. *That's O.K. A Heckler & Koch will fire wet. But so
will a Browning or a SIG.*

The next lightning flash was still well to the south, but it
was nearer. And brighter. It was a gigantic lateral bolt that
hissed and crackled across the sky. He scanned left. The
woman had moved closer. She was sixty feet away from him,
still tight against the mesa. *Good, but not really good.* She
fired at him and missed by four feet. It was a hasty shot and
her arm was still swinging in from the south. *The south? She
figured I'd moved away.* He felt mildly insulted and leveled
his arm and fired back. The incoming thunderclap buried the
sound of the shot. *Probably a miss. Eight left.*

Then it was back to the calculations. *What will she do?
What will she figure I'll do?* She had been wrong the last
time. *So this time she'll gamble. She'll guess I'll move in
closer. So she'll move in closer too. She'll go for the killing
shot immediately.*

He stayed in a crouch, exactly where he was. *Triple-bluff.*
He tracked his gun hand left-to-right along the theoretical direction she must be moving. Waited for the precious lightning. It came sooner than he expected. The storm was ripping
in fast. It exploded not more than a half-mile away and was
followed almost immediately by a bellow of thunder. The
flash was brighter than the sun. He squinted ahead. *The
woman was gone.* He jerked left and saw a smudge of vivid
blue backtracking away in the opposite direction. He fired in-

stinctively just ahead of it and the lightning died and darkness and noise and chaos collapsed around him. *Seven left.* He smiled. *But now I only need one more.*

The sound of thunder frightened her. It sounded like when Joshua and Billy had put a new roof on the motor barn. They had used big sheets of tin and they boomed and flexed when they were carrying them and made a horrible noise when they hammered the nails through. Thunder was like a hundred million billion sheets·of roofing tin all flexing and booming in the sky. She ducked her head under the sheets and watched the room light up with bright wobbling flashes of lightning outside the window.

"Are you scared?" the man asked.

She nodded, under the sheets. It scrubbed her hair, but she was sure the man could see her head moving.

"Don't be scared," the man said. "It's only a storm. Big girls aren't scared of storms."

She said nothing. He checked his watch again.

Her tactics were transparent. She was good, but not good enough to be unreadable. She was working close in to the rim of the mesa, because it offered an illusion of safety. She was working an *in-out-in-in* move. Double-bluffing, triple-bluffing, aiming to be unpredictable. *Smart, but not smart enough.* She had moved close, and then moved away. Now she would move close again, and then the next time not away again, but closer still. She figured he would begin to read the pattern and anticipate the yo-yo outward. But she would come inward instead. To wrong-foot him. And because she wanted to be close. She *liked* close. A head-shot artiste like her, he guessed her preferred range would be something less than ten feet.

He jumped out of his crouch and ran as hard as he could, like a sprinter, backward and left, curving around in a fast wide circle. He crashed through the brush like a panicked animal, big leaping strides, hurdling mesquite, splashing

through puddles, sliding through the mud. He didn't care
how much noise he was making. He would be inaudible a
yard away. All that mattered was how fast he was. He needed
to outflank her before the next lightning bolt.

He ran wildly in a big looping curve and then slowed and
skidded and eased in close to the limestone ledge maybe
twenty feet north of where he had first seen her. She had
moved south, and then back, so now she would be on her way
south again. She ought to be thirty feet ahead by now. Right
in front of him. He walked after her, fast and easy, like he was
on a sidewalk somewhere. Kept loose, trying to second-guess
the rhythm of the lightning, staying ready to hit the wet dirt.

The small dark man checked his watch again. Ellie hid under the sheet.

"Over three hours," the man said.

Ellie said nothing.

"Can you tell the time?"

Ellie straightened up in the bed and pulled the sheet down
slowly, all the way past her mouth.

"I'm six and a half," she said.

The man nodded.

"Look," he said.

He held out his arm and twisted his wrist.

"One more hour," he said.

"Then what?"

The man looked away. Ellie watched him a long moment
more. Then she pulled the sheet back over her head. The
thunder boomed and the lightning flashed.

The flash lit up the whole landscape for miles ahead. The
crash of thunder crowded in on top of it. Reacher dropped to
a crouch and stared. *She wasn't there.* She was nowhere in
front of him. The lightning died and the thunder rolled on.
For a second he wondered whether he would hear her gun
over it. *Would he?* Or would the first he knew be the sicken-
ing impact of the bullet? He dropped full length into the mud

and lay still. Felt the rain lashing his body like a thousand tiny hammers. *O.K., rethink.* Had *she* outflanked *him?* She could have attempted an exact mirror-image of his own move. In which case they had each sprinted a wide fast circle in opposite directions and essentially exchanged positions. Or she could have found a sinkhole or a crevasse and gone to ground. She could have found the Jeep. If she'd glanced backward during a lightning strike she would have seen it. It was an easy conclusion that he'd have to get back to it eventually. How else was he going to get out of the desert? So maybe she was waiting there. Maybe she was inside it, crouching low. Maybe she was *under* it, in which case he had just presented her with a Winchester rifle with two factory rounds still in the magazine.

He stayed down in the mud, thinking hard. He ignored the next lightning flash altogether. Just pressed himself into the landscape, calculating, deciding. He rejected the possibility of the flanking maneuver. That was military instinct. He was dealing with a street shooter, not an infantry soldier. No infantryman would aim for a guy's eye. Percentages were against it. So maybe she had gone for the Jeep. He swam himself through a stationary muddy circle and raised his head and waited.

The next flash was a sheet, rippling madly and lighting the underside of the clouds like a battlefield flare. The Jeep was a long way away. Too far, surely. And if she *had* gone for it, she was no immediate threat. Not all the way back there, not at that distance. So he swiveled back around and crawled on south. *Check and clear, zone by zone.* He moved slowly, on his knees and elbows. Ten feet, twenty, twenty-five. It felt exactly like basic training. He crawled on and on, and then he smelled perfume.

It was somehow intensified by the rain. He realized the whole desert smelled different. The rain had changed things entirely. He could smell plants and earth. They made a strong, pungent, natural odor. But mixed into it was a woman's perfume. *Was* it perfume? Or was it something from nature, like a night flower suddenly blooming in the storm? No, it was perfume. A woman's perfume. No question about it. He stopped moving and lay completely still.

He could hear the mesquite moving, but it was only the wind. The rain was easing back toward torrential and a strong wet breeze was coming in from the south, teasing him with the smell of perfume. It was absolutely dark. He raised his gun and couldn't see it in his hand. Like he was a blind man.

Which way is she facing? Not east. She had to be crouched low, so to the east there would be nothing to see except the blank two-foot wall that was the edge of the mesa. If she was looking south or west, no problem. *If she's looking north, she's looking straight at me, except she can't see me. Too dark. She can't smell me either, because I'm upwind.* He raised himself on his left forearm and pointed his gun straight from his right shoulder. If she was facing south or west, it would give him an easy shot into her back. *But worst case, she's looking north and we're exactly facing each other. We could be five feet apart. So it's a gamble now. When the lightning flashes, who reacts first?*

He held his breath. Waited for the lightning. It was the longest wait of his life. The storm had changed. Thunder was rumbling long and loud, but it wasn't sharp anymore. The rain was still heavy. It kicked mud and grit up onto his face. Thrashed against the brush. Brand-new streams gurgled all around his prone body. He was half-submerged in water. He was very cold.

Then there was a split-second tearing sound in the sky and a gigantic thunderclap crashed and a bolt of lightning fired absolutely simultaneously. It was impossibly white and harsh and the desert lit up brighter than day. The woman was three feet in front of him. She was slumped facedown on the ground, already battered by rain and silted with mud. She looked small and collapsed and empty. Her legs were bent at the knees and her arms were folded under her. Her gun had fallen next to her shoulder. A Browning Hi-Power. It was half-submerged in the mud and a small thicket of twigs had already dammed against one side of it. He used the last of the lightning flash to scrabble for it and hurl it far away. Then the light died and he used the after-image retained in his eyes to find her neck.

There was no pulse. She was already very cold.

Deflection shooting. His third bullet, instinctively placed just ahead of her as she scrambled away from him. She had jumped straight into its path. He kept the fingers of his left hand on the still pulse in her neck, afraid to lose contact with her in the dark. He settled down to wait for the next lightning flash. His left arm started shaking. He told himself it was because he was holding it at an unnatural angle. Then he started laughing. It built quickly, like the rain. He had spent the last twenty minutes stalking a woman he had already shot dead. *Accidentally*. He laughed uncontrollably until the rain filled his mouth and set him coughing and spluttering wildly.

The man stood up and walked over to the credenza. Picked up his gun from where it was lying on the polished wood. Ducked down to the black nylon valise and took out a long black silencer. Fitted it carefully to the muzzle of the gun. Walked back to the chair and sat down again.

"It's time," he said.

He put his hand on her shoulder. She felt it through the sheet. She wriggled away from him. Swam down in the bed and curled up. She needed to pee. Very badly.

"It's time," the man said again.

He folded the sheet back. She scrabbled away, holding the opposite hem tight between her knees. Looked straight at him.

"You said one more hour," she said. "It hasn't been a hour yet. I'll tell that lady. She's your boss."

The man's eyes went blank. He turned and looked at the door, just for a moment. Then he turned back.

"O.K.," he said. "You tell me when you think it's been one more hour."

He let go of the sheet and she wrapped herself up in it again. Ducked her head under it and put her hands over her ears to block the noise of the thunder. Then she closed her eyes, but she could still see the lightning flashes through the sheet and through her eyelids. They looked red.

The next flash was sheet lightning again, vague and diffuse and flickering. He rolled the body over, just to be sure. Tore

open her jacket and shirt. He had hit her in the left armpit. It
was through-and-through, exiting in the opposite wall of her
chest. Probably got her heart, both lungs and her spine. A .40
bullet was not a subtle thing. It took a lot to stop one. The entry wound was small and neat. The exit wound wasn't. The
rain flushed it clean. Diluted blood leaked all over the place
and instantly disappeared. Her chest cavity was filling with
water. It looked like a medical diagram. He could have sunk
his whole hand in there.

She was medium-sized. Blond hair, soaked and full of mud
where it spilled out under the FBI cap. He pushed the bill of
the cap upward so he could see her face. Her eyes were open
and staring at the sky and filling with rain like tears. Her face
was slightly familiar. He had seen her before. *Where?* The
lightning died and he was left with the image of her face in
his mind, harsh and white and reversed like a photograph's
negative. *The diner. The Coke floats. Friday, school quitting
time, a Crown Victoria, three passengers.* He had pegged
them as a sales team. *Wrong again.*

"O.K.," he said out loud. "Ballgame over."

He put Alice's gun back in his pocket and walked away
north, back to the Jeep. It was so dark and he had so much
rain in his eyes he thumped right into the side of it before he
knew he was there. He tracked around it with a hand on the
hood and found the driver's door. Opened it and closed it and
opened it again, just for the thrill of making the dome light
come on inside, illumination he could control for himself.

It wasn't easy driving back up onto the limestone. The grit
that should have been under the wheels and aiding traction
was now slick mud. He put the headlights on bright and
started the wipers beating fast and selected four-wheel drive
and slid around for a while before the front tires caught and
dragged the car up the slope. Then he hooked a wide curve
ahead and left, all the way across to the seven o'clock position. He hit the horn twice and Alice walked out of the
mesquite into the headlight beams. She was soaked to the
skin. Water was pouring off her. Her hair was plastered flat.
Her ears stuck out a little. She stepped to her left and ran
around to the passenger door.

"I guess this is the storm people were expecting," he said.

Lightning flared again outside. A ragged bolt far to their left, accompanied by an explosion of thunder. The weather was moving north, and fast.

She shook her head. "This little shower? This is just a taste. Wait until tomorrow."

"I'll be gone tomorrow."

"You will?"

He nodded.

"You O.K.?" he asked.

"I didn't know when to fire."

"You did fine."

"What happened?"

He drove off again, turning south, zigzagging the Jeep to fan the headlight beams back and forth across the mesa. Thirty feet in front of the wrecked VW, he found the first guy's body. It was humped and inert. He dipped the lights so they would shine directly on it and jumped out into the rain. The guy was dead. He had taken the Winchester's bullet in the stomach. He hadn't died instantaneously. His hat was missing and he had torn open his jacket to clutch his wound. He had crawled quite a distance. He was tall and heavily built. Reacher closed his eyes and scanned back to the scene in the diner. *By the register. The woman, two men. One big and fair, one small and dark.* Then he walked back to the Jeep and slid inside. The seat was soaked.

"Two dead," he said. "That's what happened. But the driver escaped. Did you ID him?"

"They came to kill us, didn't they?"

"That was the plan. Did you ID the driver?"

She said nothing.

"It's very important, Alice," he said. "For Ellie's sake. We don't have a tongue. That part didn't work out. They're both dead."

She said nothing.

"Did you see him?"

She shook her head.

"No, not really," she said. "I'm very sorry. I was running, the lights were only on a second or two."

It had seemed longer than that to Reacher. Much longer. But in reality, she was probably right. She was maybe even overestimating. It might have been only three-quarters of a second. They had been very quick with the triggers.

"I've seen these people before," he said. "On Friday, up at the crossroads. Must have been after they got Eugene. They must have been scouting the area. Three of them. A woman, a big guy, a small dark guy. I can account for the woman and the big guy. So was it the small dark guy driving tonight?"

"I didn't really see."

"Gut feeling?" Reacher said. "First impression? You must have gotten a glimpse. Or seen a silhouette."

"Didn't you?"

He nodded. "He was facing away from me, looking down to where you fired from. There was a lot of glare. Some rain on his windshield. Then I was shooting, and then he took off. But I don't think he was small."

She nodded, too. "Gut feeling, he wasn't small. Or dark. It was just a blur, but I'd say he was big enough. Maybe fair-haired."

"Makes sense," Reacher said. "They left one of the team behind to guard Ellie."

"So who was driving?"

"Their client. The guy who hired them. That's my guess. Because they were short-handed, and because they needed local knowledge."

"He got away."

Reacher smiled. "He can run, but he can't hide."

They went to take a look at the wrecked VW. It was beyond help. Alice didn't seem too concerned about it. She just shrugged and turned away. Reacher took the maps from the glove compartment and turned the Jeep around and headed north. The drive back to the Red House was a nightmare. Crossing the mesa was O.K. But beyond the end of it the desert track was baked so hard that it wasn't absorbing any water at all. The rain was flooding all over the surface. The part that had felt like a riverbed *was* a riverbed. It was pouring with a fast torrent that boiled up over the tires. Mesquite bushes had been torn off their deep taproots and washed out of their shallow toeholds and whole trees were racing south on the swirl. They dammed against the front of the Jeep and rode with it until cross-currents tore them loose. Sinkholes were concealed by the tide. But the rain was easing fast. It was dying back to drizzle. The eye of the storm had blown away to the north.

They were right next to the motor barn before they saw it. It was in total darkness. Reacher braked hard and swerved around it and saw pale lights flickering behind some of the windows in the house.

"Candles," he said.

"Power must be out," Alice said. "The lightning must have hit the lines."

He braked again and slid in the mud and turned the car so the headlights washed deep into the barn.

"Recognize anything?" he asked.

Bobby's pick-up was back in its place, but it was wet and streaked with mud. Water was dripping out of the load bed and pooling on the ground.

"O.K.," Alice said. "So what now?"

Reacher stared into the mirror. Then he turned his head and watched the road from the north.

"Somebody's coming," he said.

There was a faint glow of headlights behind them, rising and falling, many miles distant, breaking into a thousand pieces in the raindrops on the Jeep's windows.

"Let's go say howdy to the Greers," he said.

He pulled Alice's gun out of his pocket and checked it. *Never assume*. But it was O.K. *Cocked and locked. Seven left*. He put it back in his pocket and drove across the soaking yard to the foot of the porch steps. The rain was almost gone. The ground was beginning to steam. The vapor rose gently and swirled in the headlight beams. They got out into the humidity. The temperature was coming back. So was the insect noise. There was a faint whirring chant all around. It sounded wary and very distant.

He led her up the porch steps and pushed open the door.

The hallway had candles burning in holders placed here and there on all the available horizontal surfaces. They gave a soft orange glow and made the foyer warm and inviting. He ushered Alice through to the parlor. Stepped in behind her. More candles were burning in there. Dozens of them. They were glued to saucers with melted wax. There was a Coleman lantern standing on a credenza against the end wall. It was hissing softly and burning bright.

Bobby and his mother were sitting together at the red-painted table. Shadows were dancing and flickering all around them. The candlelight was kind to Rusty. It took twenty years off her. She was fully dressed, in jeans and a shirt. Bobby sat beside her, looking at nothing in particular. The tiny flames lit his face and made it mobile.

"Isn't this romantic," Reacher said.

Rusty moved, awkwardly.

"I'm scared of the dark," she said. "Can't help it. Always have been."

"You should be," Reacher said. "Bad things can happen in the dark."

She made no reply to that.

"Towel?" Reacher asked. He was dripping water all over the floor. So was Alice.

"In the kitchen," Rusty said.

There was a thin striped towel on a wooden roller. Alice blotted her face and hair and patted her shirt. Reacher did the same, and then he stepped back into the parlor.

"Why are you both up?" he asked. "It's three o'clock in the morning."

Neither of them answered.

"Your truck was out tonight," Reacher said.

"But we weren't," Bobby said. "We stayed inside, like you told us to."

Rusty nodded. "Both of us, together."

Reacher smiled.

"Each other's alibi," he said. "That would get them rolling in the aisles, down in the jury room."

"We didn't do anything," Bobby said.

Reacher heard a car on the road. Just the faint subliminal

sound of tires slowing on soaked blacktop. The faint whistle of drive belts turning under a hood. Then there was a slow wet crunch as it turned under the gate. Grit and pebbles popped under the wheels as it drove up to the porch. There was a tiny squeal from a brake rotor and then silence as the engine died. The *clunk* of a door closing. Feet on the porch steps. The house door opening, footsteps crossing the foyer. Then the parlor door opened. The candle flames swayed and flickered. Hack Walker stepped into the room.

"Good," Reacher said. "We don't have much time."

"Did you rob my office?" Walker replied.

Reacher nodded. "I was curious."

"About what?"

"About details," Reacher said. "I'm a details guy."

"You didn't need to break in. I'd have shown you the files."

"You weren't there."

"Whatever, you shouldn't have broken in. You're in trouble for it. You can understand that, right? Big trouble."

Reacher smiled. *Bad luck and trouble, been my only friends.*

"Sit down, Hack," he said.

Walker paused a second. Then he threaded his way around all the chairs and sat down next to Rusty Greer. Candlelight lit his face. The lantern glowed to his left.

"You got something for me?" he asked.

Reacher sat opposite. Laid his hands palm-down on the wood.

"I was a cop of sorts for thirteen years," he said.

"So?"

"I learned a lot of stuff."

"Like?"

"Like, lies are messy. They get out of control. But the truth is messy, too. So any situation you're in, you expect rough edges. Anytime I see anything that's all buttoned up, I get real suspicious. And Carmen's situation was messy enough to be real."

"But?"

"I came to see there were a couple of edges that were just *too* rough."

"Like what?"

"Like, she had no money with her. I *know* that. Two million in the bank, and she travels three hundred miles with a single dollar in her purse? Sleeps in the car, doesn't eat? Leapfrogs from one Mobil station to the next, just to keep going? That didn't tie up for me."

"She was playacting. That's who she is."

"You know who Nicolaus Copernicus is?"

"Was," Walker said. "Some old astronomer. Polish, I think. Proved the earth goes around the sun."

Reacher nodded. "And much more than that, by implication. He asked us all to consider how likely is it that we're at the absolute center of things? What are the odds? That what we're seeing is somehow exceptional? The very best or the very worst? It's an important philosophical point."

"So?"

"So if Carmen had two million bucks in the bank but traveled with a single dollar just in case she bumped into a guy as suspicious as me, then she is undoubtedly the number-one best-prepared con artist in the history of the world. And old Copernicus asks me, how likely *is* that? That I should by chance happen to bump into the best con artist in the history of the world? His answer is, not very likely, really. He says the likelihood is, if I bump into a con artist at all, it'll be a very average and mediocre one."

"So what are you saying?"

"I'm saying it didn't tie up for me. So it got me thinking about the money. And then something else didn't tie up."

"What?"

"Al Eugene's people messengered Sloop's financial stuff over, right?"

"This morning. Feels like a long time ago."

"Thing is, I saw Al's office. When I went to the museum. It's literally within sight of the courthouse. It's a one-minute walk. So how likely is it they would *messenger* something over? Wouldn't they just *walk* it over? For a friend of Al's? Especially if it was urgent? It would take them ten times as long just to dial the phone for the courier service."

The candlelight danced and flickered. The red room glowed.

"People messenger things all the time," Walker said. "It's routine. And it was too hot for walking."

Reacher nodded. "Maybe. It didn't mean much at the time. But then something *else* didn't tie up. The collarbone."

"What about it?"

Reacher turned to face Alice. "When you fell off your in-line skates, did you break your collarbone?"

"No," Alice said.

"Any injuries at all?"

"I tore up my hand. A lot of road rash."

"You put your hand out to break your fall?"

"Reflex," she said. "It's impossible not to."

Reacher nodded. Turned back through the candlelit gloom to Walker.

"I rode with Carmen on Saturday," he said. "My first time ever. My ass got sore, but the thing I really remember is how *high* I was. It's scary up there. So the thing is, if Carmen fell off, from that height, onto rocky dirt, hard enough to bust her collarbone, how is it that she didn't get road rash, too? On her hand?"

"Maybe she did."

"The hospital didn't write it up."

"Maybe they forgot."

"It was a very detailed report. New staff, working hard. I noticed that, and Cowan Black did, too. He said they were very thorough. They wouldn't have neglected lacerations to the palm."

"She must have worn riding gloves."

Reacher shook his head. "She told me nobody wears gloves down here. Too hot. And she definitely wouldn't have said that if gloves had once saved her from serious road rash. She'd have been a big fan of gloves, in that case. She'd have certainly made *me* wear them, being new to it."

"So?"

"So I started to wonder if the collarbone thing *could* have been from Sloop hitting her. I figured it was possible. Maybe she's on her knees, a big clubbing fist from above, she moves her head. Only she also claimed he had broken her arm and her jaw and knocked her teeth loose, too, and there was no mention of all that stuff, so I stopped wondering. Especially when I found out the ring was real."

A candle on the left end of the table died. It burned out and smoke rose from it in a thin plume that ran absolutely straight for a second and then spiraled crazily.

"She's a liar," Walker said. "That's all."

"She sure is," Bobby said.

"Sloop never hit her," Rusty said. "A son of mine would never hit a woman, whoever she was."

"One at a time, O.K.?" Reacher said, quietly.

He could feel the impatience in the room. Elbows shifting on the table, feet moving on the floor. He turned to Bobby first.

"You claim she's a liar," he said. "And I know why. It's because you don't like her, because you're a racist piece of shit, and because she had an affair with the schoolteacher. So among other things you took it on yourself to try and turn me off of her. Some kind of loyalty to your brother."

Then he turned to Rusty. "We'll get to what Sloop did and didn't do real soon. But right now, you keep quiet, O.K.? Hack and I have business."

"What business?" Walker said.

"This business," Reacher said, and propped Alice's gun on the tabletop, the butt resting on the wood and the muzzle pointing straight at Walker's chest.

"What the hell are you doing?" Walker said.

Reacher clicked the safety off with his thumb. The *snick* sounded loud in the room. Candles flickered and the lantern hissed softly.

"I figured out the thing with the diamond," he said. "Then everything else made sense. Especially with you giving us the badges and sending us down here to speak with Rusty."

"What are you talking about?"

"It was like a conjuring trick. The whole thing. You knew Carmen pretty well. So you knew what she must have told me. Which was the absolute truth, always. The truth about herself, and about what Sloop was doing to her. So you just exactly reversed everything. It was simple. A very neat and convincing trick. Like she told me she was from Napa, and you said, *hey, I bet she told you she's from Napa, but she isn't, you know*. Like she told me she'd called the IRS, and you said, *hey, I bet she told you she called the IRS, but she didn't, really*. It was like *you* knew the real truth and were reluctantly exposing commonplace lies she had told before. But it was *you* who was lying. All along. It was very, very effective. Like a conjuring trick. And you dressed it all up behind pretending you wanted to save her. You fooled me for a long time."

"I *did* want to save her. I *am* saving her."

"Bullshit, Hack. Your only aim all along was to coerce a confession out of her for something she didn't do. It was a straightforward plan. Your hired guns kidnapped Ellie today so you could force Carmen to confess. I was your only problem. I stuck around, I recruited Alice. We were in your face from Monday morning onward. So you misled us for twenty-seven straight hours. You let us down slowly and regretfully, point by point. It was beautifully done. Well, almost. To really make it work, you'd have to be the best con artist in the world. And like old Copernicus says, what are the odds that the best con artist in the world would happen to be up there in Pecos?"

There was silence. Just sputtering wax, the hissing of the lantern, five people breathing. The old air conditioner wasn't running. No power.

"You're crazy," Walker said.

"No, I'm not. You decoyed me by being all regretful about what a liar Carmen was and how desperate you were to save her. You were even smart enough to reveal a cynical reason for *wanting* to save her. About wanting to be a judge, so I wouldn't think you were too good to be true. That was a great touch, Hack. But all the time you were talking to her on the phone, muffling your voice to get past the desk clerk, telling him you were her lawyer, telling *her* if she ever spoke to a *real* lawyer, you'd hurt Ellie. Which is why she refused to speak with Alice. Then you wrote out a bunch of phony financial statements on your own computer right there at your desk. One printout looks much the same as any other. And you drafted the phony trust deeds. And the phony Family

Services papers. You knew what real ones looked like, I guess. Then as soon as you heard your people had picked up the kid you got back on the phone and coached Carmen through the phony confession, feeding back to *her* all the lies you'd told to *me*. Then you sent your assistant downstairs to listen to them."

"This is nonsense."

Reacher shrugged. "So let's prove it. Let's call the FBI and ask them how the hunt for Ellie is going."

"Phones are out," Bobby said. "Electrical storm."

Reacher nodded. "O.K., no problem."

He kept the gun pointed at Walker's chest and turned to face Rusty.

"Tell me what the FBI agents asked you," he said.

Rusty looked blank. "What FBI agents?"

"No FBI agents came here tonight?"

She just shook her head. Reacher nodded.

"You were playacting, Hack," he said. "You told us you'd called the FBI and the state police, and there were roadblocks in place, and helicopters up, and more than a hundred fifty people on the ground. But you didn't call anybody. Because if you had, the very *first* thing they would have done is come down here. They'd have talked to Rusty for hours. They'd have brought sketch artists and crime scene technicians. This is the scene of the crime, after all. And Rusty is the only witness."

"You're wrong, Reacher," Walker said.

"There *were* FBI people here," Bobby said. "I saw them in the yard."

Reacher shook his head.

"There were people wearing FBI hats," he said. "Two of them. But they aren't wearing those hats anymore."

Walker said nothing.

"Big mistake, Hack," Reacher said. "Giving us those stupid badges and sending us down here. You're in law enforcement. You knew Rusty was the vital witness. You also knew she wouldn't cooperate fully with me. So it was an inexplicable decision for a DA to take, to send us down here. I couldn't believe it. Then I saw why. You wanted us out of the way. And you wanted to know where we were, at all times. So you could send your people after us."

"What people?"

"The hired guns, Hack. The people in the FBI hats. The people you sent to kill Al Eugene. The people you sent to kill Sloop. They were pretty good. Very professional. But the thing with professionals is, they need to be able to work again in the future. Al Eugene was no problem. Could have been anybody, out there in the middle of nowhere. But Sloop was harder. He was just home from prison, wasn't going anyplace for a spell. So it had to be done right here, which was risky. They made you agree to cover their asses by framing Carmen. Then you made *them* agree to help you do it by moonlighting as the kidnap team."

"This is ridiculous," Walker said.

"You knew Carmen had bought a gun," Reacher said. "You told me, the paperwork comes through your office. And you knew *why* she bought it. You knew all about Sloop and what he did to her. You knew their bedroom was a torture chamber. So she wants to hide a gun in there, where does she put it? Three choices, really. Top shelf of her closet, in her bedside table, or in her underwear drawer. Common sense. Same for any woman in any bedroom. I know it, and your people knew it. They probably watched through the window until she went to shower, they slipped some gloves on, a minute later they're in the room, they cover Sloop with their own guns until they find Carmen's, and they shoot him with it. They're outside again thirty seconds later. A quick sprint back to where they left their car on the road, and they're gone. This house is a warren. But you know it well. You're a friend of the family. You assured them they could be in and out without being seen. You probably drew them a floor plan."

Walker closed his eyes. Said nothing. He looked old and pale. The candlelight wasn't helping him.

"But you made mistakes, Hack," Reacher said. "People like you always make mistakes. The financial reports were clumsy. Lots of money, but hardly any expenditure? How likely is that? What is she, a miser, too? And the messenger thing was a bad slip. If they *had* been messengered, you'd have left them in the courier packet, like you did with the medical reports, to make them look even more official."

Walker opened his eyes, defiant.

"The medical reports," he repeated. "You saw them. They *prove* she was lying. You heard Cowan Black say it."

Reacher nodded. "Leaving them in the FedEx packet was neat. They looked real urgent, like they were hot off the truck. But you should have torn the label off the front. Because the thing is, FedEx charges by weight. And I weighed the packet on Alice's kitchen scales. One pound, one ounce. But the label said two pounds and nine ounces. So one of two things must have happened. Either FedEx ripped off the hospital by padding the charge, or you took out about sixty percent of the contents and trashed them. And you know what? I vote for you checking the contents before you sent them over to us. You've been a DA for a spell, you've tried a lot of cases, you know what convincing evidence looks like. So anything about the beatings went straight in the trash. All you left were the genuine accidents. But the road rash thing passed you by, so you left the collarbone in by mistake. Or maybe you felt you *had* to leave it in, because you know she's got a healed knot clearly visible and you figured I'd have noticed it."

Walker said nothing. The lantern hissed.

"The broken arm, the jaw, the teeth," Reacher said. "My guess is there are five or six more folders in a Dumpster somewhere. Probably not behind the courthouse. Probably not in your backyard, either. I guess you're smarter than that. Maybe they're in a trashcan at the bus station. Some big public place."

Walker said nothing. The candle flames danced. Reacher smiled.

"But you were mostly pretty good," he said. "When I figured Carmen wasn't the shooter, you steered it straight back to a conspiracy *involving* Carmen. You didn't miss a beat. Even when I made the link to Eugene, you kept on track. You were very shocked. You went all gray and sweaty. Not because you were upset about Al. But because he'd been found so soon. You hadn't planned on that. But still, you thought for ten seconds and came up with the IRS motive. But you know what? You were so busy thinking, you forgot to be scared enough. About the two-for-three possibility. It was a plausible threat. You should have been much more worried. Anybody else would have been."

Walker said nothing.

"And you got Sloop out on a Sunday," Reacher said. "Not easy to do. But you didn't do it for him. You did it so he could be killed on a Sunday, so Carmen could be framed on a Sunday and spend the maximum time in jail before visitors could get near her the next Saturday. To give yourself five clear days to work on her."

Walker said nothing.

"Lots of mistakes, Hack," Reacher said. "Including sending people after me. Like old Copernicus says, what were the chances they'd be good enough?"

Walker said nothing. Bobby was leaning forward, staring sideways across his mother, looking straight at him. Catching on, slowly.

"*You* sent people to kill my brother?" he breathed.

"No," Walker said. "Reacher's wrong."

Bobby stared at him like he'd answered *yes* instead.

"But why *would* you?" he asked. "You were friends."

Then Walker looked up, straight at Reacher.

"Yes, why *would* I?" he said. "What possible motive could I have?"

"Something Benjamin Franklin once wrote," Reacher said.

"What the hell does that mean?"

"You wanted to be a judge. Not because you wanted to do good. That was all sanctimonious bullshit. It was because you wanted the trappings. You were born a poor boy and you were greedy for money and power. And it was right there in front of you. But first you had to get elected. And what sort of a thing stops a person getting elected?"

Walker just shrugged.

"Old scandals," Reacher said. "Among other things. Old secrets, coming back at you from the past. Sloop and Al and you were a threesome, way back when. Did all kinds of stuff

together. You three against the world. You told me that. So
there's Sloop, in prison for cheating on his taxes. He can't
stand it in there. So he thinks, *how do I get out of here?* Not
by repaying my debts. By figuring, my old pal Hack is running for judge this year. Big prize, all that money and power.
What's he prepared to do to get it? So he calls you up and
says he could start some serious rumors about some old ac-
tivities if you don't broker his way out of there. You think it
over carefully. You figure Sloop wouldn't incriminate *himself*
by talking about something you all did together, so at first
you relax. Then you realize there's a large gap between the
sort of *facts* that would convict you and the sort of *rumors*
that would wreck your chances in the election. So you cave
in. You take some of your campaign donations and arrange to
pay off the IRS with it. Now Sloop's happy. But you're not.
In your mind, the cat is out of the bag. Sloop's threatened you
once. What about the next time he wants something? And
Al's involved, because he's Sloop's lawyer. So now it's all
fresh in Al's mind too. Your chances of making judge are
suddenly vulnerable."

Walker said nothing.

"You know what Ben Franklin once wrote?" Reacher
asked.

"What?"

" 'Three can keep a secret, if two of them are dead.' "

Silence in the room. No movement, no breathing. Just the
soft hiss of the lantern and the flickering of the tiny candle
flames.

"What was the secret?" Alice whispered.

"Three boys in rural Texas," Reacher said. "Growing up
together, playing ball, having fun. They get a little older, they
turn their attention to what their dads are doing. The guns, the
rifles, the hunting. Maybe they start with the armadillos.
They shouldn't, really, because they're protected. By the
tree-huggers. But the attitude is, they're on my land, they're
mine to hunt. Bobby said that to me. An arrogant attitude. A
superior attitude. I mean, hey, what's an armadillo worth?
But armadillos are slow and boring prey. Too easy. The three
boys are growing up. They're three young men now. High

school seniors. They want a little more excitement. So they go looking for coyotes, maybe. Worthier opponents. They hunt at night. They use a truck. They range far and wide. And soon they find bigger game. Soon they find a *real* thrill."

"What?"

"Mexicans," Reacher said. "Poor anonymous no-account brown families stumbling north through the desert at night. And I mean, hey, what are *they* worth? Are they even human? But they make great prey. They run, and they squeal. Almost like hunting actual people, right, Hack?"

Silence in the room.

"Maybe they started with a girl," Reacher said. "Maybe they didn't mean to kill her. But they did anyway. Maybe they *had* to. Couple of days, they're nervous. They hold their breath. But there's no comeback. Nobody reacts. Nobody even cares. So hey, this is suddenly *fun*. Then they're out often. It becomes a sport. The ultimate kill. Better than armadillos. They take that old pick-up, one of them driving, two of them riding in the load bed, they hunt for hours. Bobby said Sloop invented that technique. Said he was real good at it. I expect he was. I expect they all were. They got plenty of practice. They did it twenty-five times in a year."

"That was the border patrol," Bobby said.

"No, it wasn't. The report wasn't a whitewash. It didn't read like one, and the inside word is it was kosher. Sergeant Rodríguez told me that. And people like Sergeant Rodríguez *know* things like that, believe me. The investigation got nowhere because it was looking in the wrong place. It wasn't a bunch of rogue officers. It was three local boys called Sloop Greer and Al Eugene and Hack Walker. Having fun in that old pick-up truck that's still parked in your barn. Boys will be boys, right?"

Silence in the room.

"The attacks were mostly in Echo County," Reacher said. "That struck me as odd. Why would the border patrol come so far north? Truth is, they didn't. Three Echo boys went a little ways south instead."

Silence.

"The attacks stopped in late August," Reacher said. "Why

was that? Not because the investigation scared them off. They didn't *know* about the investigation. It was because college opens early September. They went off to be freshmen. The next summer it was too dangerous or they'd grown out of it, and they didn't ever do it again. The whole thing faded into history, until twelve years later Sloop was sitting in a cell somewhere and dragged it all up because he was so desperate to get out."

Everybody was staring straight at Walker. His eyes were closed tight and he was deathly pale.

"It seemed so unfair, right?" Reacher said to him. "All that was way in the past. Maybe you weren't even a willing participant in the first place. Maybe the others dragged you into it. And now it was all coming back at you. It was a nightmare. It was going to ruin your life. It was going to take away the big prize. So you made some calls. Made some decisions. Three can keep a secret, if two of them are dead."

Another candle died. The wick hissed and smoke plumed.

"No," Walker said. "It wasn't like that."

The lantern flickered behind him. Shadows danced on the ceiling.

"So what was it like?" Reacher asked.

"I was just going to take Ellie. Just temporarily. I hired some local people to do it. I had plenty of campaign money. They watched her for a week. I went up to the jail and told Sloop, don't mess with me. But he didn't care. He said, go ahead and take Ellie. He didn't want her. He was all conflicted. He married Carmen to punish himself for what we did, I think. That's why he hit her all the time. She was a permanent reminder. He thought she could read it in him. See it in his eyes. Like voodoo. Ellie, too. He thought *she* could see it in him. So taking her wasn't a threat to Sloop."

"So then you hired some more people."

Walker nodded. "They took over and got rid of the watchers for me."

"And then they got rid of Al and Sloop."

"It was a long time ago, Reacher. He shouldn't have brought it up. We were kids at the time. We all agreed we would never even mention it again. We promised each other.

Never, *ever*. It was the unmentionable thing. Like it had never happened. Like it was just a bad dream, a year long."

There was silence.

"You were driving the truck tonight," Reacher said.

Walker nodded again, slowly. "You two, then it would have been over. I knew you knew, you see. I mean, why else would you steal the files and lead us out into the desert? So I drove the truck. Why not? I'd driven out there at night before, many times."

Then he went quiet. Swallowed hard, twice. Closed his eyes.

"But I got scared," he said. "I got sick. I couldn't go through with it. Not again. I'm not that person anymore. I changed."

Silence in the room.

"Where's Ellie?" Reacher asked.

Walker shrugged and shook his head. Reacher fished in his pocket and came out with the chromium star.

"Is this thing legal?" he asked.

Walker opened his eyes. Nodded.

"Technically, I guess," he said.

"So I'm going to arrest you."

Walker shook his head, vaguely.

"No," he said. "Please."

"Are you armed?" Reacher asked him.

Walker nodded. "Pistol, in my pocket."

"Get it for me, Mrs. Greer," Reacher said.

Rusty turned in her chair and went for Walker's pocket. He offered no resistance. Even leaned sideways to make it easier for her. She came out with a small blued-steel revolver. A Colt Detective Special, .38 caliber, six shots, two-inch barrel. A small weapon. Rusty cradled it in her palm, and it looked right at home in a woman's hand.

"Where's Ellie, Hack?" Reacher asked again.

"I don't know," Walker said. "I really don't. They use motels. I don't know which one. They wouldn't tell me. They said it's safer that way."

"How do you contact them?"

"A Dallas number. It must be rerouted."

"Phones are out," Bobby said.

"Where is she, Hack?" Reacher asked again.

"I don't know. I'd tell you if I did."

Reacher raised Alice's gun. Held it straight out across the table. His arms were long, and the muzzle came to rest two feet from Walker's face.

"Watch the trigger finger, Hack," he said.

He tightened his finger until the skin shone white in the candlelight. The trigger moved backward, a sixteenth of an inch, then an eighth.

"You want to die, Hack?"

Walker nodded.

"Yes, please," he whispered.

"Tell me first," Reacher said. "Make it right. Where is she?"

"I don't *know*," Walker said.

He stared at the muzzle. It was so close, his eyes were crossing. The candle flames were reflected in the polished nickel. Reacher sighed and slackened his finger and lowered the gun all the way back to the tabletop. It hit the wood with a quiet sound. Nobody spoke. And nobody moved, until Rusty's hand came up with the tiny revolver in it. She raised it in a wavering circle and it finished up pointing at nobody in particular.

"Sloop wouldn't hit a woman," she whispered. "Those were all riding accidents."

Reacher shook his head. "He beat Carmen for five years, Rusty, almost every day they were married, until he went to jail. Broke her bones and split her lips and bruised her flesh. And that was after raping and torturing and murdering twenty-five human beings, at night, in the desert, twelve years ago."

She trembled wildly.

"No," she said. "That isn't true."

The gun wavered unsteadily.

"Point that thing at me and I'll shoot you," Reacher said. "Believe me, it would be an absolute pleasure."

She stared at him for a second and then crooked her arm and touched the gun to the side of her own head, just above her ear. The metal penetrated her lacquered hair like a stick thrust through a bird's nest. She kept it there for a long moment and then pulled it away and turned and twisted in her chair and moved it again and brought it level with Hack Walker's forehead, with the muzzle no more than two inches from his skin.

"You killed my boy," she whispered.

Walker made no attempt to move. He just nodded, very slightly.

"I'm sorry," he whispered back.

No revolver has a safety mechanism. And a Colt Detective Special is a double-action pistol. Which means the first half of the trigger's travel clicks the hammer back and revolves the cylinder under it, and then, if you keep on pulling, the hammer drops and the gun fires.

"No, Rusty," Reacher said.

"Mom," Bobby called.

The hammer clicked back.

"No," Alice shouted.

The hammer tripped. The gun fired. There was colossal noise and flame, and the crown of Walker's head blasted backward into the candlelit gloom. It just came off like a lid and splintered into mist. *Colt Super Autos with hollow points,* Reacher's subconscious mind told him. The flame died abruptly and he saw a blackened hole between Walker's eyes and his hair on fire from the muzzle flash. Then Rusty fired again. The second bullet followed the first straight through Walker's head and he went down and Rusty kept the gun rock-steady in the air above him and fired into space, three, four, five, six. The third shot splintered the wall, and the fourth hit the Coleman lantern and shattered its glass, and the fifth hit its kerosene reservoir and exploded it over a ten-foot square of wall. It blew sideways and ignited with a bright flash and the sixth shot hit the exact center of the flames. She kept on pumping the trigger even after the gun was empty. Reacher watched her finger flexing and the hammer clicking and the cylinder stepping around obediently. Then he turned and watched the wall.

The kerosene was thicker than water and had more surface

tension. It flung outward and dripped and ran and burned
fiercely. It set the wall on fire immediately. The dry old wood
burned with no hesitation at all. Blue flames crept upward
and sideways and the faded red paint bubbled and peeled
ahead of them. Tongues of flame found the vertical seams between the boards and raced up them like they were hungry.
They reached the ceiling and paused momentarily and then
curved horizontally and spread outward. The air in the room
stirred to feed them. The candles guttered in the sudden draft.
Within five seconds the wall was burning along its full
height. Then the fire started creeping sideways. The flames
were blue and smooth and curled and liquid, like they were
sculpted out of something wet and soft. They glowed with
mysterious inner light. Flakes of burning paint were drifting
on hot currents and landing randomly. The fire was creeping
clockwise, very fast, coming around behind everybody in the
room.

"Out," Reacher shouted.

Alice was already on her feet and Bobby was staring at the
fire. Rusty was sitting absolutely motionless, still patiently
working the trigger. The clicking of the firing mechanism
was lost behind the crackle of the flames.

"Get her out," Reacher shouted.

"We've got no water," Bobby shouted back. "The well
pump won't work without electricity."

"Just get your mother out," Reacher shouted.

Bobby stood completely still. The flames had found the
floorboards. The paint bubbled and peeled outward in a wide
arc and the fire started a patient journey in pursuit. Reacher
kicked chairs out of the way and lifted the table and over-
turned it on top of the flames. They died under it and then detoured neatly around it. The ceiling was well alight. Walker's
body was sprawled on the floor near the window. His hair
was still on fire from the muzzle flash. It smoked and smol-
dered with flames of a different color. The fire had found the
door frame. Reacher stepped across and pulled Rusty out of
her chair. Spun her around and straight-armed her through
the smoke and out of the room ahead of him. Alice was already in the foyer. She had the front door open. Reacher

could feel damp air sucking in to feed the fire. It was keeping low, down by his feet. It was already a strong breeze.

Alice ran down the steps to the yard and Reacher pushed Rusty after her. She clattered down and staggered out onto the wet dirt and got steady on her feet and just stood there, still holding the empty gun straight out from her shoulder, still clicking the useless trigger. Walker's Lincoln was parked next to the Jeep, wet and dirty and travel-stained. Reacher ducked back inside the foyer. It was filling with smoke. It was pooling near the ceiling and crowding downward in layers. The air was hot and paint was scorching everywhere. Bobby was coughing hard near the parlor door. The parlor was already a mass of flame. An inferno. The fire was curling out of the door. The door itself was on fire. The red-framed mirror cracked in the heat and Reacher turned and saw two of himself staring back. He took a deep spluttering breath and ran toward the flames and grabbed Bobby by the wrist. Twisted his arm and grabbed the back of his belt like he was arresting him and ran him out into the darkness. Hustled him down the steps and shoved him toward the center of the yard.

"It's burning down," Bobby screamed. "All of it."

The windows were alive with yellow light. Flames were dancing behind them. Smoke was drifting through the screens and there were loud random cracking sounds from inside as timbers yielded and moved. The soaked roof was already steaming gently.

"It's burning down," Bobby screamed again. "What are we going to do?"

"Go live in the barn," Reacher said. "That's where people like you belong."

Then he grabbed Alice's hand and ran straight for the Jeep.

17

When the storm moved north the driver knew his partners weren't coming back. It was a sensation so strong it took on the weight of absolute fact. It was like the rain had left a void behind that would never be filled. He turned in his chair and stared at the motel room door. Sat like that for minutes. Then he stood up and walked over and opened it. Looked out into the parking lot, focusing left, focusing right. The blacktop was streaming with water. The air smelled sharp and clean.

He stepped outside and walked ten paces in the dark. There was a running gutter somewhere and the gurgle of street drains and loud dripping from the trees. But nothing else. Nothing else at all. Nobody was coming. Nobody was ever going to come again. He knew it. He turned around. Wet grit slid under his shoes. He walked back. Stepped inside the room and closed the door gently behind him. Looked over at the bed. Looked at the sleeping child in it.

* * *

"You drive," he called. "North, O.K.?"

He pushed her toward the driver's door and ran around the hood. She pulled her seat forward and he racked his backward. Unfolded the maps on his knees. To his left the Red House was burning fiercely. All the windows were bright with flame. Both floors now. The maid ran out of the kitchen door, wrapped in a bathrobe. The light of the fire caught her face. There was no expression on it.

"O.K., let's go," he said.

She slammed the selector into Drive and gunned the motor. The transfer case was still locked in four-wheel drive and all four tires spun and scattered wet stones and the car took off. She slewed past Walker's Lincoln. Made the right under the gate without pausing. Accelerated hard. He turned his head and saw the first flames appear at the eaves of the roof. They licked outward and paused and ran horizontally, searching for sustenance. Steam was pouring off the soaked shingles and mixing with smoke. Rusty and Bobby and the maid were watching it drift, hypnotized. He glanced away and didn't look back again. Just stared ahead and then riffed through the maps on his knees and found the large-scale sheet showing Pecos County in its entirety. Then he reached up and clicked the dome light on.

"Faster," he said. "I've got a real bad feeling about this."

The four hours were long gone, but he waited anyway. He felt a certain reluctance. How could he not? He wasn't a monster. He would do what he had to do, for sure, but he wasn't going to *enjoy* it, exactly.

He walked over and opened the door again and hung the *Do Not Disturb* tag on the outside handle. Closed the door and locked it from the inside. He appreciated the locks motels put on their doors. A big lever to turn on the inside, a satisfying heavy *click,* smooth and oily, no corresponding catch on the outside. It helped. Absolute undisturbed security was a useful thing. He slipped the chain on and started into the room.

Alice drove as fast as she dared. The Jeep wasn't a great road vehicle. It rolled too much and rocked violently from

side to side. The steering was vague. It required constant correction. It was a problem. But Reacher ignored it and just held
the map high, where it caught the light from the roof console.
He stared hard at it and checked the scale and held his finger
and thumb apart like a little compass and traced a circle.

"You done any tourist stuff around here?" he asked.

She nodded at the wheel. "Some, I guess. I went to the Mc-
Donald Observatory. It was great."

He checked the map. The McDonald Observatory was
southwest of Pecos, high up in the Davis Mountains.

"That's eighty miles," he said. "Too far."

"For what?"

"For them to have been today. I think they'll have been a
half hour from Pecos by road, max. Twenty-five miles, thirty
tops."

"Why?"

"To be close to Walker. He might have planned on smug-
gling Carmen out, if necessary. Or maybe bringing Ellie in to
see her. Whatever it took to convince her that the threat was
real. So I think they'll have holed up somewhere nearby."

"And near a tourist attraction?"

"Definitely," he said. "That's key."

"Can this work?" she asked. "Finding the right place in
your head?"

"It's worked for me before."

"How many times? As a percentage?"

He ignored the question. Went back to the map. She
gripped the wheel and drove. Dropped her eyes to the
speedometer.

"Oh *God*," she whispered.

He didn't look up. "What?"

"We're out of gas. It's right on empty. The warning light
is on."

He was quiet for a second.

"Keep going," he said. "We'll be O.K."

She kept her foot hard down.

"How? You think the gauge is broken?"

He looked up. Glanced ahead.

"Just keep going," he said.

"We're going to run out," she said.

"Don't worry," he said.

She drove on. The car rocked hard. The headlights bounced ahead of them. The tires whined on the streaming blacktop. She glanced down again.

"It's right on *empty*, Reacher," she said. "*Below* empty."

"Don't worry," he said again.

"Why not?"

"You'll see."

He kept his eyes on the windshield. She drove on, as fast as the Jeep would go. The engine was growling loud. A gruff old straight-six, drinking gasoline at the rate of a pint every minute.

"Use two-wheel drive," he said. "More economical."

She wrestled with the drivetrain lever and wrenched it forward. The front end of the car went quiet. The steering stopped fighting her. She drove on. Another half mile. Then a mile. She glanced down at the dash again.

"We're running on fumes," she said.

"Don't worry," he said for the third time.

Another mile. The engine stumbled and coughed once and ran ragged for a second and then picked up again. Air in the fuel line, he thought, or sludge dredged up from the bottom of the tank.

"Reacher, we're *out of gas*," Alice said.

"Don't worry about it."

"Why not?"

Another mile.

"That's why not," he said suddenly.

The right edge of the headlight beam washed over the ragged gravel shoulder and lit up a steel-blue Ford Crown Victoria. It had four VHF antennas on the back and no wheel covers. It was just sitting there, inert and abandoned, facing north.

"We'll use that," he said. "It'll have most of a tank. They were well organized."

She braked hard and pulled in behind it. "This is theirs? Why is it here?"

"Walker left it here."

"How did you know?"

"It's pretty obvious. They came down from Pecos in two

cars, this and the Lincoln. They dumped the Lincoln here and used the Ford the rest of the way. Then Walker ran away from the mesa, put the pick-up back in the barn, drove the Ford back up here, retrieved his Lincoln and came back down in it for our benefit. To make us think it was his first visit, if we happened to be still alive and looking."

"What about the keys?"

"They'll be in it. Walker wasn't in the right frame of mind to worry about Hertz losing a rental car."

Alice jumped out and checked. Gave a thumbs-up. The keys were in it. Reacher followed her with the maps. They left the Greers' Jeep with the doors standing open and the motor idling through the last of its gas. They got into the Crown Vic and he racked his seat back and she pulled hers forward. She fired it up and they were on the road again within thirty seconds, already doing sixty miles an hour.

"It's three-quarters full," she said. "And it drives much better."

He nodded. It felt low and fast and smooth. Exactly like a big sedan should.

"I'm sitting where Al Eugene sat," he said.

She glanced at him. He smiled.

"Go faster," he said. "Nobody will stop you. We look just like a squad car."

She accelerated to seventy-five, then eighty. He found the dome light and clicked it on and returned to the maps.

"O.K., where were we?" he said.

"The McDonald Observatory," she said. "You didn't like it." He nodded. "It was too far out."

He tilted the map to catch the light. Stared hard at it. *Concentrate, Reacher. Make it work. If you can.*

"What's at Balmorhea State Recreation Area?" he asked.

It was still southwest of Pecos, but only thirty miles out. *The right sort of distance.*

"It's a desert oasis," she said. "Like a huge lake, very clear. You can swim and scuba dive there."

But not the right sort of place.

"I don't think so," he said.

He checked northeast, up to thirty miles out.

"What about Monahans Sandhills?"

"Four thousand acres of sand dunes. Looks like the Sahara."

"That's it? And people go there?"

"It's very impressive."

He went quiet and checked the map all over again.

"What about Fort Stockton?" he asked.

"It's just a town," she said. "No different than Pecos, really."

Then she glanced across at him. "But *Old* Fort Stockton is worth seeing, I guess."

He looked at the map. Old Fort Stockton was marked as a historic ruin, north of the town itself. Nearer Pecos. He measured the distance. Maybe forty-five miles.

Possible.

"What is it exactly?" he asked.

"Heritage site," she said. "An old military fort. The Buffalo Soldiers were there. Confederates had torn the place down. The Buffaloes rebuilt it. Eighteen sixty-seven, I think."

He checked again. The ruins were southeast of Pecos, accessible from Route 285, which looked like a decent road. Probably a fast road. Probably a *typical* road. He closed his eyes. Alice raced on. The Crown Vic was very quiet. It was warm and comfortable. He wanted to go to sleep. He was very tired. Wet spray from the tires hissed against the underside.

"I like the Old Fort Stockton area," he said.

"You think they were there?"

He was quiet again, another whole mile.

"Not *there*," he said. "But nearby. Think about it, from their point of view."

"I can't," she said. "I'm not like them."

"So pretend," he said. "What were they?"

"I don't know."

"They were professionals. Quiet and unobtrusive. Like chameleons. Instinctively good at camouflage. Good at not being noticed. Put yourself in their shoes, Alice."

"I can't," she said again.

"Think like them. Imagine. Get into it. Who are they? I saw them and thought they were a sales team. Rusty Greer thought they were social workers. Apparently Al Eugene thought they were FBI agents. So think like them. *Be* them. Your strength is you look very normal and very ordinary. You're white, and you look very middle-class, and you've got this Crown Victoria, which when it's not all tricked up with radio antennas looks like an ordinary family sedan. The FBI con helped, but basically you looked harmless enough that Al Eugene felt *safe* to stop for you, but also somehow commanding enough that he also *had* to. *Wanted* to. So you're ordinary, but you're respectable and plausible. And businesslike."

"O.K."

"But now you've got a kid with you. So what are you now?"

"What?"

"Now you're a normal, ordinary, respectable, plausible middle-class family."

"But there were three of them."

He was quiet a beat. Kept his eyes closed.

"One of the men was an uncle," he said. "You're a middle-class family, on vacation together in your sedan. But you're not a loud Disneyland type of family. You're not in shorts and brightly colored T-shirts. You look quiet, maybe a little earnest. Maybe a little nerdy. Or maybe a little *studious*. Maybe you look like a school principal's family. Or an accountant's. You're obviously from out of state, so you're traveling. Where to? Ask yourself the same question they must have asked themselves. Where will you blend in? Where's the safest place around here? Where would an earnest, studious, middle-class family go, with their six-and-a-half-year-old daughter? Where's a proper, enlightening, *educational* kind of a place to take her? Even though she's way too young and doesn't care? Even though people laugh behind your back at how politically correct and cloyingly *diligent* you are?"

"Old Fort Stockton," Alice said.

"Exactly. You show the kid the glorious history of the African-American soldiers, even though you'd have a heart attack if she grew up and wanted to date one. But you're driving a Ford, not a BMW or a Cadillac. You're *sensible*. Which means not rich, basically. Careful about your expenditure.

You resent overpaying for something. Motels, just as much as cars. So you drive in from the north and you stay at a place far enough out to be reasonable. Not the dumps in the middle of nowhere. But on the first distant fringes of the Fort Stockton tourist area. Where the value is good."

He opened his eyes.

"That's where you would stay, Alice," he said.

"It is?"

He nodded. "A place where they get plenty of earnest, striving, not-rich middle-class families on vacation. The sort of place that gets recommended in boring AAA magazines. A place where you fit right in. A place with lots of people exactly like you. A place where you won't stand out in anybody's memory for a second. And a place where you're only thirty, thirty-five minutes from Pecos by a fast road."

Alice shrugged and nodded all at the same time.

"Good theory, I guess," she said. "Good logic. Question is, were they following the same logic?"

"I hope so," Reacher said. "Because we don't have time for a big search. I don't think we have much time for anything. I'm getting a bad feeling. I think she's in real danger now."

Alice said nothing.

"Maybe the others were supposed to call in regularly," he said. "Maybe this third guy is about to panic."

"So it's a hell of a gamble."

He said nothing.

"Do the math," she said. "A forty-five-mile radius gives you a circle over six thousand square miles in area. And you want to pick one tiny pinpoint out of it?"

He was quiet again, another mile.

Roll the dice, Reacher.

"I think they were pretty smart and careful," he said. "And their priorities were pretty obvious. They were looking at the same maps we are. So I think that's how they'd have done it."

"But are you *sure?*"

He shrugged.

"Can't ever be *sure,*" he said. "But that's how *I'd* have done it. That's the trick, Alice. Think like them. Never fails."

"Never?"

He shrugged. "Sometimes."

The sleeping crossroads hamlet was dead ahead. The school, the gas station, the diner. Pecos straight on, Old Fort Stockton to the right.

"Well?" she asked.

He said nothing.

"Well?" she asked again.

He stared through the windshield.

"Decision?" she said.

He said nothing. She braked hard and skidded a yard on the soaked road and came to a complete halt right on the melted stop line.

"Well?"

Roll the damn dice, Reacher.

"Make the turn," he said.

The driver decided to take a shower first. An excusable delay. He had time. The room was locked. The child was fast asleep. He stripped off his clothes and folded them neatly and placed them on his chair. Stepped into the bathroom. Pulled the shower curtain and set the water running.

Then he unwrapped a new bar of soap. He liked motel soaps. He liked the crisp paper packets, and the smell when you opened them. It bloomed out at you, clean and strong. He sniffed the shampoo. It was in a tiny plastic bottle. It smelled of strawberries. He read the label. *Conditioning Shampoo*, it said. He leaned in and placed the soap in the porcelain receptacle and balanced the shampoo on the rim of the tub. Pushed the curtain aside with his forearm and stepped into the torrent.

The road northeast out of Echo was narrow and winding and clung to a hilly ridge that followed the course of the Coyanosa Draw. Now the big Ford was no longer ideal. It felt oversized and soft and ungainly. The blacktop was running with water flowing right to left across its surface. Heavy rills were pushing mud and grit over it in fan-shaped patterns. Alice was struggling to maintain forty miles an hour. She wasn't talking.

Just hauling the wallowing sedan around an endless series of bends and looking pale under her tan. Like she was cold.

"You O.K.?" he asked.

"Are you?" she asked back.

"Why wouldn't I be?"

"You just killed two people. Then saw a third die and a house burn down."

He glanced away. *Civilians*.

"Water under the bridge," he said. "No use dwelling on it now."

"That's a hell of an answer."

"Why?"

"Doesn't stuff like that affect you at all?"

"I'm sorry I didn't get to ask them any questions."

"Is that all you're sorry for?"

He was quiet for a second.

"Tell me about that house you're renting," he said.

"What's that got to do with anything?"

"My guess is it's a short-term kind of a place, people in and out all the time, not very well maintained. My guess is it was kind of dirty when you moved in."

"So?"

"Am I right?"

She nodded at the wheel. "I spent the first week cleaning."

"Grease on the stove, sticky floors?"

"Yes."

"Bugs in the closets?"

She nodded again.

"Roaches in the kitchen?"

"A colony," she said. "Big ones."

"And you got rid of them?"

"Of course I did."

"How?"

"Poison."

"So tell me how you felt about *that*."

She glanced sideways. "You comparing those people to cockroaches?"

He shook his head. "Not really. I like cockroaches better. They're just little packets of DNA scuttling around, doing what they have to do. Walker and his buddies didn't *have* to do what they did. They had a choice. They could have been upstanding human beings. But they chose not to be. Then they chose to mess with me, which was the final straw, and they got what they got. So I'm not going to lose any sleep over it. I'm not even going to give it another thought. And if you do, I think you're wrong."

She was quiet for another twisting mile.

"You're a hard man, Reacher," she said.

He was quiet in turn.

"I think I'm a realistic man," he said. "And a decent enough guy, all told."

"You may find normal people don't agree."

He nodded.

"A lot of you don't," he said.

He stood in the warm water long enough to soak all over, and then he started on his hair. He lathered the shampoo into a rich halo and worked on his scalp with his fingertips. Then he rinsed his hands and soaped his face, his neck, behind his ears. He closed his eyes and let the water sluice down over his body. Used more shampoo on his chest where the hair was thick. Attended to his underarms and his back and his legs.

Then he washed his hands and his forearms very thoroughly and carefully, like he was a surgeon preparing for a procedure.

"How far now?" Alice asked.

Reacher calculated from the map.

"Twenty-five miles," he said. "We cross I-10 and head north on 285 toward Pecos."

"But the ruins are on the other road. The one up to Mona-hans."

"Trust me, Alice. They stayed on 285. They wanted access."

She said nothing.

"We need a plan," Reacher said.

"For taking this guy?" she said. "I wouldn't have a clue."

"No, for later. For getting Carmen back."

"You're awfully confident."

"No point going in expecting to lose."

She braked hard for a corner and the front end washed wide. Then the road straightened for a hundred yards and she accelerated like she was grateful for it.

"Habeas corpus," she said. "We'll go to a federal judge and enter an emergency motion. Tell the whole story."

"Will that work?"

"It's exactly what habeas corpus is for. It's been working for eight hundred years. No reason it won't work this time."

"O.K.," he said.

"One thing, though."

"What?"

"We'll need testimony. So you'll have to keep this one alive. If that's not too much to ask."

He finished washing and just stood there in the warm stream of water. He let it flow over his body. He had a new thought in his head. He would need money. The others weren't coming back. The killing crew was history. He knew that. He was unemployed again. And he was unhappy about that. He wasn't a leader. He wasn't good at going out and creating things for himself. Teamwork had suited him just fine. Now he was back on his own. He had some money stashed under his mattress at home, but it wasn't a whole lot. He'd need more, and he'd need it pretty damn soon.

He turned around in the stall and tilted his head back and let the water wash his hair flat against his scalp. So maybe he should take the kid with him back to L.A. Sell her there. He knew people. People who facilitated adoptions, or facilitated other stuff he wouldn't want to inquire too closely about. She was what? Six and a half? And white? Worth a lot of money to somebody, especially with all that fair hair. Blue eyes would have added an extra couple of grand, but whatever, she was a cute little package as she was. She might fetch a decent price, from people he knew.

But how to get her there? The Crown Vic was gone, but he could rent another car. Not like he hadn't done that plenty of times before. He could call Pecos or Fort Stockton and get one brought down, first thing in the morning. He had no end of phony paperwork. But that would mean some delivery driver would see his face. *And the kid's*. No, he could hide her in the woman's empty room and bring the rental guy into his. But it was still a risk.

Or, he could steal a car. Not like he hadn't done *that* before, either, long ago, in his youth. He could steal one right out of the motel parking lot. He eased the shower curtain aside and leaned out for a second and checked his watch, which was resting on the vanity. *Four-thirty in the morning.* They could be on the road by five. Two hours minimum before some citizen came out of his room and found his car gone. They would be a hundred miles away by then. And he had spare plates. The California issue from the original LAX rental, and the Texas issue that had come off the Crown Vic.

He got back under the shower and straightened the curtain again. His decision was made. If there was a white sedan out there, he would take it. Sedans were the most common shape in the Southwest, and white was the most common color, because of the sun. And he could keep the kid in the trunk. No problem. A Corolla would be best, maybe a couple of years old. Very generic. Easily confused with a Geo Prizm or a dozen other cheap imports. Even traffic cops had a hard time recognizing Corollas. He could drive it all the way home. He could sell it too, as well as the kid, make a little *more* money. He nodded to himself. Smiled and raised his arms to rinse again.

Ten miles south and west of Fort Stockton itself, the road curved to the right and switchbacked over the top of the ridge, then fell away down the far slope and ran parallel to the Big Canyon Draw for a spell. Then it leveled out and speared straight for the I-10 interchange which was represented on the map like a spider, with eight roads all coming together in one place. The northwest leg was Route 285 to Pecos, which showed up on paper as a ninety-degree left turn. Then there were maybe twenty miles of it between the Fort Stockton city limit and a highway bridge that recrossed the Coyanosa Draw.

"That's the target area," Reacher said. "Somewhere in those twenty miles. We'll drive north to the bridge and turn around and come back south. See it like they saw it."

Alice nodded silently and accelerated down the slope. The tires pattered on the rough surface and the big soft car pitched and rolled.

She woke up because of the noise of the shower. It drummed against the tiles on the other side of the wall and sounded a little like rain coming down on the roof again. She pulled the sheet over her head and then pulled it back down. Watched the window. There was no lightning anymore. She listened hard. She couldn't hear any more thunder. Then she recognized the sound for what it was. The shower was running. In the bathroom. It was louder than hers at home, but quieter than her mom's.

The man was in the shower.

She pushed the sheet down to her waist. Struggled upright and sat there. There were no lights on in the room, but the drapes weren't drawn and a yellow glow was coming in from outside. It was wet out there. She could see raindrops on the window and reflections.

The room was empty.

Of course it is, silly, she said to herself. *The man is in the shower*.

She pushed the sheet down to her ankles. Her clothes were folded on the table by the window. She crept out of the bed and tiptoed over and stretched out her hand and took her underpants from the pile. Stepped into them. Pulled her T-shirt over her head. Threaded her arms through the sleeves. Then she took her shorts and checked they were the right way around and put them on. Pulled the waistband up over her shirt and sat down cross-legged on the floor to buckle her shoes.

The shower was still running.

She stood up and crept past the bathroom door, very quietly, because she was worried about her shoes making noise.

She kept on the rug where she could. Stayed away from the
linoleum. She stood still and listened.

The shower was still running.

She crept down the little hallway, past the closet, all the
way to the door. It was dark back there. She stood still and
looked at the door. She could see a handle, and a lever thing,
and a chain thing. She thought hard. The handle was a handle, and the lever was probably a lock. She didn't know what
the chain thing was for. There was a narrow slot with a wider
hole at one end. She imagined the door opening. It would get
a little ways and then the chain would stop it.

The shower was still running.

She had to get the chain thing off. It might slide along.
Maybe that was what the narrow slot was for. She studied it.
It was very high. She stretched up and couldn't really reach
it. She stretched up taller and got the flat of her fingertips on
it. She could slide it that way. She slid it all the way sideways
until the end fell into the hole. But she couldn't pull it out.

The shower was still running.

She put her other hand flat on the door and flipped her toes
over until she was right up on the points of her shoes.
Stretched until her back started to hurt and picked at the
chain with her fingertips. It wouldn't come out. It was
hooked in. She came down off her toes and listened.

The shower was still running.

She went back on her toes and kicked and pushed against
them until her legs hurt and reached up with both hands. The
end of the chain was a little circle. She waggled it. It moved
up a little. She let it down again. Pushed it up and picked at it
at the same time and it came out. It rattled down and swung
and hit the door frame with a noise that sounded very loud.
She held her breath and listened.

The shower was still running.

She came down off her toes and tried the lock lever. She
put her thumb on one side and her finger on the other and
turned it. It wouldn't move at all. She tried it the other way. It
moved a little bit. It was very stiff. She closed her mouth in
case she was breathing too loud and used both hands and
tried harder. It moved some more, like metal rubbing on

metal. She strained at it. It hurt her hands. It moved some more. Then it suddenly clicked back all the way.

A big click.

She stood still and listened.

The shower was still running.

She tried the handle. It moved easily. She looked at the door. It was very high and it looked very thick and heavy. It had a thing at the top that would close it automatically behind her. It was made from metal. She had seen those things before. They made a lot of noise. The diner opposite her school had one.

The shower had stopped.

She froze. Stood still, blank with panic. *The door will make a noise. He'll hear it. He'll come out. He'll chase me.* She whirled around and faced the room.

The I-10 interchange was a huge concrete construction laid down like a healing scar on the landscape. It was as big as a stadium and beyond it dull orange streetlights in Fort Stockton lit up the thinning clouds. Fort Stockton still had electricity. Better power lines. Alice kept her foot hard down and screamed three-quarters of the way around the interchange and launched northwest on 285. She passed the city limit doing ninety. There was a sign: Pecos 48 miles. Reacher leaned forward, moving his head rapidly side to side, scanning both shoulders of the road at once. Low buildings flashed past. Some of them were motels.

"This could be entirely the wrong place," Alice said.

"We'll know soon enough," he replied.

He turned the water off and rattled the curtain back and stepped out of the tub. Wrapped a towel around his waist and used another to dry his face. Looked at himself in the misty mirror and combed his hair with his fingers. Strapped his watch to his wrist. Dropped both towels on the bathroom floor and took two fresh ones off the little chrome rack. Wrapped one around his waist and draped the other over his shoulder like a toga.

He stepped out of the bathroom. Light spilled out with him. It fell across the room in a broad yellow bar. He stopped dead. Stared at the empty bed.

Inside three minutes they had passed three motels and Reacher thought all three of them were wrong. It was about guessing and feeling now, about living in a zone where he was blanking out everything except the tiny murmurs from his subconscious mind. Overt analysis would ruin it. He could make a lengthy case for or against any particular place. He could talk himself into paralysis. So he was listening to nothing at all except the quiet whispers from the back of his brain. And they were saying: *not that one. No. No.*

He took a dazed involuntary step toward the bed, like seeing it from a different angle might put her back in it. But nothing changed. There was just the rumpled sheet, half pushed down, half pushed aside. The pillow, at an angle, dented with the shape of her head. He turned and checked the window. It was closed tight and locked from the inside. Then he ran to the door. Short desperate steps, dodging furniture all the way. The chain was off. The lock was clicked back.

What?

He eased the handle down. Opened the door. The *Do Not Disturb* tag was lying on the concrete walk, a foot from the doorway.

She'd gotten out.

He fixed the door so it wouldn't lock behind him and ran out into the night, barefoot, wearing just his towels, one around his waist and the other like a toga. He ran ten paces into the parking lot and stood still. He was panting. Shock, fear, sudden exertion. It was warm again. There was a heavy vegetable stink in the air, wet earth and flowers and leaves. Trees were dripping. He spun a complete circle. *Where the hell did she go? Where?* A kid that age, she'd have just run for it. As fast as she could. Probably toward the road. He took a single step after her and then whirled around. Back toward the door. He'd need his clothes. Couldn't chase her in a couple of towels.

The low clumps of buildings petered out three or four miles before they were due to hit the bridge. They just stopped being there. There was just desert. He stared through the windshield into the empty distance and thought of every road he had ever seen and asked himself: *are there going to be more buildings up ahead? Or nothing now until we hit the outskirts of Pecos thirty miles away?*

"Turn around," he said.

"Now?"

"We've seen all we're going to see."

She hit the brakes and pulled a violent turn, shoulder to shoulder across the road. Fishtailed a little on the wet gravel and straightened and headed back south.

"Slower now," he said. "Now we're them. We're looking at this with their eyes."

Ellie was lying completely still on the high shelf in the closet. She was good at hiding. Everybody said so. She was good at climbing, too, so she liked to hide high up. Like in the horse barn. Her favorite place was high up on top of the straw bales. The closet shelf wasn't as comfortable. It was narrow and there were old dust bunnies up there. A wire coat hanger and a plastic bag with a word on it too long to read. But she could lie down flat and hide. It was a good place, she thought. Difficult to get up to. She had climbed on the smaller shelves at the side. They were like a ladder. Very high. But it was dusty. She might sneeze. She knew she mustn't. *Was she high enough?* He wasn't a very tall man. She held her breath.

Alice kept the speed steady at sixty. The first motel they came back to was on the left side of the road. It had a low tended hedge running a hundred yards to screen the parking

lot. There was a center office and two one-story wings of six
rooms each. The office was dark. There was a soda machine
next to it, glowing red. Five cars in the lot.

"No," Reacher said. "We don't stop at the first place we
see. We'd more likely go for the second place."

The second place was four hundred yards south.

And it was a possibility.

It was built at right angles to the road. The office was face-
on to the highway but the cabins ran away into the distance
behind it, which made the lot U-shaped. And concealed.
There were planted trees all around it, wet and dripping from
the rain.

Possible.

Alice slowed the car to a crawl.

"Drive through," he said.

She swung into the lot and nosed down the row. It was
eight cabins long. Three cars were parked. She swung around
the far end and up the other side. Eight more cabins. Another
three cars. She paused alongside the office door.

"Well?" she asked.

He shook his head.

"No," he said.

"Why not?"

"Occupancy ratio is wrong. Sixteen cabins, six cars. I'd
need to see eight cars, at least."

"Why?"

"They didn't want a place that's practically empty. Too likely
to be remembered. They were looking for somewhere around
two-thirds full, which would be ten or eleven cars for sixteen
cabins. They've got two rooms but right now no car at all, so
that would be eight or nine cars for sixteen cabins. That's the ratio we need. Two-thirds minus two. Approximately."

She glanced across at him and shrugged. Eased back to the
road and continued south.

He got a couple of paces toward the door and stopped dead.
There was a yellow light off to one side of the lot, casting a
low glow over the soaked blacktop. It showed him his foot-

steps. They were a line of curious fluid imprints blotted into the dampness. He could see his heels and his toes and his arches. Mostly toes, because he'd been running. The prints were filmy and wet. They weren't about to dry up and disappear anytime soon.

But he couldn't see *her* footprints.

There was just one set of tracks, and they were his. No doubt about it. *She hadn't come out.* Not unless she could levitate herself and fly. Which was impossible. He smiled.

She was hiding in the room.

He ran the final eight steps and ducked back inside. Closed the door gently and fastened the chain and clicked the lock.

"Come on out," he called softly.

There was no response, but he hadn't really expected one.

• "I'm coming to get you," he called.

He started by the window, where there was an upholstered chair across the corner of the room with a space behind it large enough for a kid to hide. But she wasn't there. He got on his knees and bent down and looked under the beds. Not there, either.

"Hey, kid," he called. "Enough already."

There was a shared bedside cabinet with a little door. She wasn't in there. He straightened up and adjusted his towels. She wasn't in the bathroom, he knew that. So where was she? He looked around the room. *The closet. Of course.* He smiled to himself and danced over.

"Here I come, honey," he called.

He slid the doors and checked the floor. There was a folded valise rack and nothing else. There was a set of vertical shelves on the right, nothing in them. A high shelf above, running the whole width of the space. He stretched tall and checked it out. Nothing there. Just dust bunnies and an old wire coat hanger and a plastic bag from a grocery called Subrahamian's in Cleveland.

He turned around, temporarily defeated.

The third motel had a painted sign. No neon. Just a board hung from a gallows with chains. It was carefully lettered in

a script so fancy Reacher wasn't sure what it said. Something
Canyon, maybe, with old-fashioned spelling, *cañon,* like
Spanish. The letters were shadowed in gold.

"I like this," he said. "Very tasteful."

"Go in?" Alice asked.

"You bet."

There was a little entrance road through twenty yards of
garden. The plantings were sad and scorched by the heat, but
they were an *attempt* at something.

"I like this," he said again.

It was the same shape as the last place. An office first, with
a U-shaped parking lot snaking around two back-to-back
rows of cabins set at ninety degrees to the road. Alice drove
the complete circle. Ten cabins to a row, twenty in total,
twelve cars parked neatly next to twelve random doors. Two
Chevrolets, three Hondas, two Toyotas, two Buicks, an old
Saab, an old Audi, and a five-year-old Ford Explorer.

"Two-thirds minus two," Reacher said.

"Is this the place?" Alice asked.

He said nothing. She stopped next to the office.

"Well?"

He said nothing. Just opened the door and slid out. The
heat was coming back. It was full of the smell of soaked
earth. He could hear drains running and gutters dripping. The
office was dark and full of shadows. The door was locked.
There was a neat brass button for the night bell. He leaned his
thumb on it and peered in through the window.

There was no soda machine. Just a neat counter and a large
rack full of flyers. He couldn't make out what they referred to.
Too dark. He kept his thumb on the bell. A light came on in a
doorway in back of the office and a man stepped out. He was
running his hand through his hair. Reacher took the Echo
County deputy's star out of his pocket and clicked it flat against
the glass. The man turned the office light on and walked to the
door and undid the lock. Reacher stepped inside and walked
past him. The flyers in the rack covered all the tourist attrac-
tions within a hundred miles. Old Fort Stockton featured
prominently. There was something about a meteor crater at
Odessa. All worthy stuff. Nothing about rodeos or gun shows
or real estate. He waved to Alice. Gestured her in after him.

"This is the place," he said.

"Is it?"

He nodded. "Looks right to me."

"You cops?" the office guy asked, looking out at the car.

"I need to see your register," Reacher said. "For tonight's guests."

It was impossible. Totally impossible. She wasn't outside, she wasn't inside. He ran his eyes over the room again. The beds, the furniture, the closet. Nothing doing. She wasn't in the bathroom, because he had *been* in the bathroom.

Unless...

Unless she had been under the bed or in the closet and then had ducked into the bathroom while he was outside. He stepped over and opened the bathroom door. Smiled at himself in the mirror. The mist had cleared off it. He pulled back the shower curtain in one dramatic sweeping move.

"There you are," he said.

She was pressed up into the corner of the tub, standing straight, wearing a T-shirt and shorts and shoes. The back of her right hand was jammed in her mouth. Her eyes were wide open. They were dark and huge.

"I changed my mind," he said. "I was going to take you with me."

She said nothing. Just watched him. He reached out to her. She shrank back. Took the hand away from her mouth.

"It's not been four hours," she said.

"Yes, it has," he said. "Way more than four."

She put her knuckles back in her mouth. He reached out again. She shrank away. What had her mommy told her to do? *If you're worried about something, just scream and scream.* She took a deep breath and tried. But no sound would come out. Her throat was too dry.

"The register," Reacher said again.

The office guy hesitated like there were procedures involved. Reacher checked his watch and pulled the Heckler & Koch from his pocket, all in one simple movement.

"Right now," he said. "We don't have time to mess around."

The guy's eyes went wide and he ducked around the counter and reversed a big leather ledger. Pushed it toward the near edge. Reacher and Alice crowded together to look at it.

"What names?" she asked.

"No idea," he said. "Just look at the cars."

There were five columns to a page. Date, name, home address, vehicle make, date of departure. There were twenty lines, for twenty cabins. Sixteen were occupied. Seven of them had arrows originating on the previous page, indicating guests who were staying a second or subsequent night. Nine cabins held new arrivals. Eleven cabins had a vehicle make entered directly against them. Four cabins were marked in two pairs of two, each sharing a vehicle.

"Families," the night clerk said. "Or large parties."

"Did you check them in?" Reacher asked.

The guy shook his head.

"I'm the night man," he said. "I'm not here until midnight."

Reacher stared at the page. Went very still. Looked away.

"What?" Alice said.

"This isn't the right place. This is the wrong place. I blew it."

"Why?"

"Look at the cars," he said.

He ran the gun muzzle down the fourth column. Three Chevrolets, three Hondas, two Toyotas, two Buicks, one Saab, one Audi. And one Ford.

"Should be two Fords," he said. "Their Crown Vic and the Explorer that's already parked out there."

"Shit," she said.

He nodded. *Shit.* He went completely blank. If this wasn't the right place, he had absolutely no idea what was. He had staked everything on it. He had no plan B. He glanced at the register. *Ford.* Pictured the old Explorer sitting out there, square and dull. Then he glanced back at the register again.

The handwriting was all the same.

"Who fills this out?" he asked.

"The owner," the clerk said. "She does everything the old-fashioned way."

He closed his eyes. Retraced in his mind Alice's slow circle around the lot. Thought back to all the old-fashioned motels he'd used in his life.

"O.K.," he said. "The guest tells her the name and the address, she writes it down. Then maybe she just glances out of the window and writes down the vehicle make for herself. Maybe if the guests are talking or busy getting their money out."

"Maybe. I'm the night man. I'm never here for that."

"She's not really into automobiles, is she?"

"I wouldn't know. Why?"

"Because there are three Chevrolets in the book and only two in the lot. I think she put the Explorer down as a Chevy. It's an old model. Kind of angular. Maybe she confused it with an old-model Blazer or something."

He touched the gun muzzle to the word *Ford*.

"That's the Crown Vic," he said. "That's them."

"You think?" Alice said.

"I know. I can feel it."

They had taken two rooms, not adjacent, but in the same wing. Rooms five and eight.

"O.K.," he said again. "I'm going to take a look."

He pointed to the night guy. "You stay here and keep quiet."

Then he pointed to Alice. "You call the state police and start doing your thing with the federal judge, O.K.?"

"You need a key?" the night clerk asked.

"No," Reacher said. "I don't need a key."

Then he walked out into the damp warmth of the night.

The right-hand row of cabins started with number one. There was a concrete walkway leading past each door. He moved quickly and quietly along it and his shoes left damp prints all the way. There was nothing to see except doors. They came at regular intervals. No windows. The windows would be at the back. These were standard-issue motel rooms, like he had seen a million times before, no doubt about it. Standard layout, with a door, a short hallway, closet on one side and bathroom on the other, the hallway opening out into a room occupying the full width of the unit, two beds, two chairs, a table, a credenza, air conditioner under the window, pastel pictures on the wall.

Cabin number five had a *Do Not Disturb* tag lying on the

concrete a foot from the doorway. He stepped over it. *If you've got a stolen kid, you keep her in the room farthest from the office. No-brainer.* He walked on and stopped outside number eight. Put his ear to the crack of the door and listened. Heard nothing. He walked silently on, past number nine, past ten, to the end of the row. Walked around the bend of the U. The two cabin blocks were parallel, facing each other across a thirty-foot-wide rectangle of garden. It was desert horticulture, with low spiky plants growing out of raked gravel and crushed stone. There were small yellow lanterns here and there. Large rocks and boulders, carefully placed, a Japanese effect.

The crushed stone was noisy under his feet. He had to walk slow. He passed by ten's window, then nine's, then crouched low and eased against the wall. Crawled forward and positioned himself directly under eight's window sill. The air conditioner was running loud. He couldn't hear anything over it. He raised his head, slowly and carefully. Looked into the room.

Nothing doing. The room was completely empty. It was completely undisturbed. It might never have been occupied. It was just sitting there, still and sterile, cleaned and readied, the way motel rooms are. He felt a flash of panic. *Maybe they made multiple bookings all over the place. Two or three similar places, to give themselves a choice. Thirty or forty bucks a night, why not?* He stood up straight. Stopped worrying about the noise from the gravel. Ran past seven and six, straight to five's window. Put himself right in front of it and looked in.

And saw a small dark man wearing two white towels dragging Ellie out of the bathroom. Bright light was spilling out behind him. He had both her wrists caught in one hand above her head. She was kicking and bucking violently in his grip. Reacher stared in for maybe a quarter of a second, long enough to sense the layout of the room and see a black 9-mm handgun with a silencer lying on the credenza. Then he took a breath and one long fluid step away and bent down and picked up a rock from the garden. It was bigger than a basketball and could have weighed a hundred pounds. He heaved it straight through the window. The screen disintegrated and glass shattered and he followed it headfirst into the room with the window frame caught around his shoulders like a wreath of victory.

The small dark man froze in shock for a split second and then let Ellie go and turned and scrabbled desperately toward the credenza. Reacher batted away the splintered frame and got there first and caught him by the throat with his right hand and jammed him back against the wall and followed up with a colossal left to the gut and let him fall and kicked him once in the head, very hard. Saw his eyes roll up into his skull. Then he breathed in and out like a train and gasped and shuffled his feet and flexed his hands and fought the temptation to kick him to death.

Then he turned to Ellie.

"You O.K.?" he asked.

She nodded. Paused in the sudden silence.

"He's a bad man," she said. "I think he was going to *shoot* me."

He paused in turn. Fought to control his breathing.

"He can't do that now," he said.

"There was thunder and lightning."

"I heard it too. I was outside. Got all wet."

She nodded. "It rained a whole lot."

"You O.K.?" he asked for the second time.

She just thought about it and nodded. She was very composed. Very serious. No tears, no screaming. The room went absolutely quiet. The action had lasted all of three seconds, beginning to end. It was like it hadn't happened at all. But the rock from the garden was lying there in the middle of the floor, nested in shards of broken glass. He picked it up and carried it to the shattered window and tipped it through. It crunched on the gravel and rolled away.

"You O.K.?" he asked for the third time.

Ellie nodded. He picked up the phone and dialed zero. The night guy answered. Reacher told him to send Alice down to room five. Then he walked over and unlatched the chain and unlocked the door. Left it propped open. It set up a breeze, all the way through the room to the broken window. The outside air was damp. And warm. Warmer than the inside air.

"You O.K.?" he asked for the fourth time.

"Yes," Ellie said. "I'm O.K."

Alice stepped inside a minute later. Ellie looked at her, curiously.

"This is Alice," Reacher said. "She's helping your mom."

"Where is my mom?"

"She'll be with you soon," Alice said.

Then she turned and looked down at the small dark guy. He was inert on the floor, pressed up against the wall, arms and legs tangled.

"Is he alive?" she whispered.

Reacher nodded. "Concussed, is all. I think. I hope."

"State police is responding," she whispered. "And I called my boss at home. Got him out of bed. He's setting up a chambers meeting with a judge, first thing. But he says we'll need a straightforward confession from this guy if we want to avoid a big delay."

Reacher nodded. "We'll get one."

He bent down and twisted one of the small dark man's towels tight around his neck like a noose and used it to drag him across the floor and into the bathroom.

Twenty minutes later he came out again and found two state cops standing in the room. A sergeant and a trooper, both Hispanic, both composed and immaculate in their tan uniforms. He could hear their car idling outside the door. He nodded to them and walked over and picked up the driver's clothes from the chair. Tossed them back into the bathroom.

"So?" the sergeant said.

"He's ready to talk," Reacher said. "He's offering a full and voluntary confession. But he wants you to understand he was just the driver."

"He wasn't a shooter?"

Reacher shook his head. "But he saw everything."

"What about the kidnap?"

"He wasn't there. He was guarding her afterward, is all. And there's a lot of other stuff, too, going back a number of years."

"Situation like this, he talks, he's going away for a long time."

"He knows that. He accepts it. He's happy about it. He's looking for redemption."

The cops just glanced at each other and went into the bathroom. Reacher heard people shuffling and moving around and handcuffs clicking.

"I have to get back," Alice said. "I have to prepare the writ. Lot of work involved, with habeas corpus."

"Take the Crown Vic," Reacher said. "I'll wait here with Ellie."

The cops brought the driver out of the bathroom. He was dressed and his hands were cuffed behind him and each cop had hold of an elbow. He was bent over and white with pain and already talking fast. The cops hustled him straight out to their cruiser and the room door swung shut behind them. There was the muffled sound of car doors slamming and the growl of an engine.

"What did you do to him?" Alice whispered.

Reacher shrugged. "I'm a hard man. Like you said."

He asked her to send the night clerk down with a master key and she walked away toward the office. He turned to Ellie.

"You O.K.?" he said.

"You don't need to keep asking me," she replied.

"Tired?"

"Yes," she said.

"Your mom will come soon," he said. "We'll wait for her right here. But let's change rooms, shall we? This one's got a broken window."

She giggled. "You broke it. With that rock."

He heard the Crown Vic start up in the distance. Heard its tires on the road.

"Let's try room eight," he said. "It's nice and clean. Nobody's been in it. It can be ours."

She took his hand and they walked out together and along the concrete walkway to number eight, a dozen steps for him, three dozen for her, damp filmy tracks left in the wet behind both of them. The clerk met them with a pass key and Ellie got straight into the bed nearest the window. Reacher lay down on the other and watched her until she was sound asleep. Then he wrapped his arm under his head and tried to doze.

* * *

Less than two hours later the new day dawned bright and
hot and the air stirred and the metal roof clicked and cracked
and the timbers under it creaked and moved. Reacher opened
his eyes after a short uneasy rest and swung his legs to the
floor. Crept quietly to the door and opened it up and stepped
outside. The eastern horizon was far off to his right beyond
the motel office. It was flaring with pure white light. There
were rags of old cloud in the sky. They were burning off as he
watched. *No storm today.* People had talked about it for a
week, but it wasn't going to happen. Last night's hour of rain
was all it was ever going to be. A complete misfire.

He crept back into the room and lay down again. Ellie
was still asleep. She had kicked the sheet down and her shirt
had ridden up and he could see the plump band of pink skin
at her waist. Her legs were bent, like she had been running
in her dreams. But her arms were thrown up above her head,
which some army psychiatrist had once told him was a sign
of security. *A kid sleeps like that,* he had said, *deep down it
feels safe.* Safe? She was some kid. That was for damn sure.
Most adults he knew would be wrecks after an experience
like hers. For weeks. Or longer. But she wasn't. Maybe she
was too young to fully comprehend. Or maybe she was just
a tough kid. One or the other. He didn't know. He had no experience. He closed his eyes again.

He opened them for the second time thirty minutes later
because Ellie was standing right next to him, shaking his
shoulder.

"I'm hungry," she said.

"Me too," he said back. "What would you like?"

"Ice cream," she said.

"For breakfast?"

She nodded.

"O.K.," he said. "But eggs first. Maybe bacon. You're a
kid. You need good nutrition."

He fumbled the phone book out of the bedside drawer and
found a diner listed that was maybe a mile nearer Fort Stockton. He called them and bribed them with the promise of a

twenty-dollar tip to drive breakfast out to the motel. He sent
Ellie into the bathroom to get washed up. By the time she
came out, the food had arrived. Scrambled eggs, smoked bacon, toast, jelly, cola for her, coffee for him. And a huge plastic dish of ice cream with chocolate sauce.

Breakfast changes everything. He ate the food and drank the
coffee and felt some energy coming back. Saw the same effect
in Ellie. They propped the room door wide open while they ate
to smell the morning air. Then they dragged chairs out to the
concrete walk and set them side by side and sat down to wait.

They waited more than four hours. He stretched out and
idled the time away like he was accustomed to doing. She
waited like it was a serious task to be approached with her
usual earnest concentration. He called the diner again
halfway through and they ate a second breakfast, identical
menu to the first. They went in and out to the bathroom.
Talked a little. Tried to identify the trees, listened to the buzz
of the insects, looked for clouds in the sky. But mostly they
kept their gaze ahead and half-right, where the road came in
from the north. The ground was dry again, like it had never
rained at all. The dust was back. It plumed off the blacktop
and hung in the heat. It was a quiet road, maybe one vehicle
every couple of minutes. Occasionally a small knot of traffic,
stalled behind a slow-moving farm truck.

A few minutes after eleven o'clock Reacher was standing
a couple of paces into the lot and he saw the Crown Vic coming south in the distance. It crept slowly out of the haze. He
saw the fake antennas wobbling and flexing behind it. Dust
trailing in the air.

"Hey kid," he called. "Check this out."

She stood next to him and shaded her eyes with her hand.
The big car slowed and turned in and drove up right next to
them. Alice was in the driver's seat. Carmen was next to her.
She looked pale and washed out but she was smiling and her
eyes were wide with joy. She had the door open before the
car stopped moving and she came out and skipped around the
hood and Ellie ran to her and jumped into her arms. They

staggered around together in the sunlight. There was shriek-
ing and crying and laughter all at the same time. He watched
for a moment and then backed away and squatted next to the
car. He didn't want to intrude. He guessed times like these
were best kept private. Alice saw what he was thinking and
buzzed her window down and put her hand on his shoulder.

"Everything squared away?" he asked her.

"For us," she said. "Cops have got a lot of paperwork
ahead. All in all they're looking at more than fifty homicides
in seven separate states. Including what happened here
twelve years ago and Eugene and Sloop and Walker himself.
They're going to arrest Rusty for shooting Walker. But she'll
get off easy, I should think, in the circumstances."

"Anything about me?"

"They were asking about last night. Lots of questions. I
said I did it all."

"Why?"

She smiled. "Because I'm a lawyer. I called it self-defense
and they bought it without hesitating. It was my car out there,
and my gun. No-brainer. They'd have given you a much
harder time."

"So we're all home free?"

"Especially Carmen."

He looked up. Carmen had Ellie on her hip, with her face
buried in her neck like the sweet fragrance of her was necessary to sustain life itself. She was walking aimless random
circles with her. Then she raised her head and squinted
against the sun and smiled with such abandoned joy that
Reacher found himself smiling along with her.

"She got plans?" he asked.

"Moving up to Pecos," Alice said. "We'll sort through
Sloop's affairs. There's probably some cash somewhere.
She's talking about moving into a place like mine. Maybe
working part-time. Maybe even looking at law school."

"You tell her about the Red House?"

"She laughed with happiness. I told her it was probably
burned down to a cinder, and she just laughed and laughed. I
felt good for her."

Now Ellie was leading her by the hand around the parking lot, checking out the trees she had inspected previously, talking a mile a minute. They looked perfect together. Ellie was hopping with energy and Carmen looked serene and radiant and very beautiful. Reacher stood up and leaned against the car.

"You want lunch?"

"Here?"

"I've got a thing going with a diner. They've probably got vegetables."

"Tuna salad will do it for me."

He went inside and used the phone. Ordered three sandwiches and promised yet another twenty bucks for the tip. Came out and found Ellie and Carmen looking for him.

"I'm going to a new school soon," Ellie said. "Just like you did."

"You'll do great," he said. "You're smart as a whip."

Then Carmen let go of her daughter's hand and stepped near him, a little shy and silent and awkward for a second. Then she smiled wide and put her arms around his chest and hugged him hard.

"Thanks," was all she said.

He hugged her back. "I'm sorry it took so long."

"Did my clue help?"

"Clue?" he said.

"I left a clue for you."

"Where?"

"In the confession."

He said nothing. She unwound herself from his embrace and took his arm and led him to where Ellie wouldn't hear her.

"He made me say I was a whore."

He nodded.

"But I pretended to be nervous and I got the words wrong. I said 'street stroller.'"

He nodded again. "I remember."

"But it's really streetwalker, isn't it? To be correct? That was the clue. You were supposed to think to yourself, it's not *stroller,* it's *walker.* Get it? It's *Walker.* Meaning it's Hack Walker doing all of this."

He went very quiet.

"I missed that," he said.

"So how did you know?"

"I guess I took the long way around."

She just smiled again. Laced her arm into his and walked him back to the car, where Ellie was laughing with Alice.

"You going to be O.K.?" he asked her.

She nodded. "But I feel very guilty. People died."

He shrugged. "Like Clay Allison said."

"Thanks," she said again.

"No hay de que, señora."

"Señorita," she said.

Carmen and Ellie and Alice drifted inside to get washed up for lunch. He watched the door close behind them and just walked away. It seemed like the natural thing to do. He didn't want anybody to try to keep him there. He jogged to the road and turned south. Walked a whole hot mile before he got a ride from a farm truck driven by a toothless old man who didn't talk much. He got out at the I-10 interchange and waited on the west ramp for ninety minutes in the sun until an eighteen-wheeler slowed and stopped next to him. He walked around the massive hood and looked up at the window. The window came down. He could hear music over the loud shudder of the diesel. It sounded like Buddy Holly. The driver leaned out. He was a guy of about fifty, fleshy, wearing a Dodgers T-shirt and about four days' growth of beard.

"Los Angeles?" he called.

"Anywhere," Reacher called back.

Turn the page for a preview
of Lee Child's new novel,

WITHOUT FAIL

available in hardcover from
G. P. Putnam's Sons

1

They found out about him in July and stayed angry all through August. They tried to kill him in September. It was way too soon. They weren't ready. The attempt was a failure. It could have been a disaster, but it was actually a miracle. *Because nobody noticed.*

They used their usual method to get past security and set up a hundred feet from where he was speaking. They used a silencer and missed him by an inch. The bullet must have passed right over his head. Maybe even *through his hair*, because he immediately raised his hand and patted it back into place as if a gust of wind had disturbed it. They saw it over and over again, afterward, on television. He raised his hand and patted his hair. He did nothing else. He just kept on with his speech, unaware, because by definition a silenced bullet is too fast to see and too quiet to hear. So it missed him and flew on. It missed everybody standing behind him. It struck no obstacles, hit no buildings. It flew on straight and true until its energy was spent and gravity hauled it to earth in the far distance where there was nothing except empty grassland. There was no response. No reaction. *Nobody noticed.* It was like the bullet had never been fired at all. They didn't fire again. They were too shaken up.

So, a failure, but a miracle. And a lesson. They spent October acting like the professionals they were, starting over, calming down, thinking, learning, preparing for their second attempt. It would be a better attempt, carefully planned and properly executed, built around technique and nuance and sophistication, and enhanced by unholy fear. A worthy attempt. A *creative* attempt. Above all, an attempt that wouldn't fail. Then November came, and the rules changed completely.

Reacher's cup was empty but still warm. He lifted it off the saucer and tilted it and watched the sludge in the bottom flow toward him, slow and brown, like river silt.

"When does it need to be done?" he asked.

"As soon as possible," she said.

He nodded. Slid out of the booth and stood up.

"I'll call you in ten days," he said.

"With a decision?"

He shook his head. "To tell you how it went."

"I'll *know* how it went."

"Okay, to tell you where to send my money."

She closed her eyes and smiled. He glanced down at her.

"You thought I'd refuse?" he said.

She opened her eyes. "I thought you might be a little harder to persuade."

He shrugged. "Like Joe told you, I'm a sucker for a challenge. Joe was usually right about things like that. He was usually right about a lot of things."

"Now I don't know what to say, except thank you."

He didn't reply. Just started to move away, but she stood up right next to him and kept him where he was. There was an awkward pause. They stood for a second face-to-face, trapped by the table. She put out her hand and he shook it. She held on a fraction too long, and then she stretched up tall and kissed him on the check. Her lips were soft. Their touch burned him like a tiny voltage.

"A handshake isn't enough," she said. "You're going to do it for us." Then she paused. "And you were nearly my brother-in-law."

He said nothing. Just nodded and shuffled out from behind the table and glanced back once. Then he headed up the stairs and out to the street. Her perfume was on his hand. He walked around to the cabaret lounge and left a note for his friends in their dressing room. Then he headed out to the highway, with ten whole days to find a way to kill the fourth-best-protected person on the planet.

It had started eight hours earlier, like this: team leader M. E. Froelich came to work on that Monday morning, thirteen days after the election, an hour before the second strategy meeting, seven days after the word *assassination* had first been used, and made her final decision. She set off in search of her immediate superior and found him in the secretarial pen outside his office, clearly on his way to somewhere else, clearly in a hurry. He had a file under his arm and a definite *stay back* expression on his face. But she took a deep breath and made it clear that she needed to talk right then. Urgently. And off the record and in private, obviously. So he paused a moment and turned abruptly and went back inside his office. He let her step in after him and closed the door behind her, softly enough to make the unscheduled meeting feel a little conspiratorial, but firmly enough that she was in no doubt he was annoyed about the interruption to his routine. It was just the click of a door latch, but it was also an unmistakable message, parsed exactly in the language of office hierarchies everywhere: *You better not be wasting my time with this.*

He was a twenty-five-year veteran well into his final lap before retirement, well into his middle fifties, the last echo of the old days. He was still tall, still fairly lean and athletic, but graying fast and softening in some of the wrong places. His name was Stuyvesant. Like the last Director-General of New

Amsterdam, he would say when the spelling was questioned. Then, acknowledging the modern world, he would say: like the cigarette. He wore Brooks Brothers every day of his life without exception, but he was considered capable of flexibility in his tactics. Best of all, he had never failed. Not ever, and he had been around a long time, with more than his fair share of difficulties. But there had been no failures, and no bad luck, either. Therefore, in the merciless calculus of organizations everywhere, he was considered a good guy to work for.

"You look a little nervous," he said.

"I am, a little," Froelich said back.

His office was small, and quiet, and sparsely furnished, and very clean. The walls were painted bright white and lit with halogen. There was a window, with white vertical blinds half closed against gray weather outside.

"Why are you nervous?" he asked.

"I need to ask your permission."

"For what?"

"For something I want to try," she said. She was twenty years younger than Stuyvesant, exactly thirty-five. Tall rather than short, but not excessively. Maybe only an inch or two over the average for American women of her generation, but the kind of intelligence and energy and vitality she radiated took the word *medium* right out of the equation. She was halfway between lithe and muscular, with a bright glow in her skin and her eyes that made her look like an athlete. Her hair was short and fair and casually unkempt. She gave the impression of having hurriedly stepped into her street clothes after showering quickly after winning a gold medal at the Olympics by playing a crucial role in some kind of team sport. Like it was no big deal, like she wanted to get out of the stadium before the television interviewers got through with her teammates and started in on her. She looked like a very competent person, but a very modest one.

"What kind of something?" Stuyvesant asked. He turned and placed the file he was carrying on his desk. His desk was large, topped with a slab of gray composite. High-end modern office furniture, obsessively cleaned and polished like an antique. He was famous for always keeping his desktop clear of paperwork and completely empty. The habit created an air of extreme efficiency.

"I want an outsider to do it," Froelich said.

Stuyvesant squared the file on the desk corner and ran his fingers along the spine and the adjacent edge, like he was checking the angle was exact.

"You think that's a good idea?" he asked.

Froelich said nothing.

"I suppose you've got somebody in mind?" he asked.

"An excellent prospect."

"Who?"

Froelich shook her head.

"You should stay outside the loop," she said. "Better that way."

"Was he recommended?"

"Or she."

Stuyvesant nodded again. *The modern world.*

"Was the *person* you have in mind recommended?"

"Yes, by an excellent source."

"In-house?"

"Yes," Froelich said again.

"So we're already in the loop."

"No, the source isn't in-house anymore."

Stuyvesant turned again and moved his file parallel to the long edge of the desk. Then back again parallel with the short edge.

"Let me play devil's advocate," he said. "I promoted you four months ago. Four months is a long time. Choosing to bring in an outsider *now* might be seen to betray a certain lack of self-confidence, mightn't it? Wouldn't you say?"

"I can't worry about that."

"Maybe you should," Stuyvesant said. "This could hurt you. There were six guys who wanted your job. So if you do this and it leaks, then you've got real problems. You've got half a dozen vultures muttering *told you so* the whole rest of your career. Because you started second-guessing your own abilities."

"Thing like this, I *need* to second-guess myself. I think."

"You think?"

"No, I know. I don't see an alternative."

Stuyvesant said nothing.

"I'm not happy about it," Froelich said. "Believe me. But I think it's got to be done. And that's my judgment call."

The office went quiet. Stuyvesant said nothing.

"So will you authorize it?" Froelich asked.

Stuyvesant shrugged. "You shouldn't be asking. You should have just gone ahead and done it regardless."

"Not my way," Froelich said.

"So don't tell anybody else. And don't put anything on paper."

"I wouldn't anyway. It would compromise effectiveness."

Stuyvesant nodded vaguely. Then, like the good bureaucrat he had become, he arrived at the most important question of all.

"How much would this person cost?" he asked.

"Not much," Froelich said. "Maybe nothing at all. Maybe expenses only. We've got some history together. Theoretically. Of a sort."

"This could stall your career. No more promotions."

"The alternative would *finish* my career."

"You were my choice," Stuyvesant said. "I picked you. Therefore anything that damages you damages me, too."

"I understand that, sir."

"So take a deep breath and count to ten. Then tell me that it's really necessary."

Froelich nodded, and took a breath and kept quiet, ten or eleven seconds.

"It's really necessary," she said.

Stuyvesant picked up his file.

"Okay, do it," he said.